…triguing Rubik's Cube of a Book'
Liz Nugent, author of *Unravelling Oliver*

'A dizzying tale of lives falling apart that has you addicted from the very first page'
Michelle Frances, author of *The Girlfriend*

'Enthralling – Spain dissects her characters' secrets with razor-sharp precision'
JP Delaney, author of *The Girl Before*

'Fabulous characters, superbly written, twists, turns & ends with a punch'
Amanda Jennings, author of *In Her Wake*

'An absolute cracker of a book, compulsive, deviously plotted and intense'
Elizabeth Haynes, author of *Into the Darkest Corner*

'A clever and unusual premise . . . punchy and energetic . . . a brilliant hook and rapid-fire ride'
*Irish Independent*

'Brilliantly crafted . . . each piece of the puzzle is gradually put together and keeps you gripped'
*Prima*

'Spain's blackly comic touch pulls us through a brilliantly dark tale'
*Daily Mail*

'Fabulous . . . Clever, pacey, compulsive'
*Sunday Mirror*

'R… …ts'

Jo Spain is a full-time writer and screenwriter. Her first novel, *With Our Blessing*, was one of seven books shortlisted in the Richard and Judy Search for a Bestseller competition and her first psychological thriller, *The Confession*, was a number one bestseller in Ireland. Jo co-wrote the ground-breaking television series *Taken Down*, which first broadcast in Ireland in 2018. She's now working on multiple European television projects. Jo lives in Dublin with her husband and their four young children.

Also by Jo Spain

*The Confession*
*Dirty Little Secrets*
*Six Wicked Reasons*
*With Our Blessing: An Inspector Tom Reynolds Mystery*
*Beneath the Surface: An Inspector Tom Reynolds Mystery*
*Sleeping Beauties: An Inspector Tom Reynolds Mystery*
*The Darkest Place: An Inspector Tom Reynolds Mystery*

# The Boy Who Fell

JO SPAIN

First published in Great Britain in 2019 by Quercus
This paperback edition published in 2020 by

Quercus Editions Ltd
Carmelite House
50 Victoria Embankment
London EC4Y 0DZ

An Hachette UK company



A CIP catalogue record for this book is available from the British Library

PB ISBN 978 1 78747 436 9
EB ISBN 978 1 78747 435 2



Papers used by Quercus are from well-managed forests and other responsible sources.

# PROLOGUE

*Dublin, 1 March 2015*

The story went like this.

Fifteen years ago, the man who owned the house had walked into the kitchen and taken a knife. The sharpest, largest knife; the one that had been used the previous day to carve the Sunday roast.

He took it and he walked, first, into the bedroom of his son, aged twelve at the time.

He slit his throat while he slept.

Then the man walked into his wife's bedroom. She had the misfortune of being awake; something had disturbed her sleep. Not the noise of her son being murdered by his father – that was carried out in relative silence. But perhaps some mother's instinct stirred in her and opened her eyes. And so she saw her husband approach with his weapon of choice, still dripping with the blood of the child they'd made together.

The woman knew her husband to be a violent man.

The papers, at least initially, would carry articles containing words and phrases like 'pillar of the community' and 'mental health issues' and 'tragedy'.

Not 'domestic violence'. Or 'wife-beater'.

But she knew. And knowing the danger had escalated, she

didn't do what she normally did. She didn't retreat into herself; she didn't seek shelter in the quiet recesses of her mind, while she cowered beneath his blows.

She fought.

Her body showed all the hallmarks of resistance when the first responders came. It was her body that caused the youngest paramedic to vomit extensively, and that was before he'd even seen the child's.

Knife wounds to her hands, arms, face. Multiple stab wounds to the chest.

The husband dropped the knife then, beside his wife's bloodied body and mere metres away from the suitcase she had stashed in the bottom of her wardrobe. The detectives discovered it filled with the smallest amount of belongings, nothing she thought her husband would miss, just enough for the mother and son to flee with when she found the courage to leave.

Her husband found the suitcase first.

He was the last to die. He laced a rope around one of the more secure beams in the high-ceilinged living room and placed the chair directly underneath. A week previous he'd researched knot-tying on the internet.

And that's where he was found. Hanging inside his €1.2 million Georgian-style family home in the pretty, affluent Dublin suburb of Little Leaf.

The house was never demolished. There were distant relatives, but no will had been drawn up and the property languished in probate for fifteen years. Gates were locked, hoarding erected, security appointed. Rot and decay set in. The ceiling leaked, the windows cracked, the wooden beams became damp and rotten. The rodents nested. The insects flourished. The ivy sprawled.

The tales grew.

The house was haunted.

Ireland. Ghosts are easy to conjure, even during the brightest of hours.

A house such as this, especially at night, was fertile ground for rumour and story.

Nobody in their right mind would go near that place. That's what they said.

But go they did. Creeping in, bottles tucked under arms, drugs wrapped in foil in back pockets, hearts pounding, adrenaline surging, teenage hormones pumping.

An empty house.

A dead family.

And now, the body of the boy lay on the ground outside. Almost a man but technically still a child.

The awkward angle of his neck, the torn flesh, the protruding bones.

A three-storey plummet, life extinguished.

A broken boy.

Another soul claimed by the house.

Another story to tell.

# CHAPTER 1

*Dublin, 16 April 2015*

It was difficult to put into words how much DCI Tom Reynolds disliked these occasions.

Perhaps it was best explained like this: if offered the choice of attending the annual police ball or repeatedly banging his head off a brick wall, Tom would already be in a coma in the intensive care unit.

Everybody around him seemed to be enjoying this one just fine. His wife, Louise, was tonight resplendent in a simple black gown, her long dark wavy hair wrapped in a complicated style that had required many thousands of small clip things and enough hair-spray to withstand a significant weather event. She hadn't stopped smiling since they arrived, the yin to his grumpy yang.

The ageing process was treating the couple terribly unfairly, in Tom's opinion. He'd cut himself shaving earlier, distracted because he had just realised the grey hairs on his head were starting to outstrip the black in noticeable numbers. The lines around his eyes deepened by the day. 'Rugged' didn't quite do it justice any more.

Louise was Dorian Gray; Tom was the picture in the attic.

Tom's team members and fellow table guests weren't the slightest bit bothered by his melancholic humour.

Ray Lennon, his deputy, the unwitting centre of attention, was oblivious to most things, including the fires he was igniting left and right. He was concentrating on the beautiful woman sitting next to him, Detective Laura Brennan. Not just his date for the night, but his fiancée these last six months. The ruby-encrusted ring on her wedding finger was a nod to her rust-coloured curls and the smattering of red freckles across her nose.

She, the more aware of the pair, saw the admiring glances of fellow female attendees (she'd overheard fellow officers whispering in the bathroom, comparing her beau to Jamie Dornan at his sexiest – in their opinion, as the serial killer in *The Fall*, not Christian Grey). The envy didn't bother Laura, who merely smiled, bemused at the irony.

Tom's other detectives were in situ. Brian Cullinane was squinting at the wine menu, hoping to find something other than the cheap Cabernet or Sauvignon Blanc being served freely with dinner. He'd brought his partner, Jimmy, whose nervousness was being managed with topped-up glasses of the aforesaid cheap wine. Brian was openly gay and nobody in the team cared a jot. Tom's station had sponsored a team in a triathlon to raise funds in support of the equal marriage referendum due to be held shortly. But the force in the main was still quite conservative and Brian was breaking barriers bringing Jimmy to an event such as this.

Brian and Jimmy's nearest neighbours, Detective Michael Geoghegan and his wife Anne, were nicely oiled themselves, ensuring they got the absolute most out of their expensive babysitter. Michael had left his tracksuit at home and brushed his spiky hair before stuffing himself into a black-tie suit hired for the occasion.

The seat booked two months ago for Detective Bridget Duffy

had been filled by criminal psychologist Linda McCarn. Bridget had been seconded to the drugs unit and was currently involved in a major operation that would eventually, Tom was sure, see her promoted.

Actually, Tom realised, Linda didn't look the Mae West. Her mouth was set in a thin sorrowful line and she hadn't cracked so much as a dirty joke all evening.

'Tom? Tom . . . ?' Double naming. How long had Louise been trying to get his attention? His wife squeezed his arm.

'Go up to the bar and see if they're serving prosecco, will you?' she said. 'Get a few bottles, save us from that vinegar they keep pouring.'

Tom snapped out of his reverie.

Why was he still assessing his staff one by one? He'd made his decision.

Hadn't he?

'Prosecco *is* vinegar, Lou,' he said. 'How about G&Ts?'

Very few things had tested Tom and Louise's marriage. The battle over which was superior, prosecco or cava, was up there.

'Don't be such a party pooper,' his wife replied.

Louise leaned in closer. He smelled something floral – a new perfume their nearly-four-year-old granddaughter Cáit had selected. It was a celebrity brand and cost approximately ninety-nine cents. Tom fell in love with his wife all over again for wearing it.

'You're blatantly staring at your potential successors,' Louise said.

Tom looked over at Ray and Laura. They were whispering something to each other and laughing, hands held under the table, so very much in love.

And he, their supportive, loyal, caring boss, was about to sow the seeds of discontent.

'Are you still deliberating?' Louise's lips brushed his ear and, despite the stress of the evening, or maybe because of it, her touch sent a thrill through him.

He shook his head, ever so slightly. He knew what he had to do. Tom was about to become management. It was what management did – made the best decisions for the team.

'God, Linda looks miserable,' Louise observed.

Tom looked back at the psychologist. Yes, Linda was ageing even faster than him. She'd always been skeletal, but tonight her face was pinched and her clothes appeared oversized and lacklustre, so very un-Linda.

'Is her son still refusing to talk to her?'

Tom nodded. *Her son.* Linda had given her baby up for adoption twenty-three years ago, but it hadn't been a willing decision. She'd never had another child, too traumatised by her first experience.

That had been bad enough. But when the young man, Paul, came of age, he had sought out his father. Not his mother. Paul couldn't forgive Linda for her decision but he'd been happy to build a relationship with his dad, Emmet McDonagh, Chief of the Technical Bureau, because Emmet hadn't known of Paul's existence.

Silence crossed the room like a Mexican wave, reaching their table, quieting those around it. An arm leaned over Tom's shoulder and placed a G&T in front of him, followed by a glass of bubbles for Louise.

'For the toast,' Garda Willie Callaghan, Tom's driver, said. Tom smiled in thanks, then his attention was seized by the man who'd taken to the podium. Chief Superintendent Sean McGuinness, the honouree at this year's ball.

A montage of photographs began to appear on the screen behind him:

Sean stuffed into his first uniform, looking very much the Kerry farmer's son – a giant, a fish out of water;

Sean receiving his first promotion, his late wife June standing beside him, beaming with pride;

Sean playing hurling for the Garda team;

Sean at a press conference, intense, serious, ready to do battle with familiar foes;

Sean laughing with the assistant chief commissioner Bronwyn Maher, now sitting at the top table and . . . yes, she wasn't watching Sean. She was watching Tom.

Sean's replacement.

His return from retirement had lasted longer than Sean had intended. But the condition he'd insisted on before he came back still stood. Tom would take over when Sean stood aside.

In four weeks' time.

Tom took a large gulp of his gin just as Sean started to talk.

'Seriously, lads, somebody turn that nonsense off. I can't have those pictures on loop behind me while I'm trying to speak. Look at the state of me.'

Titters at the renowned cantankerous humour. The screen behind him paused on an unflattering image of Sean glaring at somebody off-camera in a way that was both terrifying and, to those who knew him, endearing. Unflattering, but possibly the truest image of the man.

'Yep. That'll do. Thank you, somebody.' Sean waved his hand in the direction of the computer operator at the side of the room, hidden behind lights.

'And so, we're here.' Sean loosened his tie. 'Thank Christ, we're here.'

'No sequel this time!'

Cheers greeted the anonymous heckle, followed by laughs.

'By Jesus,' Sean said, covering his eyes with his hand to see better into the crowd. 'There's no way in hell you'll get me back again. I'd have been gone already if I hadn't been waiting for my replacement over there to learn how to tie his shoelaces.'

All heads turned to look at Tom.

He wanted to die.

'Smile,' Louise whispered through gritted teeth, her face fixed in a grin.

Tom forced his features into something resembling pleasure. It was more of a grimace.

'He can't wait, look at him,' Sean continued. 'Ah, Tom. You're the epitome of what makes a good leader – a man who doesn't want power but is willing to take it for the greater good. You'll thank us one day for making the man of you.'

'I won't,' Tom hissed, then almost yelped as Louise pinched his arm.

'But it's not easy, being in charge.' Sean grew sombre. 'You all know Tom, and many of you know his lovely wife Louise, too. Louise, you and my June were great friends so you know full well what your husband's taking on. We, the force, apologise in advance and we say to you, especially, thank you for the loan of him.'

Louise raised her glass. Her eyes glistened with tears as they met Sean's. Not for the loss of Tom to a position with even more responsibility – that she was prepared for. It was the mention of June, a woman who'd died nearly three years earlier after she'd received a diagnosis of early-onset Alzheimer's, but whose death felt as raw as ever.

'Tom, you take charge of the National Bureau of Criminal Investigation at a time of huge challenges across the entire system.' Sean's tone was grave, now. His grey brows furrowed in concentration, his mouth pursed with consideration.

'Public confidence in the force is depressingly low. Resources have never recovered from pre-recession levels. As a colleague once said, we're moving Guards from one side of the bin lid to the other trying to contain the crap inside and we all know the smell is seeping out. For a while, we had road deaths under control. Then we were carted en masse to drugs. Now, there are more fatalities on the road than ever before. Gang crime is growing. Domestic violence and sexual violence are being reported in greater numbers but we're struggling to secure convictions. Repeat offenders are walking through the prison system at speed and picking up worse habits in the short duration they spend there.'

Sean paused. Tom could feel butterflies dancing in his innards. He sipped more G&T. Waited for the punchline.

'Worse,' Sean continued, and the room held its breath, wondering what could possibly top all of that, 'men and women – good men and women – have come forward to say there are issues within our ranks in terms of how we manage ourselves and how we interact with the public. And within our ranks, those men and women have been vilified and mocked, instead of being vindicated and respected.'

Tom felt the collective intake of breath around the room. This was uncharted territory, this was pushing the envelope, this was . . . brilliant.

He sat up straighter, glanced around, clocked those who were shifting uncomfortably in their seats.

When Sean had asked Tom to take the top job – the first, and the second time (the latter had been more of an order than a request after the disastrous interim Chief Superintendent Joe Kennedy) – he'd told Tom it wasn't just because he was an excellent detective with a great solve rate. It was Tom's instinct for justice; his ability to follow procedure, but allow for flexibility; his natural inclination to serve the force honourably but not be blinded by bureaucracy or tradition. Sean, beneath the fiery, unapproachable, adversarial reputation, was a crusader. A romantic, you might say. He believed in the Blue.

And Tom, for all he knew they were in the right, also knew that he and Sean, cut from the same cloth, were virtually anarchists in a room like this. The rebels.

He bloody well loved it.

Louise caught the sudden enthusiasm on his face and raised her eyebrows, amused.

Sean lifted his glass now.

'To Kevin Leech.'

There was confounded silence for a moment. Leech was the whistleblower who had pushed the force the most over the last number of years. He'd refused to back down in the face of cajoling, threats, promises, intimidation. He was the sort of character who could break through the omertà.

The room was stunned.

Bronwyn Maher – one of the better ones in Tom's opinion – even she had a look on her face that said Sean had pushed it too far this time.

Well, best start as he meant to go on.

Tom raised his glass.

'Kevin Leech,' he called out.

And his team followed suit.

It spread around the hall. Even the reluctant officers

couldn't be seen to be too reticent. The Commissioner had, after all, apologised to Leech publicly.

It was just in the tribunal of inquiry that he was trying to have the whistleblower silenced.

'So, you see, we have much to do,' Sean said. 'But thankfully, it won't be me who'll be doing it. A toast to my successor, DCI Tom Reynolds, the man who inherits all these problems. Soon to be Chief Superintendent Reynolds, or bossy bollocks, as you'll probably call him.'

Glasses were raised with more relish this time, though Tom, with his excellent peripheral vision, could see a cautious watchfulness in some of his peers from other departments.

'You're hot when you're mutinous,' Louise whispered, and Tom felt his face burn.

'Your reign won't be boring, anyway,' Linda called across the table. Tom gave her his warmest smile, hoping it spoke to all of his good wishes and affection. She smiled weakly in return.

Later, when the dessert had been cleared and coffee served, Tom made his way to the bar to clear the bill for their table's extra drinks. Tonight was on him. It wasn't that it would be verboten in the future – after all, he and Sean had been friends throughout Tom's time on the force – but soon, socialising with his former teammates would take on a different dynamic.

Especially after he told them his plans.

'Tom.'

The inspector was just returning his wallet to his pocket when the latest well-wisher greeted him. It was Natasha McCarthy, head of sexual crimes.

Tom had a lot of time for Natasha. Like Assistant Commissioner Maher, Natasha had forged her career in a male-dominated world and she'd done it without over-playing the game and sacrificing her principles. She was progressive, very much of the 'prevention is better than watching the penal system fail to cure' mindset. And she'd done all that with the additional challenge of being one of the only mixed-race members of the force.

He was ready to offer her a drink, but the suggestion died on his lips. Natasha's face was flushed and she had bags under her eyes. She was practically oozing worry.

'What is it?' Tom asked.

'I'm sorry, I know tonight is your big night. It's just, with you still in your own job for the next four weeks, I thought . . .' Natasha looked around, desperately. The table nearest to them erupted with laughter at a shared joke; somebody bumped into Tom's arm on the way to the bar. People going about their business, unawares.

'God, what am I doing?' she said. 'This is neither the time nor the place. Sorry, Tom . . . Really, just . . . congratulations.'

She started to walk away. Tom frowned and caught up with her.

'Natasha, let's go out and get some air.'

She had tears in her eyes. Tom was horrified. This woman was practically made of steel.

Taking Natasha's elbow, and simultaneously catching Louise's eye back at their table to indicate what he was at, he steered his colleague in the direction of the exit.

Only one thing could make a woman like Natasha McCarthy so upset.

Somebody close to her was either hurt or in danger.

# CHAPTER 2

'Right. Talk to me.'

Tom and Natasha were alone outside. The mid-April day had started mild enough but the temperature had dipped as the evening progressed. The chill meant there was a notable absence of the smokers who'd usually dot the venue's gardens.

Natasha bit her lip. Tom waited, and watched.

'Well,' Natasha said. 'In at the deep end, I guess. You know my mother is Irish but my father is from Mali.' It was a statement, not a question. 'He came here to study medicine and met Mum, the most modern woman in the whole of the Midlands.'

'Modern because she married a black man?'

'Modern because after she married the black man she kept her own surname. Can you imagine what it was like for me growing up in Westmeath, looking as I do, with a name like McCarthy?' Natasha smiled thinly. Tom was happy to indulge her, though he knew she was stalling.

'My father's brother followed him over five years later. He studied medicine, too.'

'Coming over here, stealing our women and keeping our hospitals running,' Tom said, wryly.

'Ha. My mother would have chewed any Irish man alive, to be fair. Anyway, my uncle brought his wife over with him. And they had a daughter, my cousin Lizzie. Lizzie did marry here – an English man, as it happens. And they had a son.'

'Okaaay – so he's your first cousin once removed, right?' Tom said. 'And I guess something has happened to him?'

Natasha sighed.

'His name is Daniel. Daniel Konaté Jones. You haven't heard it yet because they've managed to keep it out of the news. So far.'

Tom shook his head, none the wiser.

'You know that kid they found dead at that house in Little Leaf?' Natasha continued. 'About six weeks ago?'

'Sure,' Tom said. 'Luke Connolly, seventeen. They think he was pushed out of a window on the third storey, don't they?'

Natasha nodded.

'They've had somebody in custody the last three and a half weeks,' she said.

Tom frowned, the jigsaw piecing together.

'Not your cousin, Daniel?'

'Yes.'

'Oh, Natasha. I'm so sorry.'

She stared at the ground, shook her head softly. It wasn't his pity she wanted.

'I knew they were keeping hush about it,' Tom said. 'I assumed a minor was involved. I didn't realise it was because there was a connection to somebody on the force.'

'That's not why his name is being kept out of the headlines,' Natasha said. 'It doesn't matter that he's related to me. And Daniel's eighteen, not a minor.'

'Then why . . . ?'

'It's being kept quiet because Luke's parents have asked for that. And also because (a), they're saying Luke Connolly was raped before he was pushed out that window, and (b), Daniel is black. Everybody's afraid this trial will become about race and homophobia. And there's some issue with the victim's sibling. I don't know what. All I was told was that there are sensitivities to be considered. Daniel's in isolation in a detention centre at the moment while they await a trial date. His mum doesn't have a lot of money and she point-blank refuses to let me pay for a proper brief. She's old-fashioned, sees it as charity. But Tom, they won't keep him in isolation. And when the connection *is* made that he's related to me, it will be horrific for him.'

Tom frowned again.

'The investigators are certain it's Daniel? I'm sorry, Natasha, I have no knowledge of the ins and outs of this case. We weren't called in, they had their guy almost immediately. And I've been distracted with all this job-move stuff.'

Natasha swallowed.

'They say they're certain,' she answered. 'They have witness statements that put the two of them alone at the scene. And . . .' She hesitated. 'They lifted Daniel's DNA from the victim. Daniel is gay. But, apparently, Luke was not. They arrested Daniel formally three weeks after the file was opened.'

Tom breathed deeply. He knew, he always knew, in every crime, behind the suspect, stood a family about to be crushed. But he'd never had it happen to somebody close to him.

He placed his hand on Natasha's arm, gave it a squeeze.

'I'm heartbroken for you, Natasha,' he said. 'And for your family. Your cousins, his parents, must be devastated.'

'It's just his mother, Lizzie. Daniel's dad left when he was a kid. She's inconsolable. But Tom, I need more than sympathy.'

Tom held his breath.

'Daniel is a . . . challenging kid. He has been, for the last few years. Before that he was a cheeky chappy, real happy-go-lucky.

A smile for everybody. But . . . male teen with an absent father, black in a white neighbourhood, poor – every cliché you can imagine – it's all taken its toll.'

Natasha inhaled sharply.

'But, Tom, I've worked in sexual crimes for more years than I care to remember and I'm telling you, *I am telling you*, Daniel is not a rapist. He's not a killer. And I'm not saying that because I'm related to him. Daniel has never hurt a fly. Messing with drink and drugs, bunking off school, moody, secretive, sullen – yes, he has all of that down. But violence, no. He's not violent. Not to that extent, not to the point of it being intentional. Raping somebody and then pushing them out a window, that is utterly beyond him.'

Tom opened his mouth but Natasha was still speaking.

'And I know it's going to be impossible to convince you otherwise, that you're going to assume my heart has overtaken my head on this, but I'm still going to ask you because we've been friends for a long time. And if you only do it for that, and not because you think he's innocent or because you think I have the capacity to be objective—'

'Natasha. I'll look at the case file,' Tom interrupted.

Natasha stopped.

'You'll . . .'

'I'll look at it.'

'Are you sure?'

'You asked,' he said. 'I trust your judgement. And if you're wrong in this, at least you will know that you did everything you could to make sure you were wrong.'

'But you've only got four weeks left until you step into the Chief's role. You must have work that needs to be wrapped up, you must . . .'

'Are you trying to talk me out of this?'

'You'll be stepping on people's toes,' Natasha said weakly, unable to keep the gratitude and hope from her voice.

'Did you miss the Kevin Leech toast?' Tom smiled. 'All I'm going to do is look at the file. Ask a few questions. Get you some peace of mind. You were right to come to me.'

Natasha opened her mouth to reply. Nothing came out – she was lost for words.

Behind them, the door opened. Sean McGuinness emerged, wearing an expression on his face akin to Steve McQueen's in *The Great Escape*. That was something else Tom and he shared: a dislike of large social gatherings.

Natasha, deciding to substitute action for words, leaned in and gave Tom a tight hug.

'Leave it with me,' he said.

She passed Sean on her way back into the building. He paused in lighting his cigar to bid her goodnight.

When he joined Tom, he handed the inspector another cigar from his pocket.

Tom held the match to the end and puffed until it took light. He coughed as the strong tobacco hit his throat.

'She told you, then,' Sean said.

Tom arched his eyebrows, surprised.

'What colour is my underwear, all-knowing one?'

Sean snorted.

'Tell me you didn't say you'd look into it?' he said.

Tom took a pull from the cigar, said nothing.

'Tom, Tom, Tom.'

'Don't even try to tell me you wouldn't have done the same.'

'Of course I would,' Sean replied. 'If I thought there was something in it. But they have DNA. They have witness testimony that places Daniel as the last person with the victim. And most importantly – did she tell you what the most important bit is?'

Tom shook his head, an unpleasant feeling in the pit of his stomach. He knew enough of Natasha to know she was as honest as the day was long. He also understood that, when it came to family, one could feel the need for ruthlessness to get something done. So, what had Natasha left out?

Sean exhaled loudly.

'I've all the time in the world for that lass. I've a pain right here,' he patted his chest, 'imagining what she's going through. And there's no way it won't get out who that lad is related to. He will suffer inside, no doubt about it.'

'What did she not tell me?' Tom asked.

Sean looked him directly in the eye.

'Daniel hasn't denied he did it. In fact, he won't talk about it at all.'

# CHAPTER 3

Two days passed before Tom found the time to call out to the station where the Luke Connolly case was being handled.

He could have had the case file sent to him in headquarters. He'd certainly have got to it faster. But the inspector figured his interest would provoke less attention if he examined the file quietly. Tom had committed, in advance of taking the top job in the NBCI, to travel to the various stations around the capital and larger cities to speak to senior detectives. He'd covered most of the ground already but, as it happened, hadn't got to the Little Leaf station. So if anybody asked, this would just be seen as another polite visit.

In addition, he knew the station sergeant in Little Leaf. Ian Kelly had worked with Tom in west Dublin for a time. He knew Kelly would help him, even if the detectives in charge were aggrieved at his interest.

Willie Callaghan was driving him that day. He waited patiently while Tom ambled down his driveway, carrying his coffee in a pink Disney princess travel mug.

'Thought your Maria and Cáit had moved out,' Willie said, stroking his army-marshal-like moustache, eyeing the mug as Tom got into the car.

'They have,' Tom replied. 'Three months, now. Oh, this.' He looked down at his granddaughter Cáit's old mug. 'I guess I'm just secure in my masculinity, Willie. A pink cup doesn't bother me. Also, it doesn't leak.'

Willie raised an eyebrow and shrugged.

'Where's your other half, anyway?' he asked.

Willie had been assigned to Tom for a number of years, but more often than not, Tom ended up travelling with his deputy, Ray Lennon. Tom used to like driving himself, before a series of bad car buys and breakdowns led him into the habit of taking lifts from all and sundry.

Tom said nothing.

'Ah,' Willie said. 'Like that, is it? He's asked you to be best man at his wedding, you're going to have to stop avoiding him at some point. What about this stag you have to organise?' Willie put the car in gear. 'What are you thinking? Lap-dancing clubs in Prague? A survival weekend in the bog? Flaming shots of sambuca, then tying him naked to a lamp post?'

Tom sighed. The elation and flattery at being asked to be Ray's best man had evaporated about sixty seconds after the inspector had accepted.

'I was thinking we'd just go to the pub for a few pints,' he said.

Willie eyed him sideways and mumbled something under his breath that sounded like *boring bastard*.

Tom ignored him. It wasn't the wedding that was worrying him. When he broke his news, there was a good chance his invite might be revoked.

The police station in Little Leaf had been designed to blend into its pleasant surrounds. The locals wanted a visible Garda presence to protect their upmarket location, just not ugly-visible. The building that housed local law enforcement had the look of an old vicarage about it, a stone front and church-like arched windows. In the garden, daffodils and irises were in bloom.

It was all very quaint and Miss Marple-esque. And yet, Tom was heading inside to pick up a file containing details about the rape and murder of a seventeen-year-old.

Ian Kelly was pleased to see him. Still bald as a coot and edging close to plump these days, he had the kettle on in the back office downstairs before Tom had even removed his coat.

'You landed on your feet here,' Tom said, throwing his suit jacket over the back of a chair. The file, he was pleased to see, was already on the desk. 'I bet if you ask nicely, they'll bury you out front under the daffs when your time comes.'

'Bored out of my effin' tree,' Ian replied. He reached into a drawer and pulled out a packet of Jaffa Cakes. 'Look at the girth of me. I've gone up three trouser sizes in the last year. I mean, it's not that I'm happy about what's happened, but when this case came in . . . Let's just say, our usual work revolves around Neighbourhood Watch meetings, road safety, the odd burglary and speeding fines. Mind-numbing.'

'How good of the Connolly family to shake things up,' Tom said. He sat down and pulled the file towards him. 'The detective in charge?'

Ian shrugged.

'She's been around the block. By the numbers, bit uptight. She knows you're looking, she's not worried. They're home and dry on this, I'm sorry to say. For Natasha's sake, not for the Connolly family. Do you want me to fetch her in?'

'Sure. I'll relieve you of your duty to those biscuits, contribute to the diet effort.'

'I didn't say I was going on a diet. Just that I'm getting fat. You haven't changed a bit, still blunt as you like.'

Tom grinned and picked up the case file. He opened the folder and scanned the official document at the front – the date and time the body was found; the location. There was something about that address that resonated in Tom's mind, some old history. *Glenmore House, Little Leaf.*

No, it was beyond him for the moment.

The detectives in charge of the Connolly case were listed; Detective Jackie McCallion was the Senior Investigating Officer. Tom had looked her up. Twenty-five years on the force, fairly pedestrian career advancement. Single, devoted to her job. Worked across the country, returned to and settled in Little Leaf for the last number of years. 'Efficient' was the most glowing reference he'd seen. He'd no problem with that. Sometimes the best police work was in piecing information together and sifting through admin. Mundane and procedural, not the gutted revelations or the heightened drama people liked in their TV shows.

The next page was a summary of the medical report. Luke Connolly, aged seventeen, had been in perfect health before his untimely demise. A rugby player, he'd sustained minor injuries over the years, broken bones, cuts. Nothing that had left him damaged in any significant way.

Everything had been one hundred per cent until the night his body broke on the ground.

In his system, they'd found traces of cocaine. He had a blood alcohol level of 0.10, high enough to be drunk but not incapacitated. He'd eaten taco chips at some point that evening.

Minor rectal bleeding from anal fissures and small mucosal tears had been found. No definitive conclusions but a speculative '*indicative of rape*' had been typed. Tom frowned at that, noted it for later.

Two of the victim's fingernails were missing. The Technical Bureau's crime scene analysis had discovered the nails on the floor inside the window from where the victim had plunged to his death. There were also scratch marks on the inside of the window frame, signs he'd tried to save himself.

Death was instantaneous upon impact. Falling backwards, Luke's head had hit a low stone wall that surrounded the property's overgrown lawn. The trauma to the brain, even if he'd somehow survived, would have been irreparable. His neck and two arms had been fractured. There were multiple contusions to the chest, ribs, back and legs.

Tom turned the page. The first photo was of Luke Connolly alive, smiling. A school photograph, posed unnaturally in bad lighting, and yet he was so handsome it was appealing. Sandy blond hair, Justin Bieber teeth. Strong, broad shoulders, well-built without looking like a body builder.

The next photograph showed Luke dead on the ground, the head at an unfamiliar, disturbing angle, one arm twisted unpleasantly sideways.

Tom shuddered.

The door opened behind him, the draught hitting his neck. Tom looked up.

'Chief Superintendent Reynolds, it's an honour to meet you.'

Detective Jackie McCallion held out her hand. She was a tall, serious-looking woman. Her hair was brown, maintained in a short, unfussy bob. She wore a grey suit, ill-fitting but practical. Everything about her said professional and Tom's reaction was to giggle like a girl.

'Sorry,' he said, blushing. 'That's the first time somebody has addressed me like that. Chief Superintendent. I'm waiting for the real adult in the room to pop out.'

He smiled.

Her face contorted in confusion.

Tom straightened his. She wasn't the humorous sort, so.

'I'm still DCI for the next few weeks,' he explained.

'Oh. Yes, of course. My apologies.'

She indicated the chair beside him and he nodded. There was an awkward moment where they both reached at the same time to pull it out from the desk. Tom withdrew his hand and she sat down.

'I see you're reading the file. I didn't know the suspect had a relative in the force until recently. Not that it would have made any difference, obviously.'

Tom nodded. Obviously. He felt the same way – of course he did – but there was something in the way this woman delivered the line, with such certainty, such a . . . lack of compassion, that it made him uncomfortable. He was the first to stand up and say the Guards shouldn't act like a club, they shouldn't protect their own at any cost – it was exactly for that reason he had supported the whistleblowers and opposed Joe Kennedy when he was Chief Super. But Tom was also a realist. A human being. One could at least show sympathy, especially if they were dealing with good people.

'The case has gone to the Director of Public Prosecutions and you're waiting on a trial date, am I right?' he asked. 'It's moved fairly fast, hasn't it?'

'That's correct. We established fairly quickly – within a few days, in fact – that Mr Konaté Jones was involved. I made sure we were happy with forensics before we moved, but we've had him in custody for almost four weeks.'

She spoke in a staccato-like rhythm, sharp and with little intonation.

'Hmm,' Tom said. 'There are a couple of things I've already spotted in here I want to ask you about, if that's alright? I'm not expressing doubt. And obviously the DPP wouldn't have agreed to let this go to trial unless he was convinced by your case file, so it's not about my feelings either way. But if no trial date has been set yet, there's time. I just want to ensure we've ticked all the boxes. Given the . . . sensitivities.'

Jackie shrugged to signal she had no problem with his interest. But there was a little tic on her face, a twitch at the side of her eye. What, he wondered, was she worried about him asking?

He started with the obvious.

'According to this, Luke Connolly was drunk and had taken cocaine. Sure, scratches were found on the window frame and two nails on the floor. But what led you to believe he hadn't just stumbled backwards and scrambled to save himself at the last minute?'

She nodded, once. She wasn't worried about this one.

'Okay, from the beginning,' she said. 'We know he fell backwards. As well as the scratches and nails, we found splinters in his hands. The window frame was old, wooden. Most of the glass panes were missing, otherwise we'd have seen more cuts. Good glass, too, once upon a time. Tempered. It shattered into smithereens, not shards. The back of his body took the full impact of the blow, but of course, that doesn't mean bruising wouldn't be apparent on the front. What was telling were the contusions to the sternum. I interrupted you reading mid-file. If I can just . . .'

She reached across Tom for the folder. He sat back, let her turn the page. He caught the smell of deodorant and underneath it, the slight, pungent smell of body odour.

She was sweating. Nervously.

'This picture here captures it best.'

Tom turned his attention to the file. She'd opened the full medical report at the back. Luke Connolly had been stripped and laid out on the pathologist's table. The injuries on his chest had been recorded and photographed prior to the post-mortem. It was as clear as day. Fingers – spread, forced; ten little bruises and crescent palm-shaped markings where hands had met flesh.

'I'm not saying the drink and drugs didn't affect him,' Jackie said. 'Perhaps he could have resisted the shove more if he had been sober. Average hand size, before you ask. It's impossible to tell if it's a man or woman because they're fingertips and we don't know if the hands were spread wide or the fingers bunched. But he was certainly pushed.'

'Good,' Tom nodded. 'So, you're sure of how he died. Now, suspect. Daniel isn't talking to us, but has he indicated anything that happened, or are you relying solely on witness statements?'

'You're correct. Daniel won't talk to us, or his solicitor, either to confirm or deny he attacked Luke. But we have several witness statements about the night and leading up to it. Luke's friends have told us Daniel had an unhealthy obsession with the victim. They said Luke was friendly to him and, diplomatically, Daniel took that up the wrong way. Daniel is openly gay but there's no steady boyfriend on the scene. The witnesses confirm Daniel was with Luke that night and stayed when they all left.'

Jackie took a breath.

'Our theory is that, after imbibing alcohol and cocaine himself, Daniel used the opportunity to assault Luke, who was equally drunk. It was most likely premeditated, given the friends' statements. Luke's best friend, Jacob, said Daniel was always orchestrating scenarios where the two of them, Luke and Daniel, ended up alone. So on this night, Luke may have been too inebriated to fight Daniel off, or scared to. But when it was over, or he came to, he reacted. Maybe he told Daniel he was going to report him. Either way, they must have argued. And at some point in the fight, they were standing close to that window and Daniel pushed him. To make sure he couldn't tell anyone.'

'Whoa, hold up,' Tom said. 'If they fought and Daniel pushed him, then it wasn't premeditated. Unless he went upstairs with the intention of throwing Luke out that window, it's manslaughter. Heat of the moment. That's what his legal team will most likely counter with. And has he any history of assaulting young men? Any priors?'

'His barrister hasn't suggested any plea yet because as far as I know, Daniel is not talking to him either,' Jackie said, cutting across Tom. 'And we are going for murder because Luke was thrown from the window after he was raped. Luke may have been running to safety, scared, trying to get help. Instead, he was attacked and he was pushed from a window on the top floor. There was intent to kill. Daniel has no prior for sexual assault, but he's also only eighteen. Unfortunately for Luke, Daniel's first criminal act proved fatal.'

Tom took a deep, worried breath. He stroked his jaw, looked down at the file. Jackie waited. Out of the corner of his eye, he saw her knee jiggling up and down, just ever so slightly.

'So you're basing the murder charge on the fact he was pushed after being raped. But where's your proof it was rape?'

The knee stopped. She swallowed. This was where she was

weak. Tom had realised it as soon as he'd read the report. Rape was notoriously difficult to prove if it wasn't extremely violent. Even in cases where the victim was alive and making the complaint, medical evidence – unless backed up with extensive bruising and/or injury attached to the assault – was mostly irrelevant. And as many rape victims tended to freeze during an attack, there were often no physical indicators to show that it was forced, no extensive bruising to show resistance. It was never clear-cut.

'The pathologist and coroner identified anal sexual activity . . .'

'I've read that. I'm asking you what confirms that this was rape and not just sexual intercourse. It says "indicative". I'd pull that apart in court. Especially as we know Daniel was gay. What's to say Luke wasn't gay, too?'

Jackie glanced sideways.

'Luke had a girlfriend,' she said.

'And?'

Jackie nodded.

'He's had girlfriends since he turned twelve,' she continued. 'Very popular, by all accounts. And according to his friends, he was even a little homophobic. They are all in agreement – they found it strange when Luke, of all people, brought Daniel into the group. But they reckoned it was because Daniel was involved in the club scene and could get them into gigs, things like that. He was cool enough for his sexuality not to matter. Every one of them, though, was weirded out by how Daniel was around Luke.'

'According to his friends,' Tom echoed.

'And his family,' Jackie added. 'His parents have confirmed Luke wasn't gay.'

Tom shook his head. He wasn't happy with that. He wasn't happy with it at all.

'Natasha McCarthy mentioned the parents wanted this kept as quiet as possible. What's going on there? Are they worried the rape aspect will come out?'

'They're . . .' Jackie blushed. 'They're not entirely happy about it. Also with the suspect being of mixed race, the trial has the potential to be, well, distasteful.'

'And?' Tom said. There was an *and*. He could sense it.

'They're traumatised,' Jackie said.

'All parents of murder victims are.'

'No, it's not just this,' she frowned. 'Has nobody told you?'

'Let's assume I'm learning about this in bits and pieces,' Tom said, and accompanied it with a sigh.

'Luke was a twin. His brother Ethan is in hospital.'

'Because of this?'

'No,' Jackie said. 'He's been in and out of hospital since he was thirteen. He has acute myeloid leukaemia. He's dying. As in, right now. He's dying and only has weeks to live.'

Tom swallowed. He looked down at the file again, at the picture of Luke on the table. Perfectly healthy, the report said. Up until he died.

'The Connollys only have weeks left with Ethan,' Jackie said. 'They can't cope with the media attention all this would bring. They want justice, but they want it without fanfare.'

And on that final sentence, her voice quivered. It unsettled Tom. The situation for the Connollys was appalling. Anybody who'd spent time with them, who'd had to break the news of their son's death and learned of the fate of his twin, couldn't help but be moved.

Did that in turn mean Jackie McCallion was desperate to help them?

So desperate, she wasn't doing her job properly?

'There is more than Daniel refusing to tell us what happened,' she said, picking up the file and flicking through the pages again. She stopped on one.

He looked down. It was a phone record.

'These are Daniel's records,' she said. 'Luke died between 12 a.m. and 2 a.m., according to the coroner. Before we informed him of Luke's death, we asked Daniel to account for his movements that night. Daniel claimed he was home by 12.15, which would have meant him leaving Little Leaf before midnight, approximately 11.30 to make that journey on foot, which he says he did. But Daniel's mobile pinged on the phone mast nearest to Glenmore House at 12.30. Daniel lives closer to the Dún Laoghaire mast. His mobile didn't ping there until 3 a.m. He lied about what time he got home. He tried to alibi himself, but he was in that house with Luke when he died. The only one who was.'

# CHAPTER 4

The pool house was warm, toasty even, compared to outside. The drizzling rain formed a speckled effect on the glass panels that served for walls, making inside seem even cosier.

Jacob was floating on the large pink pool inflatable his parents had bought for his little sister. It was meant to be a swan. It looked like a chicken with a long neck.

His feet were submerged in the tepid water; the fingers of one of his hands trailed lazily alongside the rubber float. In his other hand he held an ice-cold bottle of some hipster ale Brian had brought over. He took a sip now and again, enjoying the fact he was just nicely buzzing, but still alert, still listening to the inane squawking of his friends.

If you could call them that.

Christ, he already missed Luke.

The olds were away for the fortnight. They'd taken their darling princess with them, scarpered off to the house in Chamonix. There was still snow on the mountains; they'd get some last-minute skiing in before the season turned. Then it would be on to the villa in Santorini, where his father would get pissed in a taverna on vintage Greek wine and his mother's eyes would be on stalks watching young Greek men.

Jacob might still be in school and in an exam year but he was eighteen. A man. He didn't need parenting. Or shouldn't. That's what his parents said, anyway.

Not even after what had happened.

Luke's body hadn't even been released for the funeral yet but when it was, Jacob knew he'd probably be going alone. He'd be surrounded by people, but he'd be alone.

Luke had got it. They'd started in the same school aged five. They'd been in the same class ever since. They hadn't had to try, back then. Same interests, same rugby team – the same girls, more often than not. Luke was the only one that Jacob really talked to. He had his own issues with his folks; he knew where Jacob was coming from. They weren't there for Jacob but they also expected him not to fuck it up. There was a lot of emphasis on not fucking it up. Whatever 'it' was.

Jacob had no brothers. Luke had one.

But Jacob and Luke were the real brothers.

Jacob picked out Hazel's voice amongst the babble over on the loungers.

They always ended up here, in his house. Not the largest, but the most frequently adult-free.

Though they were all adults now, weren't they? Or about to be. All except Luke.

And Ethan, his twin.

'Don't be so fucking moronic, Charlotte,' Hazel was saying. 'We gave our statements. They've charged that . . . animal. It's over. We can get on with our lives. Why would you speak to your father's solicitor? Are you some kind of fucktard?'

Jacob raised the bottle and sipped again. So very Hazel. Straight to the un-PC insulting point.

When her mouth was shut, when you had her naked in your

bed, docile and controlled, she was gorgeous. You could almost forget what a mean bitch she was.

They'd both had her. Jacob and Luke. They'd offered her to Ethan because he was too sick to go out looking, and no matter what girls said – and no matter the actual facts – most of them seemed to have this notion that it wasn't right to be with a boy dying from cancer. They probably thought you could catch leukaemia or something.

Hazel, though, she could be talked into it. Or, well, plied into it. Once she'd necked a bottle of vodka, she didn't really care who or what was being done to her.

Daddy issues, Luke used to say.

'Give her a break, Hazel.' This was Dylan. Dylan Keating, seventeen, an absolute mummy's boy, afraid of his own shadow. He'd agree to anything. He was an embarrassment.

Luckily for him, his parents were two of the wealthiest people in Dublin. If not Ireland. Which meant he'd been foisted on their little gang by virtue of Jacob's parents and their ever-desperate need to network, i.e. shove their tongues up the arses of their betters and feel superior because they were in proximity.

'I wasn't speaking to you, asswipe,' Hazel shot back. 'Why don't you fuck off and get me another vodka? Do something useful.'

'Stay where you are, Dylan.' Jacob lifted the Armani sunglasses off his eyes, pushing them back onto his head. He glowered at Hazel.

'Put your fat arse in gear and get your own vodka,' he said. It was targeted and it was cruel. Hazel had suffered on and off with bulimia for years; they were all aware of it. She turned bright red. Her eyes glistened with automatic tears.

'Screw you, limp dick.' She stood up. 'Charlotte, come on.'

Charlotte blushed too. With his glasses off and his head raised, Jacob could see Brian sitting between the girls, watching them, watching Jacob, trying to guess how this would go. Brian was always watching.

'*Come on?*' Charlotte repeated, her voice incredulous. 'You just called me a fucktard because I made a very important point. Yeah, the police have charged Daniel. But he still has to go to trial. And if the courts mess it up, if he's found not guilty, what then? What if he talks? We don't know what Daniel knows. That's what I want to ask my dad's solicitor about. Confidentially. There is such a thing, you know. I want to find out where I stand.'

'I didn't mean it, I just . . .' Hazel struggled to finish the sentence. A big fat tear rolled down her cheek. Jacob rolled his eyes. Brian and Dylan looked away, embarrassed.

It had the desired effect on Charlotte, though.

'Fine, Hazel, forget it. I know you didn't mean it. You never do. Your mouth is faster than your brain.' She stood up. She was a good-looking girl, Jacob could acknowledge that, but over the last few weeks she'd started to slide. Her hair was greasy, her skin blotchy and dotted with spots. There were bags under her eyes. She needed a makeover, or whatever it was that females did when they were going through a shit patch.

Charlotte noticed Jacob studying her as she wrapped her scarf around her neck.

'You're a pig, Jacob Quinn Delaney.'

Jacob smiled, gave her his cheekiest wink.

She'd refused to give it up to him when she was with Luke.

Luke hadn't been the problem. He didn't care. They had a code. Bros before hoes. At least until things were serious. And neither of them planned to get serious until they were forced into it, well into their thirties.

Charlotte simply refused to drop her knickers for anybody. Not Luke, not Jacob, nobody they knew of, either. She was keeping her virginity until marriage or some other such shite.

And yet, everybody knew she was head over heels for Luke.

Jacob would work on her now. He'd make it his mission. He'd pop Charlotte's cherry. For his buddy.

Hazel slammed the door so hard on the way out, it nearly smashed.

Brian whistled and they all laughed.

Jacob smiled indulgently and lowered his sunglasses again.

It was fragile, this thing they held between the five of them. So very fragile.

It really couldn't withstand hormonal females and hissy fits.

# CHAPTER 5

'. . . because Laura's family – and I'm not being funny, right – but I'd really only met her gang in Dublin. The ones who'd moved up from Kerry. But Tom, seriously, they left the masses behind. There's about forty thousand in her family. I think the Brennans *are* County Kerry.'

Ray threw his hands out in despair.

Tom took off his reading glasses and peered at the lenses. They were grubby from where he kept accidentally touching them as he pushed the frame up his nose. He was unused to having anything sitting on his face. He puffed warm air on the glass and proceeded to rub it with the sleeve of his sweater. He'd seen people do that; he'd had no idea how quickly he'd become one of them.

A day had passed since he'd read Daniel's file and it was still playing on his mind.

In fact, it was all he could think about.

'So, we've gone from a moderate-sized wedding to . . . well, I'm not sure how you'd describe this circus,' Ray continued. 'And then, last weekend I visited my mother and she said she expects me to invite her neighbours to the afters. *Her* neighbours – they're not even the same people I grew up next door to!'

Tom sighed, loudly.

'I know, boss,' Ray said. 'I'm boring myself and it's my wedding. It's insidious. One minute you're just agreeing to stuff, the next you've spent your life savings and you're the star attraction in the event of the century. And Laura, Jesus, she's the love of my life but she has changed. You know what she's calling her bridesmaids? Brideslaves. I kid you–'

'Ray, I can't. I just can't.' Tom held up his hand.

Ray baulked.

'Sorry. I'll shut up.'

He picked up the file on Tom's desk, started to flick through it.

'So, you're looking into it, then? Natasha's cousin's case?'

'Hmm,' Tom said. 'There's something about it that doesn't sit right with me. What are you on at the moment – you still chasing that bloke for the ex-wife?'

'Yeah. His mother is giving him his alibi. He . . .'

Tom had stopped listening. He was distracted. Something had jogged his memory. He turned to his computer as Ray continued to talk and tapped in the address where Luke Connolly had been found. Glenmore House.

'I knew it,' he said. 'I knew I'd heard it before.'

'What's this?' Ray leaned over the desk to get a better look at the screen.

The article, one of the first to pop up in the search, contained a fifteen-year-old photograph of Glenmore House. Forensic officers in white suits were sealing off the garden and property and a uniformed Guard stood beside a growing pile of flowers at the main gate.

'We weren't called in on that one,' Tom said. 'You probably don't remember, anyway, I'm not sure you were even on the team at that stage. The husband was a dentist. He murdered his son first, then his wife, then he hanged himself in the sitting room.'

'Christ,' Ray said. 'And that's where Luke Connolly was found?'

'Yeah.' Tom nodded. 'It's obviously derelict and now we know why. I can imagine it all: empty, deserted house; teenagers, drink, drugs. I don't know what they pay these security companies for.'

Ray shrugged. 'You know what kids are like. Mice. They find ways in everywhere, especially when they're not supposed to. Do you need a hand on this? Laura has just handed over the case file on the shooting in North County Dublin to the DPP.'

'Isn't she due holiday leave?' Tom asked, his eyes still on the screen.

'Please – you'll be doing me a favour by keeping her busy.'

Tom snorted and sat back in his chair. He studied Ray. Maybe now was the time.

'Ray, there's something I've been meaning to talk to you about.'

Ray sat forward eagerly. Tom knew they were all waiting for this. Everyone assumed they knew what was going to happen.

The door to the office opened. It was Sean McGuinness.

'One of my fellow football coaches is a deputy governor in Cloverhill, where the Konaté lad is on remand. We can get you in there, under the radar, to have a little chat.'

Sean eyeballed Ray. Taking his cue, Ray stood up to leave.

'Eh, we'll have that chat later,' Tom said. Ray nodded and left.

'You need to pull that plaster off, man,' Sean said. 'You can't leave him hanging.'

'I know,' Tom said. 'It's just . . .'

'How do you break it to a man that you're promoting his missus over him?'

Tom groaned.

'Yes. That.'

'You just do it and hope he has a bigger pair of balls than you're giving him credit for,' Sean said, shrugging. 'Anyway, are you sure about talking to Konaté?'

'I'm sure. There's . . .'

'Something in your gut,' Sean completed the sentence. 'You have that look on your face. Just so you know, this will ruffle feathers, to resort to clichés. And to use another one – do you know who Luke's father is?'

'Darth Vader?'

'Funny.'

'No, I don't know who his dad is.' Tom sighed. 'I thought my whole approach to this would be more fun if I was drip-fed pieces of information every other day, rather than somebody telling me the whole story at once. Jig things up a bit.'

'Don't be a smart arse,' Sean said. 'It's not your investigation. It's not anybody's. It's done and dusted our end and now we wait for the judge and jury to decide based on the evidence. Why would anybody tell you everything? Anyway, Luke's daddy is Chris Connolly.'

'Means nothing to me,' Tom said.

'Let's just say, when the top bankers were quaffing champers at those fancy dinners way back when and thinking about how to screw Joe Public good and proper, Connolly was the man who gave them their accounting advice. He's the head of auditing at Moore, Connolly and Alderman. And he came out of the financial crash smelling of roses, maybe even wealthier, because he's also a clever son of a bitch.'

'Still, an unlucky one.'

Sean came into the office proper and sat down heavily in the seat recently vacated by Ray.

'True. You wouldn't swap your life for his, for any money. One child murdered, one dying. It's amazing the parents are still standing. Anyhow, the point is, Chris Connolly is a monied man with access to an exceptional legal team. He wants justice for his son and he's only human; that's entirely allowed. Konaté is in custody awaiting trial and Chris now thinks justice is being done. So, you can't just ride in there asking questions and shaking things up and not expect kickback.'

'I won't just ride in. I'll call and email first. And I'm all about the justice, whether Daniel is the right man or not. Surely it's better to get a safe conviction than a false one? That's what I'd want. By the way, you keep calling him Konaté. Isn't he Daniel Konaté Jones? That's what Natasha said.'

'My pal Robert, the deputy governor, said the kid doesn't want his father's name used. Never has, not since the dad left. Issues there, I think.'

'Fine,' Tom said. He stood up, put his computer in sleep mode. 'Do I need to ring Cloverhill or can I just ride in there?'

'We'll go now.'

Tom paused.

'We?'

There was a tiny hint of red in Sean's cheeks. Tom squinted at his old friend. This was interesting. What was Sean at?

'Don't make me spell it out,' Sean said.

'Please, spell it out.'

Sean met Tom's eye.

'When I retired the first time, it was to take care of June after the Alzheimer's diagnosis. When I came back, it was partly because we'd messed up so badly by putting Joe Kennedy into the top job – of course, you'd turned it down, so we didn't have much option. But, hand on heart, I was glad to be back. And sure, it's gone on a bit longer than I intended and it's time for me to step aside. But . . . the house is a lonely place. I'm going to miss all this. And all I'm doing upstairs for the next few weeks is answering emails from well-wishers and accepting invites to speak at events. I'd rather stick pins in my eyes at this stage. I'd like to go out feeling I've done something.'

'Okay,' Tom said, processing what he'd just heard. 'What if the something you do is see Natasha McCarthy's cousin banged up? What if I'm wrong?'

'Then you're wrong and a young man's murder has been solved – well, proved correctly solved.'

Tom mused on this.

'I have to admit, I'm not keen on spending too much time with Ray or Laura at the moment,' he said. 'And I have the other lads clearing up old cases so the new team can start with a clean-ish slate.'

'Well, that's decided, then.' Sean grinned. 'Partners at last.'

Tom grabbed his jacket and shoved an arm in, pointedly ignoring Sean. The door to his office opened again. This time, it was Laura.

'Oh, sorry, boss. Are you heading out?'

'I'm taking the old man for his walk. Do you need something?'

Laura's eyes widened. She was still far too respectful of the exiting Chief to even smile at a joke at his expense.

'No, I just wanted to let you know they have a trial date for the gang hit and I've just got word from the courts: twenty years for that man who killed his neighbour with the pipe bomb.'

'Good work, Laura,' Tom said. 'I'll catch up with you later. We'll get the team out for a drink to celebrate. That was a tough case.'

He and Sean made their way out of the office and headed in the opposite direction to Laura.

'You made the right choice,' Sean said as they walked. Tom glanced over his shoulder at Laura's retreating back. He didn't think it was his imagination; she turned and gave him a funny look as she rounded the corner. Like she knew what was on his mind.

'I did,' he said, answering Sean.

Along the corridor and before she entered the open-plan team office, Laura paused. She couldn't go in there just yet. Ray was waiting at her desk with the sandwiches they'd brought in – they'd promised themselves they'd keep to a strict budget until the wedding and that meant home-packed lunches. But Laura had no appetite.

And it was getting harder and harder not to say something, especially as Ray – in his frustration with Tom's silence – was talking more and more about when their boss would break the news about who was taking over as DCI.

Laura knew it was her. She'd guessed it months ago. She'd caught Tom looking at her on occasion, studying her, and knowing him as well as she did, she knew there was absolutely nothing sexual or off about it. He was sizing her up. And then he started asking about her cases. Not just what conclusions she was drawing from evidence, but *how* she'd got there, *why*. Her objective thinking outside the nitty-gritty.

Ray – God, she loved him to pieces but he had his limitations – was completely oblivious. His ability to be unaware of basically everything that was happening around him in his own life was precisely why Tom had chosen her, she was sure of it. In the middle of an investigation, Ray could zone in on motives, he could see things others didn't, he could read suspects. He was excellent on the small stuff – just not on the bigger picture.

Laura was five years younger than Ray. And five fewer years in the murder squad, even though she'd joined early and had a good few detective years under her belt. She was a woman, and for all the Bronwyn Mahers and Natasha McCarthys, it was still unusual for women to take the senior jobs, especially when they were skipping a promotion or two along the way. In an organisation where everything rested on bureaucracy, even she was surprised that Tom might push the boat out for her.

She'd assumed that, at some point, the inspector would have realised he had no option and appointed Ray, the obvious successor. But as time wore on, she knew there could be only one reason he was stalling.

Laura closed her eyes and breathed deeply. Ray had always treated her as an equal. But, at the back of it, he'd done that knowing he was technically more senior than her.

This would be a test for them.

Just three months before they were due to get married.

# CHAPTER 6

Daniel Konaté didn't look his eighteen years.

He had been skinny already. After four weeks on remand, he was angular, all sharp edges and a waif-like frame. His hair was shorn tight, his eyes wide, scared. He'd pass for fifteen.

And he was absolutely beautiful. In another life, thought Tom, and with a tiny bit more bulk, he'd be a model. Calvin Klein would kill for that face and those cheekbones.

It was an odd threesome. Sean, Tom and Daniel. None of them speaking. Daniel had shuffled in and plonked himself on a chair, hands shoved firmly in his pockets. He looked left, right, at the floor, anywhere but at the two men facing him.

They weren't in the visitors' room. The prison's deputy governor had organised for Daniel to be brought into one of the offices. Daniel was already in isolation – the other prisoners had heard the whispers, thanks to loose-lipped Guards. Rapist. If word spread he'd sexually assaulted a man and he was a copper's cousin, Daniel's life wouldn't be worth living. And this was just a remand centre. When he ended up in one of the high security jails with serious criminals . . . Tom didn't like to think of what was coming.

Tom leaned forward, rested his elbows on his open knees. He was doing his best to appear unthreatening, congenial. To compensate for the fact that beside him, Sean was sitting ramrod straight with his arms crossed, giving Daniel his best narrow-eyed stare.

Somewhere, somehow, on the trip over to Cloverhill, Sean had decided to play bad cop.

Tom looked down at the floor, shook his head slightly and sighed. When he looked up, he caught Daniel watching him.

'We're only here for your benefit,' Tom said, hoping this would break the five minutes of silence on Daniel's part.

Daniel sucked in air and kissed the back of his teeth. He looked like he was going to continue ignoring them, but instead he met Tom's eye.

'Nah. You're here for my cousin's benefit, innit. The pig. She's morto there's a crim in the family.'

His voice was deep. He sounded more manly than he looked. But then, maybe he'd looked more manly before he'd been arrested and spent four weeks incarcerated.

'Her benefit, your benefit, what does it matter if you do well out of it?' Sean said, his voice gruff, unsympathetic. Tom had to resist the urge to kick him.

'How can I do well?' Daniel said. 'I'm going down, amn't I? What jury's going to find me not guilty? Come on, to fuck. I read my history, I know how this shit works.'

He lifted his arm, dragged the back of it across his nose. Tom noticed a bracelet of bruises around his wrist.

How had he got that in isolation?

'Why are you speaking like that?' Sean asked.

'Like what?'

'Like you're in an east London squad. You're from the south side of Dublin, aren't you? What history have you been reading? The race wars in the States? It's hardly comparable, is it?'

Daniel narrowed his eyes at Sean.

'Racism is still a fucking *thing*, man. And I might live on the south side, but not all of it is posh.'

'I know,' Sean said. 'I live there.'

Tom turned to his boss.

'You live in one of the posh bits,' he said.

'So does he,' Sean said, nodding his head at Daniel.

'No. I live on the edge of the posh bit. In an apartment that me ma pays two grand a month for. A shitty two-bed apartment. And she works three jobs to keep us in it. Has done for years. She keeps us afloat. And I know this ain't the States. If it was the States, I'd already have been shot. That don't mean you ain't all a shower of black-hating pricks. I know I'm going to get done.'

'If you can embellish that sob story a little more, you'll get to the final ten on *X Factor*,' Sean said.

'Christ almighty,' Tom muttered under his breath.

Daniel stared at Sean like he could kill him. Then he shook his head, laughed, started biting his fingernails.

'What does she do?' Tom asked.

Daniel ignored him.

'Your mum,' Tom tried again. 'You said she does three jobs. How does she keep that going?'

Daniel exhaled. Tom knew he was right to push through the bravado. To appeal to the boy, not that act.

Natasha had given the inspector a photograph of Daniel, taken a few years ago. It showed Natasha's house at Christmas time and Daniel had been helping another kid build a Scalextric set. Sure, you couldn't tell everything from a picture, but Daniel had a kind face. He might have hardened, but the softness was still there, underneath the harsh words and the snarling.

Natasha had also told Tom that Daniel's grandparents hadn't wanted anything to do with his mother when she married the English man. He was 'unsavoury', that was how they put it. Daniel and his mother were alone in the world and they hadn't had it easy.

'She works in a supermarket during the day,' Daniel said. 'She cleans offices at night. And she takes in people's ironing. Bags of it. Other people's clothes all over our sitting room.'

'That's tough,' Tom said. 'On your mum, I mean. She must be exhausted keeping all that going. And now . . .'

Daniel bowed his head.

'So, how did this come about?' Sean asked. 'We haven't met these other kids yet, the ones who gave statements about you, but I can see from their addresses that Luke and his pals all moved in certain circles. They're a certain class. Your mother is working three jobs. You attended a local secondary school until last year; you weren't in the privileged private college those lads go to. You haven't got a job – at least not on the books – and you haven't applied to university. As you're keen to point out, you're a different colour to the rest of them and I bet if you cut their veins, they bleed blue. How did you meet this gang? How did you meet Luke Connolly?'

'We hung around together.'

'We've heard,' Tom said. 'But how?'

'In a club they all went to.'

'Just "in a club"?'

'I DJ.'

'Right,' Tom said. 'Cash in hand, so.'

Daniel looked away.

'And you met Luke and his friends and started to party with them. Two years ago, isn't that right?'

'Yeah.'

'So you're partying with these rich kids,' Sean said. 'Must have been tough enough keeping up with them. How and ever. This one night, you get shit-faced and, what? Did you think you were in love with Luke and he just hadn't figured out he was gay, too? So you chanced your arm and it all went wrong? Or did Luke say or do something to upset you and you decided to teach him a lesson? Was he homophobic? And you thought, I know how I can show this smug little shit how small he is, how powerful I really am?' Sean paused. 'Or maybe he did nothing; you just saw a victim and pounced. What happened?'

Daniel shrugged and stared down at his fingers again. He'd bitten one of the nails so short it was starting to bleed. He glanced up at Sean with disdain. Then he caught Tom's eyes. And he looked away, embarrassed. Distressed.

'You don't know anything,' he said. 'I was always going to take the flak for this. Always. I'm the outsider. The black dude. Nice and exotic, for about five minutes, though I hung on for longer.'

'Did you rape Luke?' Tom asked.

Daniel looked down at his hands again.

Tom sighed, frustrated.

'Nobody planted your DNA on Luke Connolly,' Sean said. 'Nobody's stitching you up for the sex. It happened. There's proof.'

Daniel laughed, thinly, harshly.

'Really? Nobody's stitching me up? You haven't met these fuckers yet; you've no idea. They're sick. The whole lot of them.'

'What are you saying?' Tom pressed. 'Daniel, you have to talk to us, defend yourself. Is that what you're saying? That we have this wrong?'

Daniel shook his head.

'Nah. I'm not saying that. I'm not saying that at all.'

He stood, his hands back in his pockets, staring at the floor.

'Why did you lie about what time you got home?' Tom asked. 'You were still in or around Glenmore House at 12.30 a.m. but you said you were home by 12.15.'

'Can I go?'

'It's getting you nowhere, not talking to the police,' Tom said.

Daniel frowned, shook his head again.

'Can I go?'

Tom shrugged. He waved at the prison guard outside the office window. The door opened and Daniel walked through it, shoulders hunched forward, brow furrowed. He couldn't hack it being with Tom and Sean but he wasn't happy to be going back to his cell either.

'Well,' Sean said.

'Well,' Tom echoed.

They sat in silence for a moment.

'What was with the Popeye Doyle carry-on?' Tom asked.

'No point pretending I'm the kid's best friend,' Sean said. 'I've nearly fifty years on him and I still remember the first time I saw a black man in Ireland. What the hell do I know about his life?'

'Eh . . . okay. I'm just saying, attacking him doesn't seem like an ideal route to get him to talk.'

'He has no dad.'

Tom shrugged. What had that got to do with anything?

'He has no dad,' Sean repeated, 'and I guarantee you, the hand-wringing liberal brigade have been in and out of here already, telling him to play on the poor-black-kid-victimised-by-rich-white-boys angle.'

'You mean free legal aid,' Tom said.

'Yeah, them. That tactic won't work in court, no matter what they've told him. And it's not him. A kid like that doesn't survive unless he's learned to be tough. He doesn't walk in and out of other people's worlds unless he's tough. And he needs to get tougher to survive whatever's coming in here. That's why I went hard on him. He doesn't need our sympathy, Tom. We need to see how he reacts to pressure, whether he'll flinch under it. Because then we'll know whether or not he's telling the truth when he does open his mouth and start talking.'

Tom sat back and crossed his arms.

'If he ever talks to us,' he said.

'Pfft. Maybe he did kill that kid, but if he did, there's more to it than we know about.' Sean sighed. 'And correct me if I'm wrong, but what I picked up from him, despite all the machismo, is that he is terrified out of his wits.'

# CHAPTER 7

Louise was defrosting the freezer when Tom got home. Either that, or she was battering somebody to death.

He walked into the kitchen and found her surrounded by ice, bashing away at the shelves with the meat hammer. Her hair was tidied away under a scarf, her cheeks flushed from exertion. Boxes of food were stacked around the counters and floor, cardboard coverings becoming soggy as the ice on top of them melted.

This didn't look good. Tom was starving.

'Other people turn it off overnight and let it defrost,' he said, pointing at the freezer.

'Other people have husbands who do this kind of thing for them,' Louise answered. She sat back on her hunkers and rubbed the sweat from her forehead with the back of her forearm. 'I haven't made dinner. Pick one of the boxes. I'll be here a while.'

'Want wine?' Tom asked. 'Everything is better with wine.'

She nodded.

Tom selected a frozen pizza and garlic bread and crossed to the cooker to turn the oven on, before perusing the wine rack.

'Well, how did it go?' Louise shouted over her resumed banging.

'He's very hostile,' Tom called back. 'He's hiding something.

We both sensed that. There's a reason he's not talking to us and it's not necessarily to do with the fact he's guilty.'

'I meant how did pairing up with Sean go? Laura called by earlier.'

Tom paused mid-turn as he unscrewed the cork from the wine bottle.

'Laura called here?'

'She wanted help selecting readings for the wedding ceremony.'

'And she didn't think to have that conversation with her husband-to-be?'

'She may have been scouting to see if you were here, too.'

'Why would she be looking for me?'

Tom turned back to the bottle and popped the cork.

Louise stood and approached the counter, where he was now pouring the wine. She waited impatiently, then took her glass and drank from it.

'Easy there, alco in training,' he said. 'Oh, shit.'

'Shit what?'

'I told Laura I'd bring her out for a drink to celebrate some cases she's cleared.'

Louise shook her head.

'She's made plans for tonight. Her sisters are due over. For more wedding talk. And to answer your other question, I sense, and don't quote me on this, she's avoiding Ray.'

'Why would she be doing that?' Tom asked, feigning nonchalance.

'She knows,' Louise said.

'No.'

'Seriously, love? You've chosen her to replace you for a reason.' She kicked at some stray ice with her foot, both of them watching as it skidded off under the kitchen table. 'Anyway, Sean? How did it go?'

Tom widened his eyes and exhaled loudly.

'Sean? Sean is reliving his youth. We're Sherlock and Watson, Poirot and Hastings, Starsky and Hutch . . .'

'Cagney and Lacey. Stick three pizzas on. And clean up the floor, will you? It's the least you can do.'

Louise pulled the scarf from her head and took her wine to the sitting room.

'Why not?' Tom called after her. 'I just take orders these days.'

'I have a PhD in English and I refuse to become your full-time skivvy,' she countered.

He opened the cabinet where the brush and pan were kept, before standing upright again.

'Did you say three pizzas?'

Linda McCarn wasn't in the humour for eating. Or men. The pizzas, and Tom, were wasted on her.

So Tom sat in the kitchen alone, eating his dinner and drinking wine, but unable to tune out Linda's booming voice.

She had turned up at seven, in a crisp, conservative black skirt suit that caused more alarm in Tom than any of her typical out-there attire. Linda had changed ever since she'd learned her son had got in touch with Emmet a couple of years previously. Vivacity and bombast had ebbed from her like life itself, the grief over her loss twenty-three years ago hitting just as hard the second time. Harder, perhaps.

'. . . not like I haven't tried, Lou. Borderline harassment, that's what Emmet said. Paul was on the verge of reporting me. So I've pulled back. May I have more wine, darling?'

'Sure, but eat some of that pizza, Linda, please.'

The kitchen door opened and Louise came in. She looked frazzled.

'What's the crisis?' Tom mouthed.

Louise gave him an exasperated look, as though Tom knew full well.

'I mean today,' he added. 'Right now.'

'Oh. They were meant to have a mediation meeting,' Louise whispered. 'Emmet set it up. But Paul didn't show.'

'I think the thing that gets me most' – Linda was hovering in the kitchen door frame, watching the two of them – 'is that Paul attributes none of the blame to Emmet. Emmet insists he's told him the whole truth – how little choice he'd left me with, how he chose to stay with his wife . . .'

'She did have cancer,' Tom interjected. Louise flashed him a warning look and he clamped his mouth shut again.

'She recovered from that pretty quick, didn't she?' Linda snapped. 'Was it even real, that's what I wonder. You know, Emmet has had the best of both worlds right from the start. His wife has apparently met Paul. *She's* met him! But I haven't even been able to tell Geoffrey that Paul has been to Ireland. That I know his name. Geoff's condition when he took me back was that I never mention Emmet or the baby again.'

A look of fury passed over Linda's face, so raw and terrifying that Tom held his breath. He could imagine her smashing the near-empty glass of wine she held in her hand, then finding her husband, and Emmet, and glassing them with it.

But then it passed and was replaced with resignation. Sadness.

Tom had come to realise that Linda was very much of a generation and background that accepted their lot in life, no matter how unfair. Even if Linda was outwardly feminist, outwardly progressive, she was, bizarrely, quite traditional at heart. There was only a decade between her and Tom and Louise, but the years, added to her monied background, made all the difference. Tom and Louise hadn't had it beaten into them from a young age that other people's opinions were more important than their own feelings. Linda challenged that belief somewhat with her mad clothes and overblown manner and the satisfaction she took from putting people on edge. But when her family threatened to disown her and she'd realised that she was about to be on her own with a baby – not to mention she'd lose her job and her name would be disgraced among her circle – she'd made the only decision she thought she could. It was tragic.

Both women were looking at Tom now. He swallowed, uncomfortably, aware of what was coming.

'You wouldn't . . . would you?'

Tom blinked. The last time he'd tried to put himself in the middle of Emmet and Linda, both of them had told him, not so politely, to remove himself. And Emmet was the Chief Superintendent of the Technical Bureau, somebody Tom had to work with regularly.

'I'm not sure . . .'

'Just have a word,' Louise egged him on. 'See what's going on in Paul's head, if there's anything Linda could do differently.'

'Try to find out if Emmet is actually telling me the truth about the situation,' Linda added.

Tom looked down at his last pizza slice. He'd thought when their daughter Maria moved out it meant the end of women ganging up on him.

He shrugged, which they took as acquiescence. Louise

grabbed another bottle from the wine rack, an expensive Merlot, not that she noticed or cared – it was crisis time, after all – and the two women left the kitchen.

Tom let out the sigh he'd been holding in. Then he pulled his phone towards him and googled Chris Connolly, Luke's father. It was best if he lost himself in his work for a while. It kept him sane.

# CHAPTER 8

The following morning saw Tom and Sean in the Connolly house.

Chris and Rose, the twins' parents, both looked like somebody had cut them open, taken out their hearts and sewn them back up.

Though the April winds were blustery and on the cool side, they'd invited Tom and Sean to sit in the back garden of their large Little Leaf property. As Tom walked through the vast house and out onto the expansive lawn, he couldn't help but think how quiet the building was, how *big* it was for just two people. No wonder they wanted to be outside, where at least the birds sang and the leaves whispered.

But the garden was yet another stark reminder of what had been lost. An old trampoline sat to one side of the lawn. A tree behind it held a wooden house that had been built among the branches. The remnants of the Connolly children's younger lives, before horrific tragedy struck.

'It was good of you to come out to speak to us,' Chris said when they'd settled. 'We appreciate your seniority, I mean.'

The husband was clearly trying to adopt a practical approach to the situation he found himself in. He was the one who brushed the leaves off the wrought-iron patio chairs, who poured the coffee and made sure the two men were settled. He wore a suit. It was probably no different to the ones he'd usually wear to work, though Tom suspected the belt in his trousers had been tightened a notch or two recently as the weight fell off due to stress. And in Chris's voice, the slightest quiver betrayed his true feelings.

Rose couldn't make an effort. She was haunted, almost dead behind the eyes. Her hair was white at the roots, growing quickly into the expensive blonde dye-job she'd once maintained, probably weekly. Her skin was pasty, not even the sun's rays giving her warmth, and the whites of her eyes were dimpled and bloodshot. She'd thrown on an oversized sweater that had seen better days, a comfort blanket of sorts.

The inspector imagined she was trying to reserve all her strength for visits with her still-living son, Ethan. At those, she'd smile and try to behave like he still had a chance, like her world wasn't about to entirely implode, even while she knew it was. It was always more difficult for the mother, Tom felt, even though he was a father himself. It was Rose who had carried the twins, given birth to them. And if she'd taken on the more traditional role, she'd also have been the one at home with them from the start. She'd have bought them their first shoes and seen their first steps and brought them to playgrounds and kissed cut knees and folded their soft clothes in drawers painted blue and cream.

No amount of money, no expensive house, no stream of sympathetic well-wishers would ever replace what she'd lost, what she was about to lose. According to Jackie, Ethan had been diagnosed with leukaemia just after his thirteenth birthday. The Connollys had been through enough before all this.

'I always thought they should knock that house,' Chris said. 'Glenmore. Jesus, with its history. You know, it was even more tragic than they made out, later, when the domestic violence emerged. I heard a rumour that the wife . . . well.' He glanced at the two policemen and looked away uncomfortably. Tom gave him a moment to say more, wondering where he'd been going, but Chris had decided to change tack.

'So, when will Konaté go to trial?' he asked.

Tom and Sean exchanged a glance.

'A date will be set as soon as possible,' Tom said. 'He's only been in custody for four weeks. The court schedule fills up months in advance and there will be a rush between now and summer to get through as much as they can. But it might not be until September, if they can't squeeze it in before the recess. I really can't say for definite.'

In Tom's own mind, he feared it would be sooner. The prosecution would interpret Daniel's silence as guilt and they'd be eager to get a trial under way and over before the kid changed his mind and decided to defend himself properly.

'Oh.' Chris looked from one to the other of the detectives. 'I thought that was why you were here. To tell us when it would all start. We have to prepare, you know. Just in terms of Ethan, we need to know how much time will be required for court appearances and when we can be in the hospital. The doctors can't tell us when–'

'Why are you here?' Rose interrupted her husband, her voice hoarse, cracked.

'Well, we, um, we just wanted to find out a little about the case,' Tom said. 'To talk to you about Luke. Ask what you know about Daniel.'

Chris opened his mouth, shrugged, like he didn't know where to start.

'Why?' Rose was still studying Tom. 'We went through all

this with Detective McCallion. Daniel murdered Luke. She told us the case is solid. That the evidence is all there and it doesn't matter that he won't confess. In fact, she said he wasn't saying anything at all, which is proof, really, isn't it? An innocent person would defend themselves. So, why are you asking us these questions now?'

She was watching him with such intensity that Tom actually felt himself grow hot under the collar.

'Things like this aren't easy to prove,' Sean answered. 'Luke's case getting to court does not automatically equal Daniel Konaté going to jail. Unless evidence is watertight, it's very difficult to secure a conviction. And while he might not be talking now, he could talk in court, and that's a problem when we don't know what he's going to say.'

'But the evidence is watertight, isn't it?' Chris said. 'They have the DNA –' he flinched as he said it – 'and they have Luke's friends' statements. And ours. We know Luke wasn't gay, so whatever happened that night was non-consensual. And Konaté lied about his whereabouts. It's obvious he's guilty.'

'He doesn't think it is,' Rose said, nodding at Tom.

Tom cocked his head.

'Applying a little doubt is a good thing,' he said. 'It tests the evidence before the defence get to, makes sure they can't spring any surprises on us.'

'Do you have children?' Rose asked. 'Sorry, I know you've probably been asked that a thousand times before. But it matters.'

'Yes,' he said. 'I have a daughter and a granddaughter.'

Rose nodded, satisfied.

'Well, then, you'll understand this,' she said. 'I want justice for Luke. But I want real justice. I don't want the wrong person going to prison for what happened to him. If . . .'

Tom found himself edging forward on the chair. He was desperate to hear what Rose Connolly would say next. But it was Chris who spoke.

'Daniel Konaté Jones is not the wrong boy, though, darling. He . . . he raped our son, Rose. Raped and then murdered him. As hard as it is to say it out loud, that is what happened. Luke had a lovely girlfriend. They could have got married and had kids. Or there might have been another, later. He was expecting great results from his exams; we knew that from his mocks. He had his choice of colleges. He was a talented sportsman – could have played rugby for Ireland. Any number of options lay ahead for him and that man took them all. He robbed Luke. He robbed us.'

Rose didn't reply. She kept her eyes fixed on Tom.

This was not good, was all he could think.

She knew something.

And for the victim's own mother to have a sliver of doubt – that was worrying.

'Will you go speak to our other son, Ethan?' Rose said.

'Well, yes, sure,' he replied. 'We can do that. He wasn't there that night, though. Do you think he might have something to add?'

Chris frowned and made a dismissive sound, but Rose ignored him.

She nodded.

'They were twins,' she said. 'If anybody can talk to you about Luke, it's Ethan. He'll want to talk to you.'

# CHAPTER 9

There was no time like the present. Tom and Sean drove straight from the Connollys' to Ethan's hospital.

It was private, as Tom had expected.

No, that wasn't true. He hadn't been expecting a hospital at all. He'd been expecting a hospice. They knew Ethan Connolly was dying, so the inspector had assumed the boy would be in that final terminus, the place where angels worked amongst the living, easing pain, soothing patients towards their end.

But Ethan was in a small private hospital near Dublin Bay. A turn off the coast road and a short drive up a tree-lined avenue revealed its white walls and large glass windows, affording patients an exclusive view over what was today a calm blue sea.

Apparently, the hospital had a cancer specialist on site, one of the country's leading experts. Hence Ethan's residency.

'One of the many perks of private healthcare,' Sean said, returning to the car after looking in vain for a meter or a card machine. 'Parking is free.'

'Parking but not the bed,' Tom said. 'What do you reckon it costs for a night's stay in here?'

'Probably more than we earn in a week, put it like that.'

Sean had driven, giving Tom the chance to google everything he could find on Ethan's diagnosis, acute myeloid leukaemia.

He'd learned it accounted for half of leukaemia cases diagnosed in teenagers and young adults. That it was the most common acute leukaemia in adults. He'd read through the technical aspects, unable to get his head around the unfamiliar terms, baulking at the mentions of bone marrow, bleeding, bruising, and frequent infections.

He'd spent twenty minutes on healthcare sites and his head was spinning. Tom guessed were he to ask Rose, Chris or Ethan Connolly himself to talk about the disease, they could have given him a bachelor's degree.

If his Maria or Cáit became ill, he would research it until he thought he'd found a cure.

Ethan had first been diagnosed with leukaemia shortly after his thirteenth birthday. Tom imagined there had been despair but a resignation to the condition; a hope, a presumption even, that a young, strong boy would be able to fight the pervasive cancer.

And fight he did. Chemo, followed by remission. Followed by relapse. Again and again. Now, at seventeen, time was running out for Ethan. Chris had mentioned chromosome abnormalities and a high white blood cell count on the latest diagnosis, which had apparently affected Ethan's chances of any effective treatment this time around.

It turned Tom's stomach.

'What's going on with those parents?' Sean asked, as they walked towards the entrance. He'd been quiet in the car, letting Tom read. 'It's rare you see it that way round – the dad insistent, the mother hesitant. Normally the mother wants the suspect suspended from the testicles and beaten to within an inch of their lives. But I felt like she was interrogating us – not because she was worried we'd question Daniel's guilt, but because she wants to know if we have doubts.'

Tom shrugged.

'I know,' he said. 'There's no hard and fast rule where parents' reactions are concerned but it's worrying that she's not convinced. Why, though? What does she know? Did you notice what the dad said, as well?'

Sean nodded. 'I did. *He had a lovely girlfriend he was going to marry*. First thing out of his mouth in the list of what Luke had going for him.'

'Perhaps the rape is clouding his overall vision?' Tom ventured. 'A little homophobia goes a long way.'

The revolving doors rotated for the two men as they approached and then they were inside, breathing in the fragrant scent of fresh-cut spring flowers, listening to low classical music, basking in the artificial warmth of the glass ceiling.

'I think this is heaven's waiting lobby,' Tom whispered.

'How very undiplomatic of you,' Sean replied, and walked over to the reception desk, where a supermodel waited to assist.

In her teens, Tom's daughter Maria had gone through a phase of watching young-adult movies and reading books where all the plots revolved around the main protagonist or their siblings dying from cancer. He'd come across her in her room more than once halfway through a box of Kleenex, bawling her eyes out as some (still good-looking) bald boy, wearing a hospital gown, wept through his goodbyes with his on-screen nearest and dearest.

'Why would you do this to yourself?' Tom would ask.

'It's just a film,' she'd reply. 'Though, you know, it does

prepare you. Irish cancer rates are very high, Dad. Any one of us could get it.'

'Mm-hmm, and I'm sure it looks nothing like that,' Tom would answer, not really knowing because, strangely, nobody very close to him had died from cancer. His parents were alive and well, just suffering with the ailments of being elderly. His siblings were all fine. His grandparents had died from old age in one instance, a heart attack in the other.

Ethan Connolly bore some resemblance to his brother Luke, even though they weren't identical. But Ethan was ghostly pale and had lost all his hair. He was dreadfully skinny, although he also had a protruding stomach that looked painfully bloated.

But he wasn't hooked up to tubes, he wasn't using a ventilator. He wore a tracksuit, and lay on his back in the bed, head turned towards the window.

A nurse was with him when Tom and Sean arrived, a young woman, no older than twenty.

If there was a nurse selection process, clearly all the best-looking ones got to work in this hospital, Tom thought. The Connollys had told them that Ethan had been assigned a small team of nurses and a doctor who would take care of him until he died, so he would have consistency and familiarity.

Rose had also intimated that that hadn't been said to Ethan, who was struggling to come to terms with the news there would be no more treatment.

Tom watched as she filled out a clipboard at the end of Ethan's bed.

'Police,' Tom mouthed quietly, when she looked up and saw them.

Her mouth formed an O.

'Visitors, Ethan,' she said, eyeing Tom and Sean nervously.

'Did you sign in downstairs?' she asked them. 'Use the sanitiser on your way up?'

Tom nodded. Ethan turned to look at them. Realising he didn't know them, he struggled to pull himself into a sitting position. The nurse rounded the bed, pulled him forward easily and raised the bed up slightly.

'I'm Claire,' she told Tom. 'If you need me, I'm just down the hall.'

'Thanks,' Tom said, standing aside to let her leave the room. She paused momentarily.

'Really, just down the hall,' she repeated, then added, quietly, 'if he gets bad. Please, don't keep him too long.'

Tom nodded, to show he understood how serious it was.

'I think your parents rang ahead,' Sean said, taking one of the comfortable armchairs facing Ethan's bed.

'Dad texted,' Ethan replied. His voice was still strong. That or he was making an effort. 'My folks have this thing: they like to message instead of ring because they're convinced placing a mobile phone too close to my head will give me cancer.'

Tom and Sean looked at each other. It took a beat to realise the kid was joking.

'There it is,' he said, and smiled, weakly.

Tom took the other seat.

'You're here to talk about Luke,' Ethan said.

Tom nodded. 'We don't want to tire you. We don't want to be here at all having this conversation. But . . . you were his twin. Your mother said you were close and that your brother visited you regularly.'

Ethan shrugged. 'We were as close as two teenage brothers can be, I guess. As in, if I had the strength, I'd have beaten him up when he came in here that time wearing my Barcelona jersey. He said it suited him better, the little shit. But then, on Valentine's Day, he did organise a kissogram.' Ethan snorted. 'You should have seen the reaction of the staff. But . . . Daddy's money and all that. Plus, I think Father dearest is on the auditing board for the hospital. It was only a kiss, anyway; it's not like she was here to pluck my cherry. Though Luke had promised to try and sort that out before I shuffle off the mortal coil.'

Ethan fell silent. He stared out the window again, unable to meet their eyes. Because he was tearing up, Tom realised.

'You know what I think,' Ethan said quietly. 'I think I hate the word "sick". I'm not sick. God is fucking sick. It was meant to be me. We'd prepared for it, in case. We'd talked about it. I'd told Luke – if it happened, he had to live the life I didn't have. He had to see the world and eat everything, drink everything, experience everything. He had to live twice as much. I never stopped hoping, but it didn't hurt as much, knowing that if I died he was going to carry on. My brother, my twin. It would be like part of me was still living. What kind of messed up . . .' Ethan broke off with a half-sob. At his sides, his fists clenched in anger.

Tom leaned across and placed his hand on the boy's arm. Sean stared down at his lap, uncomfortable with the boy's distress.

'It's . . . I'm not even going to say unfair,' Tom said. 'It's an evil, what's been visited on your family. I'm sorry. I have no other words.'

Ethan sighed.

'Forget it. I just . . . I just have these moments when I feel rage. I want so badly to live. I'm happy to fight for it. But now I feel like I want to die. Then I feel guilty because I know it will be worse for my parents if I'm gone.'

Tom frowned. *If* Ethan died? *Fight it?* The inspector understood now what Rose Connolly had meant. There were no *ifs.* Only when.

'It's all wrong,' Ethan continued. 'It's so wrong. If I could change it . . .'

'It's not within your power,' Tom said. He sat back, let a few moments pass in silence. Enough time for Ethan to collect himself.

'You haven't asked why we're asking questions about Luke,' Tom said, at last. 'Aren't you curious as to what we want when the man they suspect of killing Luke has already been charged?'

'No,' Ethan said. 'I was waiting for somebody to come in and ask something sensible. When the woman was in – what's her name?'

'Detective McCallion?'

'Yeah. That one. I wasn't – I wasn't like I am now. I'd no energy. It comes in fits and starts. I've good days, good nights, and then I'm just, well, you know. Nearly dead. Sometimes it depends on the treatment I've had – they give me transfusions. Other times it's simply because I'm exhausted. Anyway, when she was in, I could barely lift my head off the pillow. I guess, along with everything else, it had just hit me. What had happened. But I still tried to tell her. I did try, honestly. It was like she didn't want to listen. Like she was determined to make my answers fit her questions.'

'What do you mean?' Sean asked. 'What did you try to tell our colleague?'

'She kept going on about Daniel. All this evidence they had on Daniel and she was going to get me justice. And I was like, no way, there's just no way. She was speaking to me like I was some kind of halfwit. I've seen nurses speak to people in here with Acquired Brain Injury better than she spoke to me.'

'And you told her you didn't think Daniel would harm your brother?' Sean said. 'So, you know Daniel well?'

'Sure I do. He came in a few times. We weren't friends or anything but I knew him through Luke. And it's not just that Daniel wouldn't harm my brother. He *loved* Luke. He'd prevent harm from happening to him, I'm absolutely sure of it.'

'Loved, how?' Tom asked. 'Like a brother? Like a best mate?'

Ethan frowned.

'Shit, no. Proper love. In love.'

Tom and Sean exchanged a glance.

'Daniel had nothing to do with Luke dying, I'm sure of that,' Ethan continued. 'You need to talk to Luke's friends.'

'Ethan, was Luke gay?' Tom asked. 'Is that what you're saying?'

'You need to talk to Luke's friends,' Ethan repeated, looking away, uncomfortable. He stared down at the blanket that covered him. 'Daniel wouldn't have hurt him. But them . . .'

Tom wanted to pursue it. He wanted to know more about Daniel and Luke, but he realised Ethan was starting to tire. They'd only been there a few minutes, but already the boy's voice was weakening a little, his body slumping. If there was a deadline on this conversation, Tom wanted to know why Ethan was pushing the notion that Luke's friends were of more interest than the boy they had in custody.

'Luke's other friends – they're not your friends as well?' Sean asked, and Tom smiled thinly. They'd both come to the same conclusion.

'They're definitely not my friends. I've known them – well, nearly all of them – since I was a kid. We were all in the same school from primary – the boys anyway. The girls came later.'

'Do you think they could have been involved in your brother's death?' Tom asked.

Ethan shrugged.

'I just know they are a nasty little shower of pricks. They're liars, all of them. And not one of them has been in here to offer their sympathies. Make of that what you will.'

Tom raised his eyebrows. There was real vehemence in Ethan's voice. He believed something had happened involving them, even if nobody else did.

From Tom's memory, there had been five other kids in the house at the start of that night, before Luke and Daniel were left on their own. Three boys and two girls. Had one of them lied? Had they all lied?

Ethan reached out and grabbed Tom's arm. His hands were large, man-like, but his grip was weak, like that of a child's.

'Inspector, if I give you my number, will you keep me up to date with what's happening? I'd really like to know. My parents think talking about it is too stressful for me. Well, my dad does, anyway. But I would swear on my life that Daniel wouldn't hurt Luke.'

'Sure,' Tom said. 'I'll keep you informed, *if* anything changes.'

'Can you . . . can you promise me you'll look at his friends? That you'll find out if they've done something? For Luke. For me. And for my mum.'

Tom swallowed. No, of course he couldn't promise that. For all he knew, they already had the person who'd killed Luke Connolly in custody.

But Ethan was dying. And Tom couldn't bear to take his hand away, to remove a life raft of hope.

'I'll do my best,' he said.

Ethan nodded. In his eyes, Tom could see, the boy had already decided Tom's best would be good enough.

And now they had a pact.

Tom's heart sank.

He never did that with relatives. Never. But then he'd never met the dying brother of a victim, either.

Shit.

## CHAPTER 10

It was later that day when Tom finally made it to the pathologist's office.

Moya Chambers was in her lab, washing down steel tables and puffing furiously on an e-cigarette. It didn't seem to be working for her at all – neither in giving her the nicotine fix she craved nor in keeping her calm.

The eyes in the back of her head, though, were working just fine.

'Please, let this be a social call,' she said, without turning around. 'I just cut open a sixteen-year-old girl and I can't cope with anything else being dumped on my heavily burdened shoulders right now. And you always bring the toughest asks, Tom Reynolds.'

'It's not social,' he said, 'but it's just a simple query and I come bearing gifts.'

Moya knocked off the hose and dumped the blue gloves she was wearing in the bin. She turned and looked up at the inspector. She'd had her hair cut since Tom had seen her last – the missing inches meant her Dolly Parton curls sat even closer to her small head, feathering her face and making her entirely pleasant-looking. God love the intern that made the mistake of judging the book by the cover. Moya was a fabulous woman, once you got to know her. And what you got to know was that she'd crush your balls as soon as look at you if you took any liberties with her.

'McDonald's?' she said, spotting the brown paper bag. 'You brought me a Big Mac? Is this a joke? Other Chief Supers bring me to five-star restaurants and suck up.'

'You're trying to give up smoking,' Tom said.

'Wow. Best detective on the force, I always said. Relevance?'

'You're trying to give up smoking and I bet you are craving every unhealthy thing under the sun, little Miss Cranky.'

Moya smiled. 'Okay, Mr Smartypants. Give me all the salt and sugary soda drinks.'

She held her hand out for the brown paper bag, then looked inside.

'Oh, there's a McFlurry in here too, you big sweetheart. Right, sit your ass over here on these high stools and hit me with your question. Two blinks for yes, one for no. Don't mistake the purring noises I make when I'm eating for anything other than sheer delight.'

Tom laughed and pulled out the pathology report he'd managed to lay his hands on. Moya hadn't performed the autopsy on Luke Connolly; one of her deputies had. So what Tom was about to do was both useful and difficult. Moya would be irritated he'd come straight to her and over a protégé's head. But if she discovered the report had missed something, she'd chew her student alive.

'This is an Irish case?' Moya asked, looking at the first page of the file Tom had opened on the counter. She peered up at the inspector quizzically.

'Six weeks ago. You were . . .'

'In London at a conference. I left Lucy Silva in charge.'

'Would she have had assistance in the lab?'

Moya raised an eyebrow.

'It's the pathologist in charge who signs off on the report. What's the problem?'

'There may not be a problem. But I just want your opinion on a particular aspect. Will the photos of the body and post-mortem be on digital file?'

Moya crunched down on the first bite of her burger like it was Tom's head. She pulled her laptop towards her and opened it.

'Name,' she mumbled through the food.

'Luke Connolly.'

Moya glanced down at the report's index number and summoned a file on screen. Tom watched as she speed-read through the findings and then waited while she swallowed her food.

'Nothing jumping out at me as extraordinary here,' she said. 'I'd have come to the same conclusions based on the distance he fell, the chest contusions, the ancillary evidence noted at the scene and so forth. What's your beef?'

'My beef,' Tom said, flicking through the report, 'is this.'

He turned to the page which highlighted the evidence of sexual activity that could be *indicative of rape*.

Moya read the highlighted section of the page he'd left open, then looked up again, puzzled.

'It's inconclusive. That's fine, Tom. You know what this is like. Unless it's particularly violent, if the victim was inebriated or concussed during the assault, it's very difficult to ascertain rape. But, given it is a *he* we're talking about, presumably those around him had some indication of his sexual inclinations. Was he gay?'

'Father says no. Friends say no. Girlfriend says no. Brother indicates a soft yes. Mother might have doubts, but I'm speculating. Moya, I know you can tell when there's repeated sexual activity.'

Moya sighed and popped a chip into her mouth and turned back to the laptop.

She pulled up some files and began to read. Tom helped himself to tepid, soggy chips as she did. When she finished, she placed her chin on her hand and sighed.

'Hmm.'

'Hmm, you have something for me or hmm, I wasted my fast food gift?' Tom asked.

'He was young. But, historical tears to the anal lining. Micro, no real damage. He may well have had previous intercourse. That doesn't mean, of course, that he wasn't raped on this occasion.'

'Of course not,' Tom agreed. 'But it does mean his sexuality might not be clear-cut.'

Moya shrugged. She looked back down at the report.

'I'm not going to lie: I would have been more cautious indicating a possible rape conclusion based on those previous abrasions. I'd have at least included them.'

'Don't go too hard on your colleague,' Tom said, stroking his chin. 'She may have been guided by our side in her conclusions.'

Moya shook her head, clicked her tongue impatiently.

'By the way,' Tom said, taking his coat off the back of the stool. 'You need to know I'm going to be exactly the same person when I become Chief Super. If you want a five-star restaurant, you'll have to bring me.'

He escaped just in time.

# CHAPTER 11

It was the modern-day version of a mixed tape. Charlotte pulled up the YouTube playlist that Luke had made for her and sat back in her favourite armchair in the conservatory, earbuds in.

The morning light streamed in, an April shower fell lightly on the glass roof. She pressed play on the first track, a Coldplay song Luke hated but knew she loved. And she let the music fill her head and reach down inside her, as she pulled her hoodie tighter and wrapped her arms around herself.

Everybody at home was being so nice. Not that that was unusual. She was the youngest of a large family and had always been spoiled, but never so much that it affected her in any negative way. Sure, she could wheedle things from her sisters and brothers and parents, but she also had to suffer eternal slagging about being the baby.

That was why she'd kept news of her first boyfriend from them. Plus, her parents were really strict about that kind of thing, ever since the whole religion craze had kicked off.

Charlotte had kissed boys before but it had never felt serious. Not like it did with Luke. It was real, what they'd had.

'What are you doing, squirt?'

Her older brother leaned over the back of the chair and read the title of the track she was listening to.

'"Fix you"? Jeez, Sis. Cheery.'

She pushed him in the arm, gently but firmly, and he shoved her back. Then he gave her a tight hug, his arm wrapped around her neck, and kissed the top of her head.

They thought Luke had been Charlotte's friend. That was all. A good friend, so she was entitled to be upset and thrown.

They had no idea how upset and thrown.

She'd been in love with him. Even when he . . . even after *that* happened.

Love is blind, they say.

Charlotte's brother was back. He placed toast on the small wicker table in front of her and a glass of orange juice. With ice.

Charlotte frowned.

As it turned out, her family were blind, too. They had no idea what Charlotte was capable of.

Their little girl. The baby of the bunch.

How could she ever do anything bad?

# CHAPTER 12

Thankfully, Sean had an appointment he couldn't miss that morning.

Tom wanted to talk to Daniel again, but he wanted to do it alone. He wasn't entirely convinced his boss's method of going hard on the kid was the best one, regardless of Sean's theories on toughening Daniel up or seeing what would break him.

Tom was just about to leave the station car park when the passenger door was opened.

Laura's head appeared.

'I think we need to have a little chat,' she said, her voice firm and stern.

Tom sighed and stared out the windscreen. It was like being summoned by the headmistress.

'I'm on my way—'

'To talk to Daniel Konaté again, I know,' she said. 'Seeing as I'm going to be the next detective chief inspector of the murder squad, consider this ongoing training.'

She got in and slammed the door shut.

Tom took a deep breath and put the car in gear.

'It's 2015,' Laura said as they left the car park and joined the line of traffic leaving the Phoenix Park, the site of headquarters. 'Take the Chapelizod Road and come out at Palmerstown; don't go via Heuston.'

'Sorry, what does that have to do with the year?' Tom asked.

'Nothing. It's the shortest route. And I'm pointing out it's 2015, so why is it so hard to tell a man there's going to be a woman in charge?'

'It's not–'

'Wait until I tell you the conversation I overheard in the canteen,' Laura interrupted.

Tom shut up and concentrated on driving. Laura didn't want his answer. She just wanted to speak.

'Michael, our Michael, well, his Anne has been offered a job. You know she used to work in IT? Before the babies. Anyway, they're offering her this huge package, six-figure salary, private healthcare, car, pension, etc., etc. But Michael and Anne don't want to put their kids in a crèche, which is what would happen if they were both working. I mean, can you tell me what the problem is?'

'Well, Michael really likes his job . . .'

'He's on, what, €50,000 a year?' Laura said. 'Anne gave up work for six years, Tom. Six. Years. Including the miscarriages, before those two rainbow babies came. He can't take a career break to let her get started? You know what the problem is? It's not that he'd miss his job. It's him not being able to get his head around being a stay-at-home dad while she's earning the big bucks. And, no!'

Laura held her hand up.

Tom hadn't even got a word out this time, he'd just opened his mouth.

'Don't you dare tell me Michael is more progressive than that,' she said. 'He isn't, Tom. He just isn't. I've spent more time with him than you. I love him, he's a great detective, but he's not a modern man. Not in the sense we'd all like to think exist. 2015!'

Laura shook her head and stared out the window.

'What do you want me to say?' Tom asked. 'Am I allowed to say anything? I'm a modern man, aren't I? I know you're right for the job even though I know it's going to cause headaches.'

'Are you, though?' She looked at him sideways. 'Would you have given a heartbeat's thought about breaking the news before now if you'd decided on Ray and it was him you were asking?'

'That's different. Ray has more experience, he's the natural choice. I'm going against the obvious route and putting somebody's nose out of joint – not just somebody, a close friend.'

'If we were both the same age, had the same experience?'

'I wouldn't even need to think about it,' Tom answered.

He felt Laura studying him. And he started to blush. But that was the truth, wasn't it? He wouldn't have hesitated. Tom didn't differentiate between female and male officers, did he?

He swallowed. Okay, maybe a little. Like when he asked Laura to accompany him to break bad news to people because he figured a woman in tow would be better.

But it was Ray he'd ask to accompany him when he thought a suspect might be dodgy.

That was just common sense, though, wasn't it?

Wasn't it?

Well, this was uncomfortable.

'Suddenly realised you're a man, have you?' Laura said.

'I'd always suspected,' Tom joked, half-heartedly.

Laura turned back around in her seat so she was facing forwards again.

'You're so far ahead of the vast majority of men I know, Tom, I wouldn't let it worry you for a second. I think what I'm really struggling to come to terms with is how *I'm* reacting to all this. When I realised what you were planning . . .' She hesitated. 'I was going to come to you and talk you out of it. I was going to say I wasn't ready. Because, you know, I'm marrying Ray. Jesus, how could it even cross my mind to turn down such an opportunity? How could I even think that he wouldn't be thrilled for me? And he will, of course he will. But it will make things difficult, no matter how we try to work it out. And I don't want to lose him from the squad, because he's good. But what if he can't work under me?'

Tom chewed the inside of his cheek. She was speaking aloud the conversations he'd had in his own head.

If Laura and Ray weren't together, it would be very different. He'd expect Ray to just man up and Laura to handle him.

But it was his fiancée, his wife, that he'd be taking orders from. And she'd be bossing around her husband, having jumped ahead of him in the promotion stakes.

Yep. That had entered Tom's head. He was ashamed of himself.

'Tell him,' Laura said. 'Just tell him and get it done. He's starting to think I'm crazy for going on about this wedding so much, just for something to talk about that's not work. I can't pretend to be that interested in cakes any more. Who gives a damn what's in the third tier? Seriously, who cares?'

Sean had rung ahead to ensure Tom had access to Daniel again, but this time, the inspector was brought down to the visitors' room. Tom's trip coincided with normal visiting hours, so if he played it right, Daniel still wouldn't appear to be getting any special treatment.

Nevertheless, before they went in, Tom glanced through the window next to the door to check out the men sitting at the various plastic tables and chairs in case he recognised anybody.

'I did that little scumbag for GBH and attempted murder two years ago,' Laura said, turning her head so she had her back to the room and couldn't be seen. She indicated a man over her shoulder on the far right. 'He got away with it and here he is again. *Quelle surprise*. I'll wait out in the car for you. No point in causing a scene.'

Tom nodded and let her go. He'd spotted Daniel coming into the room. He took his seat at the desk belligerently, sneering at the visitor at the next table.

He was playing the hard man extra special today, for the company.

It must kill his poor mother to see him like this, Tom thought, as he entered the hall. He hadn't met Lizzie Konaté yet. He hadn't seen the need. Natasha had given him the family angle on Daniel. There wasn't a mother alive, Tom knew, who would say a bad word about a child she loved when he was facing adversity like this. And Tom didn't want the weight of any more relatives' hopes bearing down on his shoulders.

'Ah, for f–'

Daniel glared at Tom when he sat down.

'I thought it was somebody interesting,' he said.

'Nope.'

Tom looked around at the other inmates and visitors. Some of them were looking over at Daniel, their faces hostile, one or two sniggering.

'You want something from the machine?' Tom asked, indicating the chocolate dispenser.

'What am I, five?'

'You certainly act petulant enough.'

Daniel snorted.

'Where's your buddy? Bad cop?'

'It's just you and me today. So, we can have a proper conversation.'

Tom leaned closer, lowered his voice.

'And we're going to talk about your relationship with Luke Connolly.'

Daniel blinked. His leg started to jig up and down. He glanced around to see who, if anybody, was listening.

'Why should I talk to you? You going to believe me, are you? Look at where I am.'

'I can see where you are. You won't say anything to convince me or anybody else you shouldn't be here. And I really want to know what happened between the two of you. The truth.'

Daniel looked around him again.

'I'm not talking to you. No point.'

Tom could see it now in high definition. Daniel was hiding something. Was he *afraid* to talk to the inspector? Who had told him he shouldn't?

'I'm wondering about Luke's sexuality, Daniel. Was he gay?'

Daniel pursed his lips.

'Dunno.'

Tom rested his chin on his hand.

'He had a girlfriend, and yet the medical report tells me he may have been in a relationship with a man.'

Daniel stared down at the table.

'That would be . . . that would be cruel,' Daniel said.

'If he had a girlfriend on the go but he was gay?' Tom asked. 'Yes. It would be, wouldn't it.'

Tom watched as Daniel winced. It wasn't just that he was hiding things from the inspector; Daniel was in pain.

'Let's say, hypothetically, that on the night he died, you two had sex. That you didn't rape him. Why wouldn't you tell us something like that? Why wouldn't you be shouting it from the rooftops? You know what happens to rapists in places like this. That's why you're in solitary. Why would you not want to defend yourself? Has somebody told you to stay quiet?'

Daniel started biting the skin around his nails again. Tom watched him, sizing up the situation.

'You know who doesn't believe you had anything to do with Luke's death?' Tom said. 'His brother, Ethan.'

Daniel shrugged, but there was something on his face. Surprise, Tom thought. And, perhaps, hope.

'He's a good kid,' Daniel said. 'But he doesn't know what he's talking about.'

'Well, he doesn't think you raped Luke. He says you were in love with his brother and I suspect he thinks you two were together. It's weird, that, isn't it?'

'What?'

'Twins. The bond they have. One can always tell when the other is lying. I think we're starting to form a little bond, Daniel. And I know bloody well there's something you're dying to tell me.'

Daniel glanced sideways, his cheeks burning.

Tom leaned forward.

'I'm going to keep coming back, son. You can take that as a promise.' He stood up, readied himself to leave. If the room had been any louder, he wouldn't have heard it.

'I loved him.'

Tom sat back down, brought his face close to Daniel's.

'Say that again?'

'I loved him.'

'Did you kill him?'

Daniel looked down. This time, he was the one who stood up to go. Tom watched his retreating back, more puzzled than ever.

# CHAPTER 13

Little Leaf had a more modest name than the area and its properties should have inspired. Tom had no idea of its origin – whether some developer had decided at some point that the main thoroughfare and its surrounding cul-de-sacs and roads would all be christened under the term Little Leaf, or if it had some meaning attached to the original land. The neighbouring seaside town of Dún Laoghaire came from the Irish for 'Fort of Laoire', after King Laoire established a port there.

Little Leaf was certainly beautiful but it also had an obnoxious air of wealth that Tom found off-putting. It wasn't the old, settled, comfortable wealth of places like Vienna or London. It was a forced, ostentatious wealth, new, designed to scream *We're not inferior, we're as good as the rest of the world.* The post-colonial mentality.

Tom wasn't exactly poor, but he lived in a more diverse part of Dublin, along with a whole load of other regular people, all terraced houses and small gardens. Average-sized homes to go with average-sized egos and no complicated societal norms.

Around here, everybody drove big four-wheel-drive jeep variants and kept their fences and bushes high around large detached houses. The paths outside the houses were pristine, the patches of grass surrounding the ornate lamp posts lush and trimmed. It felt very much like a pretty southern English village, but without the warmth. It was mimicry, but not the best sort.

Glenmore House, though, stood apart.

It was rare for Tom to give much store to 'atmosphere' in empty buildings, though it had happened a couple of times before – once in an old Magdalene Laundry and then again in a deserted psychiatric hospital. A feeling that bad things had happened there.

But then, he and Louise had stayed in an alleged haunted castle once, a novelty anniversary gift from one of their siblings. He'd woken up the next morning, happy and refreshed after a great night's sleep. Louise, however, had bags under her eyes and a ghostly pallor, and claimed she'd been awake half the night, shivering in the icy cold that had apparently descended on the room when the lights went out.

He couldn't put his finger on what it was about Glenmore House. He knew the building's history, but he'd been in plenty of places where horrible things had happened.

No, this place had something more to it. An aura of evil that didn't sit well in Tom's stomach, that made him uneasy. He knew instantly what the attraction was for teenagers looking for some sort of adrenaline rush, a thrill before they raced home to their comfortable, inviting, safe homes. This place felt more haunted than a graveyard.

A general air of neglect and decay oozed out of the building's three storeys. The last of the day's sun was shining brightly outside when he arrived, reflecting on the glass panes not yet broken in the windows. The ivy that draped over the wooden frames and down along the front of the stonework had begun to bud, hiding the worst of the discolouration and damp. If you squinted, you could imagine the home as it once was – a

Georgian-style build, expensive, impressive – and yet, still cold. Still unwelcoming. Could any good have ever been associated with this house?

Nobody had known what was going on inside the walls before the first murders took place. Everybody had jumped to the extremely politically-correct conclusion. They'd assumed the husband had had a nervous breakdown and, deciding his own life wasn't worth living, had also come to the conclusion that his family couldn't survive without him. Much was made about the lack of mental health resources, the cuts to special facilities, etc., etc.

Until the doctors came forward.

The woman of the house had been careful – she was listed as a walk-in at several different clinics for her various injuries. Broken ribs, wrist, nose, burn marks, blood clots. Each time she'd claimed a minor accident: a car crash, a fall, a sporting injury. Collectively, alarm bells would have rung. Individually, and with her so dismissive and articulate, nobody asked too many questions.

Then they read about what had happened.

Her husband had been beating her for years before he snapped and killed her. She'd been isolated from her family, her friends. He was estranged from his family. But at work and with their neighbours, he'd presented such a respectable front.

'This place has been sitting empty for fifteen years,' Laura said, breaking Tom's train of thought. 'In the middle of the worst homeless crisis the state has ever seen.'

'Would you live here?' Tom asked, surprised.

'Jesus, no. But I'd have knocked it and built apartments or something. Prime real estate.'

'There was no will and a lot of distant relatives climbing out of the closet,' Tom told her. 'Though I guess that's their only option when it's all settled. Who on earth would buy it now?'

The rooms inside were bare and cold. In the crime scene photographs from seven weeks ago, there had been the assorted detritus of many late-night visitors. Cigarette butts, empty plastic and glass bottles, cans and food wrappers.

The floors were clear of everything now. It had all been bagged up and brought back for fingerprint and DNA sampling by the Technical Bureau – hours and hours of probably pointless work.

'There's Emmet McDonagh ringing now,' Laura said.

'Speak of the devil,' Tom murmured.

'He's outside, I'll go open the gate again.'

She left the inspector to wander around on his own.

On the second floor, he walked to the end of the corridor and stopped outside a large bedroom.

He'd looked up the original crime scene photographs from fifteen years ago.

This was the room where the child had died. He'd gone to sleep and never opened his eyes, according to the coroner. Small mercies.

Tom touched the door, then covered his face with his hands. What made people so evil? He couldn't fathom the inner workings of a man who'd murder his own child just to punish his wife.

Tom shuddered again as he remembered reading the papers' editorials at the time, the innocent and hopeful at best, ignorant at worst. The inspector had known, even then, that something smelled rotten.

He'd seen the trend – men murdering their families and people jumping to the conclusion of a disturbed mind and diminished responsibility.

Like domestic violence wasn't one of Ireland's greatest problems.

Like the alternative – that evil walked among us, smiled at us in the post office, kept its garden mowed and its car washed and achieved success in work – was too difficult to contemplate.

'You wouldn't be long getting to ten thousand steps living in this house.'

Emmet joined Tom on the first landing. He glanced at the Fitbit on his arm and smiled, content with himself.

Over the last two and a half years, the Tech Bureau chief had, if not completely slimmed down, certainly lost a good deal of the excess weight he'd been carrying. It was partially prompted by the diabetes and heart condition warnings from his doctors. But more particularly, it had been due to the arrival of his son in his life.

He'd decided to get healthy, fit. He'd even stopped dyeing his hair that unnatural dark brown colour he'd been at for years. The grey suited him, suited his age.

He looked well; content. Entirely the opposite of Linda McCarn.

Tom sighed.

'Another flight,' he said, pointing up.

'Oh, I know,' Emmet replied. 'I've been here. Both times, in fact.'

He looked at the room beyond Tom and shivered.

On the third floor, they headed directly for the room from which Luke had been pushed.

'What's on your mind, pal?' he asked Tom. 'I'm sure you've seen the pathologist's notes. Combined with these . . .'

Emmet crossed to the window frame. Wooden boards had

been placed over the broken window, ostensibly for safety and to maintain the crime scene, but really to prevent long-lens media opportunities. On the wooden slats, white chalk was still visible where various markings had been left by the crime scene team.

Tom joined Emmet and dropped to his hunkers. He examined the scratches that had been left on the window frame. Four fingers on each side; the thumbs had just missed their grips, not that it would have mattered.

Emmet moved Tom aside and stood with his back to the boards.

He placed his hands on either side of the window and demonstrated to Tom how Luke would have been backed into it.

'He *was* pushed,' Emmet said.

'I had to see it,' Tom said. 'Something has come up which makes me wonder . . .'

'If I'm capable of doing my job.'

The voice was female, and certainly hadn't come out of Emmet's mouth.

Tom turned around. Jackie McCallion was standing in the doorway behind Tom. She was bristling and trying to look suitably respectful of authority at the same time.

'There's a pub around the corner,' Emmet said. 'Meet you there when you're finished.'

'Chief Superintendent,' Jackie said, standing aside for him.

Emmet nodded at her and left the room.

Tom crossed his arms and studied the detective. He waited a moment before speaking, to let her stew.

'I'm not saying you're not capable of doing your job, Detective. But I do have some concerns.'

'Which are?'

'There were a group of teenagers here the night Luke died.'

'Yes. We know that. It's in the report. We've spoken to all of them. They left before Luke. Before Daniel. They left the two of them up here, alone.'

Tom nodded. 'I've read the report. One of his friends – Jacob, was it? – said, and I quote, "Luke was out of it". Don't sound like good friends, do they? Why did they leave him if they thought that, again, to quote: "Daniel was obsessed with Luke"?'

'There was a lot of drinking,' Jackie answered. 'And quite possibly a lot of drugs, though none of them would admit to it. They were *all* out of it. Well, bar one of the girls.'

'Not so out of it that their collective memories weren't identical about who'd stayed in the house. Not so out of it that they didn't remember exactly what time they'd left and who was walking with whom.'

Jackie shrugged, the colour rising in her cheeks.

'According to the pathologist, it wasn't the first time Luke Connolly had sex with a man,' Tom said.

'I wasn't told that,' Jackie responded.

'Did you ask?' Tom said.

She tightened her lips, shrugged.

'Why did you immediately conclude it was rape?' Tom said. 'Because Daniel is gay and Luke was allegedly straight?'

'Seriously? Is that why you're doubting me?' Jackie's shoulders slumped. 'Every one of the boy's friends, his parents, his school teachers, his *girlfriend*, told me he wasn't gay. You think I wouldn't check that? And so what if he'd had sex previously? We have no proof Daniel didn't do this before.'

'You're now alleging Daniel raped Luke more than once?' Tom asked, his voice incredulous.

'I don't know. He could have drugged him before and Luke didn't know, and maybe this time he woke up or something. Luke wasn't gay.'

'I can't understand why you are so quick to believe Luke mightn't have had secrets,' Tom said, shaking his head.

'Look, if it had just been his parents,' Jackie replied, 'I mean, absolutely, I'd see where you're coming from. Some people are funny about homosexuality, even in this day and age, *even* in the teeth of a bloody referendum on gay marriage. Which most of the country seems to want passed. And before you ask, I certainly don't have any issue with it. But Luke was seventeen. He didn't have to keep it hidden from all his friends. He would have confided in somebody, even if it was just to say he was having doubts about his orientation. They're all young, they're a different generation.'

'What about his brother?'

She flinched. There it was, that tic to the side of her eye again.

'Ethan told you that Daniel and Luke were close,' Tom said.

'Close but . . .'

'He thinks Luke was gay.'

'Ethan never told me that,' Jackie snapped back. 'He said Daniel loved Luke.'

'Perhaps he was sworn to secrecy. Sure, this is a different generation, but, like you say, we're in the teeth of a referendum on gay marriage. On the one side, there's a hugely positive yes campaign and it's all about equality and love. And on the other, there are the old conservatives, same as usual, out bleating about how wrong it all is, how gays are off to hell and the sanctity of marriage is about to be destroyed. For God's sake, this is Ireland. Nothing changes fast. You don't know for sure how his parents felt about it all. Maybe they'd been having conversations in their house and Luke decided he was better off keeping quiet.'

Jackie opened and closed her mouth.

Tom sighed.

'Your premise for a murder over manslaughter charge is rape prior to the attack. If there was no rape, then even if Daniel was the one who pushed Luke, his defence team can argue manslaughter. But I just saw him and you know what he told me? He said he loved Luke Connolly. I think he's going to start talking.'

Jackie threw her hands in the air, exasperated.

'Right, and now he's willing. Has it occurred to you that he's shit scared?'

'Chris Connolly is a wealthy and powerful man,' Tom said, gently. 'Luke comes from a good family. His brother is dying. You're in a rush to close this one.'

'I just want to get some bloody justice for the boy. He was . . . he was just a kid. I'm not in a rush!'

'You are,' Tom said. He was trying to remain calm in the face of her escalating emotions. 'And, Jackie, I have serious reservations about securing a conviction in this case on the basis of your evidence. I'm surprised the DPP took it on. It doesn't look good, but it might be better to reopen the investigation than leave ourselves exposed if the case against Daniel is torn asunder.'

'I thought this was the very thing you stood against.'

Jackie's words were quiet. She picked at imaginary fluff on her jacket sleeve, not able to meet Tom's eye.

'Excuse me?'

Jackie met his eyes directly.

'You know what they'll say? That we're trying to cover up because he's related to one of our own. You think that won't get out?'

'That's not how I operate,' he said. 'If the boy is guilty, he'll go down for it. But I'm not allowing shoddy, rushed police work to be responsible for an erroneous conviction. Not on my watch. That's not what I stand for.'

Jackie lowered her eyes, unable to look at him.

Tom watched her.

'I'm going to talk to his friends,' Tom said. 'See what they have to say for themselves, see if they've any little secrets that might pop out at trial. Are you sure Luke was on good terms with all of them? Have you gone through his social media, his phone and so on?'

Jackie cringed.

'We looked at his social media accounts,' she said. 'There are no arguments, no fights. He got on fine with his friends.'

She stopped. The twitch was there again, the side of her face. Nerves.

'And his phone?' Tom said.

'We can't find his phone.'

'Can't find it?'

Jackie shook her head.

'You've searched Daniel's house?' Tom asked.

She nodded.

'Then where is it? Had he reported it missing? Have you asked his parents?'

'Yes!' Jackie snapped. 'It's gone. We think he lost it that night. He was drunk, remember.'

Tom frowned.

'Hold on. Have you pursued this?'

'We've looked in the suspect's house and Luke's home. There's no sign.'

'What about his phone records?'

Jackie shrugged the slightest amount.

'It didn't seem relevant,' she said. 'We know where he was that night. We've gone through his accounts. We spoke to everybody in his life. We even had access to his computer. His phone is turned off. He must have dropped it somewhere and somebody just picked it up. It's an iPhone.'

Tom took a deep breath, tried to calm down.

'Get those records,' he said coolly, and stormed from the room.

The pub was upmarket with tall tables and stools, Sky Sports on widescreen TVs, and cocktail menus on the bar counter.

Lovely surroundings and the poorest Guinness Tom had ever tasted.

He put his pint down, a bitter film in his mouth. Still, he needed the drink.

Laura had joined them and was nursing a pink cocktail that had cost him twelve euro. She seemed determined to teach him a lesson today.

'Piece of work, isn't she, Jackie McCallion?' Emmet said, raising his glass. He put it down almost as quickly as Tom had. 'Jesus. They should be shot for crimes against pints.'

'What has McCallion done to you?' Tom asked.

'She sent my team about two hundred snotty emails asking if they'd finished examining all the evidence picked up on site. It started twenty-four hours after we were summoned to the scene.'

'That confirms my suspicions, then,' Tom said. 'She was panicking.'

'That will all come out at trial,' Emmet replied. 'Just what the force needs, another botched job.'

'Possibly,' Tom said. He felt depressed just thinking about it. 'Daniel Konaté's not doing himself any favours, and Jackie and the DPP might be banking on that. I guess some people feel a prosecution, even the wrong one, is better than a case not solved.'

Tom's phone buzzed on the tabletop. It was a text message from Sean, but he noticed underneath his boss's name he had three missed calls from Natasha. She needed to back off a little, let him do his job. She shouldn't be talking to him at all.

He'd sit down with her and explain.

'I'm going up to order the eight-euro triple-cooked chips with sea salt,' Laura said. 'Want anything?'

Both men shook their heads. Tom planned to have a nice rib-eye steak with pepper sauce that night. There was no way he was spoiling his appetite in a pub that couldn't get Guinness right but still charged the earth for it.

'Come on, spit it out.' Emmet took another tentative sip of his pint and eyed Tom.

'What?'

'Who asked you to talk to me about Paul? Your wife or that bloody woman?'

Tom's eyes widened.

'How do you know anybody asked me to talk to you about anything?'

'You looked pissed off when Laura said she'd come for a drink with us and I know you like her. Plus, you've been giving me shifty looks since we met at the house. We've no business outside of this case at the moment so it can only be something you shouldn't be sticking your nose into. And might I remind you . . .'

'This never ends well. I know, I know.'

Emmet sighed.

'Look, Tom, for your own peace of mind, it's not like I haven't tried talking to the lad. Paul is . . . well, when he makes his mind up on things, it's made up. He's stubborn.'

'I wonder where he gets that from?'

'Ha. Ha.'

'Emmet, does he know everything that happened between you two back then? Everything? Have you been straight with Linda?'

'What do you take me for, Tom? You think I'm that petty? I told Paul I treated his mother badly. And I did, I do see that. A little. I should have told Linda as soon as I found out my wife had cancer. She might have understood then why I was staying put and blanking her. But I'm not going to make myself out to be a total villain. Linda never told me she was pregnant and if she had, everything could have been different.'

'Because then you'd have left your wife and you two would have raised Paul together, happy families?' Tom said. 'You'd have ignored what your wife was going through?'

Emmet blinked. He had no answer for that.

Tom took another sip from the bad Guinness.

'Why is Paul so angry, Emmet? He's, what, twenty-three now? It's old enough to get your head around being adopted, especially if your mother does want to make the effort. He's had a few years now to be convinced of that.'

'He didn't have a good life,' Emmet said. 'His adopted family had a son naturally almost immediately after they got Paul. He hasn't mentioned abuse or anything like that but he certainly felt like the cuckoo in the nest. As soon as he could, he left home and soon after that, he went looking for us.'

'And found you first?'

Emmet shifted uncomfortably.

'Emmet?' Tom said.

'He found Linda first. Obviously. Her name was on his birth certificate. Mine wasn't there. He even approached her.'

Tom was astonished.

'What? When?'

'He'd moved over here by then. He was working as a barman and got a job at an event she was attending.'

'Why didn't he speak to her?' Tom asked, his breath held, imagining how close Linda had been to her own son and not knowing. To the best of the inspector's knowledge, she'd only seen one or two photos of him, the ones Emmet had been willing to give her.

'She was drunk and she – get this – she flirted with him.'

Tom felt himself cringing. He could imagine the scene. Linda dressed in some God-awful outfit, being loud, obnoxious, playfully flirting with the nearest bloke, all completely innocent – but how would anybody know that who didn't know her?

How could her son know that?

'He was able to track me down just by talking to people who worked with her because, you know, our business is everybody's goddamned business, thanks to her, and people really don't give a shit what they're saying about each other these days. Or to whom.'

'She needs a chance to apologise,' Tom said. 'To explain. She's not coping well, Emmet. She really isn't. I hear she's planning to take a sabbatical from work.'

Emmet shrugged.

'There's more to it than that, Tom. Paul . . .'

Emmet stopped talking. Laura was back, slipping into her

seat, frowning because she could see from their faces they'd been talking about something private.

'I can't finish that,' Emmet said, pointing to the beer.

'Aye, fair enough,' Tom said. He switched back into work mode. 'Before you go – give me something more on the scene, eh? Was there anything of interest?'

'You read the report.'

'Emmet.'

The other man sighed.

'McCallion didn't consider it relevant.'

'You shock me,' Tom said wryly. 'There's a lot she didn't consider relevant. What is it this time?'

'We picked up a semen sample – Konaté's DNA.'

'On the floor, yes. Trace. Probably before or after the sex.'

'Yes.' Emmet nodded. 'Except it wasn't in the same room.'

Tom frowned.

'Sorry?'

'The same room where Luke was pushed from the window, I mean. It was in the room across from it.' Emmet shrugged. 'That's all I can tell you. There was sex in one room and the window attack occurred in the other. There might have been sex in both rooms, but we didn't pick up anything in the second one.'

Emmet briefly closed his eyes.

'Fifteen years and I find myself talking about that house again and what might have happened in it. Makes me sick.'

Tom rubbed his chin. Something had popped into his head, something Chris Connolly had said.

'Somebody alluded to there being an even more tragic element to that case than what the press managed to get hold of,' he said. 'Did something else happen I'm not aware of?'

Emmet glanced around, almost to see if anybody was listening, then leaned closer.

'I heard a rumour,' he said. 'Unsubstantiated, but we spoke about it amongst ourselves at the time.'

Tom and Laura drew closer.

'They say the wife went to the local station and tried to report the husband.'

Tom felt his stomach tighten.

'You're kidding me,' he said.

'Whether it was some cynic of a desk sergeant or a newbie who didn't know his arse from his elbow, nothing happened. Fifteen years ago, Tom. It wasn't the eighties, but it still wasn't great when it came to husbands and wives and the cops interfering. Anyway, there was no record of it and nobody came forward to admit knocking her back or failing to follow up. The rumour only started because one of the doctors, a woman, claimed she suspected something and gently suggested a visit to the police station. But the woman told her she'd already been and got nowhere.'

Tom sighed. It was unbearable, to think the woman had possibly reached out for help from the police and not received it. That her and her son's murder may have been prevented.

Emmet looked at his watch.

'I have to run, Tom. Got to finish a report for court and I need a thousand more steps to reach my target.'

Tom nodded. When Emmet had left, he turned to Laura.

'How the hell would you live with yourself if you'd let that go?' he said.

'I don't think I could have,' she said. 'I'd have struggled to come into work. I know shit happens all the time that we can't stay on top of but . . . with a kid involved? I'd say if you went back through the records of Little Leaf station and found somebody packing it all in a few months later – you'd pin down who the woman tried to talk to.'

Tom found himself nodding in agreement.

'And now we've this,' he said. 'McCallion is working on the assumption Daniel raped Luke and they fought afterwards. Let's say Luke tried to get away, tried to escape from Daniel. Once you'd emerged from a room on the third floor, wouldn't you take the stairs down? Why would you run across the hall into another room, one with no exit bar a window?'

'If you were high, you might not be thinking straight,' Laura said.

Tom rubbed his jaw, considered it.

'It's falling apart and we're only scratching. Did McCallion really think this would stand up under a judge? I know we can talk down legal aid but, Christ on a bike, the kid deserves to have half a chance to defend himself.'

'It's pointless, though,' Laura said. 'If Daniel doesn't want to fight; if he's uncooperative.'

She twisted the stem of her glass in her hand, still contemplating.

'I think there's another point that would have raised a flag for me, though.'

'Yeah?' Tom said.

'Yes. Luke and Daniel are roughly the same size, right? Well, it's difficult for a bloke to overpower another bloke and rape him, one on one. So, McCallion's obviously working on the assumption Luke was too drunk or drugged to fight back. In which case, why was he pushed to his death? You have a boy, you've just raped him, maybe he's crying, angry, saying he's going to tell everybody – and he's too out of it to run away; you know that because you've just managed to overpower him. You'd strangle him, wouldn't you? Or kick his head in, or bang it off the floor a few times. It just doesn't feel to me that pushing somebody from a window is a crime that follows rape. I guess if you wanted it to look like an accident but . . . you'd already raped him. There isn't a person alive who doesn't know about DNA at this stage.'

Tom took another drink, forgetting again the bitterness of his pint as he swallowed with discomfort.

Laura really was very smart. What she'd just said was exactly the reason Tom had told Natasha he'd look into the case. Death in sexual crime usually occurred through strangulation or suffocation of some sort, sometimes stabbing.

Pushing somebody out a window was the best way of making a death look accidental. Everybody knew that sexual assault left evidence, but not everybody would be aware of the ways in which it could be ascertained that a body had been pushed from a height, as opposed to an accidental fall.

So, what if the sex and the murder had involved two separate people?

# CHAPTER 14

Dylan Keating hated his life.

He hated his parents. He hated his friends. He hated his school. He hated exams.

Hated, hated, hated.

Sometimes, lying in bed at night, wide awake because masturbating hadn't done its job and staring at the ceiling was getting him no closer to sleep, he'd think about all the bullying, the nastiness, the cruelty, everything he'd ever swallowed.

Everything he'd ever been weak enough to swallow.

Sometimes he wished he could shoot everybody, then kill himself.

Dylan thought about killing himself a lot.

He'd looked up the various methods – hanging, wrist-slitting, tablets.

The problem was, Dylan didn't like pain. Basically, he'd had enough of it to know it wasn't something you invited in.

So, really, the only route he would even consider was tablets, but then, you could never be sure, could you? He'd read horror stories. People not taking enough or taking the wrong sort and dying slowly, agonisingly.

'Do you want jam and butter, sweetie, or just jam?'

Dylan looked up from the kitchen table, where his history

texts were spread out in front of him, pages opened on the Industrial Revolution.

His mother was holding toast in one hand and a knife in the other. She was wearing an expensive designer dress and high heels and had had her hair done that day, yet there she was, making his tea in the middle of their top-brand kitchen. And there was nothing incongruous about it at all. She liked to look good for his father, she always said. And Dylan would say nothing, because what *could* he say?

'Just butter.' He smiled.

'I need to feed you up, sweetie. All this studying you're doing, you'll wear yourself out. Let me put a biscuit on the side.'

Dylan rolled his eyes. He'd spent his early childhood fat as a fool, thanks to his mother's need to feed him up. She would spend fifteen hours a day in the gym if she could, but Dylan had to be fattened like a calf for market.

She'd actually, unintentionally, been responsible for a lot of the bullying. If he hadn't been such a large target, maybe he would have escaped their notice.

His father had stepped in when he was thirteen. He began to take Dylan hiking. They'd walk for miles and miles, Dylan huffing and puffing behind while the old man banged on and on about whatever shit he was handling in work that week.

Dylan hadn't been sure back then exactly what it was his father did, except that it involved *a lot* of money. Later, he'd learned his father didn't just do one thing. His work involved having his fingers in many pies: media, a horse stud, property; he even had a small share in a Premiership team.

His dad was minted.

They talked a lot about money on the hikes, before, during and after.

What they didn't talk about were the beatings Dylan Senior gave Dylan Junior when they reached the summit of whatever hill they were on.

*Fat little piggie fuck.*

Dylan Jr hated his life.

By contrast, Jacob Quinn Delaney lived a charmed life. He moaned a lot about his parents never being around. Well, he liked to pretend it wasn't moaning, that it was all a big joke, but Dylan knew it upset him. He wanted to grab Jacob and shake him and tell him he should be glad his parents left him alone. That it was Dylan's dream – to move out, to get away from his father. And his mother.

His dad hadn't given him a hiding in years. The last time, Dylan, aged fifteen, had threatened to tell everybody. But the real reason his father had stopped hurting him was because after two years of hiking, all that fat had turned into lean muscle. Dylan was towering over his dad, who clocked in at a very modest five foot four.

They all lived a charmed life, his *friends.*

But they were a toxic little mix of money and meanness and boredom.

What was it Luke Connolly had said to him?

'It's like you stole the life Daniel should have had, you little twat. Imagine Daniel with everything he has going for him and having a bit of money on top of that? Life's not fucking fair.'

No, it wasn't fair, was it, Luke? Not that Luke realised how lucky he had it.

Luke couldn't even be grateful for what he had in the face of his own brother dying. Ethan was the only decent one of the lot, and definitely the nicer twin, and look what life had handed him.

Dylan's mother placed the toast in front of him and kissed the side of his head. She'd added jam, a gateau bar and a packet of crisps.

Dylan smiled through gritted teeth.

Nothing was fair.

# CHAPTER 15

Tom wore his full suit into work the next day. Which was madness, because his office was half packed up and the movement of so many old files and books had left a sheet of dust on almost everything.

'Do you have a secret hoarding habit?' Willie asked, throwing papers from 1999 into one of the trash bags.

'Hey, that's the New Year's Eve paper before the turn of the century,' Tom replied, rescuing the one on top.

'I rest my case,' Willie said, exiting with the bag before Tom could salvage any more of his treasures.

Tom was nervous. So bloody nervous. He could hear Ray's voice out on the corridor, growing louder with each approaching step.

Maybe he should have brought him for a drink. Broke it to him over pints. Not made it so . . . official.

'Hey, boss.'

Ray was wearing his full suit, too. He'd got a haircut. He was looking his absolute most professional.

Tom's heart sank.

'Howya. Eh, take a seat. Just, em, close that door.'

Ray did as he was told.

'Laura says you're going to be talking to the Connolly kid's friends?' Ray said. His voice was expectant. Hopeful. 'Sounds like an interesting case. Dynamite for the media. Rich, middle-class boys and the gay, black outsider.'

Tom nodded. He opened his mouth. His tongue was dry.

'You alright, boss?'

Tom nodded again. Why couldn't he find the words?

'Eh . . . your stag, Ray?' he said. 'Do you want a weekend, or just a night?'

Where the hell had that come from?

'Just a night?' Ray answered, confused. 'I don't really care, to be honest.' He sat back in his chair.

'What's up? I know you didn't ask me in here during office hours to talk about my stag.'

Tom took a deep breath.

'I wanted to talk to you about who's going to be taking over when I leave this position.'

The colour started to rise in Ray's cheeks. Tom steeled himself.

'You're a fantastic detective, Ray. One of the best and one of the most experienced. I've no doubt you're going to rise up the ranks.'

Ray blinked. He looked down at his hands, back up at Tom. It was the inspector's tone, not just his words. Ray got it.

'They're bringing somebody in, aren't they?' Ray's voice was small.

'No,' Tom said firmly. 'The decision has always been up to me. It was a condition I asked for.'

His deputy looked confused now.

'I'm offering Laura the promotion,' Tom said, as quickly as he could get it out.

Ray's mouth fell open. When he closed it, his face was a picture of confusion and hurt.

'It's not that I think she's a better detective than you,' Tom said. 'It's just, this job requires a certain managerial skill. Sometimes that's all the job is, even more so than actual police work. It's a step on the ladder to full administrative management, which is exactly where I'm heading now. Laura is good with people; she has good organisational skills. She's . . .'

'I get it,' Ray said. He smiled, weakly. 'I can hardly be jealous of my own fiancée, can I? I'm thrilled for her. You're right. She'll make an excellent DCI.'

'Ray, I know this isn't going to be easy—'

Ray held up his hand.

'It's fine, Tom. Don't underestimate me. I'm pissed off for myself – I mean, I'm not going to lie, I'd have liked the promotion. But Laura is a great fit. I know that. I know you'll have spent a long time making this decision.'

Ray dropped his eyes.

'It stings. A bit. But when I go down the hall, I'm not going to show her that, not even for a second.'

Tom didn't know how to react. Ray's response was simultaneously making him feel proud and like the worst shit in the world.

'When are you going to tell her?' Ray asked. Already his face was beginning to even out as he consciously replaced the shock with calm acceptance.

'Em, I'll officially offer it to her today.'

'Officially . . .' Ray hesitated. 'She already knows, doesn't she?'

Tom glanced sideways.

'I didn't tell her. She just guessed.'

'And you talked about it?'

Tom nodded.

On the other side of the desk, Ray grimaced.

'Did you talk about me?'

Tom said nothing. Ray waited, in the silence.

'Well. I guess she is a better detective than me, after all,' he said. 'I had no idea this was coming.' He stood up. He hesitated for a few seconds, but whatever he was going to say, he changed his mind. Ray pushed back his chair and headed for the door.

'Ray,' Tom said.

His deputy stalled, his fingers already gripping the door handle.

'She was going to refuse it. For you.'

Ray didn't turn.

'That would have been really stupid, wouldn't it?' he said, and then he was gone.

Tom sat there, feeling like a quiet hurricane had just blown through the office.

What had he done?

The door closed; Tom had barely time to breathe before it opened again.

This time it was Natasha McCarthy.

'Are you avoiding my calls?' she said.

Tom stood up, felt in his pockets. Where had he left his car keys? To hell with it; Sean could drive that afternoon.

'Yes, I'm avoiding you, Natasha,' he said. 'And I'm going to be avoiding you for as long as I'm looking into Daniel's case. I would have thought that you, of all people, would get that.'

The last sentence was snapped. Tom instantly regretted it. He rested his hands on the table and steadied himself with a deep breath.

'Sorry,' he said.

Natasha nodded. She raised her hand to her chest, began to fiddle agitatedly with the buttons on her cardigan.

'Don't be. You're right. I just . . . I just need to know what you think.'

Tom had already pissed off one friend today. He didn't want to mess with another relationship.

'If Daniel was involved, I'm not sure it was deliberate,' he said. 'But I don't know, Natasha. I just don't know. I'm not happy with the investigation, or what I've seen of it so far. But in the grand scheme of things, that means very little.'

The look on Natasha's face was pure relief.

'Oh, thank God.'

Tom shrugged.

'That's a long way from proving he's not guilty.'

'I owe you for this, Tom.'

'No,' he said. 'Don't say that, Natasha. Because if he is guilty, the evidence I find will leave no room for doubt in a jury's mind.'

'He's not,' Natasha said. She shook her head adamantly. But in her eyes, there was the tiniest glimmer of doubt. Almost imperceptible, but there.

She'd seen too much in her career. She knew there was very little innocence in the world.

It was probably that doubt that Daniel had seen when Natasha had tried to speak to her cousin, Tom realised. That's why he wouldn't talk to her, or any police. If he felt his own family didn't believe him, what hope was there?

# CHAPTER 16

'So, do you think we'll take the Six Nations this year?'

Sean was getting along quite well with Jacob Quinn Delaney. They'd found common ground on the subject of rugby. While football, especially Gaelic, was Sean's primary love, anything that involved a ball held appeal for him.

It was an area in which the chief and the inspector diverged. Tom enjoyed watching the Premiership and GAA, but his sport of choice outside of those was golf. Not that he played it much. He found viewing it relaxing, especially the Masters at Augusta; he dreamed of going there, if only to see the magnolia trees and sip warm southern bourbon.

There was something about rugby that didn't do it for Tom. Perhaps it was the possibility that at any moment somebody might break their neck.

In all likelihood, though, it probably stemmed from the fact that Tom's upbringing had been working class. And where he came from, on the north side of Dublin, he'd always considered rugby the preserve of well-off lads in the better schools on the south side. Well-off, entitled, privileged lads.

He sat back as Sean and Jacob discussed the merits of Ireland's defence. He was happy to observe Jacob for now.

The lad had an air of arrogance to him, but Tom was seasoned enough to read between the lines.

He'd answered the door of his huge house and told them he was home alone. Dark, close-cut hair. A square chin and wide shoulders. A rugby jersey and tight jeans. And a desperate, determined attempt to exude a sense of maturity and confidence that Tom wasn't entirely sure was completely in residence.

Sure, Jacob had recently turned eighteen. A man. But Tom was surprised, given what had happened in recent times and with his best friend's funeral imminent, that his parents had chosen that fortnight to head off on holidays.

And it had clearly crossed Jacob's mind, too, for all the bravado.

'What position did Luke play?' Sean asked.

'Scrum-half. He was a good team player.'

'And you're captain,' Tom confirmed.

'I'm a good leader.' Jacob shrugged. 'The lads look up to me.' He said it like it wasn't a boast, just fact.

'Luke's other friends who were in Glenmore House that night – Brian Power and Dylan Keating – are they on the rugby team, too?'

'Brian is. He's the one on his way over now. Dylan isn't into rugby. Not tough enough.'

'Me neither,' Tom said. Jacob gave him a look – he was sizing him up. And then he nodded, a hint of superiority and condescension on his face.

Tom smiled, bemused.

'Daniel,' the inspector continued. 'How did he feel about rugby?'

Jacob grunted.

'I don't want to talk about that little runt. Not after what he did.' Jacob looked like he wanted to spit.

'What he's accused of doing,' Tom corrected.

Jacob watched him, quizzically.

'Accused by your lot. You've arrested him, haven't you? You don't do that unless you're sure.'

'And you seemed fairly sure in your statement about Daniel's guilt,' Tom said.

Jacob stood up, walked to the expensive Gaggia on the kitchen counter. He filled the reservoir at the back of it with water and turned on the switch.

'We should have told him to fuck off years ago. He wasn't one of us.'

'In what sense?' Sean asked. 'He wasn't from your school? From money? Or . . .'

'I don't give a toss that he's black,' Jacob clarified.

'So why did you hang out with him?' Tom asked.

'I didn't. Luke did. And Luke was my best mate, so.'

'Your best mate. Not Daniel's best mate.'

Jacob shook his head.

'But they were close,' Tom added. 'Ethan, Luke's brother, seems to think they were very close.'

'Bollocks. Ethan doesn't know what he's talking about. He's been in and out of hospital for the last four years. *I* was more like a brother to Luke than Ethan was.'

'That seems harsh,' Tom said. 'The boys were twins. It's not Ethan's fault he's ill.'

Jacob opened his mouth, then thought better of it.

'No,' he said. 'Fair enough. But have you any idea what a pain it was for Luke? Constantly having to visit? It's bad enough when your parents force you to hang out with your sibling when they're well, let alone . . . There's only so much fucking poker at a bedside you can play before you're bored out of your wits.'

Tom narrowed his eyes. He pitied anybody who ever got sick around Jacob. His Florence Nightingale gene seemed to be entirely absent.

'You don't think they were close, then?'

Jacob hesitated.

'They were. Of course they were. It's just, on this, Ethan is imagining things. It must be the medication he's on. He obviously implied something like that to that other cop, what's her name – McCallion – because she asked me about it. I told her, not once, not *once*, did Luke even remotely hint that he was gay. Nor did anything like that come out of Daniel's mouth, for that matter. And I'd have known, wouldn't I? It's nonsense. Luke was with Charlotte. Charlotte Burke. She gave a statement. We all knew they were together. Daniel's gay. Luke wasn't. Daniel . . . he ra–'

Jacob couldn't say it.

Tom and Sean caught each other's eye.

'Is it possible, lad,' Sean said, 'that Luke was keeping it secret because of how people would react around him? That maybe Ethan was closer to his brother than you were, or think you were – that he picked up on it and you didn't?'

Jacob looked uncomfortable.

'No. What, I wouldn't have a gay friend? Shit, I'm as tolerant as the next bloke. There's a gay lad in our class; we've never, like, gay-bashed him. Sure, there's a bit of joking. A bit of slagging. Nothing nasty, like. Luke would join in. Luke was probably worse than the rest of us. I called him out on it once, for being a bit homophobic. It's not like it's catching. Anyway, we're all making badges in school for a Yes in the marriage referendum. It's only the really weird kids – let's face it, the ones who are probably gay – who don't join in. Luke would have known we'd be fine.'

Jacob laughed, but it was hollow.

'Luke was my mate,' he said. 'I knew him, inside out.'

For all his naivety and stupidity, Jacob really did miss his friend, Tom realised.

And in that moment, Jacob looked dreadfully young and alone.

The coffee machine started to hiss. At the same time, the doorbell rang.

'It's Brian,' Jacob said, looking away from the two policemen. He left them and went out to open the door.

'You think times have changed,' Sean said, quietly. '*Only the weird kids are gay.*'

'Times have changed,' Tom said. 'It's just . . . it's still hard, when you're a teenage boy and surrounded by other lads all trying to out-machismo each other. It takes a strong personality to suck up that . . . bit of slagging, was that what Jacob called it?'

They both frowned.

A few seconds later, Jacob was back, accompanied by Brian.

They looked nothing alike: one dark-haired, one mousy-haired. Brian was shorter than Jacob, less stocky. And yet, in their almost-matching uniforms of Leinster jerseys and jeans, Adidas with the tongues loose, and identical crew cuts, they were near twins themselves.

Who set the style? Tom wondered.

He wasn't long figuring it out. For every question, Brian deferred to Jacob with a look first. For every thought of Jacob's, Brian was able to finish it. Brian was the follower.

'Brian, you also remembered Daniel and Luke still being in the house when the rest of you left?' Tom asked.

'Yeah, we all left and, like, it was Daniel and Luke upstairs?' Brian said.

'Was it?' Tom asked.

'Sorry?'

'It's just you said that like it was a question.'

'Oh.' Brian tilted his head. 'No, I mean, they were.'

He glanced at Jacob. He was tacitly seeking permission to speak, Tom realised.

'Did you go to Glenmore House often?' Tom asked.

'Sometimes, yeah. It was, like, just one of the places we'd hang out to get some peace from the olds, you know?'

'That night, why did you leave Daniel alone with Luke?' Tom asked.

'We, uh, we'd been drinking? Luke wanted to stay out but we wanted to leave. Daniel was there, so.'

'You said they were both upstairs and that Luke was "out of it".'

'Yeah. But, like, we thought he was safe?' Brian shrugged. It said, *None of this is my fault.*

'Did Luke seem happy to stay with Daniel?' Tom paused and rubbed his chin. 'I mean, you didn't think there was anything to worry about, did you? There was absolutely no indication that Daniel was a danger to Luke?'

Brian shook his head, adamantly.

'No. Like, we wouldn't have left him . . .'

'What's the point of all this?' Jacob asked. 'We know Daniel attacked Luke. You're the ones who have the evidence.'

Tom ignored him and turned back to Brian.

'So, there's no way you would have left Luke if you thought he was in danger and yet, in your statement you also said that Daniel was acting weird around Luke and that he was *obsessed* with him. You both used that word.'

Brian looked over at Jacob. His friend's face was burning; he knew Tom had deliberately walked Brian into a trap of his own making.

'Okay,' Tom said. 'Moving on. When you all left together, who was with who?'

Brian and Jacob looked at each other again. Checking in, Tom mused.

'Jacob, me, Dylan walked behind. The girls were walking up ahead.'

'And you all went home to your individual houses; nobody was staying over with anybody?'

'No,' Brian said. 'We parted ways, as they say, and went home.'

Tom watched both boys. And then he and Sean exchanged a glance. And something unspoken passed between them.

The boys were lying.

'Did you notice Luke using his phone that night?' Tom asked. 'Nobody picked it up, or brought it home by accident or anything?'

Jacob and Brian shrugged.

'The woman detective asked had we seen his phone,' Jacob said. 'I can't remember if he had it.'

Tom nodded. On that, Jacob appeared to be telling the truth.

He watched as the teenager crossed to the coffee machine and pressed the button to release the liquid into the waiting cup.

Then Jacob picked up a bottle of whiskey from the counter, uncapped it, and added a measure to the coffee.

# CHAPTER 17

Ray had been staring at the same bunch of flowers for at least ten minutes. He could feel the eyes of the saleswoman boring into his back. She'd already asked him if he needed help.

Sure, he'd answered in his head. How big and expensive should the bouquet be to convince my fiancée she's the love of my life and I don't resent her getting the big promotion I should have had?

'No, just looking,' he'd actually said.

Jesus, what was he doing? Laura would see straight through flowers, wouldn't she? They weren't that kind of couple.

He crossed to the door of the shop and opened it, the little bell jingling.

Then he closed it, walked back in and picked up the largest bunch on display.

Laura was in their apartment, cooking dinner. She didn't notice him come in. She had the Bluetooth player on and connected to her phone. Music was blaring and Laura was watching a pot of pasta bubbling. Her curls were tied up in a high ponytail, swinging against her black fitted top with each movement. Ray stood in the door frame of the kitchen, watching as she lifted a glass of red wine to her lips. She took a large gulp. Then she returned to stirring the pot, even though it didn't need it.

Wine, pasta – the only meal she could really put together without setting fire to the place. She was planning to tell him tonight. He could see the tension in her shoulders, slightly raised; the way her fingers gripped the glass stem, the fact the bottle was already half empty.

'I already know,' Ray said aloud. He just had to get it over with. They had to deal with this, and quick, before the rot set in.

She jumped, then turned.

'Tom told me,' he added.

She hesitated. Then she blinked furiously, pale, anxious.

'I'm sorry.'

And in a moment, Ray's head was completely clear. He placed the ridiculously sized bunch of flowers down on the table and crossed the room. He put his arms around Laura and squeezed her with all the love he felt.

'What the hell are you sorry for?' he said. 'What have you done? Other than be absolutely brilliant at your job?'

'You thought the promotion was yours. We all did.'

'Screw what I thought. If he'd given it to Michael Geoghegan or Brian Cullinane, I might have been miffed. Not you. You can buy and sell all of us in HQ.'

'I think they're making a conscious effort to promote women.'

Ray shook his head, angry. He leaned back, cupped her face with his hands.

'Don't you dare think that. This has nothing to do with your being a woman. It's got everything to do with you being better than the rest of us.'

The relief that filled Laura's face made everything else irrelevant. Ray could barely feel the stone in his stomach any more.

'I bought you flowers – the biggest in the shop. I was coming home to congratulate you anyway. I nearly didn't buy them because I thought you'd think I was making too much of an effort.'

She laughed and pushed him gently.

'I was making you this fancy dinner so I could break it to you . . . I was terrified you were going to say you were planning a transfer or something.'

'How did you know . . .' Ray blinked and tensed.

Laura looked up at him. She sensed the change in atmosphere.

She froze.

'Oh, Ray,' she sighed. 'You're not, are you?'

The two of them looked at each other, saying nothing.

# CHAPTER 18

It was late, but it seemed the gym only really came alive around 7.30 p.m. Tom and Sean had gone straight there from Jacob's house. They flashed their badges at the guy on reception and he'd let them through the gates.

So there they were in their suits, standing in the middle of a giant room, people on the left using various elliptical machines, people on the right pumping iron and Stealers Wheel playing in Tom's head.

TV screens blared MTV and the room smelled of body odour, rubber and a distinct lack of fresh air. The two men were already sweating.

'I feel unhealthy just being in here,' Sean said, as they strolled up the green carpet aisle that ran through the centre of the workout area. 'What's wrong with a field and a ball and not breathing in everybody else's body fluids?'

'What's wrong with watching a movie or reading a book?' Tom replied, acutely aware the closest he came to exercise these days was taking the stairs in HQ.

They found Charlotte Burke and Hazel Brophy on the cross trainers, both in luminous pink cropped vests and black leggings, their hair tied up in identical high buns and, Tom noted, both wearing full make-up.

Charlotte hopped off her machine immediately upon Tom

showing her his badge. Hazel slowed but kept the rhythm going – up, down, up, down – while she studied the two men.

'Is this legal, you coming here to talk to us on our own?' she said. 'We're both still seventeen, you know. Should we call our parents?'

Tom shrugged.

'One of your friends is about to stand trial for the murder of your other friend. This isn't a formal interview. We just want to chat – but of course, you're absolutely entitled to have appropriate adults with you. If you'd like to ring them, we can all head back to the station and do this there.'

'Hazel,' Charlotte said, a warning note in her voice.

'Oh, fine. We've only just started, but I've a spin class at eight, so can we do this quick?'

Hazel stopped the machine and grabbed her water bottle, petulantly.

'There's a juice bar over there,' Charlotte said, pointing in the direction of the back of the gym.

'Oh, lovely,' Sean replied. 'I'm in the humour for something green and . . . algae-y.'

Charlotte smiled shyly. Her friend rolled her eyes dramatically.

'What's the point of this?' Hazel said, repeating the sentiment they'd been on the receiving end of since Tom and Sean had launched themselves on this escapade. She sipped on the six-euro juice Tom had bought her and looked up at him again. 'We all know what Daniel did. Are you afraid he's going to get off? Because, I can tell you, that will be a total head melt. Somebody will have to sue or something. We always knew there was something not right about him, didn't we, Charls?'

Charlotte jutted out her bottom lip. So far, it didn't feel like Charlotte and Hazel's friendship was a replica of Jacob and Brian's relationship.

Tom got the impression she didn't always agree with her friend but, in this instance, she couldn't deny it.

'He was . . . intense,' Charlotte said.

'Intense?' Hazel said, mockingly. 'You said he was a creepy bastard. Remember, he was always staring at you and Luke when you were together.' Hazel turned to Tom and Sean. 'We thought at first he was into Charlotte. That he was faking the gay thing. Turns out . . .' She raised her eyebrows, made a *now we know* look.

Charlotte stared at the floor, said nothing.

'You and Luke were an item, is that right?' Tom asked. 'You told our colleagues you were his girlfriend?'

'I *was* his girlfriend,' Charlotte said.

She reached up to the bun in her hair and loosened it, like it was hurting her head. Long brown hair fell onto her shoulders, kinky from the damp sweat. She was pretty in a much softer way than Hazel, whose face was remarkable for its high, harsh cheekbones and slanted eyes.

'For how long?' Tom asked.

'Six, seven months?'

'Five and a half,' Hazel corrected.

Charlotte flashed her a look.

'What?' Hazel said. 'I know because *I* was with him before that.'

Charlotte's lip curled in distaste.

'Oh,' Tom said, shaking his head. 'I didn't realise. That's . . . interesting. How did you two end things?'

Hazel shrugged, casually.

'It just happened. Luke and I split, and I went with Jacob.'

'Any other couple swaps we should know about?' Sean asked.

Charlotte paled. Her eyes sought anywhere that wasn't Sean or Tom.

Hazel's features contorted in anger.

'We already spoke to Jackie about this,' she said. 'Luke wasn't gay.'

Jackie, Tom noted.

'It's sick, what Ethan is saying,' Hazel continued. 'That shit about Daniel loving Luke. His own brother, too. Whatever about Luke and Charlotte, Luke and I were . . .' She caught herself, coloured. 'Well, it's just, Charlotte has this thing about after marriage and all that shite. I'm – you know – normal. I think women should own their bodies. We're beyond all that slut-shaming crap that used to go on back in your day.'

Tom and Sean caught each other's eye and smiled.

Charlotte sighed, the resigned sound of somebody familiar with a thinly veiled insult.

'It's not really normal, though, is it, to shag half the rugby team and claim it's empowering?' Charlotte turned back to Tom before Hazel could retort. 'My parents are Mormons.'

'I see,' Tom said. 'Your parents – so you are, too?'

'Pretty much.'

'Pretty much,' Hazel said scornfully. 'She doesn't drink, smoke, screw – sorry – so, yeah. Boring as fuck, Charls, these days. Aren't you?'

Charlotte grimaced.

'We became Mormons two years ago,' she said. 'It's been hard for my *friends* to adjust.'

'So, of everybody there the night Luke died, you were stone cold sober?' Sean said.

Charlotte nodded.

They'd given more weight to her statement in the case file, Tom remembered. It made sense now.

'And you remember leaving with everybody and Luke and Daniel staying behind?' he continued.

'Yes,' she said. 'There was me and Dylan and the other three were behind.' There was a momentary flash of something on her face and then it was gone.

'And, as for your other question,' she said, blushing, 'what Ethan is saying is nonsense. I wouldn't sleep with Luke. But that didn't stop him from trying. I mean, why would he even bother, if he was gay? He could have just pretended. But he wasn't pretending, he was really romantic. He loved me.' Her eyes started to water. She reached for the phone strapped to her arm in a sport's pocket and took it out. Then she scrolled through until she found something.

'Look,' she said.

Tom took the iPhone from her and found himself looking at a WhatsApp conversation:

*L. I'm thinking about you, Charlotte. Your gorgeous hair, your beautiful eyes. Your lovely boobs.*

*C. Stop, you idiot.*

*L. I'm kidding (unless you want to show me them?). You know how much I love you, right?*

*C. Show me on Valentine's.*

*L. I've bought you the biggest teddy bear. A teddy bear from your teddy bear.*

*C. Aww . . . totes adorbs.*

Tom scrolled along the message. It was the same sort of silly stuff, right up to a day or so before Luke died. He felt Charlotte's eyes on him. She wanted the phone back and he detected a note of urgency.

The phone still in his hand, he exited the message and scanned the messages folder without changing facial expression.

There. 'Gang.'

He opened it. All their names were in it – Hazel, Luke, Jacob, Dylan, Brian, Charlotte herself. Tom scrolled up quickly, speed-reading through nonsense. He'd just caught the end of an exchange – *What the fuck we do now?* – when Charlotte reached over and actually took the phone out of his hand.

'Sorry,' she said. 'It's a bit embarrassing.'

How far back had that been? Tom wondered. Twelve, thirteen weeks?

He watched as Charlotte tucked the phone back in its pocket, her face red. There was something on that phone she didn't want him seeing. Had it been that last message he'd read?

'By the way, have you any idea where Luke's phone ended up?' Tom asked.

Both girls shook their heads.

'Who got the drugs that night?' Sean asked.

'There were no drugs,' Hazel said.

'Oh, come on,' Sean insisted. 'There were drugs in Luke's system.'

'Then he must have taken them after we'd left. That sicko must have given them to him.'

'Were there drugs?' Tom asked Charlotte.

She shook her head again but refused to meet his eye.

'Just drink. That was all.'

'And you were all hanging out in one of the old bedrooms,' Tom said.

The girls nodded, quiet suddenly, even mouthy Hazel.

'The one where a woman was murdered fifteen years ago.'

'Well, like, yeah. It would have been disturbing to hang out in the room where the kid was killed.' Hazel shuddered in disgust.

'I'm not sure I'd hang out in either,' Tom said. 'I can understand you wanting an empty house – that's teenager stuff – but why one of those rooms? Were you telling ghost stories or something?'

Hazel laughed, but it was a cover.

'Ghost stories are for babies,' she said.

Tom met Charlotte's eye. She was staring at him now, unblinking.

'We had a Ouija board,' she said. 'We'd done it before.'

'A Ouija board?' he repeated. 'There was nothing about that in your statement.'

'It was just a joke. We were messing. It didn't seem important.'

Charlotte tugged on her bottom lip with her finger and thumb.

And right then, Tom got the distinct impression there was a lot more she wanted to confess. She wasn't accidentally letting things slip out.

She was intentionally trying to get his attention.

# CHAPTER 19

Dylan Keating was their final stop of the day, but he was still in study group. His mother had gone to collect him, so only his father was home.

Tom and Sean spent a couple of minutes chatting with Dylan Keating Sr, arranging to talk to Dylan Jr the next day. He was a charming man, smaller than Tom had imagined him. More accessible than he would have guessed, too. The Keating home had an electronic security gate but it was still on a normal road in Little Leaf (if any of the roads around there could be described as normal). Although the inspector had heard Dylan Keating Sr had houses in several places, including Monte Carlo, London, Madrid and New York, so perhaps rather than investing a lot in a single mansion in Ireland, he'd decided to spread the load.

'My son is traumatised,' he told Tom and Sean. 'We're just hoping it doesn't affect his Leaving Certificate, you know. Couldn't have come at a worse time, all this. He's studying hard. He doesn't want – and I wouldn't want it for him – to be dependent on my money. Fair play. He needs a good college and a degree. To find his own way in the world, that sort of thing.'

Charming, friendly – Tom couldn't quite figure out what it was about the man that set his antennae buzzing, but there was something. And Sean obviously felt the same way.

'He probably has a gimp costume in the back of his wardrobe

and makes his wife wear a saddle while he roars "giddy-up" during lovemaking,' Sean said, as they drove back down the Keatings' driveway.

Tom burst out laughing.

'He is hiding something, isn't he?' he said. 'It's not just me.'

'Of course he is!' Sean said. 'Nobody that rich is just a regular chap, no matter the aura they try to give off.'

'That's true,' Tom said. He fell silent, mulling over what he'd learned.

'What's on your mind?' Sean asked.

'There was something in a WhatsApp group chat on Charlotte's phone,' Tom replied. 'I didn't get a chance to read it properly.'

'Yeah?'

'Some sort of argument or panic, a few months ago. It stood out because the rest of the messages were all chit-chat and gossip. But in this message, she'd said, "What the fuck do we do now?" '

'I see,' Sean said. 'That's interesting.'

They turned out of Little Leaf, Sean heading for the coast road.

'So, Charlotte,' Sean said. 'The girlfriend, as we're calling her, she was sober. You have to believe she's telling the truth. You would hardly resist losing your virginity as part of your religion but lie about throwing booze into yourself. She insists the five of them, the three lads and two girls, left together, leaving Daniel and Luke behind in Glenmore House.'

'But, it's the first time we've heard a discrepancy,' Tom pointed out. 'Charlotte said she was walking with Dylan. Jacob said the girls were together up ahead and the lads were lagging behind. The five statements, if I recall correctly, all said the same as Jacob's.'

'Ah,' Sean said. 'This is true. So. What's the truth then about

Luke? Was he playing Charlotte very well, or is she conning herself?'

'Or do we have it wrong?' Tom lifted his hands. 'I don't know. There was no need for him to send her those messages if she was just a front for him. Daniel said something, by the way, when I met him–'

'Would you look at that little shit!'

A car had overtaken them using the oncoming traffic lane, barely pulling into the correct lane on time.

'You want to chase him?' Tom asked, grabbing the passenger door armrest.

'My arse. This is a Volvo, Tom, I'm not making it do anything it doesn't want to do. What did Daniel say?'

Tom exhaled. He pulled out his phone and texted the licence plate of the car ahead to Ian Kelly.

'He said that Luke could be cruel,' he said. 'In so many words.'

'Hmm.' Sean considered this. 'And yet he was still his buddy. Perhaps even his lover.'

'Those closest to us are the ones who see our real flaws, though, aren't they?' Tom said.

They drove in silence for a minute or two.

'The courts won't take forever to set a date,' Sean said. 'What's our plan? Where are we going with this?'

Tom shrugged.

'Honestly, I don't know. Let's talk with Dylan Keating. Find out more about Luke and Daniel. Maybe talk to Daniel's friends, if he has any outside of that little gang. I don't know how much or how little pressure was brought to bear on those kids by McCallion, but you know as well as I, teenagers are not good at keeping their mouths shut. With the exception of Daniel, unfortunately.'

'You think one or more of them hung back in that house and Daniel and Luke weren't on their own?'

'Yeah,' Tom said, nodding. 'I'm considering it. I'm considering everything, including the people nobody else seems to have considered.'

'Like?'

'The adults. The proper ones, I mean, not the recently-got-my-voting-card ones. The parents.'

Sean said nothing for a moment. Then he smiled.

'A Ouija board. Are they still a thing?'

'Fecked if I know. Maria is a bit old for one and Cáit doesn't need a device to summon the devil; she just opens her mouth and screams.'

'Are we all that stupid when we're young and we just grow out of it, or are today's kids particularly dumb?'

'Jesus.' Tom gave a short laugh. 'Sean, you really are old if you think we were any less idiotic.'

Maria was in the house when he got home. Cáit was with her other grandparents and Maria had agreed to help her mother empty the attic – yet another job Tom had allegedly been promising to do for several years.

'Are you feeling broody or something?' Tom called up from the landing at the top of the stairs. Through the open door over his head he could hear all sorts of grunting and shunting of various boxes and bags. 'Is this nesting?'

Louise's head appeared in the door space.

'I'm spring cleaning, Tom. It's occurred to me that when you start in the chief's job, I'll see even less of you, so I've decided to tackle your list. I thought that was blatantly obvious after the freezer. Nesting, Jesus. What are you doing, anyway?'

'I have to do some research. Eh – what's my list?'

'Oh my God, don't even talk to me. You know like when I say, "Tom, can you do something for me, love of my life?" and you say, "Of course, Louise, I'll put it on my list".'

'Oh, yeah.' Tom squirmed. 'That list. Can I help with something now?'

'Yes. We want Chinese. Beef in black bean sauce for me. Maria?'

Tom heard a muffled reply.

'She wants shredded duck. Thank you!'

'This is why I'm getting fat,' Tom called up.

Louise disappeared. Tom shrugged and returned downstairs.

He placed the order with the Chinese restaurant, then turned on his laptop.

The IT department had sent him links to the Little Leaf teenagers' social media platforms. All of them, bar Daniel who was positively restrained with only one or two accounts, were on Facebook, Twitter, Instagram, Tumblr and Snapchat. Tom felt his head spin. How much energy did it take to keep on top of all these things? When did they study, let alone socialise?

Tom prided himself on knowing his limitations and letting the experts do their jobs. When he needed advice on information technology in a case, he went straight to the Guards who specialised in it. He wasn't cut out for Silicon Valley parlance, and while he knew that left him out of date in the world he lived in, he sort of hoped everything would come full circle and people would eventually realise social media was all a big load of nonsense. His dearth of knowledge might pass by without anybody being any the wiser. That, or he'd have to start attending those bloody classes they kept offering.

Even with his lack of knowledge, though, he was aware of the inescapable Facebook and Twitter.

He tried Facebook first but the Little Leaf's kids' privacy settings were excellent. Tom was proud of them. They'd obviously heeded the cautionary tales.

So he went on Twitter to stalk them there.

The first handle he looked up was Jacob's. He didn't tweet much and when he did, it was rugby scores, links to articles about players and a few derogatory remarks about management strategy. Tom scrolled through the timeline – Jacob had tweeted so little, it was easy to reach the start date.

Dylan's was fairly similar but had dried up almost completely when he entered his final year in school. Tom suspected all of Dylan's social media accounts would show the same. Extra study classes at night; he was taking his exams very seriously.

Which begged the question: why had he been out with the gang that night at all?

Hazel's twitter account was a different beast. She'd posted thousands of tweets. Her profile declared her 'Feminist but not afraid to be feminine, love men, hate misogynists'.

'Hmm,' Tom murmured, and scrolled through her tweets. Hazel's brain was a mass of contradictions. She appeared to be a huge fan of women being able to wear whatever they liked. She cited Ariana Grande as a role model – Tom jotted her name down on the pad beside him – and had also retweeted multiple times about some strong, inspirational woman called Nicki Minaj.

'Nicki Minack? Nicki Minich?'

'What are you doing?' Maria walked into the sitting room carrying a brown paper bag. Her long brown hair was tucked behind a hairband, her cheeks streaked with dirt. 'Didn't you hear the doorbell?'

Tom shook his head.

'It's Min-*aage*,' she clarified. 'And what, why or how are you interested?'

'Is she a feminist?' Tom asked. He was squinting at the photo on Hazel's page. 'She wears very small thongs a lot.'

'So we're upstairs clearing out filth and you're down here looking at it? Hmm. Depends on how you define feminist. She's a singer who's into teeny tiny clothes and rapping about penises.'

Maria disappeared out of the room. When she reappeared a few minutes later, she'd plated up his roast pork kung po.

'You're a star,' Tom said, balancing it on the arm of the chair. He nodded his head at the laptop screen.

'This girl doesn't seem to like her gal pals very much – for a feminist, I mean.' He'd just encountered some particularly nasty tweets about some girl in Hazel's class.

Maria frowned and came around to see what he was looking at. She leaned over and scrolled through the tweets.

'Feminist, my eye,' she snorted. '"Hazel Brophy" is one of those idiots who seize upon an *ism* to defend themselves when they choose to be complete arseholes. Really unpleasant and nasty and if anybody challenges them, it's because they have an issue with the *ism*. Anyway, should I be worried you're stalking teenage girls on Twitter?'

'Your mum is getting older,' Tom said. 'Time to look for a replacement model.'

Maria swiped at the back of her dad's head.

He smiled. 'I'm keeping an eye on a whole gang of kids – they have about four thousand social media accounts between them.'

'That sounds about right.'

Tom took off his glasses and turned to Maria.

'Do you have accounts like this?'

Maria laughed.

'I have a nearly four-year-old daughter and a college course, that's what I have, Dad. I'm on Facebook, that's about it. So's Mam.'

'Is she?'

'Yeah. You are, too.'

Tom's eyes widened.

'They give you accounts even when you don't want them?'

'Jesus Christ, Dad. What century is it? No, they don't give you accounts. We set one up for you. In case you ever wanted one.'

'But I don't want one.'

'Well, that's okay then. Your blue anonymous head can remain anonymous. Can I go? My food is getting cold and I have to call Mam down. She's probably trapped under a box of your old records and long johns.'

'Very funny,' Tom said. 'So, you were never, like, bullied on social media or anything?'

Maria laughed out loud.

'What?' She pointed at the tweets on the screen in front of Tom. 'God, you think that's bullying? Slagging off somebody for being chubby without even tagging her so she'll see it? Wow, Dad. You should hear what kids actually say to each other these days.'

Maria was at the sitting-room door, about to leave.

'Like what?' Tom asked.

'Oh, I don't know. Like, "Why don't you fucking kill yourself, you ugly fucking bitch." Lovely stuff like that. And, no, don't worry, I never had any of it.'

Tom let her go.

He chewed distractedly on forkfuls of his dinner, going through the rest of the Twitter feeds. There didn't seem to be anything violent between these kids.

Luke was his penultimate search.

Any negative interaction he found between the lad and the rest of his friends could only be described as sparring, nothing more.

Luke's page, in fact, was about as interesting as his male friends'. It was mainly sports and music, though he did seem to be marginally more curious about the world around him. He'd shared some satirical articles on politics and current affairs, even linking to pieces about US politics, Catalonia and Palestine.

There were photos of Luke with the other lads, including Daniel. He could only find one with Ethan, a picture taken at Christmas. It was a sad, distressing picture – Ethan in a hospital bed, his family gathered around, a small Christmas tree, everybody, including Ethan, wearing tinsel around their necks. Forced smiles. Luke had written the caption *Making the best of a shit Christmas.* Plenty of people had tweeted back hearts and sad face emojis.

Daniel's Twitter feed was sparse enough, consisting mainly of retweets of YouTube music videos.

Tom sighed. His eyes were swimming from reading the screen. He made himself concentrate and went back into Charlotte's profile, looking for anything resembling the comment he'd spotted on her phone. He found nothing.

He heard Maria and Louise in the kitchen, talking and laughing.

'Maria!' he yelled.

Her head appeared in the door a few seconds later.

'Want me to take your plate and get you tea now, is it?' she asked, an eyebrow raised.

'No, I'm still eating, but tea would be nice after. Before you go – is there an easier way of searching Twitter accounts for tweets you want to see? Can I put in a search word or something?'

'Not unless it's a hashtag.'

'What?'

Maria clapped her hand to her forehead.

'What are you looking for, Dad?'

'I don't know. An interaction that might have taken place a while ago. I can't see anything. It doesn't matter.'

'Are you looking at "Tweets" or "Tweets and Replies"?'

Tom frowned, puzzled.

'Top of the page. Go into "Tweets *and* Replies".'

When she'd closed the door, Tom did what she suggested. Now Charlotte's account was even longer.

He'd gone as far as the end of January, four weeks before Luke had died, when he saw something. Charlotte had tweeted, *Jesus. Delete that.*

Tom clicked into the tweet, feeling a frisson of excitement. What had she wanted deleted?

She'd been replying to Jacob.

He'd tweeted a moving image – a GIF. It was a cartoon character running around in flames. Tom hadn't clocked it the first time he'd scrolled down Jacob's wall.

Brian and Luke had liked it. Underneath Charlotte's tweet, Hazel had tweeted, *You're sick, Jacob.*

Tom sighed. There was nothing there, except the age-old tradition of teenage boys having bad taste and teenage girls being disgusted by it.

The sitting-room door opened; Louise appeared this time.

'Right, your break is over,' she said. 'I have a few boxes out here and we're giving them to charity. I want you to put the boxes in the back of your car and under no circumstances are you to open them.'

'Why, what's inside them?' Tom asked.

'It's better you don't know,' his wife said, mysteriously.

And suddenly Tom was racking his brains, trying to remember what he'd been storing for safekeeping and nostalgia's sake in the attic.

# CHAPTER 20

'Stay still or I'll poke you in the eye.'

Hazel held her little sister's forehead and started to apply the liner to Mia's eyelid. She didn't really need it. Mia had always been naturally dark and people often stopped their mother when they were out to comment on her beautiful brown eyes and long lashes. When they were younger, Hazel would flick her hair and try to look adorable, and be completely ignored. It used to upset her.

'Ouch!' Mia flinched as Hazel brought the liquid liner up a little too hard on the curve at the edge of the eye.

She hadn't intended to hurt Mia. Her phone had beeped, yet again. Another whiny text from Charlotte.

Jesus, that girl. She just couldn't let anything go.

'Sorry,' Hazel said, and dabbed at the side of Mia's eye with a baby wipe. 'There. You're beautiful.'

She held the mirror up for the ten-year-old to admire herself. Mia's eyes widened. She looked like a little doll. And that's what she was, really. Hazel's doll.

Hazel had realised early on that jealousy of her baby sibling was getting her nowhere. So she changed tack. She made Mia hers. After all, you can't be jealous of what's yours. Only proud.

'I look like a grown-up,' Mia said, voice awed.

'You do. But we'd better get it all off before Mum comes and finds you like this. She got her knickers in a twist about a bit of lip gloss. The full RuPaul is probably a bit much. Take a picture and send it to your pals on Instagram, quick.'

'When do you think Mum will let me wear make-up properly?' Mia asked. 'What about for my Confirmation? I'll be twelve, then.'

'I think there's more chance of her letting you mainline heroin than wear make-up to your Confo,' Hazel said, starting to scoop up the various bottles and concoctions. 'Anyway, you don't need it.'

Hazel's phone was beeping again. She glanced at it and barely heard her sister speak again.

'Hazel? Hazel! I said, can you help me make some cakes? Or give me money?'

'What? For what?'

'We have to bring in cakes for a school bake sale.'

'Jesus, get my purse,' Hazel snapped. She knew Mia would have preferred baking the cakes, but if their mum was too busy, there was no way Hazel was making them. She'd once asked her dad how to boil an egg and he'd said, 'Just put the egg in the pot on the cooker.' So she did just that. Without water. Cooking wasn't her strong point.

Nor was money. Hazel's family was nowhere near the level of her friends and it cost a fortune to keep up with that image. But she wouldn't let Mia down.

Mia crossed to the other side of the room and started opening various bags and purses hanging on the side of the dressing chair.

Hazel picked up her phone and looked at the screen.

'For fuck's sake, Charls,' she muttered, and opened the ten messages that had been sent.

Didn't Charlotte realise Hazel was stressed, too? It wasn't fair, her acting like she was the only one grieving in all this, like she was the only one who was sad and worried.

Like she was the only one who was innocent.

Charlotte had the *good girl* act down pat. Even when she'd essentially stolen Luke from under Hazel's nose, nobody reacted. It was like they expected Hazel not to feel hurt, like Charlotte couldn't do anything wrong.

But Hazel had been hurt. Deeply. By both of them.

Hazel shook her head. She couldn't think about that now. She hated getting too emotional. It was weak. Strong women didn't cry over men and they especially didn't fight with other women over men.

She scrolled through the increasingly desperate texts until she got to the last one.

*I need to know*, it said. *What happened when he went back into the house?*

## CHAPTER 21

Only a few days had passed, but Ethan Connolly was weaker the second time Tom and Sean met him. He'd texted Tom requesting a visit. Tom had nothing to tell the lad but, Christ, he felt sorry for him. Luke's brother needed company and, at the very least, they could ask more about Luke and Daniel's relationship.

Rose Connolly was sitting by Ethan's bedside that morning, knitting and talking animatedly, when Tom opened the door and announced their presence.

'Come in,' she said, brightly. 'Ethan, it's the detectives.'

Ethan turned his head a little in their direction.

'Hey,' he said, his voice barely above a whisper.

'Gosh, look at me, sitting here knitting.' Rose smiled and stood up. She held out the needles almost apologetically. 'I took it up when we first started doing chemo. Just to have something to do with my hands. Turns out I'm a natural. Not very fashionable, I know, but I'm knitting comfort toys for preemies. Premature babies? Have you heard of them? The toys, I mean. They put them in the cots. My father was a paediatrician, so I know a bit about it.'

They let her talk. After a minute or so, Rose's cheeks flushed. She knew she was rabbiting on.

'It's good of you to call in. Ethan's a bit tired, though. I'm not sure he's up to questions.'

Tom shrugged.

'That's fine. We won't be long. We can sit with him for a few minutes if you want to go down and get yourself a coffee or something?'

Rose looked down at Ethan uncertainly. He nodded his head, the tiniest movement.

'Sure,' she said. 'I could do with stretching my legs.'

When she'd left, Tom and Sean took the armchairs again, drawing them a little closer to Ethan's bed.

'How are you feeling, son?' Sean said. 'Are you actually tired or feigning it so your mum stops talking about babies and knitting?'

Ethan smiled weakly.

'Oscar-winning performance,' he said. 'You talk to Daniel?'

'Yes,' Tom said. 'Well, we talked, but he wouldn't say anything.'

Ethan's lids fell heavily over his eyes. There was a small sighing sound. He opened his eyes again; it looked like a struggle.

Tom watched the boy in the bed for a moment, then decided to just come out with it.

'Ethan, did Luke ever actually tell you he was gay or are you just guessing?'

Ethan flinched. He said nothing.

'Because . . . he was gay, wasn't he?' Tom said.

There was a slight nod of the head. Ethan had confirmed it.

'I see,' Tom said. 'Why was he so concerned about telling other people? Why did it have to be secret? The whole thing with the girlfriends – was he confused or . . . ?'

Ethan took a breath.

'Lying.' The effort to make a complete sentence seemed to exhaust him.

He sighed, then steadied himself.

'He was cruel to the girls.'

Tom made a note. There was that word again. *Cruel.*

It was cruel, to have pretended. Teenage girls had fragile hearts. If Charlotte had found out he'd been using her . . . or Hazel . . .

'His friends are adamant he was straight,' Tom said. 'Jacob in particular. We haven't spoken to Dylan yet.'

'Not . . . surprised.'

'Why's that?' Sean asked. They both leaned closer, trying to hear Ethan.

'Jac . . . ob. Rugby. I always thought it was . . .' A deep breath. 'All a bit homoerotic. Maybe they're in the closet.' He smiled.

Tom stroked his chin, considered for a moment.

'Ethan, do you remember anything happening with your brother and his friends a few months ago?' Tom asked.

'Like?'

'I don't know. A falling-out? An argument over something?'

Ethan closed his eyes. He looked like he was thinking about Tom's question but the inspector had the distinct feeling that he'd closed his eyes to give himself time to think about his answer.

Twins knew everything about each other, didn't they?

The door opened and Claire, the nurse from the other day, came in.

'I heard you had some special visitors again,' she said. 'Oh, dear. Not even sitting up today, Ethan?'

It was funny, Tom thought, how she spoke to her patient. She couldn't be more than a couple of years older than him but she had that nurse way of speaking. Like she'd been doing it for decades.

She approached the bed and took his vitals. Her face contorted with concern as she held Ethan's arm and watched the blood pressure monitor.

'I might just pop down and grab some coffees,' Tom said, giving Sean a sideways glance. Sean nodded. He got it. Tom wanted to speak to Rose Connolly on her own.

Ethan barely responded.

Tom left the room with Claire in tow; she called cheerfully to Ethan that she was going to get his doctor and would be back in a mo, false jollity in her voice.

'Should I tell his mother to come up?' Tom asked, seeing the expression of concern on her face once the door closed.

Claire shook her head, her blonde curls bobbing.

'No, it's fine.'

'Is he . . . How long does he have left?' Tom asked.

Claire pursed her lips.

'His blood transfusions are more frequent now,' she said. 'That's never a good sign. And he has less and less energy each time. He used to have spurts of it but . . .' She sighed. She looked genuinely distressed.

'He thinks he's going to get better,' she said. 'But he's not. Not this time.'

'It must be very hard,' he said. 'To see it happen to somebody so young. So close to your own age, too.'

She shrugged.

'You know what makes it even worse?' Her voice was harder now, angry. 'That brother of his. It's knocked Ethan for six. It's hard when they're at this stage to get any length of time out of them, but when they suffer a shock? Jesus. Luke had the world at his feet. And he threw it all away, while Ethan never even had a chance.'

'Well, I don't think he threw it away, as such,' Tom said.

'I'm sorry, but wasn't he off his face on drugs and drink?' Claire continued. 'Whether he was pushed or he fell, you don't go down that route and expect to live happily ever after. It's playing Russian roulette with your life.'

'Plenty of kids take drugs,' Tom said, surprised at how unforgiving she was.

'Yes,' she said, turning on her heels and starting to walk away. 'And plenty of them end up in places like this having their stomachs pumped.'

He watched her retreating back, her shoes clipping away on the linoleum, and supposed she was right. When you worked with patients like Ethan, you saw life's injustices in high definition. It wasn't fair, when there were some people who had no choice, that those who did could have so little respect for their own lives.

Rose was sitting outside the canteen in the small patients' garden. She'd perched herself on a bench, her cardigan wrapped tight around her, a cigarette in her hand.

'I know,' she said, looking up at Tom, smoke drifting into the air. 'And in a hospital that specialises in cancer treatment.'

'Needs must,' Tom said, sitting down.

They enjoyed the silence for a few moments. She smoked like she was inhaling oxygen. Tom stared back through the window of the canteen, watching the queue of hospital visitors and patients at the self-service counter as they chose from plastic-wrapped sandwiches and tried to work a complicated coffee machine.

'So, Luke was gay,' he said, after a time.

Rose shrugged.

'I . . . I don't know. Maybe.'

'Ethan knew. Is that why you told me to speak to him?'

Rose nodded.

'Why didn't you say it when my colleagues suggested Luke had been raped? You know the fact that everybody said he was straight impacted on that assessment?'

'He never told me,' Rose said and her face was pained. 'And I was in such shock at what had happened . . .'

'Why didn't he tell you?' Tom asked.

'He was . . . he was only seventeen. Just a child. It's easier, sometimes, to talk to your brother than your mother.'

'But children often turn to their parents when they're confused – it's not unheard of.'

'Yes, well, my husband,' Rose said, like that explained everything.

'Chris would have had a problem with Luke being gay?'

'He'd have had a problem with Luke being anything other than what Chris perceives as perfect.' Rose sighed. 'God, how do I put this? I know it sounds contradictory, but Chris isn't homophobic. Well, not classically so. But these are special circumstances. When Ethan first got his diagnosis, Chris came to terms with where it was leading quicker than I did. He didn't overtly give up on Ethan, but there was – um – a transfer of ambition. All his hopes and dreams were funnelled into Luke.'

Rose pushed the still-blonde strands of hair that had fallen into her eyes back behind her ears. Tom noticed her manicured nails were chewed, the colour of the polish fading. But she'd put on lipstick and a nice dress to visit her son, confirming Tom's earlier speculation that she reserved all her energy for the hospital.

'Luke would be our only son,' she said. 'So he would be the

one who achieved academic success, who won rugby games, who went to discos, learned to drive, got married, had grandchildren. Who did everything by the book.'

Tom whistled.

'Wow. That's a lot of pressure.'

'He ticked most of the boxes,' Rose said. 'For his father's sake. Luke used to be more into books than sport but he let his intellectual side slide. He joined the rugby team, not the debate team. But it . . .' She winced. 'It made him difficult, at times. Angry. Bitter. It's hard to be the twin who's dying but, my God, it's hard to be the twin who's living.'

Tom nodded, thoughtfully.

A pained look fell across Rose's face.

'I loved Luke so much,' she said. 'He was the second born. Just a quirk of fate. It was a C-section; they took Ethan out first, then Luke. He didn't cry for a minute and I thought my heart would stop. It was like, *That's it; because they're both so small, only one of them will survive, and I should be grateful for that.* But I didn't feel grateful. I was greedy for both of them. Then he cried. He's been my baby ever since. He was, I mean.'

She stood abruptly.

'Now, I'll have neither of them,' she said.

'I'm truly sorry,' Tom said.

'What are you sorry for?' She looked down at him. She'd been beautiful, once. A smiler, you could see it in the creases around her lips and eyes. Tom wondered how she'd ever smile again. He couldn't, in her position.

'You really don't think Daniel killed Luke, do you?' she said.

Tom lifted a shoulder slightly, then said, 'I don't know.'

'I think they were close,' Rose said. 'But I don't think that means he didn't hurt him. You can still hurt the ones you love.

We all know that, don't we? But I want you to make sure. It all felt so rushed with the other detective. I mean, it made sense, but it didn't make sense. I'm sorry I didn't say anything about my suspicions that Luke was gay. It got lost in the middle of everything. It felt like, I don't know, I was betraying him. After all, it's not like he wanted people to know.'

'Look,' Tom said, 'as you say, it could still be rape and murder, even if Daniel and Luke were together. Even if they were . . . in love. If Luke had, I don't know, dumped Daniel or said he preferred girls, something like that. It could have made Daniel angry.'

Rose watched him for a few seconds.

'Find out,' she said. 'Because I keep thinking about Daniel's mother, too, and wondering how she's coping with all this.'

Rose lowered her eyes and walked off.

Tom sat in the April sun for another few minutes, waiting for Sean. He thought of Rose, and how remarkable she was to have such charity in her heart. It was too easy to make assumptions about people based on where they lived or what they worked at or whom they'd married. He'd seen nothing in Rose that didn't indicate goodness.

He checked his texts. One was from Louise, reminding him to ring his sister and wish her happy birthday. For yesterday.

The other was from the assistant commissioner, Bronwyn Maher, asking him to call into her later. Not good, Tom thought.

And one from Laura. She'd written '*Armageddon*'.

Ray, Tom realised. He must have pushed the transfer button.

But Tom had too much on his plate to deal with that at the moment.

Shit, shit, triple shit.

# CHAPTER 22

Tom and Sean went straight from the hospital back to Dylan Keating's house, and this time, he was in.

Having already met the other four kids in the Little Leaf gang, Tom instinctively knew Dylan Keating did not fit in with his friends. He looked different, for a start. He had an actual hairstyle, not a crew cut. He was paler, his chin a little weak, his body language more deferential than arrogant. His clothes may have been expensive but they didn't hang on him well, mainly because his posture was so bad, crouched forward like he was constantly prepared for an attack on his person.

He was polite, offered to make tea, fidgeted nervously in the face of Tom and Sean's authority. His family was the wealthiest of the set, that much was obvious, yet he was humble. None of the swagger or the arrogance of his pals.

The kitchen they sat in had a country cream theme but there was little that was homely about it. Somebody had put a lot of money and thought into the design. The taps were space age and the fridge and other unattractive utilities were nowhere to be seen, hidden behind the glistening cupboard doors. Expensive Denby crockery was on display on some shelves, as well as a set of champagne glasses.

The kitchen opened back into a large conservatory, with

floor-to-ceiling windows. Beyond that, an expansive lawn ran to the woods at the rear of the property.

Tom looked down the green and counted in his head how many houses could be built on the patch of land and still leave the Keatings with a large garden.

'You're not on the rugby team,' Tom addressed Dylan. 'Jacob mentioned. How did you all end up friends, so?'

Dylan shrugged.

'Same school. And our parents.'

'Parents.' Sean raised an eyebrow in solidarity. 'Been a while since I had that problem, lad, but I'm familiar with it. Mine had a thing about me hanging out with a girl from the farm near ours. You ever seen *The Field*?'

'We studied the play,' Dylan said. 'John B. Keane.'

'Course you did. My part of the country was a bit like that. Her father was the devil, according to mine. Didn't stop me wanting her to join me in the far fields at the bottom of our farm.'

Dylan blushed.

'We take your point, Chief,' Tom said. He turned to Dylan. 'Do you get on, though? You, Jacob and the others?'

'They're alright. In small doses.'

'What about Luke and Daniel, what were they like when you were all hanging out?'

'Daniel was okay. Luke was . . .' Dylan winced and fell quiet.

'Don't speak ill of the dead?' Tom said, suspecting that was the cause of the pause.

'You've met Jacob,' Dylan answered. 'Luke was Jacob, except smarter. Sharper. He had a way with words that Jacob doesn't, really. Jacob was the brawn; Luke was the brains.'

Tom nodded.

'In your statement, you said the five of you left the house that night, leaving Daniel and Luke upstairs. You, Jacob and Brian were together and Charlotte and Hazel walked ahead.'

'Yes.'

'So you weren't with Charlotte?'

'What?' Dylan looked innocent enough, but Tom could see the calculation running behind his eyes like a ticker tape. *Who's said what?*

'Were you walking up ahead with Charlotte?' Tom repeated.

'I don't know. Maybe for a minute.'

'Hmm,' Tom murmured, but added nothing. Clever, that, to allow for some doubt, but only a fraction's worth.

'And you all went home to your individual houses?'

'Yeah.'

'It's interesting,' Sean interjected, 'that Charlotte was happy to go home alone, leaving her boyfriend behind. Did nobody offer to walk her home? It was late. You'd all taken something, bar her, so presumably she had her wits about her.' Sean paused as Dylan cringed. 'She'd have known it was dangerous to stroll home on her own at that hour. You seem like a gentleman, lad. Didn't it cross your mind to accompany her? Did Hazel walk home alone?'

Dylan glanced sideways. He wasn't a good liar.

'Hazel was with Jacob and Brian,' he said. 'I can't remember if I offered to walk with Charlotte. It's not something we usually do. It's not dangerous around here, anyway.'

'Dangerous enough, if what happened to Luke is anything to go by,' Sean said.

'Yes, but Daniel did that.'

Dylan lowered his eyes, stared down at the marble countertop. Was he, too, having doubts, the inspector wondered?

'So, if you were up ahead, even for a couple of minutes, there might have been a window,' Tom suggested. 'There might have been a few moments where not everybody knew what everybody else was doing, or where they were. You might have been talking to Charlotte, distracted.' Tom paused. 'She's a pretty girl. Seems nice.'

Dylan shrugged.

'Did you get into trouble with your parents, afterwards?' Tom said. 'When they found out where you'd been that night and that you'd been drinking? I'm guessing they were happy to have you safe and well, after what happened, but – well, you seem to study a lot. I'm guessing they're strict.'

'I wasn't drinking that much,' Dylan said, shaking his head. 'And they're not strict.'

Tom was surprised at the vehemence.

'I study a lot because I can't wait to get the fuck out of here. I hate Little Leaf.'

'That's, eh . . .' Tom paused, looked to Sean for help.

Sean shrugged.

'You feel strongly about it,' Sean said. 'This seems like a nice house, a nice place to live. Your parents have money; you don't go without, I'm guessing. They're not strict, you say. So what are you running from? Your friends?'

'I can handle them,' Dylan said. 'Luke was . . .'

He clamped his mouth shut. Tom watched him. He'd a feeling he knew what Dylan had been about to say. *The worst.* Luke was the worst.

'It's not one thing or the other,' Dylan said. 'It's everything.'

His face, Tom noted, had such a lost quality to it. Dylan Keating was not a happy kid. But why? Because of what had happened recently? Or was there more?

'What was Daniel like to be around?' Sean asked.

'He was fine,' Dylan said. 'He was . . . nice. The others could be a bit snobby about Daniel, but I liked him.'

'And Luke liked him?'

'Yeah,' Dylan said. 'I know what's been said. Look, Luke seemed to be into Charlotte. He seemed to be into Hazel, too. But Luke had this talent of knowing how to act in whatever way he was supposed to. Like in school – he could be talking away, joking, getting up to all things, but as soon as a teacher turned their head towards us, he was Mr A Student, good as gold. He never got caught.'

'Do you think he was acting at being straight?' Tom asked.

'I don't know,' Dylan said. 'That's the problem when you're a good actor. You're good. How can anybody know? But there was something between him and Daniel. None of us can deny that. They had a . . . thing. I wouldn't have cared. But Jacob and Brian – they talk the talk about being all modern and shit, but they'd feel something, you know?'

'Yes. I know,' Tom said. He found Dylan interesting. And, honest. For the most part.

The kitchen door opened and an attractive woman walked in. She was in running gear, a Nike T-shirt and shorts, her blonde hair in a ponytail. She'd obviously just finished exercise, but she wasn't sweating; she looked probably as good as she had when she left the house, maybe just a little windswept.

As she approached them, Tom noticed the smoothness of her forehead and skin around her eyes and cheekbones. The slightly bee-stung plumpness of the lips.

Botox, he realised. It wasn't that he hadn't seen it on people before, but that was generally on TV, not in somebody's kitchen in Dublin. Hollywood's ways hadn't quite hit Ireland in the same manner as elsewhere.

'Oh, my goodness,' she said. 'I didn't realise you were here. Look at the state of me!'

Tom and Sean stood up. Dylan, Tom saw, rolled his eyes, ever so slightly.

'DCI Tom Reynolds and Chief Superintendent Sean McGuinness,' Tom said, introducing them.

'Of course! I'm Dylan's mom.'

What was with the Americanisation of everything, Tom wondered? It seemed a peculiarly South Dublin thing.

'If I'd known you were coming, well, I'd have at least showered,' she giggled.

'You look great as you are,' Sean said, smiling benignly. For all his crankiness, Sean could always turn it on for a good-looking woman. Although this one seemed to think of herself more as a girl. She blushed and tugged at the bottom of her ponytail, almost cooing in the wake of Sean's praise.

'You don't even have refreshments,' she said, noticing the empty table, her expression scandalised. 'My goodness, Dylan. Guests!'

'I offered,' he said, weakly.

'What can I get you?' she continued, ignoring her son. 'Coffee and cake? I have a lovely Victoria jam sponge. Or apple tart. Or perhaps you'd like sandwiches? I can do bagels and cream cheese?'

'Really, we're fine,' Tom interrupted, before Sean could order a double course. It was amazing, the amount of food the woman seemed to have, considering they could see none of it in the minimalist-designed kitchen and she herself looked like a crumb never passed her mouth.

'Oh, what a shame,' she said. 'Well, the offer is there. So, do we know when that man will stand trial for what he did to our Lukey? It's utterly appalling. He was quite a favourite of yours, wasn't he, Dylan? I'm just so glad you came home safe that night. That's awful of me to say, isn't it? It's just how I feel.'

'Not awful,' Tom said. Beside him, Dylan was bristling. He'd been a ball of tension since she arrived. The inspector was starting to understand why the kid wanted to escape.

'Dylan,' he said, turning to the lad. 'Do you know Ethan, Luke's brother?'

'Not very well. We were in different primary schools and obviously, by the time he started secondary school, he'd been diagnosed. Why do you ask?'

'No reason. He seems to have liked Daniel, too.'

'Liked Daniel?' Dylan's mother clasped her hand to her breast. 'Honestly, does that matter now? After what happened?'

Tom shrugged.

'It's important because Ethan doesn't believe Daniel would have hurt Luke. What do you think, Dylan?'

Dylan opened his mouth to say something. Then he looked at his mother and closed it again. He rubbed at his neck with his hand, considered for a moment.

'He must have done,' Dylan said. 'He was the only one left with him.'

# CHAPTER 23

'Where is he?'

Jacob was agitated. Brian wasn't used to seeing his friend so unsettled. Jacob was the cool one. The relaxed one. That's why he was the captain of the team. In the face of chaos and panic, it was Jacob who knew how to steady them, how to inspire them, how to look defeat head on and beat it.

But since Luke's death, the world was on its axis. Jacob had lost his power. And as it was he and Luke who held the group together, that was not good.

Brian picked up his phone again. He'd two missed calls from his mother – she'd left a voice message reminding him to pick up a box of chocolates for his grandmother, who was coming for dinner later. There was nothing from Dylan.

'He was meeting the cops today,' Jacob continued. 'How long does it take?'

Hazel planted a glass on the table in front of him. They were in Jacob's TV room. Brian was sitting on the couch, a box of Domino's chicken bites on his lap. Charlotte was lying on the chaise longue in the corner, one arm hanging languidly off the side, the other twirling the curls in the ends of her hair.

Jacob was perched on the edge of an armchair. He'd moved from the couch to the window seat, from standing to pacing, all in the space of the short half-hour they'd been there. He couldn't relax.

'Drink that and chill, will you?' Hazel said. She'd been raiding Jacob's parents' drinks cabinet all week. As far as Brian could tell, she'd no intention of replacing the alcohol, either. That was what she always did, got stuff for free. Flash you a teasing smile and expect you to pay for everything.

Not that she'd ever delivered on any of her promises to him. Which had made him frustrated. And angry. And bitter.

'I don't want sloppy seconds,' he'd said to Jacob one night, purely to hurt Hazel, knowing she was listening. 'Or is it sloppy thirds? I've lost count.'

'What are all these questions from the cops about, anyway?' Jacob continued. 'Why do they keep asking whether there were drugs? Just because they know Luke took something – why assume? We can't have that shit getting back to school. We can't have it getting back to coach.'

'They're not concerned about the drugs,' Charlotte said, from the corner. 'They don't give a shit about the drugs. They're trying to figure out if it was one of us who pushed Luke. They think we're covering up for each other.'

'Don't be stupid,' Jacob snapped, then looked panicked. 'They have somebody in custody. They have Daniel.'

'They're not happy with that,' Charlotte said. 'That's why they're still asking questions. Like where Luke's phone went. By the way, do any of you happen to know anything about that? Because there are some pictures on there I'd like to get hold of.'

Hazel glared at Charlotte. There was something going on between them, Brian thought. Lots of meaningful looks and sniping.

As if on cue, Charlotte got up and moved towards the room's double doors. She paused with her hand on one of the white wooden panels and stared at Hazel.

Seconds later, Hazel followed Charlotte. Jacob didn't seem to notice. He was knocking back the drink Hazel had given him.

Brian chucked a chicken piece into his mouth and stood up.

'Want anything?' he asked Jacob.

'Get me another one of those.' Jacob nodded at his glass.

Brian picked it up and moved to the door. Jacob was already fiddling on his phone, oblivious to the fact he'd just been deserted by everybody.

The girls weren't in the kitchen. Brian took a litre of milk from the fridge and slugged from it. He wiped the lid with his fingers before putting the carton back in the door of the Smeg.

He wandered through the ground floor of the house – the reception room, the study, the library. To the best of Brian's knowledge, nobody in the Quinn Delaney family read books. And yet they'd a library full of old tomes that he'd bet cost a fortune. Brian knew Jacob's father's favourite pastime was trying to make as much money as Dylan Keating's dad. And Jacob's mother's hobbies included getting her hair done and chasing younger men. She'd once drunkenly made a pass at Brian. Maybe she'd done it with Luke, too. The woman was a nympho.

Brian couldn't see Charlotte and Hazel anywhere.

He went upstairs, pausing at the bathroom on the first landing. He could hear the girls talking inside.

Brian dropped to his hunkers and peered in the keyhole.

Hazel was on the toilet, her knickers around her knees. Charlotte was staring at her reflection in the mirror over the sink, examining a small scar on the underside of her chin.

The girls looked annoyed with each other.

'I haven't answered you because I don't fucking know what you want me to say,' Hazel said. 'No matter how many texts you send me or calls you make. And you acting like a crazy woman is not helping. Why did you say that to Jacob? Don't you think he's panicking enough?'

'Maybe he has reason to panic,' Charlotte said. 'Maybe you should blow him, help calm him down. Isn't that what you do?'

'For fuck's sake, Charlotte.' Hazel stood up. Brian smirked as he got full sight of her nakedness before she reefed her knickers up. Nice. 'It was just the once and me and Luke were out of it. I don't see what entitles you to get annoyed. *You* took him from *me*, remember? Little Miss Innocent. And then you just left him hanging. His balls were bursting by the time *I* got to him.'

'Do you have to be so crass?' Charlotte snapped. 'Do you think that's cute? It's not. It doesn't make you sound hot; it makes you sound like a tramp.'

'I can do what I like with my body,' Hazel spat back.

'Sure. It's just other girls might object if you do what you like with *their* boyfriends' bodies.'

Hazel pushed Charlotte away from the sink and washed her hands.

Charlotte sat on the edge of the bath. She was twirling the ends of her hair again, frowning, a picture of stress.

'Anyway,' she said. 'I don't think Luke was exactly hanging.'

Her voice was so small, Brian almost felt sorry for her. He edged slightly sideways to get a better look at her. Fuck Hazel, anyway. Mean bitch. Though, now, even Hazel glanced sympathetically at Charlotte's pitiful frame.

'You hate Daniel, so what's the problem?' Hazel continued. 'I don't get it. Why are you making such a big deal?'

'Yes, I hate Daniel, but I want to know my friends aren't psychopaths. If somebody else pushed Luke, if it wasn't Daniel . . . I want to know.'

'Charls, you've lost the plot. Why would anybody else push him?'

'Luke was starting to feel guilty. About . . . about what happened.'

Hazel froze at the sink. She turned to Charlotte. The atmosphere in the bathroom had turned to ice. Even Brian felt it, and he was outside the door.

'We said we'd never talk about that again,' Hazel said.

Outside the door, Brian's thighs had grown tired from hunkering. He put his hand out to steady himself against the wall but he missed. His hand hit the door. Hazel and Charlotte jumped.

Brian had time to straighten up and reach for the door handle before it opened, and then the two girls were standing there, staring at him.

'You both in here?' he said, walking past them, already undoing his flies. 'Dirty bitches. You know there are four bathrooms in this house?'

'Were you perving at us through the keyhole?' Hazel accused, her eyes narrowing as Brian started to urinate into the bowl, not even waiting for them to leave.

'Sure,' Brian said, not looking at them. He was blushing, but they couldn't see, standing behind him. 'I like nothing better than watching girls wee-wee.'

Charlotte was already stomping downstairs. Brian felt Hazel staring at his back for a few seconds more, then she slammed the door and was gone.

She was a liability. They both were.

# CHAPTER 24

Bronwyn Maher was not impressed.

Tom had tried to avoid her but she'd demanded he come in and see her that night. So, here he was, suffering her wrath, desperately wishing he could go home.

He couldn't remember the last time he'd seen her in a mood this foul, but what he did know was that time he hadn't caused the irritation, so while he'd been awestruck by it, he wasn't terrified.

Unlike now.

'Did you know Jackie McCallion has been hounding the DPP's office to get a court date?' she said. 'Like the State Prosecutor can just make magic happen. And he, in turn, is hounding me. He wants to know, Tom, what the hell is going on? The kid is only in detention, what, less than four weeks? Why the frantic urgency on a case everybody assumed was home and dry?'

Tom tried to get comfortable on the hardback chair that faced Bronwyn's desk. There was no way of relaxing in it, and that was the very reason she'd had it installed.

Her chair, however, looked particularly snug. Tom thought he might order one of those when he moved offices. Seeing as he'd be spending more time at his desk.

'Is this a policeman's midlife crisis?' she continued. 'One last Tom special before you have to sit at the grown-ups' table?'

'You know full well why I'm looking into this,' he said, prickling just a little.

Bronwyn frowned. She tugged on the cuffs of her fitted navy jacket with such ferocity, Tom felt sorry for them. A flick of her carefully styled hairdo – not too flouncy, but professionally attractive, perfectly chosen for the cameras – and she was studying him again.

'I know,' she said. 'You know who else knows? All the people who don't like you. And who don't like me. Or Natasha McCarthy, for that matter.' She hesitated. 'I didn't tell you this at the time, Tom, but when we moved Joe Kennedy sideways out of the Chief Superintendent's job, I argued that he be fired.'

Tom cocked his head sideways. That was interesting.

'Of course, we don't tend to fire public servants of that seniority,' Bronwyn continued. 'Especially not ones who know where the bodies are buried. So, I was overruled. But I said at the time and I say it now – when you've somebody in your ranks like that, you ignore them at your peril. You remember the circumstances that caused your first clash with Kennedy?'

'Bronwyn, what is this?' Tom sighed. 'I know full well what my issues with Joe Kennedy were – I was there. The man played fast and loose with the rule book and not in a good way.'

'Joe Kennedy believed,' Bronwyn interrupted, 'that when doubt is cast on anybody within the force, the answer is to close ranks.'

'That's not what I'm doing for Natasha. If I'd met her cousin and believed in his guilt, if Jackie McCallion had convinced me of his guilt, I'd have taken Natasha out for a commiseration drink.'

'I'm angry at her for asking you to get involved at all,'

Bronwyn said, shaking her head. 'With the position you're about to take on, it was incredibly blinkered.'

'What would you do if it was your family?' Tom asked.

'Oh, stop. We all know you're the best detective on the force. Put aside your ego for a moment, can you? Think of the media. Who are about to become your new best friends. Put yourself in the shoes of the best investigative reporter you can think of. How would you write this story if it was handed to you?'

Tom said nothing.

Bronwyn pushed her chair back from the desk and walked to an oak cabinet at the side of the office. She pulled out a swing drawer from behind one of its doors; a decanter of golden liquid and some crystal cut glasses sat inside.

'I didn't know you were a fan of *Mad Men*,' Tom joked. 'Office drinks?'

Bronwyn ignored him.

'Don't change the subject. I'll tell you what that journalist would write, Tom.' Bronwyn cleared her throat and deepened her voice. ' "The soon-to-be-appointed Chief Superintendent of the National Bureau of Criminal Investigation, former DCI Tom Reynolds, spent the last few weeks in charge of the murder squad attempting to get a relative of the head of Sexual Offences off a rape and murder charge".' Bronwyn stopped. 'This is you, driving me to drink.'

She filled the bottom of one of the glasses with liquid from the decanter.

'Well, when you put it like that. Maybe pour me one too.'

Bronwyn splashed some liquid into a glass and placed it in front of Tom.

'Jesus,' he said, as the raw Scotch hit his throat. 'I always saw you as a vodka-and-tonic kinda gal.'

Bronwyn eyed him over the rim of her glass.

'If you think this promotion entitles you to call me "gal", you're going to be sorely disappointed.'

Tom raised his glass in salute.

'Anyway, it's a present from the commissioner. I rarely drink, Tom, but when I do, I make sure it's the best. So. Fill me in on where you're at. At least then I can talk to the DPP with a modicum of knowledge about what my new chief is doing. God knows, I've no control over the old one any more.'

So that was why Sean was in absentia and Tom had to face this meeting alone.

'I'm nowhere,' Tom said. 'Except for the fact that I believe Daniel Konaté and Luke Connolly were actually in a relationship. Which means that what probably happened that night wasn't the rape of Luke Connolly, but consensual sex. And I believe several of his friends lied in their statements. So, maybe Daniel wasn't on his own with Luke or, at least, wasn't the last one with him.'

'And you say you're nowhere, eh?' Bronwyn's eyes widened. 'And how did Jackie McCallion miss this, yet you managed to waltz in and figure it all out in the space of a week?'

'Jackie arrested Daniel Konaté three weeks after Luke was murdered,' Tom said. 'She moved too quickly.'

'She had forensics and witness statements, didn't she?'

'But no confession,' Tom sighed. 'The only reason he's in a cell is because his mother can't afford a good legal team and won't take "charity" from Natasha or other family members. Jackie was in a rush to get an arrest, I'm telling you.'

'Why?' Bronwyn frowned.

'The Connollys' other son, Luke's twin, is dying,' Tom answered. 'Jackie wants it solved. You know she hasn't even found Luke's phone. God knows what's on it, if somebody saw fit to make it disappear.'

'Maybe it's just bloody lost, Tom.' Bronwyn rolled her eyes, then took a breath. 'You really think Daniel is innocent? That he's being framed?'

'I don't know how deeply the other kids are involved,' Tom said. 'Maybe one of them went back and the others didn't notice?'

'Sure,' Bronwyn said. 'But if they are lying – one of them will crack. That's for certain. And Tom, believe me when I say this: that's the only outcome that can justify your involvement in the case. New evidence.'

'And if I do get it – I've made an enemy of Jackie McCallion for life,' Tom added.

'Yes.' Bronwyn nodded. 'They do seem to be stacking up, don't they?'

Tom didn't go directly back to his own office. It might have been the thumb of Scotch. It might have been that he was feeling disconcerted. But something made him brave. He called into Emmet McDonagh's office.

It was late and Emmet wasn't there, but the door was open. Tom strolled in anyway – he'd been in there before on his own plenty of times. Emmet never had a problem with it.

He sat in front of the desk for a minute or two, browsing through the pages of the newspapers delivered to his friend that morning. Article after article on whistleblowers in the Gardaí. Tom flinched. Too raw, too much of a reminder of what was at stake. And too reminiscent of what Bronwyn had just lectured him on.

Tom looked up. He noticed it, then. The photo frame on

Emmet's desk. That was new, he thought. He turned it around to face him.

The picture showed Emmet and Linda's son, Paul. And in Paul's arms – a newborn.

'You're kidding me,' Tom blurted out, picking up the frame.

'Is there no privacy to be had in this building?' Emmet came in behind him. He snatched the frame from Tom's hands.

'Does your son have a son?' Tom exclaimed.

'No,' Emmet growled. Then he looked away from Tom's eyes. 'He has a daughter.'

'And does Linda know she's a grandmother?'

'She won't be finding out from you, Tom Reynolds,' Emmet snapped.

'Of course not,' Tom said, shocked Emmet would even think it. 'But don't you think she has a right to know?'

Emmet sat down heavily in his chair.

'The child is the reason Paul wants nothing to do with her, Tom. For heaven's sake. I had him this close.' Emmet paused and made a pincer movement with his finger and thumb. 'The mediation meeting was set up. Then his girlfriend had the baby. Paul took one look at her and said no decent person could give away their child.'

He sighed and placed his head in his hand.

Tom took the picture off Emmet again and studied it. Paul's face as he stared at his new baby daughter was a mix of emotions. Mainly love, but you could tell it had hit him: how painful and how demanding the love of a child could be. He looked desperately confused and overwhelmed.

An idea hit Tom.

'Emmet, do you remember Kilcross?' he said.

'What?'

'The Magdalene Laundry. The case a few years ago; the nuns who were killed? Jesus, are you going senile?'

'Of course I remember the bloody thing. I just don't see the point of you referencing it.'

'There was a nun there, Sister Gladys. She delivered a lot of the babies for the women. The women who were forced to give them up.'

Emmet lifted his head from his hand.

'I hope you're not going where I think you're going with this, because you just said it yourself: *made* to give them up. By the Church.'

'No,' Tom said, shaking his head. 'The Church was involved, but a lot of the time, those girls had been sent in there by their families. By poverty. By circumstance. That's what their children came to understand when they reconnected years later.'

'It's not the same,' Emmet said.

'No,' Tom agreed. 'Not exactly. But there are familiar strands, you have to admit. Linda didn't have as much choice as Paul has chosen to believe she did. You know what her family were like. They were willing to estrange her just for wanting to leave Geoff. Her father did – he never spoke to her again. She needs Paul's forgiveness for what she had to do, even if he doesn't want her in his life. She's dying inside, Emmet.'

Emmet spun his chair sideways and stared out his window.

'What do you suggest, Tom? That I try explaining it to him in Magdalene Laundries' terms?'

'No. I'm not suggesting you try anything at all. I think he should meet Sister Gladys.'

Emmet looked astonished.

'Wasn't she, like, one hundred and two or something, four years ago?'

'She's elderly. But she still has her faculties.'

'How do you know?' Emmet asked.

'She emails me once a month thanking me for the booze I send down,' Tom said.

'And why would he listen to her and not me?'

'Sometimes,' Tom said, and sighed, 'it has to come from an outsider. Nobody would have believed Natasha McCarthy when she said her cousin was innocent of rape and murder. Of course she'd say that; she's his relative. But now I'm saying it . . . I think. I don't believe he did what he's accused of. And now it matters, because it's coming from a stranger.'

'You're so bloody . . . annoying,' Emmet said. He pressed a button on the side of his Fitbit, bringing up his BPM, heartbeats per minute. 'You're making my blood pressure rise.'

'Am I annoying and right?' Tom asked.

'Maybe,' Emmet said, begrudgingly.

# CHAPTER 25

Jacob was still in bed but he wasn't sleeping. He'd been looking at the clock strike every hour since 6 a.m.

Last night, he had done what he'd never thought he'd do: he'd rung his father.

It was all getting too much.

It felt like it was falling apart.

Jacob wasn't worried about Daniel Konaté talking. He was sure he knew nothing. For all that Luke had inflicted him on their group, Jacob knew that, for the most part, he had kept Daniel separate from their business. Which meant that Daniel, when not in Luke's immediate company, tended not to hang around with the rest of them or care what they were doing.

Daniel had come nowhere near the others in the house the night Luke died, so he hadn't overheard them talking, Jacob was sure of it. When Hazel had taken out that stupid fucking Ouija board, that was when it had all started. She'd started going on about summoning the dead and Charlotte had got upset and said nobody was dead.

Technically, not true. Nobody was dead, *yet*. And there were other spirits in the house to call, Hazel had said, laughing.

Then Charlotte, in a move that took even Jacob by surprise, had grabbed Hazel by the hair and started pulling.

All the while, Daniel and Luke were upstairs, listening to

that shit rap Daniel was always playing, obscure Brit bands nobody had ever heard of. When Luke came down earlier in the evening, Jacob could already see he was off his face. Jacob didn't mind snorting the odd line, but they had a match coming up the following week. He just fancied a few drinks that night, maybe some weed.

But since Daniel had appeared on the scene, Jacob felt like he was running to stand still with his best friend. Like he had to keep up with Daniel if he wanted to compete.

Anyway, there was no way Daniel had heard anything. Jacob was sure of it.

But not positive.

Not that it mattered. They were convinced Daniel would be sent to jail for what had happened to Luke. And if he was convicted, who'd believe what he had to say?

But if he wasn't convicted and he started talking – what if he *had* overheard?

This was all down to that fucking runt, Ethan. If he hadn't opened his mouth and started pushing all those lies about Daniel and Luke being ... being ... for Christ's sake. It was ludicrous. But it had opened everything up, the possibility that Luke hadn't been raped; that he'd had sex with Daniel and then somebody else had pushed him.

Jacob's father was coming home.

Not out of any great desire to be a better father to Jacob. But he hadn't put all that money into Jacob's education, into protecting Jacob's future, for his son to go and blow it all now over something so – accidental. That was the word for it.

An accident.

It hadn't even been intended.

It had just got out of hand.

# CHAPTER 26

Ray was running. Of course, he was running. When Tom called to the apartment that morning, Laura opened the door, pale and sleep-deprived.

'He won't talk to me,' she said. 'I mean – he'll talk to me about everything else. But not this. We're getting married in a few months, Tom. I keep thinking I should turn down the promotion but then I talk myself out of it because you can't give it to him now, anyway. I actually took a new case yesterday instead of giving it to one of the lads. It's like I'm trying to scupper this.'

'Laura, I don't plan on changing a thing. Where does he run?'

'There's a park up the road.'

'Got a spare tracksuit?'

It wasn't his imagination: Laura had definitely smirked after the shock passed.

Well, at least he'd cheered her up.

The park wasn't that big, which meant Ray was doing laps. Tom waited until he saw his deputy pass the pedestrian gate near the inspector's parking spot before he started jogging behind him. The borrowed runners were a size too big and the tracksuit jacket was too tight around his midriff, but at least Tom could match Ray's pace.

For about a lap. The inspector didn't have long to talk his deputy out of his planned transfer. He thought of Dylan Keating's mother, desperately clinging to her youth with the endless exercise and Botox. Really, some people should just learn to age gracefully. Sedately. Like him.

Tom approached Ray without the other man realising. It helped that Ray had headphones in and was too busy being angry at the world to notice he was being stalked. He turned and looked at Tom and for a moment there was no surprise, like it was totally normal to see his boss running beside him.

Then he yanked the headphones from his ears.

'What the hell? Are you wearing my tracksuit?'

'That's the first thing that came to mind?' Tom answered.

Ray shook his head. He kept running.

So, it was going to be like that.

'What, are you moving in with me and Laura, now?' Ray said. 'Is that the plan?'

'If that's what it takes.'

'You can't change my mind, Tom. I already spoke to Bridget Duffy. The drugs unit would be happy to secure me.'

'Absolutely, they would.' Tom was already panting slightly. 'Does that mean they should?'

'It makes sense,' Ray snapped. 'It's hard enough for me and Laura working together every day as a couple.'

'You've managed well enough for the last three years.'

'As equals.'

'What would you say to Laura, if she was planning the same?'

Ray bit his lip.

'I'd understand,' Ray lied.

'You wouldn't,' Tom said. 'Here's the conversation we'd be having. You'd say, "Tom, I can't let her leave the squad. She's too good a detective. I need her. I'm not going to be the sort of boss that pulls rank, doesn't she see that? We can work together just fine. She has to give me a chance." That's what you'd say.'

'It's different.'

Tom sighed, which came out more as a gasp.

'Used to be a time when I was the old fogey and you were the new, progressive kid on the block.'

'This is not because I'm a man and she's a woman, for f–'

Ray pulled up short. Tom ground to a halt, leaned over and rested his hands on his knees. When he straightened up, he was almost euphoric from the air hitting his lungs. At last. More talking, less running.

'How much of an arsehole do you think I am?' Ray demanded, staring at his boss. 'Is that what she thinks, too? That I've an issue taking orders from a woman? That's not it at all!'

'Then what is it?' Tom asked.

Ray, despairing, threw his hands up in the air.

'I'm embarrassed, okay? I'm mortified. It's nothing to do with Laura getting the top job. It's me being passed over and having to keep working with lads who know you didn't think I was good enough.'

Tom opened his mouth to reply but he couldn't find the words.

'Yeah,' Ray said, kicking at the grass. He turned and started to walk away.

'Damn it,' Tom muttered. He began to follow, trying to ignore the phone ringing in his pocket.

'You'd better get that,' Ray called back.

Tom pulled it out. Natasha. He'd *told* her to stop calling.

He answered it, purely out of irritation.

'Tom,' she said, breathless, before he could say anything. 'It's Daniel. He's been admitted to hospital.'

# CHAPTER 27

It looked worse than it was. When Tom peered in through the window of the hospital room and saw the extensive injuries, he'd been worried. The lad's head had swollen to the size of a watermelon – if the inspector had been told by a medical professional that Daniel had bleeding on the brain, Tom would have believed it.

Ray had come with him; they'd continued their talk in the car, but he was waiting outside now. Still stewing, Tom imagined, on everything that had been said.

'It's all superficial,' the deputy governor from Cloverhill told Tom, when he joined him at the window. 'I don't mean it's not bad, it's just not dangerously bad.'

'Thanks for getting me in, Robert,' Tom said, shaking his hand. 'Was it a fight?'

The other man sighed. He was shorter than Tom by a head or so, and the inspector could see that Robert's scalp was thinning and what hair he had was combed over in a nod to the ridiculous. Not that Tom could mock. For now, it was only the colour of his hair he worried about, but no doubt, in a year or two, he'd be on his own journey to a monk's cap, like his father before him.

'We told his family,' Robert said. 'It was self-inflicted.'

'Yes, but was it self-inflicted, self-inflicted,' Tom continued, 'or is he just afraid to say who did it?'

'He was on the isolation corridor,' Robert replied. 'In his cell, alone. He started headbutting the door. The warden saw him on the CCTV but he'd done plenty of damage before we got there. He was lucky he chose that part of his head. To the side a bit and he'd have knocked himself out and quite probably have given himself serious problems.'

'I see,' Tom said. 'I'm only asking because he was also in isolation the first time I met with him and yet he had bruises on his wrist. Like somebody had grabbed him.'

The deputy governor jerked his head, irritated. He was old school; police meets civil servant, officious. But now he was pissed off and it showed.

'Nobody on my staff did that and he hasn't been near the other prisoners.'

Tom stared through the window, satisfied. Robert wasn't the sort to lie, he could tell.

'Who's in there with him?' Tom asked, already guessing at the answer. The woman who sat beside Daniel was holding his hand with both of hers. Her eyes were closed tight and she seemed to be praying.

'His mother.'

Tom nodded. He left the deputy governor and walked into the room.

The woman looked up. She seemed too young to have a son, her dark skin smooth and pretty, her hair braided. She looked tired, and not just from the vigil she was keeping at her son's bedside. This woman had exhaustion etched into her face, the sort that can only find itself on the features of somebody working three jobs and rearing a child alone.

'Mrs Konaté?' he asked.

'Mrs Konaté Jones,' she answered. From the bed, Tom heard a murmur of annoyance. Daniel was lucid, anyway.

'Who are you?' she said. 'Are you media? Did you trick the staff to get in here?' She looked Tom up and down.

The inspector was still wearing Ray's tracksuit. He blushed. In his haste to get to the hospital, he and Ray had jumped in the car without returning to the apartment to change.

'No,' he said. 'I'm a detective. Apologies for my appearance, I wasn't in work when I got the call.'

'He's too ill to talk to any more police,' she said, her voice firm.

'I'm DCI Tom Reynolds,' he returned. 'Natasha . . .'

This made her sit up straighter.

'Oh. Oh, I see. Natasha's colleague. Then, thank you. Thank you for coming. DCI Reynolds, you said?' She pronounced the first part of his name as 'Ray'.

'Yes, but you can call me Tom.'

'Lizzie,' she said, and nodded. They were friends now, in her mind. 'Daniel –' she raised her voice – 'it's the proper detective.'

Tom couldn't help but smile. Daniel turned towards him, one eye barely open, the other shut tight. It was getting a bit much, seeing all these young men in hospital beds and on slabs.

'Hi, Daniel,' he said, sitting on the edge of the blue blanket that covered the lad's legs. 'Rough day, eh?'

The half-open eye blinked rapidly, and then a tear appeared, making its way around the lid and dropping onto Daniel's cheek.

'Son,' Lizzie said, and her voice filled with pain. 'Tell the man what happened.'

'Nothing happened,' Daniel said, voice choking. 'I just lost it.'

'What made you lose it?' Tom said.

'Isn't it obvious?' his mother cut in, eyes wide and disbelieving of the circumstances she found herself in. 'He's going mad in that place. It's not natural, locking up a young man like that, nobody to talk to. Especially when he is innocent. He has given up.'

Her voice broke into a sob.

'Is that it?' Tom asked. 'Are you giving up, Daniel? Because, you know, I'm trying to help you. I'm doing everything I can.'

'It's not about me,' Daniel said. 'It's about Luke. It's my fault. It's my fault he died.'

Tom stiffened. When he opened his mouth to talk again, he had to make a conscious effort to keep the emotion from his voice.

'How? Talk to me, son. Was there an accident? What happened that night?'

Daniel turned, painfully, to look at his mother, then back to Tom.

'I can't,' he said.

Tom wanted to bite his own tongue with frustration.

'Daniel, why are you doing this?' Tom said. 'Where is it getting you? How is it helping? Doesn't Luke deserve the truth to come out? Don't his parents?'

Daniel blinked. More tears sprung forth. The room fell silent while Tom waited and Lizzie hoped and Daniel considered.

'I was angry with him.'

Tom and Lizzie exchanged a glance. She, too, knew this was significant.

But Tom was kicking himself. He should have brought Ray in with him. If the lad confessed in his hospital bed with only his mother there as a witness, Tom would have messed up big time.

Jackie McCallion would be thrilled. And Bronwyn would have Tom's nuts for dinner.

'And I left him.' Daniel breathed out and it was like the sound of a dying man. 'I knew he was high as a kite. I knew those arseholes he called friends didn't care about him. If they did, he wouldn't have had to lie to them. But I just left him there. I walked away.'

'Daniel, I need you to be absolutely clear on this,' Tom said. 'When you left Luke, he was alive and well, bar having taken drugs?'

Daniel nodded.

'And was he alone? Was there anybody else in the house?'

'I didn't think so.'

'How long were you alone? Minutes? Hours? Think.'

'It wasn't long. We were upstairs. We'd gone up to the third floor and . . .' Another glance at his mother. She bit her lip and looked away. 'They were doing stupid stuff downstairs. Kids' stuff. Messing with a Ouija board.'

Lizzie blessed herself.

'I'd no interest, Ma,' Daniel reassured her. 'Nor did Luke. So we left them, went upstairs. I think Luke went down once or twice. I didn't bother. And then we heard them leaving. I guess about an hour had passed.'

'Did you see anybody hanging around when you left?' Tom asked. 'Outside, I mean?'

Daniel shook his head, as much movement as he could make without hurting himself.

'I wasn't looking,' he said. 'Before I left I . . . I told him I was sick of hiding. Of pretending. For his sake. I've never pretended. I've always been honest and yeah, I knew it would be hard for him, but I'd have supported him. But he didn't care about me as much as he cared about what his mates would think. What his da would think. It was like he needed them more.'

The tears started to come, faster, proper. His mother leaned in, placed her forehead against her son's.

'It wasn't your fault,' she said. 'It wasn't.'

Daniel barely heard her. He was staring at Tom. Trying to impress on him his guilt.

The guilt Daniel felt, anyway. He raised his hand to the side of his head, winced at the pain. Whatever pain relief he was on, he needed more.

'You've no idea what they're like,' Daniel said. 'You think I'm the bad guy. You've no idea.'

'What are they like?' Tom asked.

Daniel was silent.

Tom tried again.

'Why did you say you were home earlier than you were, Daniel?'

'Tell him, son,' Lizzie said.

Daniel looked at his mother, then back to Tom.

'I panicked, when the cops called. I didn't know what it was about but I felt something –' he placed his hand on his stomach – 'in here. I knew it was bad. I don't know why I lied, but I did. Detective McCallion asked me where I'd been between the hours of midnight and 2 a.m. and it just made sense to say I'd been home since 12.30, because it took me a half-hour to get from Little Leaf to Dún Laoghaire. So whatever had happened, I could pretend I wasn't there. I thought she was going to ask about the drugs.'

'But you didn't get home until close to three,' Tom said. 'Where were you, if you weren't with Luke?'

'I just walked around,' Daniel said. 'I know what it sounds

like. But I was pissed and stoned and I needed to clear my head before my ma saw me.'

Tom nodded. It did sound bad, but not as bad as lying.

He studied Daniel. There was more he wasn't telling Tom. Why?

'Daniel, has somebody told you not to talk to me?'

Daniel didn't answer. But he glanced at his mother, briefly. His face filled with concern. Worry. He didn't want to be causing her this pain but there was nothing he could do about it.

If somebody wanted to keep Daniel quiet, all they had to do was threaten the one person in the world he had left who meant something to him.

His mother.

Ray had turned up the radio in the car and was blaring some pop song Tom had never heard.

The inspector got in and rubbed his face with his hands.

'Anybody have anything to say about the fact you look like you're undercover?' Ray asked.

'Not really. But let's head back to yours so I can pick up my suit.'

'I think you should leave it on,' his deputy replied. 'Walk in my shoes for a few hours, see how it feels.'

'Ha, ha.'

Tom turned to Ray.

'I'm sorry,' he said.

Ray put the car in gear.

'For what?'

'For not thinking through all the ripples of my decision. I only thought about the impact on your and Laura's relationship. I didn't think through the rest of it. And, funnily enough,

I've done nothing but think about it for months. I'm a flawed individual and, apparently, not very smart.'

Ray shrugged.

'I know,' he said.

'I understand why you want a transfer. But I think you are underestimating the lads on our team.'

'Maybe,' Ray said. 'Though you mightn't think that if you heard what Michael was saying about leaving work so his missus can go back to her job.'

Tom sighed.

'I heard,' he said. 'He's an idiot.'

'Top drawer.'

Tom didn't speak for a moment. He had to tread carefully. But this was the time for honest conversation.

'Don't lose it with me,' he said, 'but you might be letting Laura down a bit. She'll need you. Badly. Like I needed you. When people are questioning her appointment or acting the gobshite, like Michael, you're the one who'll be batting for her.'

Ray stuck the indicator on and looked down the road they were about to turn onto.

'Yeah,' he said. 'Perhaps.'

They drove in silence for a few minutes. Then Ray spoke again.

'These many flaws you speak of,' he said.

'I'm not sure I said *many*,' Tom replied.

'Do these include completely abandoning plans for my stag?'

'Not abandoning.' Tom coughed. 'Just . . . delegating.'

'Delegating to who?' Ray asked, suspicious now.

Tom muttered something.

'Who?' Ray repeated.

'Willie Callaghan,' Tom said.

Ray said nothing. They pulled up at traffic lights. He turned to Tom.

'I feel you're determined to wreck our friendship.'

Tom smiled. With relief. There'd been a hint of something like mirth in Ray's voice.

# CHAPTER 28

Charlotte had many things to do before she could get away that afternoon.

She'd fallen behind with her schoolwork to such an extent that her tutor had mentioned it to her parents. She'd got a free pass for a short time but her parents were determined she'd still get a good Leaving Certificate. It couldn't and wouldn't be derailed by the death of a friend, no matter how tragic.

So she'd applied every ounce of brainpower and speed she could summon to get several essays finished to an acceptable standard before their deadlines, one of which her tutor would hopefully flesh out without too much prompting from Charlotte.

Then she'd cleaned her room – cleanliness brought the soul peace, her mother was fond of saying. Cleaning stressed Charlotte out, but she didn't say that. Nor did she point out that nearly all her friends had cleaners. According to her mother, no matter how wealthy they were, her children would not be taught the lesson that money was the answer to everything.

Finally, she'd spoken to relatives in the States who'd been sending endless messages of support for their darling Charls and were awaiting her polite replies – she'd played devastated but positive very well on the Skype calls, she felt.

And then she made herself look nice and turned her phone

off, so if Hazel tried to ring, she wouldn't have to ignore her. She could tell her the battery had died.

After blanking her for days, suddenly Hazel wanted to keep a very close eye on her. It was because of what Charlotte had said at Jacob's house. Hazel looked at her strangely now, like Charlotte was a loose cannon.

Her dad was leaving the house at the same time, for his weekly round of golf, when Charlotte let herself out the front door. She stood in the porch trying to decide if the hood on her raincoat was sufficient protection from the April rain that had been falling on and off all afternoon. Rain was kryptonite to Charlotte's fine, straight hair – it made it spring up and curl like she'd never met a straightener. And Charlotte wanted to look good. Even if it didn't matter, she wanted it for *him*.

'Need a lift, Princess?' her dad called out.

'No, I'm fine,' she said. The last thing she wanted was her dad knowing she was going to the hospital. He'd have so many questions. Plus, he was picking up Chris Connolly on the way to the golf course. As far as Charlotte knew, Mr Connolly wasn't a big golf fan, but she'd overheard her parents speaking earlier in the week about how everybody had to be there for the Connollys and sure, Chris could just sit in the clubhouse and have coffee if he wasn't on form for the course. At least he'd have company.

Charlotte did not want to be around Mr Connolly.

And for good reason.

She'd seen him.

She'd seen him *there*.

'Charlotte, have you left the planet?' Her dad's voice snapped her from her reverie. 'I said, it's raining, are you sure?'

'Sorry, Dad. Just trying to remember if I have all my notes for the library. I'm going to walk. I need the air to clear my head before I take out the books again.'

Charlotte's dad smiled and nodded.

'Good girl,' he said, getting into the car.

Sometimes she even amazed herself with how easily the lies just slid out of her mouth.

Charlotte took the bus that left her near the hospital. She walked the last half-mile, stopping at the flower shop across the road from the main entrance. She bought a small bunch of roses, the girl behind the counter smiling in recognition.

Charlotte had been in the shop before. She'd visited him before, too.

If her friends found out – they'd kill her.

# CHAPTER 29

'I was worried you'd abandoned me,' Sean said, when Tom met him back at police headquarters after leaving Ray and Laura's apartment. 'Thought you might have gone back to your old partner.'

'When we're having all this fun?' Tom said.

'I'm going to take that at face value. Anyway. Where to?'

'Back to school,' Tom said. 'Little Leaf College. Let's go hear some eulogies for Luke.'

Detective Jackie McCallion met them at the entrance to the private secondary school Luke and his friends attended. She was leaning against a pillar outside the front door, arms folded, sunglasses on, her short bob tucked neatly behind her ears. Her suit was ironed to the point of almost standing by itself; her blouse was a shade of shimmering white that would shame the angels.

'When I grow up,' Sean said, as he parked the car in one of the teaching spots, 'I want to be in the FBI like Jackie.'

'You're being mean,' Tom said. But still, when he got out of the car he made sure his shirt was tucked neatly into his trousers and his jacket was straight.

'Chief McGuinness, DCI Reynolds,' Jackie said, standing to attention. 'I informed the headmaster you were en route. He's gathered some of the teachers in the staffroom.'

'Very organised of you,' Tom said.

Jackie pursed her lips.

'I'm not sure how much they have to tell you,' she said. 'Daniel didn't attend here, so . . .'

'We're going to his old school, too,' Tom said.

Jackie said nothing but her face betrayed her feelings. And they said Tom was wasting her time and chasing his own tail.

'Luke was an honours student,' Jackie said, as they walked. 'He'd sat his mock exams in preparation for the Leaving and he'd got all As. Good sportsman, sociable. An all-rounder. He was well liked.'

'Are you giving his funeral oration?' Tom asked.

'Should I be critical of the victim?' Jackie asked.

'I don't want you to be critical,' Tom said. 'I want you to scratch the surface of what you're being told.'

'What would it matter if he wasn't a saint? He didn't ask to be pushed.'

'This isn't about victim blaming. It's about getting to motive. If it wasn't Daniel, who was it and why?'

'But it was Daniel.'

Tom and Sean exchanged a glance. Sean took over.

'It's not a watertight case, lass,' he said. 'We can see that, after only a short time.'

'It's not for you to decide,' Jackie snapped back. She was angry and struggling to maintain her natural inclination to be respectful of their authority, even if she privately thought they were both nuts. 'And I don't appreciate being called "lass".'

'My apologies,' Sean said, the colour flaring in his cheeks. 'It's just a turn of phrase that comes to me naturally.' He hesitated, thrown. 'Look, neither of us are implying that you haven't done a decent job here. But there are questions and it's better they're answered this side of a court hearing than in the middle of it. If I was your DS, I'd have pointed that out to you from the word go.'

'I don't have a DS,' Jackie said. 'Cutbacks.'

The three of them looked at each other. They'd reached an impasse. Jackie was prickly, offended, resentful. But Tom and Sean were trying to make sure the job was done properly and they couldn't wilt in the wake of her feelings.

'Let's go see this headmaster, will we?' Tom said.

Jackie nodded curtly, then turned on her heel and walked briskly ahead.

'Any word on those phone records?' Tom called after her.

'They're coming.'

Tom sensed she wasn't applying a whole lot of urgency to them.

He bit down on his frustration and followed her.

The headmaster was also a fan of Luke Connolly's.

'We're all devastated,' Principal Lynch told Tom and Sean as soon as they met in his office. They spent only moments there before he began walking them in the direction of the staff-room. He was an overweight man but also vain, dressed in a smart, expensive suit and polished leather shoes. His hair was cut a little too long for his age and brushed back into an extravagant style.

'Luke was an absolute star student and very popular,' he said. 'Of course, we immediately offered counselling to the students, particularly those in Luke's year facing exams. However, they've been stoical – no less than we'd expect from our boys and girls, but still. You have to be ready to offer support. You never know when it will be needed. We learned that two years ago.'

'What happened two years ago?' Tom asked.

Principal Lynch slowed his stride for a moment and lowered his voice.

'A suicide,' he said. 'A Leaving Certificate student at the time. It wasn't just the stress of the exams. There were family issues. But we've had to be on the lookout for other potential victims. There can be a domino effect.'

'Anything to do with Luke Connolly and his circle?' Sean asked.

'No. They were two years behind. Kids don't tend to mix across the divide. Two years is a massive gap at this age.'

'My colleague here says Luke was an honours student,' Tom said.

Principal Lynch smiled at Jackie.

'That's right. All higher-level subjects. Eight in total. Despite everything that was happening with his brother.'

'What was Ethan like when he was here?' Tom asked.

'Well, technically, he still is. A student, I mean. Although . . . well. We made many provisions for him over the years but I don't think he will be sitting his final exams, after all. He was a nice student. Bright, possibly even more so than his brother. Not very sporty. Quieter. But he'd only started here and then he was diagnosed. Such a sad, sad story. The poor parents.'

Tom nodded. He had the sudden sense that all he would get from this man was platitudes and generalised statements. Little Leaf College had over one thousand students. Lynch may have been more aware of the Connollys because of Ethan's condition and now the tragedy with Luke, but he wasn't the sort of man to invest in individual students.

Most of the teachers sang from the same hymn sheet. One, a woman who taught history, came across as timid and likely a target for smart-mouthed kids; she intimated Luke had been a bit cheeky in her class. But she too was sticking to the line. They all missed him; he'd been a great kid, friends with everybody.

As they listened to the staff wax lyrical, the inspector noticed Jackie McCallion standing ever straighter. She was being validated in her views. She'd yet to accept that what teachers and friends had to say about the deceased held little stock in the overall picture. Not this soon post mortem. In time, maybe, true feelings might be spoken. For now, people were being respectful.

But Tom knew. No kid was *that* good in school. Death just martyred them.

The teachers were equally flattering about Luke's friends. Though perhaps not as enthusiastically. Jacob was considered a charmer. Brian was not a great student but was in with the right crowd. Dylan was reserved but studied hard. Charlotte, too, was 'good'. Praise for Hazel was double-edged. 'Confident', 'full of strong opinions' and 'determined' were some of the words used.

'Are all Luke's teachers here?' Tom asked, as time drew on. They were getting nowhere with this bunch.

'We're missing Coach Walsh,' Principal Lynch answered. 'We had a friendly practice game of rugby this afternoon against a rival school. But he should be back by now. We like to get the students home by teatime. If he is, he'll be in the club rooms beside the pitch.'

'You have your own rugby pitch?' Tom asked.

Lynch nodded like it wasn't that unusual.

'We have rugby, soccer and cricket pitches; tennis courts and, of course, access to the athletics stadium in the university nearby. Sport is a big part of the package we offer here at Little Leaf.'

'I suppose, if you're charging through the nose, you have to offer something extra,' Sean said.

'Well . . .'

They stood aside as the other teachers began to take their leave.

'How much are we talking, actually?' Tom asked the headmaster. 'In fees, I mean.'

A shutter came down on Principal Lynch's features. Everything they heard from here on out would be from the handbook of private school spin.

'It depends on the student,' he said. 'We offer scholarships, of course. And some parents are in the fortunate position of being able to avail of the additional tutoring we offer in the evenings during exam years, extras like that. But our basic rate works out at approximately €4,000 a term; considerably better than some of the more expensive options and with, we believe, more value for money. Of course, we don't offer boarding but it's something we might consider in the future.'

Tom zoned out as the headmaster continued to defend the fees. He searched his memory for details of Maria's school year.

'It's three terms a school year, am I right?' he asked.

Principal Lynch nodded. He was starting to look slightly embarrassed, as if discussing money was undignified.

Tom blew a low whistle. So, the Connollys alone were paying the school €24,000 a year for the boys to attend. This principal was probably on more money than half the headmasters and mistresses in Dublin put together.

Tom and Sean politely refused his offer to walk them out to the rugby clubhouse, stressing they could find their own way and didn't want to hold him up any longer. In reality, Tom wanted to hear what a teacher, any teacher, might have to say about Luke et al. out of the earshot of their boss.

'Jackie, you probably know the way, do you?' he asked, when they left the main building.

'No. I haven't met the coach.'

'Oh?' Tom said. 'I'm surprised, given what a large role rugby seemed to play in Luke's life. Two of his best mates are on the squad.'

'Yes. But Daniel isn't.'

And again, Tom found himself pondering how quickly she had ruled out everybody else for Luke's murder.

They found Coach Walsh where Lynch said he would be. A gang of lads were streaming out of the clubhouse, fresh from showers. Tom spotted Jacob and Brian among them. Jacob looked red-faced and his eyes were bloodshot.

He waved his hand in greeting. They returned the gesture but as soon as they'd walked past, Tom could see Jacob and Brian, heads together, talking furiously.

'How was the game?' Tom asked, as a man he suspected was Walsh approached. He looked different to the other teachers. If Tom had been asked to choose a word to describe that lot as a collective, he'd have selected 'privileged'. Walsh, on the other hand, looked rough and ready; he was stocky, broad-shouldered and thick-necked, with a weather-beaten face. Fit as a fiddle, the tracksuit wasn't just for show; not like when Tom was forced to wear one.

And Walsh wasn't young. He was at least late forties; maybe even around Tom's age, early fifties.

'Could have gone better,' Walsh said. 'Doesn't help when the captain is playing like he's been on the rip since last week.'

Already, Tom knew this conversation was going to be different.

'I need to clean out these locker rooms, do you want to come in?' Walsh asked. 'I take it you're the cops. The teachers' WhatsApp group on my phone is exploding with warnings.'

'Warnings?' Sean said.

'Sure. We're all on-message. Especially as the Connollys and all their little gang are such well-respected patrons of this wonderful bastion of education.'

Tom felt like kissing Coach Walsh. How refreshing. He could see Jackie visibly flinch.

They followed the teacher into the locker rooms, which smelled of teenage boys' sweat, muck and ozone.

Walsh picked up a hose and began showering the tiled floor, muddy water running off into the drains at the side.

'Luke was a good player,' he said, concentrating on the spray of water. 'Don't get me wrong. He'll be missed. Not least because Jacob seems to have lost the plot the last seven weeks without his little buddy.'

'But?' Tom asked.

'But?' Walsh repeated.

'There sounded like there was one.'

Walsh smiled thinly.

'Ha. Yeah. *But* he wasn't the saint everybody above is making him out to be.'

'What makes you say that?' Tom asked.

Walsh stood up straight, considered, the water splashing aimlessly as he did.

'How can I put it? In the freezing rain, in the mud, staring into the face of a lad who wants to drive you into the dirt and trample all over you to get to the other end of the field, you really do see a person's mettle. You have to be fierce in rugby but it's also a gentleman's sport. None of that pansy, petty shit they get away with in soccer. You hurt a lad, you respect the fact he's hurt and you offer him your hand.'

'So . . . Luke wasn't a gentleman?' Tom said.

Walsh shrugged.

'Luke had courage but he could also be mean.'

'Are you thinking of a specific incident?' Sean said. 'Or are you speaking generally?'

'I am indeed thinking of one in particular, sir,' Walsh answered. 'I couldn't tell you if anybody else saw it, but I did. We were winning a game against St Pat's. Good team, solid in their defensive line. We'd cracked it and were miles ahead; there was no need to do anything but keep the ball out of their hands and run down the clock, as it were. I kept my lads focused but they went into that final scrum more or less just to maintain the lead. Standard tactics, you know. Then one of the opposing team's players slipped. Luke saw the opportunity to get a try, rare enough for his position on the field. So he climbs over this chap, stamping on him with his spikes, and then he slips on the same greasy patch that brought down the fallen guy. Ball is thrown forward, penalty for the other team.'

'Stamping happens,' Sean said.

'Sure. Except Luke didn't just take it as fair's fair when he fell too. He blamed the guy underneath him, thought your man had grabbed his leg or something in the heat of the tackle. So, he kicked him in the whatsits while the lad was still on the ground.'

Tom winced.

'Nobody else noticed?'

'Maybe one or two of Luke's teammates but not the crowd and certainly not the ref. They were too busy following the ball.'

'Why did he do it?' Tom asked. 'Did he have a temper issue?'

'Damn right he did. I've never seen a kid that age swallow so much anger so often. It's like he was boiling with it. Maybe it was because the brother was dying, I don't know.'

'Luke, though, is not about to go on trial for killing somebody.' Jackie spoke, her voice sharp. 'It doesn't matter if he had a temper. He didn't push himself out the window.'

'No.' Walsh turned off the spray and looked across at Jackie. 'I'm just saying, you can provoke somebody into giving you a shove. That's what I thought, when I heard what had happened. It's still not right, but that's my honest opinion. That guy he kicked during the match would have been well within his rights to get off the ground and thump Luke's head in – but with nobody having seen the kick, that would have looked quite something, hey?'

Jackie shrugged. She lifted the sleeve of her jacket and noticeably checked her watch. Like she had somewhere better to be.

'Did you ever see him fall out with any of his pals?' Sean asked. 'Jacob Quinn Delaney or Brian Power?'

Walsh jutted out his bottom lip, tilted his head thoughtfully.

'Nope,' he said. 'That little gang is tight. I have the girls, Charlotte and Hazel, on my track team. I take care of athletics too. I'm under no illusion with those two: they do it to keep slim; there's no competitive edge. Which is a real shame, because that Hazel one could run for Ireland if she put her mind to it.'

'What about Dylan Keating?' Tom asked.

'There's a kid who's never been on my radar,' Walsh said. 'Closest I've come to spending time with him is supervising detention.'

'Detention?' Tom was surprised. Dylan hadn't struck him as the type to get into trouble.

'Sure,' Walsh said. 'He stabbed his pencil into another kid's hand in third year. Only reason he wasn't expelled was because of his last name. You know who his father is?'

Tom nodded.

'You know who he stabbed?' Walsh continued.

This time, Tom shook his head.

'Luke Connolly.'

'Luke . . . are you serious?' Jackie just about got her jaw off the floor to ask the question. 'But they were friends.'

'There are friends and there are friends,' Walsh said, and shrugged. 'They made up afterwards, apparently. Mammies and daddies made sure of it. This whole school is a big network. You're in the elite here. It's all sewn up. In the future, half of them will be in business together. Somebody's uncle or aunty will get somebody else a job. If any of them get into trouble, one of the others will bail them out. It's the way it goes.'

Jackie looked at Tom, her eyes wide, surprised. Maybe a little doubt was creeping in. Just a little.

'I'm guessing you don't know Daniel Konaté?' Tom asked.

'Well, I saw him at one or two games,' Walsh said. 'He stood out. Tall, skinny, black. You can count on one hand the number of black kids in this school and none of them are on my squad, so it wasn't anybody's brother in the crowd.'

'Right,' Tom said. He didn't know what else to ask, and yet he felt like this was one of the first honest conversations he was having about Luke Connolly.

'Ethan Connolly,' he asked. 'Any experience of him before he got sick?'

Walsh shook his head.

'He was always sick,' he said. 'But he used to come and watch his brother, the odd time.'

'We hear Luke was quite devoted to him.'

Walsh said nothing. He began to pick up discarded jerseys, throwing them in a black sack he'd just torn off a roll.

'Who told you that?'

'Isn't it true?'

'Ah, look. Luke was a teenager. Teenagers are selfish. His brother had been sick for years. His parents made him visit him a lot and he'd miss things, you know. Training. Nights out. Time with his mates. Can't have been easy. My father died from cancer, asbestos in his lungs from the job. It went on a while. I loved him, but I also resented him – when we couldn't do stuff other families could, when we had to be in the hospital, all that crap. I wouldn't buy into the whole "Luke was the best brother alive" story. And maybe it was understandable. That's all I'm saying.'

'Sure,' Tom said. It made sense. Luke could love Ethan but still carry a lot of anger about how much his life was affected by his brother's illness.

'You've been very helpful,' he told Walsh. 'Just one more thing. Do you remember something happening a few months ago involving any of that gang? Were the lads off their game for a period? Fighting over anything?'

Walsh scrunched up his face.

'After Christmas, you mean?'

'Could have been.'

'Yes. Perhaps. I came in here and interrupted Luke and Brian having a bit of an argument. Didn't hear much, but they'd had a bad game, fluffed passes, things like that, and when the rest of the lads left I noticed the two of them hadn't come out. I came in to check they were alright. I wasn't eavesdropping, that's not my thing. From the mouths of babes comes an awful lot of crap. But I heard Luke saying something about his da.'

'Chris Connolly?' Tom asked.

'Hmm. Something about his job. Couldn't tell you a thing more than that.'

'Can you remember the exact words?' Sean asked.

Walsh hesitated. He closed his eyes while he thought, then opened them.

'"He has enough problems as it is. If he hears about this, he'll kill me."'

Tom and Sean both frowned, bemused. Jackie couldn't have looked any more startled.

'Luke Connolly thought his father might kill him?' Sean repeated.

'No,' Walsh said, dismissively. 'That's just what he said. We all say that, don't we? If Principal Lynch finds out I've been this frank with you lot, he'll kill me.'

'But, his dad had enough problems? Didn't that ring any alarm bells for you, when Luke was actually killed?'

Walsh put down the bin bag and held out his hands.

'Why would it? You lot arrested somebody within weeks. I barely knew the boy was dead and you had somebody for it. And, anyway, most of the parents in this school have problems. Chris Connolly more than most, I'd guess. Another world to you and me, but there nonetheless. Trust me.'

Tom looked over at Jackie.

She looked back, still defiant. This wasn't game, set and match, by any stretch. But she was definitely conceding some ground.

# CHAPTER 30

'Where were the parents the night Luke died?' Tom asked Jackie as they walked back to their cars. Sean had strolled on ahead. His son had rung and Sean was doing his level best to get out of a family dinner. In his words, his children and their various spouses had been henpecking him since June had died. Sean wasn't averse to a bit of minding but he was also keen to remind Tom that he was still in his sixties, not ready to be mollycoddled into his nursing home just yet.

'His parents were at home,' Jackie answered. 'You know, I did check all this. I didn't just go looking for the nearest black, working-class kid and try to hang a heinous crime around his neck.'

Tom stopped abruptly and faced her. 'We have to get beyond this, Detective,' he said, curtly.

Jackie's lips set in displeasure.

'Get beyond what?' she said. 'Me trying to ensure somebody is prosecuted for Luke's murder and you trying to blow a hole in the case? How can I get beyond that?'

She started to walk away. Tom looked at the back of her head.

He'd known, hadn't he?

He'd realised early what was driving her, but it hadn't formed itself into a proper thought until now.

'It was you,' he said.

Jackie stopped and turned her head, looked at him quizzically.

'I've been racking my brains as to why you're so insistent that you're right on Daniel, why you are so determined to forge forward with his prosecution in the face of all the contradictions. I've told myself you're dogmatic, persistent – all good qualities in a detective – but not when the detective is also blinkered. But there's much more than that behind all this, isn't there?'

Jackie's face twitched, her lips pursed. She was unsettled, still unsure where he was going.

'You've been stationed in Little Leaf for the last few years. Before that, you worked around the country. That might have been what put me off. But you started in Little Leaf, didn't you? You worked there for ten years. And then, you put in for a transfer. Out of character for you, I think, but you probably told your superiors you wanted to gain more experience. And they didn't suspect one of their more experienced detectives. They thought it was probably a newbie or a junior who'd failed to help that woman and her son.'

Jackie's face flushed bright red. Her lips started to quiver.

'The wife from Glenmore House. She came to you. You didn't, for whatever reason, follow through. And she died. That's why you need Daniel prosecuted. When you said Luke was just a kid and you needed to get him justice – it wasn't just Luke you were thinking of.'

Tom got to Jackie before her knees crumpled. He stopped her from falling and helped her to stand straight again. The tears were flowing from her eyes now. She was breathing heavily, too, veering into panic attack territory.

'Calm,' Tom said. 'Breathe, just breathe. Tell me what happened.'

'I . . . It wasn't like they said,' she whispered. 'It had been busy, weirdly busy for us, and this woman just came in. There wasn't a mark on her and she spoke so well. There were no tears, she was in complete control and all she said was that her husband had been violent towards her. I asked her what he'd done and she . . .' Jackie looked up at Tom. 'I mean, I realised, after, she was too embarrassed to tell me. She was embarrassed that her life wasn't what it looked like, that her husband beat her. But at the time, all she said was, *Well, he gets rough*. She didn't seem frightened. I've gone over and over it in my head. If she'd been scared or bruised or . . . But I didn't deliberately not help her.'

'What did you say to her?' Tom asked.

'I told her she would need physical evidence to make a case. That if he laid a finger on her, to come to the station immediately, or take photos or ring the doctor and get the surgery to contact us. I told her if he was properly violent, we would pursue it and she should start readying herself to leave him. Maybe pack a bag for her and her child. I asked her did she think he'd be violent to the child, and she . . . she said he'd never laid a finger on him. I asked her did she want me to open a case file, go out to the house and interview the husband. But she wanted to get out of the station. The kid was waiting in the car. I don't know what I should have done. I think she thought when she walked in that we would send her and the kid to a refuge or go arrest the husband immediately. I don't know, Inspector. I don't know.'

Jackie sobbed, and covered her mouth, shocked.

'It had crossed my mind, in the days that followed, when I was less busy. I wondered if I'd see her back. I even considered calling out. A week later. That's when they were found dead.'

Tom put his arms around Jackie. He could see the burden she carried was far worse than anything he or anybody else might say to her all these years later. Perhaps, at the time, she should have told her superiors what had happened but, on the basis of what she'd just told him, there wasn't anything technically wrong in how she'd handled the situation. Domestic violence cases were complicated. It might seem like a huge step for the spouse to go to the police station for the first time, but really it was only a baby step in the right direction. Blame the law, blame technicalities, blame anybody – Jackie blamed herself, but it wasn't entirely fair.

Crippling, but it hadn't been her who'd killed that woman and her son. It had been the husband.

'Jackie, I understand,' Tom said. 'And I won't speak about this again. It's fifteen years ago and by the sounds of it, you did everything by the book. I think you should have confided in your chief back then but I expect you were in shock and blaming yourself a lot more than was necessary. Look, we can speak about it again, if it helps. I can get you counselling. But, in the immediate term, now it's out in the open, I think you have to accept it's influenced you in this case.'

Jackie nodded, meekly, wiping her nose with her sleeve.

'I'm sorry,' she said.

'Don't be sorry,' Tom said. 'Be aware. You can't get justice for that woman and her son. But we can for Luke. It's not too late. And, you know, even with all these questions to be answered, I'm not saying we mightn't turn up the same result. You might be completely right about Daniel, despite some blindness around the circumstances. At least this way, though, we can be sure of it. Yes?'

She nodded. He'd thrown her a bone and she was grateful for it.

'The question you asked, about Chris and Rose,' Jackie said, straightening herself, trying to be professional again. 'They were at home together. But the house is huge so I followed protocol. What were you watching, reading, did you talk to anybody on the phone. She was in bed, but awake. She was waiting for Luke to come home. It was her who rang us. At 6 a.m. He'd never stayed out that late before and he wasn't answering his phone. It rang out a few times, then it was off, like it had run out of battery. None of his friends were answering either. Chris said he'd been working, then watched some TV. He was in bed by midnight, slept until his wife woke him.'

'Okay, good. You asked the right questions. So, Chris wasn't worried?'

'No,' Jackie confirmed. 'He thought his wife was being paranoid. Understandable, but unnecessary. They knew who Luke was with and they thought he was over in Jacob's house. She rang us, lodged her concern, then drove over there and subsequently went around all the friends. When we arrived later that morning, they were all ready to talk. They hadn't been in Jacob's; they'd gone to the haunted house, as they called it. Well, the girls did. They'd had a few drinks, messed around with a Ouija board, did shit kids do. And then they left, but Luke and Daniel stayed behind. We went over to the house and saw Luke immediately. He'd obviously been dead all night. Daniel was our next port of call.'

'What did Daniel say initially?'

'That was the thing. He held out his hands and said, "Go on then. Arrest me." And I asked him where he'd been in the two hours we were already narrowing in on and he said he'd been at home. He was obviously lying. But he . . .'

She stopped.

'Go on.'

'When we told him Luke was dead, he said he thought we were there to arrest him for the drugs. I said, no, this is about Luke Connolly being pushed to his death and he just froze. He clammed up.'

'Could he have been in shock?'

'Too in shock to say "I didn't do that"?'

'It can happen,' Tom said. 'He was expecting one thing and got another. And was he the one who got them the drugs?'

Jackie shook her head.

'You know, it's the one thing we haven't gone after anybody for. It was just a recreational amount and there was no drug dealing per se, from what I can establish. Traces in Luke's system and Daniel's urine. We couldn't test the others. No cause. With Daniel working in a club and everything, it's an easy leap to assume he supplied them. But I don't think the drugs came from him.'

'Who do you think got them?'

'I don't know. I'm just saying, the kids in this area have money and they know where to get things.'

'Who bought the alcohol?' Tom asked.

'That we do know. Jacob and Luke were caught on CCTV going into the Little Leaf off-licence earlier that evening and coming out with two carrier bags.'

Tom walked in silence for a few seconds.

'It is understandable that Luke's mother would be worried that he didn't come home,' he said. 'It's less understandable that Chris wouldn't be. I mean, they're not ordinary parents. He's not a regular, relaxed dad. Rose Connolly said something to me: she said Chris had poured all his hopes and dreams into Luke when he realised Ethan was dying. So why wasn't he concerned that the kid wasn't home at six in the morning?'

'You don't really think . . .'

'What do we know?' he said. 'What if the father saw the two of them together – Luke and Daniel? Rose doesn't think he'd have been too happy to know his son was gay. Say he caught them, was furious, waited until Daniel left and then he and Luke fought.'

Jackie gestured dismissively.

'If Chris saw them together and wasn't happy, he'd have killed Daniel, surely? Not his own son.'

Tom said nothing; he was still mulling the possibilities.

Jackie shifted awkwardly from foot to foot, looking distinctly uncomfortable.

'Well, anyway, Rose said she didn't hear Chris leave the house at any point.'

Tom stared at her, said nothing. Then he repeated what she'd just said.

'She didn't *hear* him leave?'

'No.'

'Don't you mean she didn't *see* him?'

Jackie sucked the insides of her cheek.

'She didn't hear him. She didn't say anything about seeing him.'

'Because . . .' Tom prompted. He knew what was coming, but he wanted her to say it, to realise its gravity.

'Because they sleep in separate bedrooms,' Jackie said.

Sean was finishing his call as Tom got in the car.

'What was happening there?' Sean asked, after he'd hung up.

'You wouldn't believe me if I told you. Though I've got my head around why she's so persistent on the Daniel thing. We might start to make some progress. Anyhow, how are your kids?'

'June is dead almost three years, God rest her,' Sean said. 'I really thought they'd have run out of steam at this stage. *Are you eating, Dad?* I mean, do I look like I'm fading away to you, Tom?'

Sean pinched at the small tyre sitting atop his trousers.

'They worry about you, you should be grateful,' Tom said. 'Speaking of food, do you want to come back to ours for dinner?'

'That's out of the blue. I'm not being used as a body shield, am I? That's the other problem with being a single man: couples think they can throw you in between them when they're fighting.'

'We're not fighting,' Tom reassured him. 'Though, Louise is doing so much house cleaning lately, I'm half expecting to wake up one of these mornings at the bottom of a skip.'

'Ah. Making her way through your list, is she?'

'Seriously?' Tom said, surprised. 'You know I've a list, too?'

'We all have a list,' Sean said. 'Trust me, you won't get near it when you go into my job, son.'

'Have you two talked about this?'

Sean smiled.

'You know,' Tom said, 'Rose and Chris Connolly sleep in separate rooms. Why do you think that is?'

'Maybe when Ethan's at home, they take turns caring for him,' Sean suggested. 'Maybe they got into the habit of having their own rooms so whoever was off on any given night could get some sleep. Myself and June did the same when the youngest came. Just for a time. She couldn't get Annie to take the breast so she decided to have a night on, night off. It was a first for me. Quite distressing, I tell you.'

'God love you.'

'Tom, do you think I'm offensive? When I called Jackie McCallion "lass", she was really peeved. Is lass such a bad thing?'

Tom swallowed.

'Well, Sean, I've always seen you as an equal opportunities insulter. You call women girls and lass, and you call men jumped-up little shitbags and arseholes.'

'It's just a . . .'

'A turn of phrase,' Tom completed the sentence. 'I know. But if you called me "boy", I'd take issue.'

'I see,' Sean said. He started to drive. 'I'll stick with arsehole, will I?'

Tom snorted.

Sean leaned over to the CD player and turned it on. Albinoni's 'Adagio in G Minor' filled the car. Tom leaned his head against the headrest and listened.

Sean and his best pal Louise made themselves comfortable in the sitting room while Tom made dinner. He didn't have the gall to point out to his wife that he'd been in charge of dinner every night for the last week. He suspected it would result in a lecture on how busy she was and he guessed (though he could actually see no discernible difference in their home, despite the black bags piling up in the hall for various charities or the dump) that she was within her rights.

So he chopped chicken and vegetables and garlic and made a stir-fry, blaring Puccini on the laptop and wondering what the two of them could be laughing so hard about in the sitting room.

'Is there a party in there?' he asked, when the smell summoned them into the kitchen.

'You know what he's taking up when he retires again?' Louise asked.

'Watching more sport on TV?' Tom suggested.

'There is no more sport to watch,' Sean said. 'No, it's something I've wanted to do my whole life.'

'I'm at a loss,' Tom said.

'Dancing.'

Tom didn't think he'd heard Sean correctly.

'You know,' Sean said. 'A man and a woman.' He grabbed Louise's waist and began to twirl her. She giggled and let him. 'But I have to find a woman. Louise has turned me down.'

'Let me get this straight,' Tom said. 'Dancing? You're built like a brick shithouse. What do you mean? Ballroom?'

'Well, it's hardly going to be interpretive, now, is it? And don't mock me. Dancing is for everyone.'

Tom raised his eyebrows.

'It's not for me to judge. Emmet McDonagh is wearing a Fitbit, after all. But where are you going to find a woman?'

'I don't know. I looked on Tinder but they're just after sex. I only want them for the dance lessons.'

Tom stopped what he was doing and caught Louise's eye. He'd no idea if Sean was pulling their legs, but he suspected from her pained effort to keep her face straight that his boss was deadly serious.

'You could ask Linda McCarn,' Tom suggested. 'If ever a woman needed a distraction right now, it's her.'

Sean frowned.

'Oh, do,' Louise said. 'Really, Sean. She needs to get out of the house and you can be sure of one thing.'

'What?'

'She won't be looking for any romance.'

Tom turned Puccini down as he ladled out the dinner, but the strains of 'Va, Tosca!' could still be heard. They took their seats, Louise pouring large glasses of water when she saw how many chillies Tom had chopped into the stir-fry.

'So, are we going to start poking around in Chris Connolly's business now?' Sean said, through a mouthful of food. 'Because, you know, he's a well-connected little problem.'

'I don't know,' Tom said truthfully, shifting rice around his plate. 'It's a stretch, a father killing his son just because he's gay. A bit, I don't know, 1950s.'

'It's the stupidest thing I've ever heard,' Louise said.

'Is it, though?' Sean said. 'Some lad got murdered by a gang in Russia last week for being gay. In places in India, they murder their own daughters for sex outside marriage.'

'We're about to hold a referendum on gay marriage!' Louise exclaimed, laughing. 'This is Ireland.'

'And look at the polls,' Sean replied. 'There's still a high percentage opposing equality.'

Louise shrugged.

Tom chewed thoughtfully.

'But you still think those kids are keeping something from us,' Sean said, watching him.

'Don't you? Aren't kids always keeping something from somebody?'

'Yup. What's your team like at the moment? Who's not on a case?'

'They're all doing something,' Tom said.

'Sure. But who can spare a few hours for a day or two?'

Tom put his fork down.

'You're not suggesting what I think you're suggesting? Tailing five kids for no apparent reason other than I think they might be hiding something?'

'Hiding something that could result in an innocent kid getting prison time.'

Tom reached over and placed his hand on Sean's forehead. He was hot, but that could have just been the chillies.

'If I'd suggested something like this to you in the past, you'd have had a nervous breakdown,' Tom said.

Sean nodded.

'But I'm not really the boss any more, so I don't have to worry about resources,' he said. 'And also –' he studied the fork of food in front of him – 'I'm fairly certain it was one of those little shits who pushed Luke. Not Chris Connolly. Daniel is their fall guy. There's no other reason for them all to back each other up. He's the outsider; he's been designated to take the blame. I don't like that. It doesn't sit right with my sense of . . . fairness.'

'Interesting, that,' Tom said.

'What?'

'The term *outsider*. It's how Daniel described himself. And, even more interesting, he really seems, aside from the family, to be the only one truly mourning Luke. But I want to look at Chris Connolly a bit more. Just to be sure.'

# CHAPTER 31

The pitch was like a mud bath after the previous day's steady rainfall. Sean stood at the side and watched his grandson and his teammates slide from one end to the other, trying to pass the ball and not break their necks at the same time. Saturday afternoon football had never been so dangerous.

He stomped his feet to keep warm and took a sip from his flask. A particularly large kid skidded into a tackle on Sean's grandson and brought him crashing to the ground.

'Jesus, ref, straight red,' Sean yelled, nearly rupturing the eardrums of the woman standing beside him. 'What's he doing on an under-fourteens team anyway? He's practically a full-grown man. Cheat!'

'That's my grandson, the nerve of you.'

Sean's old pal Robert, the deputy governor from Cloverhill prison, came to stand beside him.

'Your grandson will make a great Guard,' Sean said, back-tracking with flair. 'Good genes in that family. Whoever his real granddad is. What are you, four foot?'

'Fuck off,' Robert replied. 'You're lucky I'm here. That little pup you gave a promotion to practically accused me of police brutality at Daniel Konaté's bedside.'

'Bollocks,' Sean said. 'You're too sensitive. And, by the way, that young pup is fifty-three.'

Sean's grandson ran over and joined them.

'Did you see what that boy . . .' he started to say as he held out his hand for his water bottle.

'It was nothing,' Sean said, shoving the bottle into his grandson's hand and turning him around at the same time. He gave the boy a push back onto the pitch.

'You have something for me?' Sean asked his friend.

Robert stuck his hand into his anorak and pulled out a plastic bag.

Sean took the bag and reached into his own coat for a similar one. His was heavy; it contained a bottle of Powers whiskey. His friend had just given him paper.

'All the requests for visits to Daniel Konaté since he became our guest,' Robert said. 'I think you'll be surprised at a couple of the names on there.'

Now Sean was interested. The whistle had just blown on the match. His grandson's team had lost.

He tucked the bag into his coat pocket and patted his friend on the shoulder.

'Gotta bring the lad out for fast food, cheer him up.'

They parted ways as the visitors' list burnt a hole in Sean's pocket.

## CHAPTER 32

Ray left Michael sitting in the car. He was having an argument with his wife on the phone, so Ray was the obvious candidate to jump out and follow Jacob Quinn Delaney into the snooker hall.

But Ray had been glad to get out of the car in any case. Listening to Michael fight with Anne over which one of them should be working and where was a bit too uncomfortable, especially considering the conversations he and Laura were currently having. Or not having, as the case may be.

Bridget had texted that morning to ask if he wanted to come in on Monday and start filling out the paperwork for the transfer. Ray had looked across at Laura sleeping and for the millionth time tried to talk himself out of leaving the murder squad. Finally, he'd texted Bridget back – *Busy, will call soon.* Bridget didn't know yet that he'd approached her before he'd talked to Laura and Tom.

And in retrospect, Ray was kicking himself. If he'd said it to them first, before contacting another unit, then there'd have been less fallout if he did change his mind.

He could tell himself it had been wise to scout whether there was an opportunity for a transfer. In his heart, though, Ray knew it had been a knee-jerk reaction.

Would it be more embarrassing or less if he was forced into a retraction?

Ray shook his head. It was all too messy. And right now he needed his head on the job.

The snooker hall was a barn of a place. To the front was a small bar and a few empty chairs and tables. Two Premiership teams were playing on a TV mounted at the end of the counter, but nobody was watching. Customers brought their drinks down to the sixteen snooker tables arranged in rows in the larger space at the rear of the hall. Low lights hung over each table. A few tables were in complete darkness – this was the kind of joint where you paid for the light. Ten minutes a go, probably a euro each time.

He couldn't immediately spot Jacob. But he had to be in here. Ray had followed him in mere seconds after the lad had entered.

Ray crossed to the bar and waited for somebody to come out and serve. He cast an eye over the tables.

It seemed a strange spot for Jacob to rock up. The snooker hall sat on the edge of an industrial estate beside an area Ray was very familiar with from his days in uniform. 'Problematic' would be the word he'd use to describe it. And he was familiar with the sorts of problems. It wasn't a million miles away from where Ray had grown up.

When Jacob had got off the bus beside the industrial estate, Ray and Michael had been instantly interested and alert. It wasn't just off the lad's beaten track; this place was a whole different world.

Then he'd gone into the snooker hall and that too had defied logic, because it didn't take a genius to imagine that a house the size of the Quinn Delaneys' more than likely had a games room that included a snooker table.

So why take a bus to the other side of the city to hang out here?

'Can I help you, mate?'

A young barman appeared and Ray ordered a pint of Carlsberg and a box of snooker balls. The barman gave him his change in euro coins.

Ray thanked him and walked further into the hall. He'd located Jacob at the very back.

To Jacob, Ray was an unknown. Just a man out on a Saturday afternoon for a pint and a game of snooker. Ray hadn't dressed down as much as Michael generally did, but he was still just wearing a sweater and a pair of jeans.

The table two down from Jacob was in darkness. Ray made his way over and rested his pint on the counter at the wall.

The room was quiet, bar the sound of balls knocking against each other and the low murmur of males talking. Ray inhaled and smelled his youth. He'd often hung out in places like this. He felt nostalgic and magnanimous. Maybe Jacob just needed to escape the stuffiness of Little Leaf every now and again. Maybe he had friends outside the usual cohort and he was more comfortable visiting them in their domain than having them in his.

Because the lads that Jacob was sitting with would certainly stand out in Little Leaf.

Ray popped a euro in the box on the wall to turn on his light, then made a show of looking for cue chalk.

The two blokes on the table beside him were in the process of chalking their own cues so Ray walked past them to Jacob's table.

Jacob was sitting on a high stool, drink in hand, while the two lads he'd joined played the table.

'Can I borrow your chalk?' Ray asked.

Jacob looked around him, saw one on the counter and handed it to Ray.

Ray watched the lads play as he rubbed the blue chalk onto the cue tip. One was tall, skinny, with a severe crew cut. The other was shorter and stockier, with one of those stupid haircuts that was more fringe and wax than anything else. He'd set up the black after potting a red so paid no attention to Ray. The other lad, though, the tall one, watched Ray as the detective blew the chalk off the top of the tip and handed it back to Jacob.

Ray stared right back until his audience lowered his eyes.

It was something that frequently stood to Ray, the fact he came from a working-class area. Most police walked, talked and smelled like cops, but Ray had authenticity.

He was so cut out for undercover in drugs, it wasn't even funny.

What was funny was that, having more or less talked himself back off the transfer ledge, he was now inadvertently scoping what very much resembled a drug deal.

Jacob was edgy on the high stool; his knee jiggled up and down and he was drinking too fast from the glass of clear liquid in his hand. He barely acknowledged Ray when the detective handed back the blue chalk; just tossed it back on the counter and returned his gaze to Little and Large.

Ray strolled back to his table, lined up the white, and broke the reds. Then he held his breath and listened as hard as he could for any exchanges on the other table.

The light on the table beside him went out.

'Fuck it,' one of the men said. 'I've to collect the kids from her anyway. Want to come over to mine later for the match?'

His friend grunted in assent; they laid their cues on the table and walked away.

'. . . not a fucking bank, Jakey-lad. You can't just pop in and ask to make a withdrawal.'

The short one at Jacob's table was speaking.

Ray held his breath and steadied his chin on the cue. He hit the white ball lightly, pocketing a red, then stood over the table as if to study his options.

'I'll pay over the odds, it's not a problem,' Jacob said.

'Do you think we just have product on us? We take snooker practice seriously. Gaz here fancies himself the next Ronnie O'Sullivan.'

The short one took a shot and missed. Both lads laughed.

'This is where I came last week,' Jacob protested.

'Yeah, but we knew you were coming last week.'

Ray botched his shot on a coloured ball. He cursed under his breath and dropped to his hunkers, eyeing his positioning on the table.

'Anyway. Too many ears in here.'

Ray didn't look up. But he could feel the stares he was getting. The tall one had spoken. Ray made a quick calculation. He mightn't have made him as police, but he could equally have suspected that Ray was on the books for another dealer. When he'd walked past two empty tables at the top of the hall, it would have given it away to anybody with a modicum of smarts. And the tall chap obviously had smarts.

Ray kept potting as the three lads walked away from their table, the light still on. The other two walked ahead, facing front. Jacob followed in their wake, throwing worried glances over his shoulder at Ray.

As soon as they were far enough away, Ray pulled his phone from his pocket and dialled Michael. Thankfully, he was off the call with Anne.

'Heading your way now,' he said. 'Jacob, Little and Large.'

'Got you,' Michael said. 'They've just come out. They're hanging about outside the front door.'

'What are they doing?' Ray asked.

'Lighting joints. Talking. Oh, wait, now the tall one is poking Jacob in the chest.'

Ray straightened up.

'I suspect they're asking him if he's being followed,' he said. 'They had me marked. What's Jacob's response?'

'He looks like he's about to lose it.' Michael paused. 'Tall guy has backed off. So would I. Did you say this Jacob lad was eighteen? Jesus.'

Ray waited, phone to his ear. He spotted an opportunistic black ball pot and took it.

'Short one just reached into his pocket,' Michael said. 'He's doing the old look-around. Hasn't spotted me.' Michael went silent for a minute. 'There it is. He's handed over a baggie. Want me to do them?'

'Nah,' Ray said. 'Did you get pics?'

They'd brought a camera on the off-chance Jacob got up to something and now he had.

'Course I got pics. I'm really good at my job,' Michael said. 'If you could let my wife know, I'd appreciate it.'

'I'll be out in five,' Ray said and hung up. His pint was still half full. He took a sip and dialled Bridget Duffy.

'It's not about the paperwork,' he said, as soon as she answered. 'If I send you over a couple of pictures of some low-level dealers, can you get me their info?'

He could almost hear Bridget smiling down the phone. She obviously thought this was all part of the warm-up. The heat in Ray's cheeks could fry eggs.

# CHAPTER 33

Rose Connolly had no problem with Tom wanting to see Luke's room while they waited for Chris to come home. She had seemed distracted when Tom called to the door. Not displeased to see him, but not able to give him any time, either. She had the phone pressed to her ear and ushered him in, then paused in her call to ask what he needed.

She was happy he wanted to look upstairs; it meant she could continue the call.

Luke and Ethan had their own rooms. Tom supposed it made sense in a house this size, though he had had some notion that twins might choose to be closer than most siblings. He'd had a couple of missed calls from Ethan's mobile yesterday, a voice-mail left each time. The kid was still searching for answers and still pushing Daniel's innocence. Luke might have resented his brother being ill, but his brother wasn't holding that against him. It didn't matter any more.

Ethan's room was beside Luke's. Their names were still on little plaques on their doors, so it was easy to spot them. Tom ran his fingers over the gilt-edged letters, wondering if Rose would ever be able to bring herself to pry them from the wood.

The bedroom was that of an invalid. All the medicine Ethan had needed to enable his care at home was still piled on a table under the window. The bed was made up with crisp white sheets. A white chest of drawers, its surface still kept free of dust or dirt of any kind, held a few selected, framed photographs – pictures of Ethan with his wider family, with his parents and with Luke.

Tom frowned. He walked back to the door and stood looking at the bed, face on.

He was right. This was where the photograph had been taken at Christmas, the one Luke had tweeted. The room had so much medical equipment in it, it looked like a hospital room, which was what Tom had assumed it was.

Had it ever looked like a normal teenage boy's room? he wondered. It was bereft of anything that spoke to personality. No posters, no old toys, no computer games, no designer trainers thrown on the floor.

He spotted it then, an interconnecting door between the rooms. So even though the twins slept separately, there was a nearness. That made more sense to Tom.

He tried the door, but it was locked. Tom shrugged and went back out onto the landing, entering Luke's room that way.

This was more what he would have expected. Luke's room was half-child, half-man. The colour scheme was grey and black, with a minimalist feel to the design. But shelves over the single bed were filled with characters from *Star Wars* and on the chest of drawers sat a Lego-built Millennium Falcon.

Luke had stuck a couple of posters on the wall with Blu-tack. The Leinster rugby team. A still from *Scarface*. An enlarged photograph of some boys taking part in a 'Hell and Back' race. Tom squinted at the faces beneath the muck. It was Luke, Jacob and Brian making the peace signs to the camera, beaming in the rays from the cold sun, their skin tinged with blue beneath the dirt and damp.

There was only one photograph on Luke's bedside locker. It was of Charlotte, pouting in that teenage-girl way they think is attractive and sexy but makes them look like anorexic fish. The picture had been cut out and stuck in a heart-shaped pink frame. Hazel had probably been the casualty of the scissors.

Charlotte had given it to Luke, no doubt. He hadn't acquired that photo frame of his own volition.

There were no pictures of Daniel visible. Or of his family, for that matter.

'I can't put anything away,' Rose said. She was standing in the doorway. Tom hadn't heard her approach. Her feet were bare beneath her leggings. 'Every time I come up here with black bags in my hand, I turn back around. I mean, that's normal, isn't it? They haven't even released his body yet.'

'It's far too soon,' Tom said.

Rose nodded, appreciatively.

'Chris is home,' she said. 'Did you – have you noticed anything up here? Are you looking for something in particular?'

'No, I'm just trying to get a sense of the lad. His relationships with people, especially his friends.' Tom pointed at the photograph from the mud run. 'They were close.'

'Ever since school started,' Rose said.

'What about this other chap who hung around with Luke – Dylan? I hear there was an incident.'

'It was nothing. Just kids.'

Tom didn't buy it. Rose had bristled. The line 'It was nothing' was something she felt she should repeat.

'Teenagers, not kids,' Tom said. 'They must have been about fifteen, right? Old enough to know better. Old enough to have a criminal charge brought, if you'd wanted it. Dylan stabbed Luke in the hand with a pencil, didn't he? That took a lot of . . . anger.'

Rose glanced away, two red dots appearing on her cheeks.

'I've always thought Dylan carries a lot of rage in him,' she said. 'Any time he was here, even when his parents brought him around to apologise, I could sense it off him, you know? When Luke came home that day – when the school brought him home – I was ready to call the police. He'd had stitches. And, like you say, they were fifteen. But, Chris . . .' Rose looked over her shoulder. 'Well. The Keating family.'

She sighed.

Tom nodded, understanding everything.

'He got on with Ethan better, though,' Rose continued.

'Luke?' Tom asked, puzzled.

'No, Dylan. Ethan is quieter, smarter. Dylan – he's not really an outdoorsy sort of boy. That can be hard when you're with a pack of lads like Luke and his friends. It was hard on Ethan, too, when he started to get sick. He used to try to keep up, even then. But he couldn't. And the irony is, Luke was making himself be that kind of kid. Had Ethan not got sick, maybe Luke would have been more bookish, a little less outgoing.'

'They think girls are complicated,' Tom said, shaking his head. 'But the dynamics of a gang of young men are a thing to behold.'

'Rose?' Chris's voice carried up the stairs.

'We're coming,' she called back down.

Tom followed her out of the room and shut the door gently behind him.

'The phone call you were on when I arrived seemed important,' Tom said, as they walked.

'Yes. It was Claire, Ethan's nurse. I'd left her a message to ring me. He was really, I don't know . . . active, this morning. Sometimes he has these moments. False hope, that's what it is.

But it's addictive. For him and us. I need somebody to remind me it's nothing more than what it is because it hurts so much to hope.'

Tom couldn't think of what to say. It was too devastating a sentence to reply to.

Chris had put on a pot of coffee in the kitchen. He shook Tom's hand out of habit, then slumped on a stool beside the breakfast bar. His shirt was already unbuttoned, suit jacket flung over the back of the chair.

'Well,' he said. 'Have you answered the questions you had? Do you accept it was Daniel Konaté who did this?'

Tom didn't respond immediately. Instead, he took a stool himself.

'You look tired,' he said to Chris, noticing the bags under the man's eyes, the sickly pallor of his skin.

Chris shrugged.

'I'm trying to fit a full week's work into half a week for the last, oh, I don't know how long. And since this, it's worse again. Calling into the office on a Saturday is the new norm.'

Rose stood behind Tom, her arms wrapped around herself. She didn't look like she wanted to be any nearer to her husband.

'I told Ethan you wouldn't be in today,' she said. 'He's in good form. Claire wanted to take him for a walk, but he was talking her out of it. He hates that wheelchair.'

Chris said nothing. He rubbed his eyes with his hands, then plunged the coffee.

'Have you an audit on at the moment?' Tom asked.

Chris flapped his hand.

'There's always *an audit* on. We've no big firms undergoing one at the moment but there's constant updating of regulations.

The government has gone mad since the crash. Legislation by the day. They've introduced more red tape to run a company in this country than I imagine they have in North Korea. It makes it impossible.'

'I guess it's necessary,' Tom said. 'After what happened. All those banks that got away with so much. And anyway, from what I hear, we're still not up there in the transparency or accountability stakes. It's not like anybody went to jail for the crash, is it?'

Chris winced.

'I don't like talking about work at home,' he said, meeting Tom's eye. 'What did you come here to ask me? Rose said you had something to check?'

'I do, as it happens,' Tom said. 'About Daniel Konaté.'

'Sure,' Chris said. 'Go for it. Whatever you need to ask.'

Tom hesitated.

'I was just wondering why you visited him on remand,' Tom said.

Chris swallowed. Out of the corner of his eye, Tom saw Rose's mouth fall open.

'How do you know I visited him?' Chris asked.

'It's not exactly a walk-in-off-the-street kind of place, Mr Connolly. You had to apply for a visitor's pass.'

'I know that. I'm just wondering why you went to the trouble of looking at his visitors. Or am I being followed?'

Tom said nothing. He and Chris were sizing each other up. The inspector didn't think for a second that Chris Connolly suspected he was being followed. What he was wondering was whether the police had made the discovery or Daniel had talked.

'It's standard,' Tom said, 'to keep an eye on who comes in to speak to suspects. That's how your name came up. We had to start looking because Daniel won't speak to us.'

Tom leaned forward on the last few words.

'I thought Charlotte Burke might have mentioned it,' Chris said.

Tom blinked.

'Charlotte? Why would she know anything?'

'She was there, too,' he said. 'Not in the visiting area. Outside, in the car park. I think she was trying to get in to see Daniel. She mustn't have realised you need to request a visit.'

'Why would she want to talk to Daniel?' Tom said.

'Maybe you should ask her,' Chris responded. 'She looked quite shifty when I saw her.'

Tom frowned.

'I'm sure she was surprised to see you there,' he said, 'visiting your son's alleged attacker. Why were you there?'

'Well, there's no great conspiracy,' Chris said, sitting back, a coffee cup now in his hand. 'I know he won't speak to you. But I hoped he'd speak to me. Open up. Maybe confess. He knows what we're going through with Ethan. It seems unnaturally cruel that he'd leave us in the dark about what happened to Luke. You lot have him bang to rights, so why not tell the truth?'

'Right,' Tom said. 'It just, it struck me from the first time I met him that Daniel seems almost afraid to speak to us. In most cases like this, suspects are protesting their innocence. We can't shut them up. They become world experts in either declaring their innocence or fabricating it. For example – we all know Daniel is gay. That's not in contention. So, I find it very strange that he hasn't tried to claim that he and Luke engaged in consensual sex, at least in an attempt to get off the rape charge. He knows full well what will happen to him inside if he's convicted of that.'

Chris shrugged.

'He knows he can't claim that because it's a lie,' he said. 'Luke wasn't gay.'

'What if he was?' Tom said. 'Would that have been a problem for you?'

'Why would it have been a problem for me?' Chris had raised his voice. He was angry, growing angrier. It was the first time Tom had seen him like this.

'You honestly think if Luke was standing in front of me now – if he was still alive – and told me he was gay, I wouldn't just put my arms around him and hug him?' Chris said. 'That I would care about his sexual orientation if he was still alive? I'd give anything, *anything*, for him to be here – gay, straight, none of the above. He was my son!'

Chris banged his hand on the countertop, making the inspector and Rose jump. He glared at Tom, full of fury.

Tom said nothing, waited for the moment of rage to pass.

'Would it have been an issue for the people you work with?'

Chris looked at Tom, astonished, then at Rose, who seemed equally taken aback.

'Why?' Chris said. 'What do they have to do with anything?'

Tom swallowed. He was starting to wonder that himself. Did Coach Walsh's networking comment have any relevance to what had happened? Chris had skeletons in his closet but his son being gay was obviously not one of them.

So why had Chris gone near Daniel? Was it possible he was telling the truth – he just wanted him to confess?

Tom was lost. He was almost starting to regret coming here.

'I don't know where you're going with this,' Chris said, shaking his head. 'It wouldn't have mattered if Luke was gay, but he wasn't. And I point-blank refuse to have people going around saying it now, whether it's you or the man who killed him. It's a lie. I'm not letting history be revised. And I won't have his reputation tarnished because somebody, somewhere, wants that . . . animal to get off.'

Rose placed her hand over her mouth. She turned away.

'You think your son's reputation would be tarnished if it came out he was gay?' Tom asked. And there it was. A tiny glimmer of the truth.

Chris blushed under Tom's scrutiny. He'd fallen into a trap that Tom hadn't even planned to set. Into the silence, Chris had said too much. And in doing so, he'd reversed his own position that he didn't care whether his son loved girls or boys.

He opened his mouth, then closed it again.

'Did you threaten Daniel Konaté?' Tom asked. 'When you visited him, did you tell him not to talk to us?' The bracelet of bruises on Daniel's wrist made sense now. Tom could imagine somebody grabbing his arm, forcing him to listen. And it showed that Chris Connolly had the potential for violence.

Chris glanced quickly at Rose.

'Of course not. I want him to talk.'

Rose frowned.

Tom watched Chris. He was hiding something. That much was clear.

'Anyway, what you should be asking me is how Daniel behaved when I visited him,' Chris said.

'Right. How's that, then?'

Chris paused. He took a sip of his coffee.

'There's nothing vulnerable about that kid,' he said. 'You're running around thinking, I don't know, he might be innocent, but he's not. When I asked him to tell the truth about what happened, he just laughed at me. He has front, I'll give him that. I begged him. I pleaded with him. And he just laughed. He said, and I quote, "You fuckers all think you're better than me but you're not." Now if those aren't the words of a nasty piece of work, I don't know what are.'

'He's acting the tough guy,' Tom said. 'But I think that's all it is. An act.'

'It didn't strike me like that. He struck me as cold. Maybe you're convinced otherwise. Maybe that has something to do with who his cousin is?'

Tom froze. He should have known a man like Connolly would find that out.

'It's irrelevant whom he's related to, if he's guilty,' Tom said. 'Nobody believes that more than I do.'

'And, yet, here you are.'

Chris squinted at Tom. All trust was gone. Beside him, Rose had turned to look at Tom, her face full of confusion and betrayal.

Tom swallowed. It was time he took his leave.

'I just want to get justice for your son,' he said to her. 'I can promise you that, hand on heart.'

Rose looked away.

'I have to go back to the office,' Chris said, standing. 'I forgot to bring files home.'

Tom stood up too. Then he paused.

'Where are your offices?' he asked.

'Dún Laoghaire,' Chris answered.

'Hmm,' Tom said.

Chris studied him.

'What's so interesting about that?'

'Lizzie Konaté Jones, Daniel's mother, has three jobs,' Tom said. 'That's one of the things Daniel did say, the first time I met him. I'm just wondering – and this would be really easy to check, Mr Connolly – whether one of them is cleaning your offices.'

Chris paled.

# CHAPTER 34

At least he had hands-free in the car, Tom thought, as he surveyed the line of traffic in front. His satnav had started flashing warning signs a couple of miles back but Tom had been busy talking to Ray on the phone at the time so he'd kept going, assuming he could pull off the road at the last minute. It was Saturday, he wasn't expecting it to be busy, but here he was.

And there were no turn-offs now. He was stuck behind a row of cars as far as the eye could see, none of them going anywhere fast. A collision on the main Little Leaf roundabout, Ray had told him, before they ended the call. The news said one fatality in a van and a family of four injured in the other car.

Tom tried not to feel impatient. There were worse things than being caught in traffic.

He dialled Sean.

'Lizzie Konaté Jones is a cleaner in Chris Connolly's office,' was the first thing Tom said when his boss answered.

'So, where does that leave us?' Sean said. He sounded like he was chewing, and Tom looked at the clock on his dashboard. Dinner time. On cue, his stomach rumbled. 'Did Connolly tell Daniel to keep his mouth shut or he'd fire his mother?'

'He says he didn't, but he's lying. There's no way he wanted Daniel revealing he and Luke were together. He didn't want his dead son's name "tarnished". His word, not mine.'

'Would that be enough to keep an innocent man silent?' Sean said. 'She can get another job. I wouldn't go to jail for rape and murder just so my mum could keep working.'

'I don't thing it's that simple,' Tom said. 'Men like Chris Connolly can be intimidating. He's Teflon – look what he's done and got away with already in his professional life. He might have used the carrot and the stick on Daniel. Offered him money if he didn't talk, a punishment if he did. At the end of the day, we have plenty of evidence that Daniel was the last person with Luke, and he feels nobody is going to believe him anyway. He decided from the off it wasn't worth protesting his innocence. So Chris turns up and says, listen, if you say you had consensual sex with my son, I'll fire your mother – and I won't just make sure she doesn't work for my company again, I'll make sure she doesn't work *anywhere* again. And then there's an offer of money. Daniel loves his mum, that much is obvious. So he does the time for a crime he reckons he's going down for anyway, and his mother is taken care of.'

Sean swallowed his bite.

'I still don't think it's enough, Tom. Would he let his mother think him capable of that if he loves her so much? Maybe Connolly threatened her with violence, too. Do you think he's capable of that?'

Tom shrugged, even though Sean couldn't see him.

'You know, he could well be. I saw bruises on Daniel's arm. Your pal the governor swears blind he didn't get them from a guard or other inmate. Chris visited him. A kid like Daniel, so close to his mum, he wouldn't be able to bear the thought of being on the inside with his mum out there, alone, vulnerable. Chris was pretty angry when I was with him. Didn't frighten me but . . . a kid? And there has to be a reason Luke didn't tell his dad he was gay, more so than just being afraid of letting him down.'

Sean made an 'ah' sound, more satisfied with that explanation.

'But Daniel has now said he didn't kill him,' he said.

'He has,' Tom acknowledged. 'In a moment of weakness. In front of his mother. He hasn't told his defence team, according to Natasha, and he hasn't been screaming it from the rooftops.'

Sean fell quiet.

'Why, though?' he asked, after a moment. 'If it possibly meant his son's real killer walking free, why would Chris be happy for Daniel to take the rap? I mean . . . unless he wanted the person who actually did it to get away with it? You don't think . . . ?'

'The father killed the son?' he said. 'I don't know. I had the same conversation with Jackie McCallion. To my mind, he seems devastated and I do believe him when he says he'd rather have Luke alive and gay than gone altogether. I think he genuinely thinks he would have got his head around it. But there's something Rose said that's playing on my mind.'

Sean waited while Tom got his thoughts together. The inspector could hear him take another bite of whatever he was eating.

'I asked about that time Dylan attacked Luke with the pencil and she said her gut reaction was to get the police involved. But I sensed that Chris put a halt to that because of who Dylan's parents are. A man like Chris, he's wealthy, powerful, but he's the sort who plays second fiddle to even wealthier, more powerful men. He's the accountant, not the banker, if you know what I mean.'

'I do,' Sean said. 'So you think one of Luke's other friends – Jacob or Brian or Dylan – could have killed the boy, and the dad would rather see Daniel take the rap than the rich kid around the corner?'

'It does sound stupid,' Tom said.

'Yep. But, to be fair, I've dealt with worse madness. Listen, what about the tails?'

'Well, Jacob is definitely the one sourcing the drugs. Ray and Michael followed him to a snooker hall and saw him do a deal.'

'You've two of them on the one kid?' Sean asked.

'No. Ray's on Jacob and Michael is on Dylan, but Dylan hasn't left the house in two days. We have him covered in case he does, though – there's a crew up the road laying new broadband wires and Ray's cousin is the foreman, so they're keeping an eye for us.'

'Innovative. You're getting good at this.'

'Thanks. Brian Cullinane is following Brian Power. I've Willie Callaghan watching Hazel, just for the craic. And Laura is on Charlotte. Which could be interesting because Connolly claims he saw her outside the prison when he visited Daniel.'

'Curiouser and curiouser,' Sean said. 'But nothing except Jacob and the drugs yet?'

'Nothing of note. Yet.'

Jackie McCallion was waiting outside the station in Little Leaf village, arms crossed.

'Did you get caught in the tailback?' she asked, when she settled into the passenger seat. The detective seemed distracted; she barely looked at Tom when she got in and the question was uttered automatically.

'For an hour,' Tom confirmed. 'So, give me directions to this school. I'm guessing it's a good bit away from the – what was it Coach Walsh called it? – the *bastion of education* Luke Connolly attended.'

'Head straight out of the village and follow the signs that say *Hell this way.*'

Tom glanced sideways at Jackie. He figured she was joking, but it was hard to tell.

St Vincent's, Daniel Konaté's old school, was lit up, though night had fallen and it was the weekend. Jackie had phoned ahead and was told by the headmistress that the school was having a concert, which meant she would be about the building until late.

It took them a while to find a space in the packed car park and Tom had to wait until a man pulled his battered Ford Mondeo out of a spot – the car behind Tom beeping all the time, either annoyed that he was blocked from driving or that Tom was taking the spot, the inspector wasn't sure.

They made their way to the front doors of the grey building, which were held open for them by two students in uniform who couldn't have looked more bored if they'd tried.

'Tea and coffee is available before you go into the hall, no mobile phones allowed, enjoy the performance,' the girl student droned.

'Eh, the headmistress?' Tom asked.

'Ask at the office.'

Tom was none the wiser.

'There's a sign for the office,' Jackie said.

She started walking ahead, head bowed. There was definitely something on her mind. Tom followed her along the corridor, wondering what it was and whether it related to the case. Was she regretting confiding in him her secret from fifteen years ago? Or was she now doubting her abilities? He wanted her to question everything, not to be paralysed by a lack of self-belief. He'd ask her later what was going on. He just hoped she'd have the sense to tell him.

As they walked, Tom noticed the class year pictures hanging on the walls, the battered trophy cabinet that held very few trophies, the scuffed tiles and peeling paintwork.

Yep, this place sure was different to Little Leaf's private school. In the photos alone he noticed far more black faces. It was a demographic he was familiar with. It was odd and yet not surprising that modern Ireland hadn't reached Little Leaf.

They were still resisting the building of a Lidl, believing it would cheapen the look of the area.

'You must be the detectives?' A woman stepped out of an office, weighed down with a box containing paper cups.

'Yes – Principal Whitaker?' Tom asked.

The woman shook her head.

'Inside. I'm the secretary. The principal is grabbing a breather from the masses. Go on in.'

The woman continued down the corridor in the direction of what Tom assumed was the hall. When she opened the door, the babble grew louder.

'She knew immediately we were detectives,' Tom said. 'Do we stand out that much?'

'Most of the parents will have turned up tonight either in tracksuits or ready for the pub afterwards,' Jackie said.

Tom raised his eyebrows. If he was honest, he didn't think this place was very different to Maria's old secondary school. A bit shabbier, maybe, but that was it.

Principal Whitaker was an older woman, pleasant – almost

sweet – but with eyes that Tom would bet could turn the blood of any adolescent cold if she so desired. In her office, with two fellow adults, she was relaxed, amiable. She tried to get them to accept tea, her hand on the door ready to go out and fetch it herself, but Tom insisted they were fine.

'Most of the teachers are here tonight but, to be honest, they'd all more or less tell you the same as I'm about to,' she said. 'Daniel was a good student when he was here. Some trouble in his last couple of years, but nothing we couldn't handle.'

Tom eyed Jackie. She'd told him that morning she hadn't called out to Daniel's school because he'd completed his Leaving Certificate exam the previous year and she didn't see the need to look for twelve-month-old character references for him. She'd been to the club he worked at instead, but they'd had little to say about him other than that he was a good DJ.

Tom had insisted they visit the school. Lizzie Konaté would sing Daniel's praises. Natasha would defend her cousin. But his teachers and his principal would know exactly what he was like and capable of. You put a kid in anybody's care for six of their formative years and those adults can tell you what that child has or hasn't a predilection for.

That's why community policing always tied in with schools.

'He did well in his exams, despite bunking off the odd time,' the principal said. 'He was generally polite, but he could be a bit mouthy, a bit moody. Typical teenage boy. What is it he's accused of doing?'

'Something serious,' Tom replied, and watched with interest as the woman's eyes widened.

'You do worry about them, especially the kids that don't have a college course lined up. In an area like this, they can fall by the wayside quickly. The country might be out of the doldrums but I know of kids leaving college with degrees who are still only getting poorly paid job offers. For children going straight from school, a good job is a tough ask. But when I say worry, I mean that they might get involved in petty crime or welfare fraud, things like that. Not serious things.'

'It's definitely something more grave than that,' Tom said, and filled her in on the charge.

'No,' she cried, when he'd finished. 'I heard in the news about the poor kid who died, but they never said who they had in custody. I can't believe it.' The principal held her head in dismay. 'Well, what can I tell you that I haven't already? I looked up his records earlier, obviously, and aside from minor misdemeanours, Daniel was never in real trouble. It was surprising, really, considering how tough it can be for boys with single mothers. We deal with a lot of machismo here, a lot of buried anger and bitterness. You probably know exactly what I'm talking about.'

Tom nodded. He did, and he could tell already he liked Principal Whitaker. She was no doubt earning a fraction of the private school headmaster's salary, and she was worth every cent of it.

'But Daniel had a way about him,' she continued. 'I didn't need to look it up to remember. He was a gorgeous lad, and he could charm his way out of a detention with a smile. He was disarmingly friendly; you got the impression that kid could get on with anybody, if he wanted to. Now, I'm not saying he was a total innocent. Once they reach fifth year in here – earlier in some cases – they're coming in on Monday morning with hangovers and bloodshot eyes. Childhood ends too quickly nowadays. And Daniel wouldn't have survived with his peers if he didn't know how to be one of the lads. Especially with, well . . . You know he's gay.'

'We do,' Tom said.

'He never kept it a secret. There's a weird thing in this school – if you're in the right gang, it doesn't matter if you're gay or black or a bit of a nerd, whatever. But if you don't try to fit in, then whatever sets you apart is problematic – and that could be as simple as being too quiet. But like I say, Daniel wasn't the sort to isolate himself. I would have hoped he'd go on to achieve something.'

'Like what?' Tom said. 'Was he musical? I'm just wondering if that was the DJ rationale. That's what he's been working at.'

Principal Whitaker frowned and cocked her head.

'Not really, no.' She looked down at the file open in front of her. 'He got a B+ in honours maths in his final exams. That was without tutoring. I think if he'd had grinds, he'd have taken the A. His maths teacher felt he was a bit of a prodigy, considering how little he studied. Across the subjects, he took honours level. Mainly Cs, but still. Seven honours in this school is extremely impressive, and I know I shouldn't be proud to say that, but I am.'

Tom shrugged. Take the rewards where you can get them, he figured.

He looked over at Jackie, a glance that implied if she'd any questions, she should go for it.

'So he wasn't involved in any physical fights when he was here, he didn't lash out at anybody?' she asked.

Principal Whitaker shook her head.

'No. As I said, as boys in this school go, Daniel was practically gentle. There was some rough and tumble but no worrying behaviour. All his disciplinary notes were for talking too much in class, being a bit cheeky to get laughs, not handing in assignments on time, missing afternoons, that sort of thing. I'd have him back in the morning. I really hope whatever he's accused of, you've got this wrong. He was a good kid.'

On the return trip, Jackie was just as quiet. Tom waited but it was apparent she wasn't going to volunteer any information soon.

'It's interesting, that Daniel could get on with anybody, but chose not to with the Little Leaf gang,' Tom said. 'If it was them blanking him all the time, then that says a lot about them.'

Jackie said nothing.

'Well,' he said. 'What do you think? Are you having doubts?'

Jackie set her lips in a thin line.

'I was,' she said.

Tom frowned.

'You were? And after that glowing reference from his headmistress, you're not? You think he's guiltier than ever?'

Beside him, Jackie turned her face and looked out the window. She said nothing.

Tom sighed.

'Detective,' he said. 'Whatever is on your mind, it's better you spit it out.'

'I don't think you want me to,' she said.

'What does that mean? I'm asking you to talk to me. I'm telling you to.'

'I'm not sure you want to hear what I have to say. I feel like . . .'

'Yes?'

Jackie hesitated.

'Leaving aside where I might have fucked up, I feel like, from the start, you've had your mind made up that Daniel is innocent. And, yes, you have been more thorough than me and I am . . .' She paused again. 'I am learning from you. And I know my head wasn't straight. But . . .'

Jackie bit her lip.

'Daniel does seem like a good kid,' she said.

Tom nodded.

'But I found out something.'

The traffic was lighter now. It was getting late, almost nine. People were home from work, well past their dinner, in for the evening. Televisions were on, children were in bed, glasses of wine were being poured. Home.

That was where Tom wanted to be. It was where Lizzie Konaté and Natasha McCarthy wanted Daniel. It was where Rose Connolly wanted both her sons. But one of them lay in a hospital bed and the other in a hospital morgue.

'What did you find out?' Tom asked.

'Daniel's father, Terry Jones – I didn't really ask a lot about him because he's not with the family any more. He's from England, and that's where he returned when he and Lizzie split up.'

Tom said nothing, just listened, the stone in his empty stomach growing a little heavier with each of Jackie's pauses.

'I don't think Natasha McCarthy is aware of this,' Jackie said. 'I only found out because I have a contact in social services who gave me a summary of the file. There were no charges filed, and it wouldn't have mattered if we had been involved because Daniel was a minor.'

She hesitated again. Tom couldn't take much more.

'Jackie,' he said. 'Can we get to the point?'

'Yeah,' she said. 'Right. Terry Jones was a wife-beater. He was battering Lizzie. And on the night it all ended, he was trying to give her a hiding. But Daniel stepped in.'

Jackie turned to Tom.

'They were living in a three-bed council house at the time. Daniel was twelve. He came out of his room and his ma was trying to get past his father on the landing, but Terry was blocking the stairs. So Daniel ran at his father.'

'To defend his mother,' Tom said.

'To defend his mother,' Jackie nodded. 'Daniel pushed his da down the stairs. He broke both his arms, along with some bruising and a concussion. Lizzie told the police she'd done it but Terry said it was Daniel and Daniel admitted it to his social worker. Now, I'm not saying . . .'

Tom nodded.

'It's okay, Jackie,' he said. 'It's not enough to scream guilt or innocence, but it's extremely pertinent and something it's good for us to be aware of. And it's really excellent work on your part.'

'I nearly wasn't going to tell you.'

'I'm glad you did.'

Tom swallowed.

'And by the way,' he said. 'You are right, to an extent. I do feel that Daniel is innocent. But I'm not perfect, Jackie. I make mistakes, too. I never let feelings get in the way of evidence, though. Good or bad feelings. Nobody in my team would.'

Jackie nodded. She believed him, now.

# CHAPTER 35

Jacob was off his face. It was almost funny. Well, it would have been funny, if he wasn't pushing Dylan repeatedly in the chest.

They'd met at Jacob's house, as usual. Ostensibly, this time, to help sort the place out. Apparently the cleaners had been in and the head one had rung his mother and told her he'd been having parties, so his father was flying home the following morning to read him the riot act. That's what Jacob had told them.

Jacob had shoved bin bags into their hands when they'd arrived.

'What do you want us to do with these?' Brian had asked. 'Haven't the cleaners actually cleaned, or did they just rat you out?'

'They won't take the bottles or do the garden or pool house,' Jacob snapped. 'They're being arseholes. Probably looking for a raise.'

'You want us to clean the garden?' Hazel asked. 'In the dark? On a Saturday night? I thought you wanted a party.'

'Just fucking help, will you?' Jacob retorted.

There certainly were a lot of bottles and cans and other assorted detritus from their gatherings over the last two weeks. They were throwing it all in bags when the fight broke out between Jacob and Dylan. None of them were even drinking, which made Jacob's erratic behaviour all the more apparent.

He'd trailed Dylan around the garden and then, when Dylan had turned around, his hands full, Jacob had pushed him. They all knew he was picking on Dylan because he could. He was just as suspicious of Charlotte but Jacob couldn't lay a finger on her or all hell would break loose.

He assumed Dylan would take it.

'What the fuck have you said to the cops?'

'I already told you,' Dylan said, trying to stay composed, trying to stop the rage from rising. 'I didn't say anything to them.'

'Well, why the fuck are they still going around asking questions, then? Charlotte's da says they were back over in the Connollys. If I find out you opened your mouth . . .'

He shoved Dylan again. This time, there was force in it. Dylan tripped backward, stopping short of falling.

'I'm not going to tell you again. Push me one more time and I'm going to–'

Dylan stopped.

'What are you going to do?' Jacob mocked. 'Tell your mammy and daddy? Come after me with a pencil?' He started to laugh.

A shadow crossed Dylan's face. Jacob was too high to see it, but the others did.

Hazel was by Jacob's side in seconds.

'Jacob, babe, cool it, will you? He's said, hasn't he? The police are talking to all of us and none of us are going to say anything. We're all in it together, aren't we?'

'Some of us are more *in it* than the rest of us,' Dylan said.

And then all hell broke out. Jacob was on top of Dylan, but, even though Jacob was the stronger of the two, Dylan had the advantage of having his wits about him. As Jacob raised his arm to swing a punch at Dylan, the boy underneath dodged sideways. Jacob's fist hit the ground and he howled. The pain was enough for Dylan to push Jacob off. He jumped up and towered over him. He landed one kick before Brian ran at him and tackled him to the ground.

'He fucking started it,' Dylan yelled, knowing he stood no chance against Jacob and Brian.

'You don't kick a man on the ground,' Brian spat in his face.

Charlotte had come out of the house and was standing next to Hazel. Both girls were shocked, scared. They were used to the boys messing about but this had the now-familiar edge to it. The nastiness and undercurrent that had been there since the night that none of them wanted to talk about.

'Stop it,' Charlotte shouted, a sob in her voice. 'Just stop it.'

Jacob was sitting on the ground, cradling his fist. Brian looked up at Charlotte and took his knee off Dylan's chest.

He offered his hand to Dylan but it was rejected.

'I think my knuckles are broken,' Jacob said.

'Serves you right,' Dylan hissed. He leaned into Brian's face. 'And as for you, you little fucking sycophant, don't talk to me about what you do or don't do to men when they're down. I'm not one of your little rugger bugger pals. And we all know that what you do to people lying on the ground is a lot worse, don't we?'

Brian blinked. The situation might have turned violent once more, but Dylan spun on his heel and walked away towards the side of the house.

'*He* is a fucking *problem*,' Brian said, watching his retreating back.

Charlotte had started to leave, too, but she stopped.

'He's a problem, Brian? So what are you going to do about it? Push him out a window?'

'What are you talking about, you stupid bitch?'

Beside Charlotte, Hazel tugged at her arm. A warning glance. Charlotte shrugged her off.

'What did you say to Luke when you went back into the house, Brian?' she said. 'When Jacob and Hazel had to drag you out? What did you say? What did you do?'

# CHAPTER 36

'So, does that change things?'

Louise was in bed already, the duvet pulled up to her chest, her Kindle resting on top of it. She was reading a new crime fiction series but there was nothing in her novel as interesting as the real life mystery her husband was involved in. And the fact he'd only feed her tidbits made it all the more intriguing.

Tom pulled a T-shirt over his head and sat down heavily on his side of the mattress. His feet found his slippers under the bed. He was bone tired, and not just from the long day.

'I don't know,' he answered his wife, honestly. 'On the one hand, no. Daniel was a twelve-year-old kid defending his mother from the man who wanted to, in that moment, kill her. That doesn't make him a monster. It makes him a hero.'

'But?' Louise said.

'But the fact Luke died from being pushed and that, in a moment of heat, anger, fear, whatever, Daniel previously pushed somebody else, resulting in injury – that's not insignificant.'

Louise nodded.

'Hmm,' she said. 'It's like that kid in Cáit's crèche who bites. He does it out of habit. He doesn't even realise how much pain he's causing; it's just what he does in the argument. But somebody got bitten yesterday and he swore blind it wasn't him.'

'Was it?' Tom asked.

'Yes, it bloody was. Half the class saw him do it. But it didn't matter. Nobody believed him, anyway.'

Tom snorted.

'Typical,' he said. 'You know, what caught my attention about this case – outside of Natasha, obviously – was the murder charge. Pushing somebody out a window is not an obvious method to murder somebody after a rape. And if it wasn't rape, if it was consensual, then why would Daniel want to murder Luke at all?' Tom paused. 'But if you take out the word "murder", and you use the word "push", well, Daniel might have done it accidentally. Though if it was an accident, he's blown his chances by lying. If he'd admitted it straight up, he could have saved himself a lot of heartache.'

Tom lay back, resting his head on Louise's stomach. He was uncomfortable for a moment, until he reached back and removed the Kindle.

He held it in his hand and scanned the page.

'What detective are you cheating on me with tonight?' he asked.

'It's a woman,' Louise said.

'Ooh, kinky. Tell me more.'

'You show me yours,' she said.

Tom closed his eyes.

'Jackie McCallion said something to me and she was right.'

'Who is this woman and how dare she take my job?'

'You're safe,' Tom said. 'She said I'd approached this believing Daniel was innocent. And yes, I trust Natasha McCarthy's judgement, even when family is involved. I trust her instinct. There are gaps in the case file, that's obvious. It was always going to be a tough case for the DPP to win. Then I met Daniel and he just doesn't seem guilty. And it's not just me. Sean feels it too. Luke's own brother and even his mother, to an extent, feel it. Can we all be wrong?'

Louise said nothing. She stroked her husband's hair, slowing every now and again. Tom had the distinct feeling she was noticing how many new grey hairs he had and keeping quiet for his sake. He'd have more soon.

'It hurts to hope,' he said.

'What?' Louise said. 'That's a bizarre thing to say.'

'It wasn't me who said it. Rose Connolly did.'

Tom's head shifted position as his wife moved. He opened his eyes. Louise was leaning over him.

'Hope is not a bad thing. It's a good thing.'

Tom smiled. He wasn't going to argue with her. But in his head, he was quietly disagreeing. He understood Rose's nervousness about hope.

It only made the ultimate outcome all the more devastating if you were wrong.

The hospital was quiet the next day, a Sunday. Visiting hours hadn't started, but Tom knew Ethan had a special dispensation. The boy had been on his mind since the previous evening and, given he'd missed a couple of calls from him, the inspector figured this was as good a time as any to call over. After what Rose had said the previous day, Tom didn't know what to expect. Would Ethan have crashed after his sudden burst of energy yesterday, proving his health professionals correct – it was wrong to read too much into the bouts of spirit – or would he still be in good form?

Ethan was sitting up and smiling when Tom arrived, even though it was just after 11 a.m. Tom watched through the window for a few minutes before going in.

Yes, seeing him like this, with such vitality, it was difficult to believe Ethan was so close to death. Tom understood now how hard Rose had to work to not feel something when it was like this.

Ethan and his nurse, Claire, were talking. Tom knocked softly on the door and walked in.

'Do they ever give you time off?' Tom asked.

Claire looked up.

'Sure they do,' she said. 'But I house-share with four other girls and they all have boyfriends that I'm fairly certain we're illegally subletting to. Sometimes, it's easier to stay at work.'

Tom smiled.

'He has a box of chocolates in that drawer,' she said, pointing at the locker beside Ethan's bed. 'Steal some, because he won't offer. I'm in since six and not a hope of a taste. He sure can't eat them.'

'They're for my mum,' Ethan said.

The nurse scoffed at him and got off the side of the bed. She made her way past Tom. Tom watched Ethan watching her.

Ah.

He took the chair beside the boy.

'She's lovely, isn't she?' he said.

Ethan shrugged, trying to look non-committal, but because he was so pale, any bit of colour that rose in his cheeks was very apparent.

'Having a nice nurse like that taking care of you has to help being stuck in here.'

Ethan stiffened.

'It makes it harder, actually,' he said. 'All it does is remind me of what I can't have. I don't want girls like Claire to *pity* me.'

Ethan blushed again and looked down at his blankets.

'When Luke was alive . . . well, it's one of the difficulties, you know? Being in this position and having a twin brother who looks close to how you would if it wasn't for poxy cancer. Claire never looked at Luke with *pity*.'

'Did it make you jealous?'

Ethan sighed.

'Envy, more than jealousy. He was my brother, so I was always torn between wanting him to have the world and resenting him for having it. Makes me sound like an idiot, I know.'

'It doesn't,' Tom said. 'It makes you honest and mature. And I can't imagine Claire liked your brother any more than she likes you. In my experience, girls tend to prefer intelligence and humour over looks.'

'None of it matters now, anyway.' Ethan's voice cracked. 'He could marry her, if it meant he'd come back.'

Tom took a deep breath. Luke's family were beginning to realise how final everything was. And they'd do anything, even make Faustian pacts, to bring him back.

'Ethan, is there any more you can tell me about Luke's life?' Tom asked. 'About his friends, especially.'

'What do you want to know?' Ethan said. 'Because I'll tell you anything. I'm just so happy to have somebody believe me when I say Daniel didn't do it. He's not capable. His friends are, though. And they should be punished.'

Tom sat back. There was such vehemence in Ethan's voice, the inspector wondered if there was more he hadn't been told.

'Who of the five of them – and I'm including the girls – is the most likely to have fought with Luke?' he asked. 'If we discount them all alibiing each other, who do you think has it in them to physically attack somebody? It doesn't have to be that they were trying to kill him. It could have just been a shove and

Luke fell, do you understand what I'm saying?' Tom paused. 'I mean, even Daniel could have done something by accident, don't you think?'

He kept his voice neutral. He didn't want to guide Ethan, he just wanted his honest opinion.

'Sure,' Ethan said. 'But Daniel didn't. If you really want my opinion about who would have pushed Luke, even by *accident* – Jacob.'

Tom was taken aback. Ethan hadn't even had to think about it. Tom had been expecting him to say Dylan, after what they'd learned about the assault two years previous.

'Jacob?' he repeated. 'Not Dylan or Brian?'

'Dylan wouldn't lay his hands on Luke,' Ethan said. 'Not after what happened before. He lost it once and attacked Luke, jabbed a pencil in his hand. Luke needed stitches. It was stupid. Our parents went into United Nations mode and Luke and Dylan were the warring countries. I think Dylan learned to do more than watch himself around Luke, I think he learned to watch himself around everybody. He has a temper, but he keeps it in check.'

'Okay,' Tom said. That was properly insightful for somebody so young. Maybe it came from being ill all the time – Ethan had more time to study people and draw conclusions.

'So, not Dylan, but not Brian either?'

'Brian doesn't do shit unless Jacob tells him to,' Ethan said. 'And Jacob and Luke were closer than Jacob and Brian, so Brian would know that to fight with Luke would be an issue. The only person who could have had an argument with Luke without it leading to recriminations was Jacob.'

'But why would he?' Tom said. 'If they were friends?'

'I don't know,' Ethan said. But there was a slight hesitation in his voice. He spoke with such assuredness when it came to the psychology of his brother's relationships, but there was something he wasn't telling Tom.

'And you don't think Charlotte or Hazel may have been angry at Luke for lying to them? A girl can give a good shove if she wants and we know Luke wasn't entirely himself that night.'

'Hazel would have clawed his eyes out,' Ethan said. 'But if Luke was lying to himself, Hazel could put him to shame; she cons herself daily. She thinks she's Miss Popular, but the other girls can't stand her and the lads just put up with her because they think they'll get a shag. And I don't think she'd ever have accepted Luke was gay unless he actually told her. But Charlotte, I think she knew.'

'She doesn't talk like she knew,' Tom said.

'She wouldn't, would she? "My boyfriend is gay." Who says that out loud?'

'They don't. They just split up.'

Ethan made a noise of protest.

'Why would she split up with him? She was enjoying rubbing Hazel's nose in it. Hazel had been rubbing Charlotte's in it for years. And anyway, Charlotte did really care for Luke. She's . . . Charlotte is kind.'

Tom nodded. He'd felt that, even in the short time he'd spent with her.

'Ethan, is there something else you're not telling me? Did something happen involving Luke and his friends?'

Ethan looked away, then back at Tom.

'Yeah,' he said. 'One of them pushed him out a window.'

# CHAPTER 37

It was only the start of the week, but Laura already had the Monday blues.

Her afternoon had been mind-numbing.

She'd been following Charlotte since she'd left school on a half-day at noon. Now, at 5 p.m., Laura was losing the will to live.

First Charlotte had gone to get her nails done with Hazel. That hadn't been too bad. Laura and Willie had met up in the cafe across the way from the nail bar and sipped cappuccinos while remarking on how much time and money teenage girls seemed to have these days.

The girls had finished up and separated; Willie told her later that Hazel had picked up her sister from school. The youngest in her family, Charlotte had no such obligations. She strolled around the shops for an hour, buying a necklace in Topshop and a scarf in Zara.

Then she sat in a cafe in Dún Laoghaire village, miserably poking at a plate of salad.

She walked from there back towards Little Leaf, but before they arrived at her home, Charlotte got on the bus. Laura nearly killed herself pelting up the road to make sure she got on the same one. Once on, she realised she'd no change and ended up giving the driver a five-euro note.

Charlotte sat up top; Laura took the bottom so she was ready to jump off as soon as the teenager did.

A half-hour later, they did just that. They were on the outskirts of the city centre now.

Laura followed Charlotte up the street until the girl popped into a flower shop.

*This is the first interesting thing she's done all day*, Laura thought, standing in the doorway of a newsagents a few stores down.

Charlotte emerged with a small bunch of flowers and they began to walk again.

Across the road, to the hospital.

Laura took out her phone, dialled, and put it to her ear.

'Tom, what hospital did they take Daniel Konaté to?'

'St James's,' Tom told her. 'Why?'

'I've just followed Charlotte Burke there,' she said. 'She bought a bunch of flowers and now she's going in.'

'It's not for Daniel,' Tom said. 'He was returned to Cloverhill yesterday.'

'She mightn't know that,' Laura said.

'True. Stay on her. She may have tried to see him in jail, too.'

Laura hung up.

Charlotte didn't bother to stop at reception. She was heading straight to the wards. She took the lifts.

Laura didn't follow her in. Instead, she took the stairs beside the lifts, racing up and opening the door on each landing to see if the lift had stopped.

On the second floor, she spotted Charlotte walking down the corridor.

Laura started to follow her, but then Charlotte stopped. She was looking through the glass perspex windows of the double doors that led onto one of the wards.

She stood there a few seconds, then turned and walked to the nurses' station.

Laura hung back and watched as Charlotte handed the nurse the bunch of flowers.

Charlotte was coming towards her now. Laura strolled past, calmly, like she was headed to the nurses' station herself. She smelled the girl's floral perfume and a tinge of nail polish and ozone.

Then Charlotte was in the lift and going back downstairs.

Laura let her go. She walked over to the nurse at the desk instead.

As she did, she read the sign that hung over the double doors Charlotte had approached.

It read *Intensive Care Unit.*

# CHAPTER 38

'This is just like the good old days,' Sean said, looking up from the water dispenser in the corner of the open-plan office. He was filling cups for everyone, unasked.

They were in the team meeting room in HQ, the building more or less empty at the late hour, but for the detectives and some special guests.

'You're imagining things again,' Tom replied. 'In the good old days, I wouldn't see you from one end of the week to the other and if you called in here, it was because you wanted to yell at me for not solving an unsolvable case.'

'Ah, yes, the really good old days,' Sean said, his eyes practically glazing over with happy memories. He crossed to the desk where Willie Callaghan had perched himself. Linda McCarn positioned herself on a chair beside them. Laura, Ray, Michael and Brian were at their own desks. Tom sat facing the room, notes on his lap, feet resting on the chair in front of him. Emmet McDonagh sat beside him. It was after hours. People were giving their time freely.

'Right, to order,' Tom said. 'We gave ourselves a few days to tail these kids but I can't redirect resources any longer without drawing attention. So far, from what you've all said, we have them hanging out in Jacob's – I find it hilarious none of them copped on to all your cars lining the streets outside – we have

Jacob buying drugs and the Burke girl calling into ICU earlier this evening. Laura checked out her immediate family and there don't seem to be any relatives in hospital care at this time. So, who the hell is she visiting? Laura?'

'Firstly, I was on foot, so there weren't that many cars,' Laura said. She was swinging her chair left and right, rotating it with her feet, as she read from her notepad. 'But, anyway, there are ten patients in the ICU. I contacted Charlotte's parents tonight and, without giving them context, read through the names to enquire if any were familiar. None were. So then I contacted Little Leaf private school. One of the patients is nineteen, a motorbike crash and head injury. I figured he might have gone there. Nada.'

'So what are our options?' Sean asked.

'The nurse said Charlotte has called in every week for the last six weeks and leaves a bunch of flowers at the desk each time. But recently, she's upped the ante. She was in there a couple of days ago, too, apparently. That might be interesting, her increasing her visits after you started talking to that gang, Tom.

'Anyhow, Charlotte never tells the nurses who the flowers are for, but just asks if the staff can keep them there. There are no flowers allowed into the ICU, anyway. Six weeks ago is fairly soon after Luke died, but nobody was admitted to that ICU around that time. There were four patients admitted in the two months leading up to Luke's death who are still in care. Two of them are close to Charlotte's age group. One of them was the kid on the motorbike. The crash was pretty horrific, from what I'm told. The bike was a fireball. Another is a guy in his twenties, overdosed on drugs. Of the two older patients, there's a woman who's in a coma following a stroke. The other, an older man, was attacked. That's all I could get in the last few hours.'

'We need Charlotte to talk,' Sean said.

Laura nodded.

'What if she's not going in for anybody at all?' Linda suggested. 'What if she is just a nice person who likes to feel she's doing something good in the world to make up for the vacuous nature of the rest of her inane little teenage life?'

Laura shrugged.

'Always possible, but I followed her for two days and for most of it she did absolutely nothing that would lead me to believe she thinks of anybody but herself. Or that she's in any way interesting. But when she went to that hospital, there was real purpose. Her whole demeanour changed, right down to her gait. She was making herself go in and she made herself walk right up to those doors and look in at the patients. And when she passed me on the way out, the relief was palpable. It just didn't strike me as a meaningless charitable gesture.'

'Six weeks,' Ray said. 'If she's going in there, it has to be tied to Luke's death.'

Laura shrugged again.

Tom said nothing. He was mulling over the information Laura had just given them. Something had struck him, which could be nothing, but . . . in his gut, he'd felt it.

'You still haven't broken them on the alibis?' Linda asked. 'They're all still maintaining they left that house together?'

Sean nodded.

'They're lying,' Linda confirmed. 'I've read their statements. You must have seen what I saw: they're mirroring each other, down to the tiniest details that teenagers just do not remember.'

'We know,' Sean said. 'But there's no CCTV in Little Leaf on the route away from that house. There's barely any CCTV at all.

It's difficult to catch them in a lie when we've nothing to back it up.'

'All of their DNA is obviously all over that house,' Emmet said. 'We've picked up their fingerprints in most of the rooms but, interestingly, not in the room from which Luke fell. Except for his.'

'Not even Daniel's?' Tom asked.

'Nope. His DNA was all over the room across the hall, as I mentioned. We did, however, pick up several sets of unidentified fingerprints in the room where Luke was pushed.'

'So it could have been somebody other than the kids?' Laura asked.

'It could have been Daniel,' Ray said. 'Let's be honest, he didn't need to touch anything in the room to give Luke a good shove. I don't know; it feels like we're pissing into the wind here. There's nothing to say any of this kid's mates had it in for him to the extent they'd kill him. So his girlfriend is visiting an IC unit; so what?'

'There's nothing to say his friends had it in for him, *yet*,' Tom said. 'Laura, can you get the files on those four people you mentioned? I have an idea about something, but I won't know for sure until I've had a look at exactly what happened to them. I think the kids were involved in something prior to Luke dying, which may be connected to the reason he died.'

'Care to elaborate?' Linda asked.

Tom was about to tell her he'd nothing to add when his phone beeped.

'It's Moya,' he said. 'They're releasing Luke Connolly's body for the funeral.'

# CHAPTER 39

'I really need to talk to you,' Charlotte whined.

Hazel had successfully avoided her all day in school, but then Charlotte had turned up at her house.

She looked like shit. Hazel sighed. She was getting sick of this now. She'd brought her friend out yesterday on their half-day for a manicure, a small attempt to make her act normal. Hazel had needed her shellac removed anyway, so she'd killed two birds with one stone, even while it had cost her. But Charlotte had been monosyllabic the whole time and then said she was too busy to collect Mia with Hazel.

Hazel knew Charlotte wasn't busy. She never was. She just lied when she wanted to be on her own. She was always lying.

'Well, come in, for God's sake,' Hazel said. 'Unless you want to stand here talking on the porch. This has to be quick. I have to go over to Jacob's later. I'm still trying to talk him out of killing you for what you said to him and Brian the other night. You're lucky he picked on Dylan and not you.'

Charlotte bit her lip but said nothing. She followed Hazel in, though, up the stairs and into Hazel's room.

Hazel had been looking at paint palettes. She was thinking of having her room redone, making it more grown-up. Less pink. She still had posters up of One Direction.

Charlotte said nothing about the various colours splashed

on the wall beside the window. She just sat on the chair by the desk.

Hazel sighed more dramatically and slumped on her bed. God, her friend was so boring these days. It was painful. She didn't even know why they were still friends. It was just circumstance, really. Shared secrets.

And then Charlotte reached into her bag and took out a bottle of white wine.

'What the hell is that?' Hazel said, eyes agog.

Charlotte followed the bottle with two plastic cups. She poured one for Hazel and one for herself.

Hazel sat up and took the cup. She didn't say anything, just stared at Charlotte in astonishment, a light in her eyes that said *I'm intrigued.*

'Do you swear you're telling the truth?' Charlotte said. 'When Brian went back in, he didn't do anything to Luke?'

Hazel rolled her eyes.

'Yes, I swear. We told you. Jacob and I were a bit worried he was going to say something, so we went back in to get him. He didn't do anything to Luke. Look, if you hadn't stormed ahead with Dylan, you'd have been with us.'

'You know why I stormed ahead,' Charlotte said. She was still holding the plastic cup. She hadn't raised it to her lips yet.

Hazel took a sip. Jesus, it was muck. Never send a Mormon to buy wine, she thought as she swallowed the acrid liquid.

'Yeah, I know,' Hazel said. 'You were afraid of why Luke wanted to stay behind with Daniel. Do you think, Charls, you might be feeling a little bit guilty about how everything went down that night? Like, if you'd stayed, Luke would have been okay? Instead of having a hissy fit because he was enjoying himself with Daniel and not talking to you?'

'And when you went in,' Charlotte continued, ignoring Hazel's dig, 'Brian hadn't gone upstairs and you and Jacob made him leave with you, right?'

'Yes!' Hazel said. Her left eye twitched. It had an awful habit of doing that, especially when somebody was staring at her with such intensity, the way Charlotte was now.

Lying didn't come as naturally to Hazel as it did to her friends. She had to make the effort.

Charlotte looked at her a little longer, then nodded.

'Okay,' she said.

'Okay, what?' Hazel said.

'I believe you. I have to be able to trust you.'

'You believe me? That's good of you. I don't see why you wouldn't in the first place, but hey, you do now, so we can all be happy and get over the fact you think the three of us are liars.' Hazel snorted. 'No, not liars. Murderers.'

'When you made me and Dylan say we were all together, did you really think we wouldn't have questions?' Charlotte said. 'Or do you just assume we're pushovers who'll do whatever you want?'

'Oh, I know you won't do *whatever* I want,' Hazel said, glaring at Charlotte.

She took another sip of the foul wine. Charlotte's cup remained full.

'What is this for?' Hazel said. 'Is there a reason you're sitting there looking like you're about to break your vows, or whatever the hell you religious nutjobs have?'

'They're burying Luke,' she said. 'His parents rang mine.'

'Oh.' Hazel looked down at her cup. 'Well, it's no big deal. He's dead weeks, isn't he?'

Charlotte took a deep breath.

'And I've been visiting him,' she said.

Hazel frowned. She'd no idea what Charlotte was talking about.

'What? Who?'

Charlotte looked up and met Hazel's eye.

'I've been visiting *him*.'

Hazel continued to look confused for a moment or two.

Then it registered. Her eyes widened, her mouth fell open.

Charlotte nodded.

'Yeah,' she said.

Then she raised the cup to her mouth and drank the wine.

# CHAPTER 40

Two days after the release of Luke's body, his funeral took place.

The students of Little Leaf College had formed an honour guard for their former classmate.

As Tom and Sean walked behind the mourners towards the church, Tom nodded at the kids he knew, Luke's friends.

Principal Lynch and Coach Walsh were there. Lynch looked traumatised. It was one thing to hear one of your students was dead, quite another to see him buried. Even Walsh's eyes were red and Tom imagined the man didn't cry easily.

The church was packed to the rafters. Tom had seen it before. Young people were never alone, even when they thought they were. School friends, family, family friends, neighbours, community stalwarts – they all turned out when life was cut short too early.

The only person close to Luke Connolly who wasn't in attendance that day was Daniel Konaté. Tom had called the prison. Lizzie was visiting with him. Natasha was still keeping her distance and it was killing her.

Tom and Sean slipped into a side pew so they could keep a discreet eye on the other mourners. Jackie had confided in Tom that she thought it was better she avoid the funeral. It had really registered with her that misplaced emotions had been influencing her in the case and seeing Luke's coffin could potentially throw her off again. She needed to detach and to focus and to do that, she had to steer clear. Tom thought that was wise. Today would be distressing.

The front row was filled with Luke's immediate family, his mother and father, grandparents, a couple of aunts and uncles.

To the side of the pew, in a wheelchair, sat Ethan. He was visibly too weak to be there, yet determined not to miss it.

His nurse and a doctor Tom had noticed in the hospital once or twice sat in the seats behind him. They had their heads bowed, except for occasional glances at their patient.

'That explains the ambulance outside,' Sean whispered in Tom's ear.

Tom had barely noticed it. He'd been too busy taking stock of the mourners.

'It must be tough,' Sean continued. 'Knowing you're next.'

The inspector shivered. It didn't bear thinking about.

The students had trooped into the back of the church. Tom was tall but he still had to strain in his seat to keep an eye on Luke's crew. There were the four of them – Jacob, Brian, Dylan and Hazel.

It took him a while to spot Charlotte. She wasn't with her friends but in another row a few up. That was interesting.

The service started and the monotonous drone of the elderly parish priest filled the church as he made his way through the Catholic ritual. Tom found himself standing automatically, kneeling, sitting, intoning the words of the prayers. It was muscle memory, nothing more. He'd been dragged to church every Sunday and holy day by his parents until he was eighteen. He suspected most of the kids around him hadn't seen the inside of a church since their Confirmations.

When it came to the homily, he was surprised to see Chris

step out of his seat and wheel Ethan to the steps at the altar. The doctor followed and he, Chris and the priest helped Ethan up to the pulpit.

Tom turned to Sean and they both raised their eyebrows.

The church was silent. Everybody there knew what Ethan was facing. They wanted to show him the utmost respect as he spoke for his twin.

But nobody could hear him at first. Ethan was nowhere near the microphone and his voice was too weak to carry.

The priest rushed over, as fast as his ancient limbs would allow, and brought it closer to Ethan's mouth. The boy looked at him, not understanding, then realised.

'Sorry,' he said, and this time everybody could hear him. 'How's that now?'

There was a murmur around the church.

'I just wanted to say a few words about my brother, Luke. My care team didn't want me to come here today but I told them I was sick of Luke stealing all the limelight. He was always at that. This is supposed to be my thing. Dying.'

There were a few uncomfortable titters around the church, mainly from the teenagers. The adults were aghast. Rose Connolly was hunched into herself, her shoulders shaking with quiet sobs. Chris looked appalled.

'I'm kidding, obviously,' Ethan continued, aware the joke hadn't landed well. 'Luke might have wrecked my head at times, but when it came to it, I loved him and he loved me. That's why I'm here. I think I can actually pinpoint the moment it dawned on me that having a twin was way better than being an only child, even if it did mean him nicking my selection box every Christmas morning. I never told you this, Mum and Dad, but I figure now is as good a time as any.'

Rose and Chris looked up. Ethan took a ragged breath and steadied himself.

'By the time we were twelve, Luke and I were starting to develop a bit differently. We were never identical but we always looked fairly similar. But, at twelve, he was starting to bulk up while I was still as skinny as fu–sorry. I was skinny. I guess I was already ill, but we didn't know that then. Anyhow, we were still in primary school, in sixth class, and there were these two other boys in our year.'

Ethan paused. He made a show of lifting his hand to shade his eyes and looking around the church. From his angle, Tom could see what huge effort that took. Ethan's other hand gripped the side of the pulpit and shook with the force of holding himself up.

'Sorry, I just wanted to check those two lads are not here before I rip the back out of them.'

This was greeted with more relaxed laughs. Even Rose looked less tense.

'Anyhow, the two of them were little, eh, let's call them brats. And they liked to use me as a punch bag when we walked over to art class every week.'

Tom watched as Rose raised her hand to her mouth, shocked. Chris bristled.

'But this is not a sad story,' Ethan continued. 'I was used to the pair of them and devised many ways of avoiding art class. I wasn't the strongest, obviously, but I was definitely one of the smartest, and I'd learned to forge my mother's signature. Did you know, Mum, I'm allergic to many of the pigments in paint?'

The laughter now was loud and easy. Rose shook her head in amazement.

Ethan smiled.

'The one person who always figured out what I was up to was Luke. And one day, he asked what I was doing handing a note to our teacher, Ms Darby, every Wednesday. So I told him I wanted to skip art class – because with Luke it was always good to give him a little truth rather than try to lie. Half the story meant he might leave me alone.'

Ethan shrugged; again, an effort.

'It didn't matter what I told him. He found out. I don't know if somebody ratted on the lads or Luke followed me one day, but he knew those two boys were beating me up. So one day, I see them in the yard and I think they're coming for me, because I've been skipping art class every Wednesday for a month. Even Ms Darby was starting to get curious because that month was pottery and there was no paint. Hey ho, next thing I notice the lads aren't coming for me. They've turned around and look like they're doing their best to avoid me.

'Being the little nosy git I am, I couldn't help but wander in their direction. And do you know what? They both had black eyes and split lips.'

Ethan smiled.

'I found Luke after school. And before he could stop me, I pulled his gloves off. His knuckles were scraped bare.'

Ethan paused, now.

'My brother had taken on both those lads and single-handedly made sure they wouldn't touch me again. I hadn't asked him to. He just did it. And we didn't talk about it. But I knew. Having a twin can be tough. People expect you to live in each other's pockets and that wasn't me and Luke. But I knew Luke loved me. And I loved him. All of him, regardless of his flaws or strengths or who he chose to hang out with or . . . love.'

Around the church, the tears flowed freely. Tom couldn't

look over at Rose Connolly any longer; she was distraught. Even Chris was struggling to hold it together, rubbing at his eyes until they were red raw.

'It wasn't meant to be like this,' Ethan said. 'He was meant to live his life for both of us. But that didn't happen.'

Ethan looked over at his brother's coffin.

'See you on the other side, brother,' he said.

And then Ethan collapsed at the pulpit.

# CHAPTER 41

'You think he's okay?' Sean asked, as they watched the ambulance take Ethan back to hospital.

'As okay as he can be,' Tom said. 'I imagine he wanted to go to the graveyard, but . . .'

'He did a good enough job for his brother,' Sean said. 'There wasn't a dry eye in the house.'

'I know,' Tom said. He could see Laura approaching the church gates. She wouldn't have come on foot; he suspected she'd had to park her car half a mile away, there were so many vehicles in attendance.

'I thought I'd have to wait,' she said, as she drew near. 'Did it finish early?'

Tom shook his head.

'Bit of an incident. They're still inside, but they're about to come out, so let's head back to your car.'

'I'll move ours out before the traffic starts,' Sean said. He stared back into the car park, squinting his eyes as he tried to spot it.

Tom and Laura began their walk up the road.

'Is it the files on the ICU patients?' he asked.

'Yeah. I don't have the actual files but I did talk to the hospital and they gave me more background on what everybody is in for. Is that enough, do you think?'

Tom nodded. It would have to be. And, anyway, he was operating on a hunch. It could be nothing at all.

Laura had had to park even further away than Tom had imagined; by the time they reached her vehicle, the funeral cortège was starting to make its way past.

They watched as Luke's coffin was driven by, followed by two black family cars.

Tom bowed his head, then got into the passenger side of the car.

'Okay,' Laura said, pulling out her notepad. 'So, because drugs were involved in Luke's case, I started with the guy who had the overdose. He's twenty-seven, from Belfast, living in Dublin the last four years. A night out with friends, according to the nurse. He took some dodgy psychoactive drug. Now, I was leaping ahead and thinking maybe he had encountered Luke's gang somewhere, but apparently the drug was taken on a stag weekend in Galway and he wasn't a regular drug user. He was transferred to St James's because they've specialists on site and for his family's sake. He's brain-dead and he'll be moved from the ICU shortly.'

'Okay,' Tom said. He'd have thought the same as Laura, but it was hard to see the link between a twenty-seven-year-old and Luke's gang.

'The next one I looked at was the guy on the bike.'

'I'm interested in that one,' Tom said.

'I know,' Laura said. 'He's nineteen, a Dubliner. Skidded on surface water on the Fonthill Road. One of those days when the organ transplant team wait by the ambulance doors for motorcyclists. He came off the bike, sustained a massive head injury, multiple fractures and broken bones. The bike then collided with a car, causing it to crash too. The driver was injured, but it was a big four-wheel-drive, so not too badly. It could have been worse, though. He got out of the car right before the bike exploded. It had ruptured its fuel tank.'

'Who was in the car?' Tom asked.

'A fifty-year-old German man. Here on a business trip.'

'And was there anybody else around? No other vehicles involved?'

'None whatsoever. It was 6 a.m. The lad was driving to his job in the industrial estate in Clondalkin; the businessman was heading to the N4 to travel to Athlone. The road was deserted when the crash happened. CCTV caught it. They reckon the lad might recover, though never fully.'

'I don't think it's that, then,' he said.

'I seriously doubt it's the old woman who had a stroke, either,' Laura said. 'She was home alone. Her daughter found her later that day, hence the coma. What is it exactly that you're hoping to hear before I tell you my last one?'

Tom sighed.

'I saw something on Twitter that stuck with me. When you said the motorbike had been a fireball, I thought that might have been it. I think it involved somebody burning.'

Laura frowned.

'You think whatever they did has to do with a fire?'

'Jacob posted this cartoon character running around in flames. It just stayed in my head, that was all.'

Laura's eyes narrowed.

'Well, if it's fire you're interested in,' she said, 'the old man is who you're after.'

'You said he'd been assaulted,' Tom said.

'No. The nurse said that. Now I have the full story. He's homeless.'

'And?'

'His tent was set on fire. While he was in it.'

# CHAPTER 42

The Burke home was one of the smaller ones in Little Leaf, but you could still fit the inspector's entire floor space into Mrs Burke's kitchen and lounge.

It was a comfortable space – Mrs Burke was relaxed and welcoming and her home spoke to that. The counters were full of cooking equipment and ingredients; a calendar was stuck to the fridge with colourful magnets, the various events of the family's lives written in boxes under the dates. The chairs all had worn but soft cushions tied to them, and a vase of wildflowers sat on the table.

'I can't offer you tea or coffee, I'm afraid,' Mrs Burke said. 'We don't drink caffeinated beverages. I can do you herbal tea or water, or perhaps a soda?'

Mrs Burke, it turned out, had been born in the States but had married Charlotte's father when he'd been living and working there. She'd returned to Ireland with him over twenty-five years ago but still had the twang of a US Midwestern accent, along with most of its vocabulary.

'Please, don't put yourself out, Mrs Burke,' Tom said. 'We really just want to talk to Charlotte for a couple of minutes.'

The inspector had brought Laura with him. Both he and Sean thought the teenage girl might respond better to Laura but, in addition, Tom wanted to see if Charlotte would recognise the woman who'd been following her. If she did, she'd realise just how much trouble she was potentially in.

'That's absolutely fine,' Mrs Burke said. 'Like I say, I just need to run out for a few errands but I'll be back in no time. If it's just informal, then that's okay, isn't it? I don't need to be here? It's just, she's a little upset following the funeral this morning.'

'You only need to be here if you want to be,' Tom said.

Mrs Burke was already grabbing her car keys from the counter. The door opened and Charlotte came in just as her mother was pulling a scarf around her neck. The teenager was in a baggy tracksuit, face cleaned of make-up, hair tied in a ponytail. She looked as young as Tom had seen her.

'Just call me, baby, if you need anything,' her mother said to her.

Mrs Burke took one more look at Tom and Laura and then, satisfied that they weren't there to traumatise her daughter, she left.

Charlotte rubbed at her arm nervously before sitting across from them at the breakfast table. She looked up – her eyes seemed to linger on Laura for a moment. Did she recognise her? She rubbed her arm again, a little harder.

'You seem a little anxious today,' Tom said. 'Is everything okay?'

Charlotte dropped her arm.

'We buried Luke this morning. I guess I'm upset.'

'You *guess* you're upset?

'I am upset.'

Tom took a deep breath.

'Charlotte, I have to say, I'm starting to lose patience with the runaround you and your friends are giving me. A young man is about to stand trial for the rape and murder of Luke

Connolly. You might think he deserves to stand trial – that he deserves to go to jail, even – but you should know, nothing is ever straightforward in a criminal case of this magnitude. For the prosecutor to be successful, he or she needs to know they have all the facts. They need to know that there's nothing the defence can spring on them and that they have the right person in the dock. If, for example, the prosecution calls Luke's friends to the stand and the defence manages to extract from one of you that you have told lies to the police, do you know how much damage will be done to that case?'

Charlotte flushed red.

'So, I'm going to ask you again, Charlotte. Did you suspect that Luke might have been in a relationship with Daniel Konaté?'

He waited, watching her blink rapidly, her brain working on overtime.

'No,' she said quietly, shaking her head.

Tom felt frustration bubbling in his stomach.

'But I did think he was cheating on me,' she said.

Tom and Laura glanced at each other.

'With whom?' Laura asked.

Charlotte shrugged.

'I know the others all wondered about Daniel,' she said. 'Well, not Jacob. He was completely blind when it came to Luke – if anything, I wouldn't have been surprised if *he'd* been a little in love with him. And Brian usually can't see anything beyond Jacob. Dylan and Hazel, though. They used to make these little jokes about how close they were. Luke and Daniel. But I . . . I never thought it. Luke really wanted to . . . he really wanted to sleep with me. He was insistent. He said Jacob was starting to give him a hard time about it.'

She looked uncomfortable now, shifting about in her chair and squirming.

'But I wouldn't,' she said. 'And after a while, he stopped harassing me, so . . .'

'So you thought he'd gone elsewhere,' Laura said.

'He was with Hazel. One time, not long after he and I got together. He was drunk, he said. She'd taken advantage. Hazel can be like that. But I knew that time he'd cheated and I sensed he'd done it again. I . . . I knew it.'

'Okay,' Tom said. 'But who did you think he'd gone off with? Hazel again?'

'No. No, definitely not. She drove him nuts.'

'Whoever this mystery girl was, she wasn't at the house that night, though, was she?' Tom asked.

Charlotte shook her head.

'We told you the truth.'

Tom paused.

'I didn't introduce my colleague,' he said. 'This is Detective Laura Brennan.'

Charlotte glanced briefly at Laura, until her eyes fell away.

'So, do you want to tell me what happened after Christmas, Charlotte?' Tom said.

'Sorry?'

Her tone said 'confused', but her face gave everything away.

'Too hard?' Tom said. 'Maybe we'll start with whether you all actually left that house that night, or whether a couple of you stayed behind? Or maybe you can tell me why you tried to visit Daniel Konaté?'

The colour drained from Charlotte's face.

'I just wanted to ask him what happened that night.'

'Don't you already know?'

'I don't understand.' Charlotte was growing more flustered, her eyes flitting from Tom to Laura and back again.

'You understand very well, I think,' Tom said. 'We told your mum this was informal, Charlotte. And that's correct. If you tell me what you know, I can have a think about what to do before any charges are brought. Because I sense, if you're visiting that man in hospital every week, you might not have been as involved as your friends. You might be a compassionate girl. Or maybe you set fire to a homeless man on your own. Please, don't lie. I know you were involved in the attack on him.'

Tears bubbled in the corners of Charlotte's eyes. There was a moment where it looked like she was considering trying to deny it. But then she looked across at Laura, squinted at her.

'You followed me,' she said. 'I felt like something was wrong but I couldn't put my finger on it.'

Laura nodded, once, curtly.

'Is he . . . Have they told you anything about how he is? I can't ask. Because then they'd . . .'

'They'd know you might have had something to do with it,' Tom finished.

Charlotte nodded. And then she started to shake all over.

'It was an accident. We didn't know anybody was inside. They didn't know. It was just a joke.'

'Who's they?' Tom asked.

'Luke and Brian,' Charlotte said. 'They were just showing off, having a laugh.'

She looked like she might vomit. Tom actually considered trying to find her a bowl or something she could catch it in but she spoke before he could move.

'And then we heard the screams.'

# CHAPTER 43

Jackie McCallion was at her desk in the Little Leaf station when Tom arrived. She glanced up, all set to return to her work, but then saw his face.

'You heard, then?' she said, nervously.

'Heard what?' Tom frowned.

'A trial date has been set for Konaté. June 5th. They're fitting it in before the recess.'

'Right,' Tom said, the stone heavy in his stomach. They were getting somewhere but he was still no closer to proving Daniel hadn't killed Luke.

'I wanted to check something with you,' he said.

Jackie sat back, fingers still poised over her keyboard as though ready to resume typing at a moment's notice.

'Another incident,' Tom said.

Jackie narrowed her eyes.

'Not something else I messed up, is it?'

Tom shook his head.

'The middle of January,' Tom said, 'a homeless man in Cabinteely Park had his tent set on fire. He ended up in St James's with extensive burns.'

'I know the case,' Jackie said. 'He was lucky to survive. I didn't handle it, but it was this station.'

'They get anybody?' Tom asked.

'No. They figured it was another homeless person, maybe somebody who wanted to steal his stuff or move him off their patch. The wardens in the park are good; there aren't a lot of places for homeless people to hang out.'

'That was the only avenue of investigation?' Tom asked.

'Pretty much. They did consider it could have been some druggie off his head, but that kind of thing, normally people can't keep it in. You pick it up in the gossip.'

'Nobody thought it might have been kids messing?'

Jackie frowned.

'Not that I know of. Why? Do you know something I don't?'

'I know Charlotte Burke is coming in to give an official statement about the involvement of Luke Connolly and Brian Power in the attack.'

Jackie blanched.

'Are you serious?'

'I'm deadly serious. According to her, they were messing in the park and the lads thought the tent was empty. They set fire to it for a laugh.'

'Shit,' Jackie said.

'Yes. Shit. And according to Charlotte, they all agreed to lie about it and cover up for each other because, after all, it wasn't intentional. And the man lived. But she's been visiting the hospital since Luke died. It obviously all got to her and she was overcome with guilt, something she didn't want to show when Luke was alive.'

Jackie looked incredulous.

'Jesus, this is crazy.'

'Daniel Konaté wasn't in the park,' Tom said. 'So something happened with those six kids that he had no hand in; possibly had no knowledge of. But if he did have knowledge of it, it could have caused tension between him and Luke. And as we know, in a tense, defensive situation, Daniel can resort to violence.'

'So ...' Jackie said, 'you don't think the other kids were involved now?'

'I wish it was that straightforward,' he said. 'Charlotte told me something else. She said Brian, Jacob and Hazel went back into the house. The three of them are claiming they did nothing and just left but Charlotte doesn't believe them.'

'Shit,' Jackie said.

'So, they were lying about that, too,' Tom said. 'Which would make you wonder: what else are they lying about?'

Sean was outside with Ian Kelly when Tom emerged.

'How'd you leave my detective?' Ian asked, stubbing out his cigarette amongst the daffodils.

'In an existential state,' Tom said. 'She's in there questioning if a chair is a chair and whether half the Little Leaf teenagers are murderous rapists.'

'I'd best leave her to it, so,' Ian said. 'Right, lads, I'll love you and leave you. Sean, make sure to call by for that drink when you're out of this madness. Sure, you'll have all the time in the world, you lucky sucker.'

They bade him goodbye and walked towards their car.

'All the time in the world is what I'm afraid of,' Sean said, opening the front gate for Tom.

'Think of all the dances you're going to learn.' Tom smiled. He pulled his keys from his pocket. 'How about we catch up with Brian Power again? Get his take on the fire?'

'Good idea. Power is over in the Quinn Delaney house. I checked.'

'Hmm,' Tom said. 'This should be interesting.'

'Why's that?'

'Jacob's father was at the funeral this morning. Daddy's home.'

Vincent Quinn Delaney was, in a word, edgy.

Evening was falling by the time Tom and Sean arrived at the house, and they had to rap on the door several times before Jacob's father answered it, reluctantly.

'Should I sit in on this?' he asked them. 'I presume all you want the lads for at this stage is to help prep them for court? But shouldn't the solicitor be doing that?'

'There's no need for you to sit in,' Tom said. 'Jacob is eighteen. I want to ask him about another incident concerning his friends. We can do this in a relaxed fashion or we can do it in a more formal way. You choose.'

Tom could see the man's internal battle raging. He didn't want to aggravate Tom and Sean but he was used to getting his own way.

'I'm going to ring my solicitor,' he said. 'Just in case. You can talk to the boys, but if this is anything other than a little chat, I'm calling a halt.'

Jacob's father headed in the direction of what Tom assumed was his office. He'd already told Tom and Sean that the boys were out in the pool house.

They found it at the end of the garden, a beacon of light behind glass windows, its yellow glow spilling out onto the dusk-lit lawn.

Jacob and Brian were lounging on wicker chairs at the foot of the pool. Music blared from a sound system in the corner. A dull, droning bass beat, no recognisable melody.

Jacob spotted them first when they opened the door and entered. Tom motioned for him to turn down the music.

Jacob lifted a remote control from the ground and pointed it at the speakers.

There were two more chairs; both looked ridiculously low and difficult to get out of once seated. Tom and Sean stayed standing.

'Jacob, we've just spoken to your father and explained there's no need for him to be part of this conversation.'

Jacob frowned.

'Brian, you're not eighteen until next month so, technically, we need to bring you into the station and do this with an appropriate adult. But if there's anything you'd like to tell us before we go there, particularly pertaining to the night Luke Connolly died, we'd be happy to hear it. Once you're in the station, everything is out of our hands.'

'She fucking told you, didn't she?' Brian snarled. He turned to Jacob. 'That bitch. I knew she'd open her mouth after the other night.'

'Shut the fuck up, Brian,' Jacob said.

Brian, for once, ignored him. He looked back up at Tom.

'I don't know what Charlotte said but nothing happened. I went back in to get Luke. We all knew what he was like with Daniel. I didn't want to leave him alone with him. But Jacob and Hazel came in and convinced me to go. I didn't lay a finger on Luke. I didn't even talk to him.'

Tom and Sean exchanged a glance. They'd planned to start with the attack on the homeless man.

'Why didn't you want Luke left alone with Daniel, Brian?' Tom asked. 'Were you afraid he might talk to him?'

Brian bristled.

'No. It was, uh, just the way Luke got when he was with Daniel. It made us all . . . uncomfortable.'

'What did you see when you went back into the house, Brian?' Sean asked.

'Nothing.'

'Nothing? Nobody? You just wandered in and then wandered back out?'

The red started to rise from Brian's thick neck right up to his forehead.

'Why are you asking all this?' Jacob asked then.

'We have new information,' Tom told him.

'I fucking knew it,' Brian said.

Jacob started to pull himself out of the chair.

'I said shut it, Brian.' He was standing now, after awkwardly hoisting himself from the chair. 'Did you actually speak to Charlotte?'

Tom tapped his chin with his finger.

'Let's talk about other places you like to hang out,' he said. 'What about Cabinteely Park?'

The sneer fell from Jacob's face. Brian looked like he might pass out.

He started to say something, but Jacob held his hand up, a halt sign.

'Don't talk to them until your parents ring your solicitor,' Jacob instructed him. He stared at Tom. 'You think you're clever, coming in here and trying to get information out of us like this. You're not. I don't care what that bitch has lied about. You just wait until her parents hear. She's not going to open her mouth again, believe me.'

Tom half smiled. He was almost amused by the balls on this kid. He also wanted to smack the cheek and arrogance out of him.

'She's in the station right now giving a statement,' he said.

'I wouldn't be so sure about that,' Jacob replied.

The door to the pool house opened. Vincent Quinn Delaney was standing there.

'Right, that's it. Gentlemen, I'm going to have to ask you to leave, unless you have arrest warrants for my son and his friend.'

'They can come to the station willingly,' Tom said.

'That can be arranged as soon as Brian's parents and I have organised solicitors. And I assume you have proper grounds for asking them to come in?'

Tom felt his phone buzz in his pocket. It was just a text and yet it felt ominous that it would arrive at this time. He pulled it out and opened the message while answering Jacob's father.

'We have grounds,' he said, then hesitated. The text was from Laura. It read:

*At the station with Charlotte, her father and solicitor. She's refusing to talk – except to say she made it all up.*

# CHAPTER 44

The inspector was furious. Sean held on to the handle of the passenger door as Tom put his foot down and weaved through the lanes on the M50.

'We've blown it,' he said. 'I should have brought her into the station myself.'

'What difference would that have made?' Sean asked. 'She's underage; her parents and solicitor would always have to have been involved and the outcome would have been the same.'

'They can't just close ranks like that,' Tom said, slapping his hand on the wheel. 'Those kids nearly killed a man and another boy is dead.'

'They can't close ranks?' Sean repeated. 'They can and they will. Have you realised nothing about how these people operate, Tom? The kids haven't licked it off the ground. Their parents are well-connected and at the top of the food chain. They mix in the circles that run the country. They'll buy silence with top-notch legal teams.'

'They can't just get away with this, though!' Tom realised how desperate he sounded. And yet, he knew the truth of what Sean was saying. These were people used to getting away with everything and anything.

'Surely,' he said, calmer now, 'the kids will crack? We can interview Jacob on his own. Charlotte is eighteen in two weeks, we can do the same there. We haven't faced Hazel down yet, but . . .'

Sean looked out the window.

'I don't know, Tom,' he said.

They drove in silence for a moment.

'You know who might be your best bet?'

'Who?' Tom asked, daring to hope that Sean had the golden bullet.

'Dylan Keating. Junior, I mean. That kid hates his buddies. And I think he might hate his folks as well. He could be angry enough to drop them all in it. According to Charlotte, he wasn't involved in the tent incident. And he didn't go back into the house that night.'

'But he's stayed silent up until now,' Tom said.

Sean shrugged.

'Yes. But maybe we weren't asking the right questions.'

Tom nodded, slowly.

'Okay,' he said.

'First, though,' Sean said, 'are you in a rush to get home?'

Tom looked at the time on the dashboard. It was almost 8 p.m.

'No mad rush, other than being tired,' he said. 'What do you have in mind?'

'Robert said he can get us in to Daniel again, if we like. I think he could do with seeing us. After missing the funeral and all.'

Tom nodded. That, he could stay up late for.

Daniel looked far better than when Tom had last seen him. He was still in solitary, and it was to his cell that Sean and Tom went when they arrived at the prison.

'They don't like me walking around too much,' Daniel said, when they arrived. He was on his bunk. There was one chair at a desk. Tom let Sean take that. He stood, resting his back against the wall.

'The head injury,' Daniel explained. 'They're worried I'll get dizzy and trip over, split my stitches or something. Then I might sue them.'

'Are you planning on suing the prison service?' Tom asked, amused.

'Sure,' Daniel said. 'I can say the voices they piped into my cell made me headbutt the door.'

Tom smiled, thinly.

'Okay, young man,' he said. 'Let's cut the bullshit. I know Luke was gay. I know you two were together. I know Chris Connolly came in here and threatened you. He told you – and this is the bit where I'm filling in the blanks – that under no circumstances were you to tell people that the sex you had with his son was consensual. That if you did, he'd make sure life got hard for your mother. And given she works in his office block, he didn't have to work too much to make you believe that. Tell me one thing: was it actually a club you met Luke in, or was it at his dad's workplace?'

Daniel blinked. He looked away from Tom, stared at the wall of his cell.

'He can't hurt your mother,' Tom said. 'And if he does, he'll have me to answer to.'

He wasn't as confident in making that statement as he would have been prior to the day's events, but he still meant it.

'And I suspect he's offered you money,' Tom continued. 'If he has, you shouldn't take it.'

'No,' Sean said. 'You shouldn't. DCI Reynolds can't say this, but I can. If you're innocent and you've been wrongly held here, do sue the prison service. Sue the Guards. Sue the State. That's where your money should come from. Not from somebody whose morals went out of fashion sometime around the eighteenth century.'

Daniel said nothing for a moment. Then his shoulders relaxed a little.

'I met Luke at his dad's office,' he said. 'I was waiting for my ma. Luke came out and we got talking. He was into music and politics and art and shit and he was really interesting. We ended up spending a bit of time together. And then I told him I DJ'd in the club and he turned up with his gang. I think he thought they'd all take me into their clique or some other shit like that. They didn't.'

'No. Well, you were probably lucky,' Tom said.

'Maybe. You know, he wasn't really like them. I mean, he wasn't a saint. Luke could be a pain in the hole. And he could be unkind. Like I said, the way he treated those girls was really cruel. He had a selfish streak in him that drove me fucking nuts. But he wasn't like that all the time. He could be funny and smart and generous. And I think it was because he'd had things so tough. He's really suffered the last few years. I know it seems weird to say it, but Ethan's illness meant Luke didn't get a look-in. It made him bitter and angry at times, but . . . he knew it. He knew what he was like. He tried to be better.'

Tom hesitated. There may have been some truth in it, but Daniel was far kinder to Luke than Luke probably deserved. Burning the tent may not have been intended to harm anybody physically, but it was still a vicious, nasty thing to do.

'Did Luke tell you what happened in Cabinteely Park?'

Daniel frowned. He shook his head. There didn't seem to be any deceit there.

'About six weeks before he died,' Sean asked, 'did he start acting funny?'

Daniel hesitated, then nodded.

'Yeah. He was avoiding me. And we had a fight.'

'Over what?'

'He asked me could I get drugs. I lost it. I'm not a drug dealer. It was insulting. Just because of where I'm from and what I do. I mean, I take the odd tab, or line. I party. But I'm not . . . anyway. He apologised. And Jacob, Mr Fucking Perfect, Mr Private School Boy, he was able to sort everybody out.'

'But Luke didn't intimate anything was going on, that anything had happened with him and his friends?' Tom asked.

'No,' Daniel said, more firmly. 'But I knew something was up. There was an edge with all of them. They were all off.'

'The night he died, when you two were together, did anybody see the pair of you?'

'I don't know.'

'You don't know? Didn't you say everybody had left?'

'Yeah, they had, but . . .'

'But what?'

'I thought . . . I might have heard somebody.'

'Ah, Daniel,' Tom said. 'Why didn't you say this before?'

'Because . . . because my ma was there. When I thought I heard something, me and Luke were, you know. I wanted to stop . . . but Luke was into it. He'd put some tunes on his iPhone and he had it blaring. I said I'd heard a noise, but he thought I was imagining it.'

Tom balled his fists with frustration.

One of those kids had seen Luke and Daniel together. Brian or Jacob or Hazel. Or all three? And had it been the fact that

Luke had lied about being gay or the possibility that he might have told Daniel what had happened that had set them off?

'But when you left, Luke remained,' Sean said. 'Why? Why didn't you leave together?'

Daniel hung his head. His regret at leaving Luke there was obvious. Painful.

'He'd got a text message,' Daniel said. 'And when he read it, he said he wanted to stay.'

'A text message?' Tom tensed. 'He had his phone?'

'Yeah, man.'

'When you left, he had his phone.'

'Yeah?' Daniel looked quizzical. 'I told you, we were listening to music on it. And he got a text.'

Tom and Sean looked at each other.

'What did it say?' Tom asked. 'Who was it from?'

'I don't know.'

'Did he seem angry? Afraid? Worried?'

'No,' Daniel said. 'He laughed.'

Tom frowned.

'Laughed?'

'Yeah. Like he thought it was funny. And I was starting to feel hungover and a bit sick, so . . . I left him to it. I . . . I thought it was from one of the girls. He was with Charlotte and he'd been with Hazel. It didn't bother him to . . . to sleep with them. I mean, I can't. But Luke thought it helped cover his tracks. Acting like he was a bit of a player. I was . . . I was hurt.'

'And when you left, you didn't take his phone?' Sean asked.

'Nah.' Daniel cocked his head, puzzled. 'Why are you even asking?'

'His phone is missing,' Tom said. 'Somebody took it. Maybe whoever texted him.'

Daniel's brow furrowed, confused, then he looked up at Tom, his face desperately sad.

'One of his mates came back, didn't they?'

Tom shrugged.

'Daniel,' he said. 'We need to talk about what happened to your dad.'

Daniel lowered his head.

'I was wondering when that would come up,' he said.

'It's one of the reasons you wouldn't talk to us, wasn't it?' Tom said. 'You assumed we'd find out what happened and put two and two together, come up with five.'

Daniel nodded.

'Fucking Chris Connolly. He knows. He threatened me. Said he'd tell my da where my ma lives. That I was going down anyway, but if I denied it, if I pled not guilty, he'd let me da find me ma. That man, mate, he's a scumbag. I was just a kid when I did that. Da was a – he was a bastard. He is a bastard. But my ma has never seen it that way. She always made excuses for him, up until it was me or him.'

'And the night Luke died,' Sean said. 'You didn't fight? You didn't let all that hurt and anger at him get the better of you? You didn't *push* him, did you?'

'No,' Daniel said. He seemed to sit up a bit straighter. 'I didn't. I fucking swear it. I didn't kill him.'

He hesitated, closed his eyes for a moment.

'I can't believe they wouldn't let me go to the funeral,' he said. 'Bastards.'

# CHAPTER 45

*Brian – She's a fucking pig. A stupid ugly pig.*

*Jacob – I wouldn't go that far. Pigs are smart. Charlotte is not smart.*

*Hazel – I don't know what her problem is. We're supposed to be best friends. Even though she's a boring bitch. First she steals my boyfriend, and now she's a rat?*

*Jacob – She's not your friend, Hazel. She's not anybody's friend. She's dead. Do you hear that, Charlotte? You're dead to us.*

*Dylan has left group chat.*
*Charlotte has left group chat.*

Brian tossed his phone on the bed. He was in his room, where his father had ordered him to stay since he'd arrived home from Jacob's house. The olds were in conclave. Vincent Quinn Delaney had just come over and they were sitting in Brian's father's study with Dylan Keating Sr, who'd brought his solicitor.

They all looked grave, angrier than Brian had seen any of them. Worried, too. But Brian knew they'd fix this.

He picked up his phone again and typed out a text to Jacob.

*Hazel and Charlotte's fathers aren't here.*

He could see from the three blinking dots that Jacob was typing something back. The text appeared from his friend.

*Charlotte won't talk. But her parents are weird. They've probably banned her from being near us and I guess they're avoiding our folks too. They'll be telling themselves she did nothing. Innocent little angel.*

Brian knew Jacob was right. His fingers flew over the screen again.

*What about Hazel?*

The reply came back in seconds.

*If her parents say anything, we'll tell them she went back into the house with us. They won't be long locking her down. But we can trust Hazel.*

Brian threw his phone down again. Fuck, if he could rewind the last three months, he'd happily do it.

Why had he gone back into Glenmore House that night?

Paranoia, that's what had driven him.

Luke had been getting watery about what had happened to the homeless dude.

It had been an accident, they'd reminded him. And it had been *his* idea. Charlotte had said she was cold and Luke had joked, 'Let's light you a fire and get rid of the smell of hobo at the same time.' They'd looked in the tent when they found it pitched in their spot in the wooded area. There was nobody in it, but it still reeked. But they were drunk and it would have taken ages to set the tent on fire with only a box of matches on them.

The next night, they returned to the park and the tent was still there, still in their spot. Brian asked Luke if he still thought it was a good idea to get a fire going. Luke had laughed and said, 'Yeah, go on.'

And Brian had taken out the bottle of liquid firelighter he'd brought from his da's garage. He'd been thinking and he'd come prepared. He wasn't as stupid as they liked to treat him. So he soaked the tent and met Luke's eye.

'Go on,' Jacob had egged him on. And Luke had laughed, lit a match and flung it at the tent. The girls started screaming, fear and adrenaline at the same time. And then they'd heard it. The other screaming.

They ran, as fast as they could, hearts racing in their chests, smoke acrid in their lungs, shins bashing against tree stumps and foreheads catching on low-hanging branches.

They read the next day that the man had got out of the tent. He was badly burnt, but he was alive.

They promised each other they'd never speak of it; they'd never tell anybody what happened.

But Luke had started to crack. Somebody was planting seeds of doubt in his ear. And now they knew it had been goody-two-shoes Charlotte. She'd even been *visiting* the homeless dude. If Brian could lay his hands on her now, he'd . . . what he'd really love to do was hold her down and humiliate her. Fuck her, the way she wanted to see them fucked.

His stomach knotted in anger at the thought of her. It was all her fault, really.

That night, when they left Glenmore House, he'd had this vision of Luke telling Daniel what had happened. And they couldn't trust Daniel. He wasn't one of them. So Brian had run back in, leaving Jacob and Hazel with their mouths hanging open.

Brian had gone right upstairs, but he'd stopped running when he got to the second floor. He'd walked up the last flight of stairs – there was something in his brain telling him to go quieter, not let the two lads know he was coming. Then he could eavesdrop.

But he couldn't hear anything, except music playing. So, he hunkered down and looked through the keyhole. And he saw them, Luke and Daniel, all over each other.

They hadn't heard him; the music was playing and they were too into it.

Brian had walked downstairs, dazed.

Jacob and Hazel had come in to get him. Hazel insisted on going up to see for herself. Jacob, though, had been furious. With Brian, not with Luke. He didn't want to see what was happening upstairs; he was just angry at Brian for bursting his bubble about his best mate.

That was nothing compared to how Hazel looked when she came down.

Her face – she was disgusted.

'He's a liar,' she said, almost choking on the words. 'A filthy, fucking liar.'

But Brian had been happy. There was no way Luke would be telling anybody about the tent because the next time he brought it up, Brian was going to tell him what he'd seen.

Brian was shaken from his thoughts by the sound of a car pulling into the driveway. Whoever was driving it must have sped in off the road, because the engine was still revving when the brakes bit, causing the tires to skid on the gravel.

Brian's room was situated at the front of the house so he got to the window just in time to see Chris Connolly hop out and slam the car door.

The front door opened downstairs and then Brian's father was outside, along with Vincent Quinn Delaney. Brian couldn't see Dylan Keating Sr or his solicitor but he imagined they were there, hanging back under the porch.

Brian opened his window so he could hear what was going on.

'Is it true?' Chris shouted. 'Damien Burke rang me. Is it true what his daughter says? That three of the kids went back into the house the night Luke died?'

'Chris, calm down and come inside.' This was Brian's father.

'I'm not coming inside. You can tell me right now, right here, what happened. Did one of your kids push my boy? I want the truth!'

'You don't want the truth,' Jacob's father spoke now. 'If you did, that wouldn't have been the first question you asked. Because I'm sure Damien told you everything Charlotte said to that cop. Including how your son and Brian set fire to a homeless man.'

'That's hearsay,' Brian's father hissed. 'From a stupid little girl who doesn't know when to keep her mouth shut.'

A cloud passed over Chris's face.

'Handy that, isn't it? Being able to blame my son for something when he's not here to defend himself. Let's be honest, all your kids have shown themselves well capable of lying, haven't they? But the only one who's dead is mine.'

His voice almost broke at the end.

And now Brian could see Dylan Keating Sr emerge from the shadows of the house. He'd been under the porch, as Brian had suspected. His solicitor hung back just behind him.

The other dads towered over Keating Sr, but when he spoke, they all listened.

'I brought my solicitor over to ensure you all had the best legal advice,' he said, so quietly that Brian had to strain to hear. 'My son wasn't involved in any of this nonsense. He didn't set fire to the tent and he didn't go back into the house that night. The man who assaulted your son is in jail, Chris. That little fucker Konaté will get what's coming to him. Now, I would suggest that rather than screaming at each other outdoors, where in all likelihood you will be overheard, you pull yourselves together and go home to discipline your children for their other actions. Unless you want to publicly display all the skeletons in your familial closets?'

'Discipline our children,' Chris Connolly spat. 'Like you discipline yours, Keating?'

Nobody said anything. Brian frowned and watched as Dylan Keating Sr and his solicitor walked towards the car they'd arrived in. Brian's father hung his head. Jacob's dad held his palms out, trying to be conciliatory.

'Chris, none of our kids hurt your son. We mightn't agree with Keating on some things, but we know who did this. The boy who's about to stand trial. We have to stay strong. Do you want him to get off while the cops flounce around not knowing their arses from their elbows? I'm planning on making a complaint about how all this is being handled. You should, too.'

Chris shook his head.

'I just want justice for my son,' he said. He turned on his heel and walked back to his car. And then Brian noticed something: Luke's mother was sitting in the passenger seat. She'd stayed in the car when her husband got out but when he got back in, she leaned over and kissed him on the cheek.

# CHAPTER 46

They drove away from the prison, mulling over what they'd learned. Tom had rung Jackie McCallion as they left the car park, reminding her of the urgency of the phone records and informing her of the new development.

She'd promised they'd have what they needed before the night was out. It was already after 9.30 p.m.

'When we get Luke's phone records, they won't show anything if it was a WhatsApp message,' Sean said. 'Or even a normal text message, for that matter.'

'And the prize for stating the blindingly obvious goes to,' Tom said.

'No need to be snarky. Aren't you a bit concerned?'

'About what?' Tom asked.

'About it being a dead end. Why would one of his mates text him? Why not just go back? They knew where he was.'

'Yes, and they knew he was with Daniel and would most likely leave with Daniel. So, they texted him and told him to stay where he was.'

'Hmm,' Sean said. 'That's your theory. You know, Daniel might be onto something about the girls. I'm just thinking about what might make a teenage boy laugh while reading a text and not share the joke.'

'Which girl?' Tom mused.

'Well, we know Charlotte is the Virgin Mary,' Sean said. 'Or whatever the Mormon equivalent is. And we *know* Hazel went back into the house. And Hazel was with Luke before, in *that* way. So, Hazel might have been incredibly pissed off if she saw her ex-boyfriend having sex with a bloke.'

'Hmm,' Tom said. 'Maybe the three of them hatched it together. Her and Jacob and Brian, and they just used her text to keep Luke there, like a honey trap. Maybe Luke was having regrets about what happened in that fire, especially if he was spending more time with Daniel and having to keep the lie up. And between those regrets and finding out he was gay, the other three snapped.'

'Sounds as good as any motive,' Sean said.

Tom shrugged. He wasn't sure. There was something he couldn't lay his finger on. He felt it. Something he was missing.

They'd ended up in the pub outside the Phoenix Park HQ. A gang of them. Ray and Laura were already there when Tom and Sean arrived. Tom buzzed Louise and suggested she stroll up from their home on Blackhorse Avenue, because he suspected it was going to be a long night of talking and possibly drowning of sorrows.

Now Louise was nestled in between Laura and Ray and whatever she was saying to them had them in fits of laughter. It didn't take a DCI to figure out his wife was telling them some humiliating story about Tom, but he didn't care. He was just happy to see them together, laughing. Transfer or no, as long as Ray and Laura came through her promotion unscathed, Tom could rest easy. And anyhow, he sensed Ray was having second thoughts. He certainly looked more relaxed than he had over the last few days.

'We're screwed,' Sean said. 'Whatever way you look at it. We can't get the kids' phones off them without warrants. We can't get warrants without cause. None of them will talk to us. They all say they went home. None of their parents will tell us what time they got in. We've no idea where Luke's phone is, so we've no way of finding out who texted him that night.'

Sean started to lay out beer mats on the table, one for each of the suspects. 'And it's starting to look like they're all capable.'

Sean was still pushing the beer mats back and forth when the door to the pub opened.

It was like a movie scene in an Old West saloon playing out. To a man and a woman, the officers and Louise fell silent and watched as Linda and Emmet came in together.

Linda took a small stool at the table while Emmet went to the bar, raising his hand to his mouth to indicate he'd get the next round in.

'I don't understand,' Tom said, turning to Sean. 'Does this mean Mommy and Daddy are getting back together?'

Linda sighed dramatically.

'Have they announced the end of the world while we've been sitting in here?' Sean asked.

'Ask him,' Linda said, pointing at Tom. 'Mr Counsellor.'

'What did I do?' Tom asked, in amazement.

'You sent Emmet in search of religious inspiration.'

Tom drew a blank for a moment, a combination of tiredness, two pints and sheer forgetfulness.

'Oh,' he said. 'No. Well, yeah. I suggested he bring your son to a nun. Remember Sister Gladys?' Tom turned to Ray and Laura, but they were too busy ogling to take part. Their heads swung back and forth like they were watching a Wimbledon final between Federer and Nadal.

'Paul hasn't gone down,' Linda said, unable to hide the

disappointment in her voice. 'But Emmet spoke to your nun on the phone. And then he rang me. And we had a long conversation.'

Tom leaned in closer. He was studying Linda's mouth. Her teeth were stained red. They'd been on the wine.

Jesus. Maybe they'd restarted the affair.

'I'm not following,' Sean said. 'Is everything fixed with your son or not? Are you all happy families now?'

'For the love of all that is holy, what are you drinking?' Linda replied. 'You've entered the realm of fantasy, darling. Isn't it enough that Emmet and I are talking to each other and not once have I pointed out how much of an arsehole he is?'

'We're only in the door but I'll take that as a compliment,' Emmet said, placing a G&T in front of Linda. 'The barman is bringing down the rest. Right so, less about our personal lives and more about how you've all screwed up this week. Pray tell. I could do with a laugh.'

'Really, don't make us go through it again,' Tom groaned.

'Are you absolutely sure it wasn't somebody outside of those kids?' Laura said, her face serious now.

'I'm not sure of anything,' Tom said, 'bar the fact after a couple of weeks it's far less likely Daniel Konaté did it. I considered the father, momentarily, but I can't see it.

'What about the mother?' Laura asked. 'I haven't met her but, I don't know. This might sound stupid, but it does feel particularly female – pushing somebody. And if she was remonstrating with him and he was giving her cheek, getting in her face, she might just . . .'

Laura extended her hands and pushed out.

'It's not the mother,' Tom said, absolutely sure of it.

Laura shrugged.

'Just a thought,' she said.

'She has no motive,' Tom continued. 'And she's . . .'

He was about to say devastated. But he stopped himself. He knew as well as any of them that grief could be feigned. But Rose Connolly – he couldn't have her so wrong.

Could he?

'Christ,' Tom said, shaking his head. 'We need to find his phone. The mother did say she was looking for him that night. She kept ringing.'

The door opened again, and Jackie McCallion walked in.

She looked around the pub until she saw the little group sitting in the corner.

Tom stood up. Jackie seemed reluctant to approach, so he made an awkward exit from his seat, squeezing past Sean's legs and crossing the pub towards her.

'I called into HQ and Garda Callaghan told me you were here,' she said.

'You really did mean tonight, didn't you,' Tom said. It was after 11 p.m., he hadn't expected her to turn up with the records at all. 'Well, work first, then you might have a drink with us.'

Jackie looked around her nervously. There was an empty table beside them, so Tom sat and indicated she do the same.

She perched herself awkwardly on the stool and reached into her bag.

'Luke's mobile records,' she said. 'I got them this evening – before you rang, in fact. I thought you'd want me to go through them first, given I have all the numbers ID'd.'

She handed the pages to Tom, lists of numbers that meant nothing to him, all leading up to the date of the night he'd died.

She'd underlined each number and put initials beside them.

Tom ran his eyes up the page. On the day he'd died, Luke had taken calls from J, Ct, Cs, D and R.

'Jacob, Charlotte, Chris, Daniel and Rose,' Jackie said, clarifying. 'The last call was from Jacob at 9 p.m. that night. That doesn't mean nobody else rang him after that, just that he didn't answer. These were calls made normally. We can't track WhatsApp calls if they've been deleted.'

Tom sighed.

'What have you spotted?' he asked Jackie, presuming she'd picked up on something. This was as animated as he'd seen her since they'd met.

'It's not on the page,' Jackie said, and Tom had to bury his irritation. She had something alright, she was just drawing it out.

'The coroner's report suggested Luke died between 12 a.m. and 2 a.m., approximately. Daniel Konaté was home just before 3 a.m., so he could have been in the house in the timeframe when Luke died.'

Jackie bit her lip. She was clearly excited that her detective work had turned up something, while kicking herself that it disproved her earlier work.

'I spoke to the phone company and to our IT guys. Luke's phone was still turned on at 3 a.m. A full hour at least after he died. They picked it up pinging on a mast in Little Leaf. Rose said she sent Luke a text at 3 a.m. asking where he was. It was delivered and read. But she got no reply. She started ringing shortly afterwards, but the phone was turned off at that stage. But Daniel was already home by then. There's no way he had Luke's phone.'

Jackie finished and stared down at the table, unable to meet Tom's eye.

'I'm sorry,' she said. 'It might have been somebody who

picked up Luke's phone, if it had been lost, but . . . given what you said about him receiving a text when Daniel was there, it seems more likely to be someone who doesn't want us seeing it.'

Tom tried to contain his anger. There was context to her actions, even if they infuriated him.

'What's done is done,' he said. 'Now we need to get to the bottom of it. This can't go to trial if we've messed up. We need to establish who had Luke's phone at 3 a.m. What area does that mast cover? All the homes in Little Leaf?'

Jackie nodded.

'We need to get Charlotte to talk again,' Tom said. 'Or one of them. Then we can secure search warrants for the houses on the basis of the tent fire. We're looking for accelerant, lighters, clothes they may have been wearing that night. And now we're also looking for Luke Connolly's mobile phone.'

'And we can only do this if one of them talks,' Jackie said. 'That sounds like a bit of an ask.'

Tom nodded, trying not to look as hopeless as he felt.

'Leave that with me,' he said. 'Sean made a suggestion earlier. He thinks Dylan might be open to breaking the code of silence.'

Jackie looked over at the crowded table Tom had recently vacated.

'Do you often do this?' she asked, genuinely interested.

'Go for a drink? Well, I'm not saying I'm a closet alcoholic or anything.'

'No, I mean, the lot of you, together. I walked in here and there's the current Chief Superintendent of the NBCI. The next Chief Super. The Chief Super of the Technical Bureau. The State's leading criminal psychologist. Leading detectives in the murder squad. And . . .' She frowned. She'd no idea who Louise was. 'It's a little intimidating,' she finished.

Tom shrugged.

'We're all friends,' he said. 'You work professionally with people over a long number of years and that's what happens, Jackie.'

He thought she looked sad. And it dawned on him – Jackie didn't have an awful lot of friends in the police force. He wondered if it had been like that before what happened at Glenmore House, or if she'd deliberately shut herself off afterwards. Either way, it was sad to see.

'Come on, let's get you that drink.'

# CHAPTER 47

Dylan Keating Sr had no intention of letting Tom and Sean near his son without a hit squad of legal eagles in attendance.

As they stood on the doorstep the following morning, Sean remonstrating with Dylan's father, Tom's phone buzzed again. A text from Ethan Connolly. Tom sighed.

He felt bad, but if ever there was a reminder not to hand out personal mobile numbers . . . He had no news for Ethan. What could he tell him: *Last night I actively considered your mother might have killed your brother*?

This time he typed a quick response: *Will call later.*

The phone buzzed again. Tom left it in his pocket.

'Mr Keating,' Tom said. 'We are aware that your son had very little involvement in all of this. That's why we want to talk to him. It strikes me that it makes sense for Dylan to cooperate when he has very little to hide. We would look extremely kindly on a material witness who never actually committed a crime himself, other than a failure to come forward. Especially a minor, which Dylan will continue to be for the next few months. But if this obstruction continues, then it does not bode well.'

Keating Sr sneered at Tom.

'You think this is how it works?' he said. 'Picking them apart one by one? I'm familiar with your style, Inspector. Divide and conquer, with empty promises all along the way. I'm not letting you within a mile of an interview room with my son unless you have a warrant and he's well-represented.'

Sean threw his hands up in the air. His theory that Dylan could be pressed would come to nothing if they couldn't get near the boy.

Tom glared at Keating Sr. There was nothing they could do. He and Sean exchanged a glance and turned on their heel.

'We'll be talking to you again,' Tom called over his shoulder.

'Don't bet on it,' Keating Sr replied.

They'd driven as far as the electric gates at the bottom of the drive when there was a rapping on the window. They hadn't spoken a word, both silently fuming at the defeat; they were so preoccupied that neither had noticed Dylan running after the car.

Tom blinked in astonishment, then rolled down the window.

'I'll talk to you,' he said, and over that, Tom could hear Keating Sr yelling. He was still at the front door, trying to order his son to return to the house.

'Can I get in the car?' Dylan asked.

'You'll need an appropriate adult,' Tom said. 'If we're bringing you in for a statement.'

'Can you ring my mother and get her to come down on her own? And can I have my own solicitor? Not my father's?'

Sean leaned around Tom.

'Absolutely. Hop in.'

Dylan jumped in the back.

In the rearview mirror, Tom could see Keating Sr barrelling down the drive now, his face purple with rage.

Dylan turned around in the backseat and gave his father the middle finger.

'Arsehole,' he said.

Tom couldn't help but snort. Sean had judged the boy's personality absolutely right.

He reached into his pocket and took out his phone to tell Jackie he was bringing Dylan in. The text message from Ethan popped up. Tom opened it distractedly just to get it off his home screen.

It wasn't from Ethan, though it had been sent from Ethan's phone.

It was from his nurse, Claire.

*It's Claire, Inspector. Ethan asked me to message. He's been very ill since the funeral. He says he knows something. But he'll only talk to you.*

# CHAPTER 48

Tom left Dylan with Sean and Jackie in Little Leaf station. His mother had been summoned and it had been explained that Dylan wished to see her on his own. A solicitor had been acquired and was already trying to slow Dylan down, but it wasn't working. Once they'd got him in the station, he wouldn't stop talking. He'd started in the car, despite Tom and Sean's warning, and he'd gone right back to the beginning – when Luke, Jacob and Brian had bullied him in school and how he'd lashed out at Luke and stabbed him with a pencil.

'I was carrying a lot of anger,' Dylan said. 'My father was using me as his own personal stress ball at the time. He'd hit me – always in the ribs and back, never on my face, so nobody would see. I just lost it.'

Tom turned and looked at Dylan over his shoulder. He was speaking so calmly, the words coming automatically and without emotion, but the mental scars he'd been carrying for so many years didn't bear thinking about.

There wasn't going to be a problem extracting a statement about what had happened in Cabinteely Park and at Glenmore House. Dylan had seen everything Charlotte had and he wasn't afraid to talk about it.

They would have grounds for the warrants and the

application was already in process. But first, Tom was going to see Ethan.

Ethan was as weak as Tom had seen him. It was like his brother's funeral had sapped his last remaining reserves. Looking at him in the bed, almost swamped by the blankets, eyes closed, the inspector instinctively knew the boy would be having no more good days.

It was coming to an end.

'Ethan,' Tom said gently. 'I got your message. You wanted to talk to me?'

Ethan's eyes flickered.

'Inspector,' he said, his voice barely there.

Tom pulled the armchair closer, brought himself as near as he could to the boy, so he wouldn't have to strain.

'I thought I was beating it. No matter . . . no matter what they said. I felt . . . strong. But now I–'

'It's okay,' Tom said. 'Don't strain yourself, son. What is it you want to talk to me about?'

'Is Daniel still . . .'

'He's still on remand, yes,' Tom said.

'I need to–' Ethan closed his eyes. 'I have to . . .'

He couldn't finish the sentence.

'It's okay,' Tom said. 'You don't have to worry about it any more, Ethan. I'm getting close. I think one of Luke's friends was involved. You were right.'

Ethan blinked rapidly. He opened his eyes again, stared at Tom.

'You . . . sure? Daniel will be let go?'

'I hope so,' Tom said. He wasn't sure, he couldn't promise anything, but what did it matter here, in this room? Ethan was dying. He wouldn't see what came to pass.

Ethan sighed.

'He changed.'

'Luke?'

'Yeah. He used to be good. Nice. But . . .'

'Still,' Tom said. 'He didn't deserve to die like that.'

'Who deserves to die?' Ethan said, a cloud of pain passing over his face. 'Do I deserve it?'

Tom had no answer. In death's final jaws, the boy was raging against fate. Even though he could barely breathe, Tom could feel the simmering fury in the body in the bed. Fury at the injustice.

'Luke told me something,' Ethan said.

Tom leaned closer.

'He . . . he said they'd almost killed a man.'

Tom straightened up, shocked. This, too, was imminent death talking. Ethan wanted to clear his conscience.

Tom pulled his phone from his pocket.

'Is this about the homeless man?' he asked.

Ethan blinked again.

'Y-you . . . asked if something happened. It did. I need to tell you.'

'Ethan, are you okay if I record this? And I'm going to ask somebody to come in here and be a witness; is that okay?'

Ethan blinked again. He closed his eyes, then turned his head away from Tom. It looked like he wanted to say more, but couldn't.

'I'll get Claire, is that okay?' Tom asked. He stood. He had to get this on tape, before the boy died.

Ethan nodded.

'You were right,' he said, breathing heavily.

Tom waited.

'I'm a little in love with her,' Ethan said. Then he fell silent again.

Later, when Tom was leaving, Ethan reached out his hand to him. It felt cold, clammy. Like there was no blood circulating in his body.

'I'm sorry,' Ethan whispered.

Tom swallowed.

'You've nothing to be sorry for,' he said. 'You wanted to protect your brother. It was misplaced but understandable. Don't think about it any more.'

'He's all I think about,' Ethan said. 'Now. I'll see him again. I don't care what happens to the rest of them. I just – I just wanted to make sure Daniel would be okay.'

On the other side of the bed, Claire coughed, burying a sob.

'I'll walk you out, Inspector,' she said. 'Ethan, your mum is on her way in. She'll be here shortly.'

With that, Ethan closed his eyes.

Tom and Claire walked down the corridor in silence. When they got to the lift, Tom looked across at the nurse.

'Are you shocked by what you heard in there?' he asked.

She stopped walking, gestured angrily.

'That his brother nearly killed somebody? No. I'm not shocked, to be honest. He was a selfish little shit. I've only known Ethan for eighteen months, but it was enough. You know, from the start, Luke used to flirt with me. Relentlessly. I couldn't get my head around it – I mean, I was flattered at first. He was a good-looking lad and he didn't seem like a sixteen-year-old. He seemed older. Most teenage boys, all you can smell is Lynx and bubblegum. He wore Creed Aventus aftershave and Calvin Klein sunglasses. But the more he flirted, the more I realised it wasn't for my benefit.'

'Whose benefit was the flirting for, then?' Tom asked.

'He was doing it to wind up his brother,' Claire said. 'He must have been jealous of how well Ethan and I got on.'

She flushed bright red.

'I should have realised then how bloody nasty that boy was. Everybody should have.'

# CHAPTER 49

They'd gone through the houses. Metaphorically and physically.

Dylan Keating Sr had followed them around his with three solicitors. They hadn't technically needed to search Dylan's house; he'd told them everything and agreed to hand over the clothes he was wearing on the night of the fire, even though they'd been well laundered.

But they were also looking for Luke's phone, something they omitted to tell Dylan.

In the Powers' garage, they'd found identical bottles of accelerant to the one discovered at the scene of the fire in Cabinteely Park. In Jacob's room, they found a scorched Leinster jersey hidden under his bed. If he'd put it in the laundry, the cleaners would have had it washed, ironed and folded by the time the Technical Bureau tried to get their hands on it. But showing his age, and possibly his arrogance, Jacob had just stuffed it behind junk.

They couldn't find Luke's phone anywhere. But they did take the phones of each member of the gang back to the station.

They'd been careful in their WhatsApp messages. Nobody mentioned the fire directly. But there were enough incriminating texts to ascertain that they'd gone to the park on that date, that something bad had happened and that they were scrambling about as to what to do.

Tom was less interested in that aspect. He was hoping to discover which of them had messaged Luke the night he died.

'There's nothing,' Jackie told him, as they sat around her desk in Little Leaf. 'One of them could have deleted the text, but we can't find it in the trash. IT are going to have to go through each phone and try to retrieve the messages. If it was sent on Snapchat, then there's a new problem – once it's seen, it's gone.'

'Christ!' Tom banged his hand on the desk. 'Nothing's easy, is it?'

He pulled Dylan's statement towards him and scanned the pages. What had they missed? What was in there that would give it away?

'Make sure they focus on Hazel's phone,' Sean told Jackie. 'I was right about Dylan cracking. Maybe I'm right about her, too.'

Tom wasn't listening. He was reading a section from Dylan's statement about the night Luke died:

*Interviewing officer – And when did you notice the other three weren't behind you, that they'd gone back into the house?*

*Interviewee – A couple of minutes. Hazel is loud, I think that's what Charlotte and I noticed. The quiet. We started to walk back. We got as far as the house and that's when they came out. Brian was laughing but Jacob, he had a face like thunder. Like he wanted to kill somebody.*

*Interviewing officer – What about your other friend? Hazel?*

*Interviewee – She was . . . I don't know. She was nothing. Just blank. She came up to Charlotte and they walked ahead. Their arms linked, whispering to each other, the way they always do. They share everything, that pair. Even lads.*

*

Tom looked up from the page. The others were still talking.

'Charlotte,' he said.

'What?' Sean looked across.

'When Hazel came out of the house, she talked to Charlotte. *They share everything*. That's what Dylan said.'

'You think she told Charlotte they'd seen Luke with Daniel?' Jackie asked.

'Why not? Why would Hazel flip and not Charlotte? She told us herself – she suspected Luke was cheating on her, but with another girl, not a bloke. She could be lying. If she knew what was happening with Luke and Daniel, she could be lying about everything. And she might have broken and told us about the fire because she comes out of that okay.'

'You'll know for sure when you get your hands on any deleted messages,' Sean said. 'How soon can IT get through the phones?'

Jackie lifted her handset and dialled a number.

'Sini? Hi, it's Jackie. Yep, all good. Could I ask a favour? Can you bump up the mobile number 0874568 . . . That's the one. Charlotte Burke. Yes. Thank you.'

Jackie hung up.

'Sini's the best,' she said. 'She'll do it as fast as she can.'

Tom nodded.

'Good work, Detective.'

And then all their phones started to ring.

# CHAPTER 50

'I don't know how those parents are expected to cope,' Ray said, as they drove towards the Connolly house the next morning. He'd collected the inspector, telling him he had paperwork for Tom to sign.

Tom sighed, unable to find any words that made sense of what the Connollys were about to go through. Ethan had passed away the previous evening, when they were still going through the kids' phones. Tom was devastated for the boy, more so for his mother and father. The inspector felt washed out. He couldn't imagine what they were going through.

And more, he had an awful feeling that Ray had brought his transfer papers for him to sign. That must have been why his deputy was less stressed. He'd made up his mind.

Tom wasn't up to it. He wanted to go home, give Louise a hug, ring Maria and Cáit and take a long soak in the tub. Then sleep until tomorrow.

'This stuff you have for me,' he said. 'Can we actually leave it for now, Ray? I've too much on my mind.'

Ray said nothing. They pulled up at a red light.

'It's not a transfer form,' he said.

'It isn't?' Tom was surprised.

'No. It's just the case file of the man who killed his ex. I have enough to close it.'

'That's fantastic work.'

The lights had changed and Ray began to drive.

'I'm not shipping out,' he said.

Tom felt a smile tug on the edge of his lips but he held it in check.

'You're not?'

'No. Don't get all smug. I've just put it on hold. I think I should give it a year. Laura needs me in there. She has some ideas for shaking up the department. I need to keep things running on the ground.'

'Okay. And after a year?'

'I'll see. I have a feeling she's just going to keep getting promoted. You know what she's like. Dynamite.'

'She sure is.'

Ray blushed.

'Let's talk about my stag,' he said.

Tom sighed. The last he'd heard from Willie, a shipment of inflatable dolls had been ordered. He'd have to get a handle on how things were going and take over.

His phone buzzed and he took it out of his pocket. Jackie McCallion.

'I told you Sini was good,' she said when he answered.

'And hello to you, too. Does this mean she found something?'

'She found everything,' Jackie said. 'She found Charlotte messaging Luke at 11.30 p.m.'

Tom sat forward, the seatbelt straining against his shoulder.

'What did she say?'

'Verbatim. *You lying scumbag. I want to see you. Now. I'm going to fucking kill you.*'

Tom cursed.

'I'm on my way to the Connollys,' he said. 'I'll call into your station straight from there.'

The Connolly house was brimming with people. Family had turned up from the four corners, people trying to prop up Rose and Chris with their mere presence. A woman Tom discovered was Rose's mother beckoned him and Ray in, offering tea and coffee and a multitude of sandwich variations. She seemed much more down to earth than the Connolly side of the family. There was evidently less money in Rose's background, but a whole lot more common sense.

'Chris is in the kitchen,' she told them. 'He's hit the whiskey. Who can blame him, but my daughter could do with a little support right now.'

'Where is Rose?' Tom asked.

'Upstairs.'

She didn't need to say where.

Tom sent Ray to get tea. He was really only at the house to offer condolences. He would find Rose and then they could leave the Connollys to their private grief. They'd an interview lined up with Charlotte Burke that afternoon which would hopefully move things along.

Rose was in Ethan's room. Tom stood in the doorway and watched as the mother lay on her son's bed, one hand wrapped around her stomach, the other under his pillow. She wasn't crying. He imagined all her tears had been shed and now were replaced with an even more painful void.

'Rose,' he said gently. She looked across at the door, registering his presence.

Her manners were impeccable. Even in her devastation, she sat up and straightened her hair, her clothes.

'I can't be downstairs,' she said.

Tom nodded. He understood.

'I just came out to tell you how terribly, terribly sorry I am. I visited Ethan yesterday.'

'So did I,' she said. She sighed heavily. 'I asked the doctor and the nurse whether I should stay last night but they said he could go on for days. He was asleep, or at least, dozing in and out of sleep. I talked to him, but he couldn't hear me. It was like, after the funeral, he just gave up.'

Tom had felt that, too. As though attending the church and giving his brother's eulogy had drained the last of Ethan's strength.

The inspector couldn't bring himself to reveal Ethan's deathbed confession about the fire. It wasn't the time or the place. They would get to that later.

'When I went to leave,' Rose continued, 'I almost couldn't stand up. I had his hand in mine, and it was so cold. Like he was already gone. My legs felt leaden. I was stuck there. But I'm so used to being practical, you know. Getting on with things. So I kissed his forehead and I pulled the blanket up and I went over to the door. And, then –' she laughed, without mirth – 'then, I couldn't move from there, either. I was looking at him, each breath coming with such difficulty, and I thought, this is it. I'm not going to see him alive again. This boy, this baby I carried for nine months, my own flesh and blood, he's going to breathe his last. But I still left. I closed the door and I walked away.'

Tom said nothing. He was struggling to find any words that were appropriate.

'What else could you have done?' he settled on. 'The medical staff were right. You could have been there all night and come home this morning and it could have happened then.'

'He shouldn't have been alone.'

'Somebody must have been with him?'

'I mean, he should have had family. I should have been there.'

Tom didn't know what to say. He'd never lost a child; he couldn't comprehend her distress. He could sympathise but not empathise. And he didn't want to ever be in a position where he could empathise.

'What did I do so wrong?' Rose asked, a desperate plea, to him, to the heavens. 'I know how Chris earns his money. I've always known. But I tried to make sure the boys were raised well, despite all that. What Ethan said in the church about Luke standing up for him; that's what I wanted. That's what I gave them. But it all went to hell when Ethan got sick. It fell apart. He was in and out of hospital and we were with him and I stopped looking out for Luke. Because he was healthy. I assumed he'd be fine. He was gone before I even knew his time was finite. I was too busy.'

She stood abruptly and crossed to the door between the two rooms. She tried to open it; Tom was about to tell her it was locked.

'You know, I realise now why Luke kept this door closed,' she said. 'Ethan took enough of us all.'

Rose was angry now. At herself, at Ethan, at the world.

She passed Tom at the door and he followed as she walked into Luke's room and sat on his bed.

'Even in the last seven weeks,' she said, 'I've kept going into the hospital. I've barely been in here. What kind of a mother does that make me?' She frowned and then her face became blank. 'Am I even a mother any more?'

Tom looked around Luke's bedroom, at the care with which it had been maintained. The expensive decor, down to the valuable Star Wars figurines. Luke Connolly was loved. You could see it in this room.

'I want to give you something,' Rose said.

She crossed over to Luke's chest of drawers and began moving aside various men's creams and aftershave. She lifted up a shower bag tucked in at the back and opened it. From inside, she withdrew a photograph.

'I found this, a few days ago,' she said. 'Ethan wanted me to look for something of Luke's to put in the coffin, some memorabilia he'd got at a concert or something. But I discovered this.'

She handed the picture to Tom. It was a photograph of Luke and Daniel together. A selfie. They were smiling, Luke's face leaning towards Daniel's, their heads touching.

They were in love. You only had to look at the photograph to know it.

'Daniel couldn't have killed him,' she said.

'No,' Tom said. 'I don't think he did, Rose. But are you ready for the truth about what happened?'

'Yes,' she said, nodding. 'I need to know. I paid Luke little enough attention when he was alive. I have to fix that now.'

Tom found Ray downstairs. He nodded in the direction of the door, indicating they could leave. Behind Ray, through several relatives, Tom could see Chris Connolly. He was slumped over the kitchen counter, a glass of whiskey in front of him, eyes and face red, nose running. He looked pitiful. Broken.

'Hang on,' Ray said. 'Follow me.'

Tom followed Ray into a sitting room at the front of the house. Hazel and Jacob were sitting together awkwardly on a couch, glasses of Coke in their hands, looking distinctly uncomfortable. And yet, they'd made the effort to come.

Jacob nodded at Tom. Hazel stood up and approached him.

'Just so you know,' she said, her voice low. 'I didn't push Luke out that window. None of us did. And anything else . . . well, it was an accident. We're not bad people.'

She was serious, there was no hint of a lie there. Perhaps her role in anything that happened had been innocent. Tom couldn't be sure.

'What did you tell Charlotte that night, Hazel?' he asked. 'When you saw Luke with Daniel. Did you tell Charlotte what you'd seen?'

Hazel blinked furiously, her cheeks reddening.

'Did it make her angry?' Tom continued.

Hazel hung her head and muttered something.

'What?' Tom asked.

She looked up.

'I said, Charlotte is not as nice as she makes out.'

# CHAPTER 51

Charlotte was flanked by her father and a solicitor, a small woman with intense, thoughtful eyes, and an expression far too exhausted for her thirty or so years.

Sean had met Tom at the station, wanting to see the case through. He joined him now, both of them sitting on the opposite side of the desk to Charlotte.

'My client has already accepted she sent the message,' the solicitor said. 'That amounts to no more than an expression of teenage anger. It does not mean she returned to that house at a later time or actually met with Luke. If this is all you have to go on, Inspector, you've no reason to have summoned her in here like this.'

Tom met Charlotte's, not the solicitor's, eye. There was no denying he'd liked the girl when he first met her. But she'd played a game with them and he was fed up. It was time to go hardball, see how she reacted to that.

'Here's what I have,' he said. 'Lies and obstruction. Charlotte refused to come forward about what happened to the homeless man her friends set fire to in Cabinteely Park. She then falsely alibied three of her friends for the timeline on the night Luke Connolly was murdered. She lied about knowing Luke was gay. She failed to tell us she messaged Luke that night and threatened him, telling him she wanted to see him immediately. She also made an admission to myself and my senior colleague here, but refused to follow that up with a written statement, retracting, in fact, everything she'd said.'

Tom rested his elbows on the table, and placed his hands together in a steeple.

'We have a man about to stand trial for the murder of Luke Connolly and half the evidence against him revolves around the fact he was the last to see Luke, according to the statements of Charlotte and others who were there that night. It strikes me that a court is going to rip that case apart, now that we've discovered that Charlotte and her friends have been lying to the police. So, at the very least, I will be looking for charges to be pressed against Charlotte for her attempt to obstruct the course of justice. How do you think that's going to play out on your college application, Charlotte? All these years of being such a good girl. I bet you had plans to travel too, huh? Maybe visit your mother's homestead in the States? You know you can't actually get a visa for America with a criminal record?'

Charlotte turned to her father, her face filled with panic.

'But I didn't go back to the house that night,' she protested.

'Charlotte,' the solicitor cautioned. The girl spun her head around.

'It's true! I was furious when Hazel told me. At first, I thought she was just stirring. But I know her. I know when she's lying. She's no good at it. And she hadn't just seen them with their arms around each other or something. She'd seen them having sex. I . . . I knew he'd been with somebody, but I . . .'

Charlotte started to cry. Huge, noisy sobs.

'I thought he was with a girl. So, yeah, I messaged him. I was angry. I wanted to kill him, but I wouldn't have actually done it. Why doesn't anybody believe me?'

'Because you've made it very hard for us to believe you,' Sean said. 'You've lied about everything else. Who is this girl you keep referencing? Where did you get this from?'

'A few months ago. Before Christmas. He . . .' Charlotte looked sideways at her dad. Whatever it was, she couldn't say it in front of him.

'Mr Burke,' Sean said, 'I think Charlotte needs a soft drink, something to keep her energy up. Would you care to accompany me?'

'No way.' Damien Burke was on his guard. 'I'm not moving.'

'Please, Daddy,' Charlotte said. '*She's* staying.' Charlotte nodded her head at her solicitor. 'Just a few minutes.'

Damien looked at his daughter, disappointment on his face. She lowered her eyes. She couldn't look at him.

He stood up, stormed from the room. Sean followed.

Charlotte waited until the door closed.

'I've already told you. At the start, Luke was pestering me to have sex. And I wouldn't, for obvious reasons. Jacob started slagging him. I heard him saying Luke had gone gay since he'd split with Hazel. He was only joking, but Luke got really defensive. Then, a few nights later, we were in the park. It was freezing and Luke had gone back to his house to get me an extra jacket. His house was closest. I heard him and Jacob coming back before they saw us. Luke said that he'd been . . .' Charlotte took a deep breath. 'That he'd been *banging some bird to clear his balls*. And Jacob said, prove it. And then they were quiet and next thing, Jacob was laughing. *You have her knickers*, he said. Then they shut up because they knew they were near us.'

Charlotte looked up at Tom, her face still flushed.

'He had sex with a girl just to get Jacob off his back. Luke didn't want anybody to know he was gay. He was never going to admit it, not until he was caught.'

'His brother knew he was gay, so he told somebody,' Tom said.

'He wouldn't tell Ethan,' Charlotte said, scornfully.

Tom frowned.

'Why wouldn't he tell his brother?'

The door to the interview room opened.

'Tom,' Sean said. 'I need you out here for a minute.'

Tom turned off the tape and followed Sean out to the corridor.

'Jackie McCallion just rang.'

'And?'

'Ethan's belongings have just been returned from the hospital to the Connolly house. She was there when they arrived; she'd called over to offer condolences.'

Tom looked blankly at Sean, waiting.

'There are two phones,' Sean said.

Tom felt his head spin.

'Two?'

Sean nodded.

'Wait,' Tom said. He opened the interview room door. Sean came in behind him. Still standing, Tom turned the tape back on.

'There was no way he'd tell Ethan,' Tom repeated. 'What did you mean by that, Charlotte?'

The girl shrugged.

'All that stuff at the funeral that Ethan came out with. It was nice and all, but Luke despised Ethan. He was sick, all the time. But it wasn't just that. He was so bossy. He kept telling Luke how to live his life. To not drink, not do drugs; who he should hang around with. Everything. Luke would have been glad to see Ethan die. Seriously.'

Jackie was back at the station. They'd plugged in what they suspected was Luke's phone and were waiting for it to charge. They could only hope it was dead from having been turned off for a period, and not damaged.

'Do we have the password for it?' Tom asked.

'Yep,' Jackie confirmed. Her face was grim, focused. And tired. She was so determined to right her previous mistakes, she was probably working around the clock, Tom realised. Once they got through this, he'd talk to her again. She was a good detective, she just needed to find some balance.

'It's the same password as Ethan's,' she said. 'And Rose helped Ethan with his phone sometimes, so she knows it. We've already checked Ethan's device but there are no messages on it. Sini has taken it to go through the SIM card.'

An Apple logo flashed on Luke's phone. Then the home screen was visible, telling them the SIM was locked and prompting them to enter the four-digit code.

Tom took the phone in his gloved hand and tapped the numbers in that Jackie gave him. The twins' birthday, 1508, the fifteenth of August.

There was a moment when he thought they'd got it wrong, that this wasn't Luke's phone, just a spare one Ethan had managed to lay his hands on.

Then the phone came to life. The screen filled with a picture of Luke and Charlotte. Seconds later, messages started to appear, sent after the phone was turned off. Sent after Luke's death.

Tom, Sean and Jackie all looked at each other.

'Shit,' Tom said. He opened the message folder, ignoring the unread alerts. He scrolled down until he got to the last read message, the one sent from Rose at 3 a.m.

And there was Charlotte's message at 11.30 p.m.

And in between them, a message from Ethan. Luke had given him the nickname *Headwreck.*

Jesus, if they'd seen that, it might have given it away before now.

*I've been liberated. You said you were partying in Glenmore? Still there? Need to talk to you. One last favour, bro?*

Underneath, Luke had replied.

*Serious? Mad bastard. Yeah, I'm here. Bit of a party, off my face. Come on. Upstairs with Daniel if I can convince him to stay. Totes respect, man. Might even get a drink into you, lol.*

A hush followed Tom's reading aloud of the text exchange.

'I don't understand,' Jackie said. 'Ethan was dying. We all saw him. How the hell did he get from the hospital to that house? I mean, even if he had the energy to get off the bed. Did he just walk out and get a taxi? None of this makes sense.'

'We need CCTV from that hospital *now*,' Sean said.

Tom was still staring at the phone as the other two leapt into action. He was scrolling back up the messages, the one-sided conversation Ethan had been having with his brother.

*Are you on the drink again?*

*Can you not just cool off.*

*Mum is worried.*

*Are you still messing C around?*

*Don't you think she deserves better?*

All met with silence from Luke.

And Tom's head was filled with everything he'd heard and seen over the last few weeks. A matrix of conversations and pictures all blurring into one solid, almost unbelievable conclusion.

'We have to go over,' Sean said. 'Tom, are you listening? We need to go to the hospital. They've CCTV on site but it will take forever to make duplicates of the tapes.'

Tom nodded.

'I know what happened,' he said.

# CHAPTER 52

Rose Connolly was standing in the station's reception area. As soon as they emerged, she launched herself at Tom. She looked crazed, her pupils dilated with fear, her skin covered in a light sheen of sweat.

'I need to know what's going on,' she said. 'Why did you take Ethan's belongings? Why is nobody talking to me?'

Tom placed his hands on her upper arms and held her steady. She actually looked like she might fall over.

'Rose, you need to listen to me now,' he said. 'I asked you if you were ready for the truth about what happened to Luke. You said you were.'

A shadow passed over Rose's eyes. That had been before. She hadn't realised at that stage that his brother could have been involved, that one of her sons could have murdered the other.

'You need to go home to Chris and to your family,' he said. 'When we know more, I will come myself and tell you exactly what happened.'

Tom looked over at Jackie.

'Can you . . . ?'

She nodded and placed an arm around Rose. She would comfort this mother to the best of her abilities. Tom nodded grimly. Jackie's story had come full circle, even if it wasn't going to have a satisfactory ending.

Tom and Sean left the station.

'I can't believe this,' Sean said. 'Cain and Abel.'

'Maybe,' Tom said. He didn't add anything. He was still considering.

They drove to the hospital with flashing lights on and parked in a loading bay. They'd deal with tickets after. This was more important.

The hospital's security chief was waiting for them.

'I've got what you asked for,' he said. He was defensive, worried he was being accused of not having done his job. 'We've narrowed down footage from that corridor and the exit routes. Like I told you, there's no way a patient walked out the front of this building after hours. Even if they'd tried to disguise themselves, we would have recognised anybody who wasn't a doctor or nurse.'

'That's fine,' Tom said. 'Nobody's questioning your security procedures. It's the other exits we're interested in, like we said.'

The security chief brought them to the viewing room and sat them either side of his chair in front of the monitor.

'Okay,' he said. 'First things first. You wanted to see if Ethan Connolly left his room that night. It's unusual, they all have private bathrooms, but yeah, sometimes a patient needs to stretch their legs. Insomnia kicks in, whatever. So, there you have it. Ethan walking down his corridor just before midnight.'

Tom and Sean leaned closer to the monitors and watched the boy leave his room and begin his journey. He was dressed for outdoors. A tracksuit, hood pulled up.

'And where's the footage of him returning to his room?' Tom said.

The security chief blinked, keeping his eyes on the monitor. He pulled up a file. The time on the corner of the screen said 3.45 a.m. There was Ethan, coming back down the corridor.

Tom shook his head. It had been here all along.

'I need the other exits now,' Tom said.

He turned to Sean.

'There's no way Ethan knew by chance how to get out of this hospital in any manner that wasn't through the front door. Somebody told him.'

Sean nodded.

'I'd just started going through that footage,' the security chief said. 'I'm giving him a few minutes to get to each one. I've checked the kitchen exit, where deliveries come in. He's not there.' He pulled up the file and they watched still footage for a minute or two as he fast-forwarded through.

'This is the equipment delivery bay,' the security chief said. He scratched at the back of his neck, angrily. He was taking it as a personal affront that somebody had got in and out of the hospital after hours without him being aware of it.

They watched the footage for a minute in real time. And then, there he was. Ethan walking through the door. He looked to his left, somewhere off-camera.

'Do you have another angle?' Tom asked.

The security chief nodded. He pulled up more footage.

This time, the camera caught the back of Ethan's head. And pulling up beside the door was a small, silver Toyota.

The driver's door opened. And Ethan's nurse, Claire, got out.

# CHAPTER 53

'How long had Ethan been in love with you?' Tom asked.

He'd placed a cup of coffee in front of Claire Doyle. It sat untouched. She was drumming her fingers nervously on the tabletop. They'd shown her the CCTV footage. It was devastating to any lies she might have hoped to tell them. And Emmet's team were right now going over the DNA they'd collected from the room Luke had been pushed from. Now they were looking for evidence of Ethan and Claire's presence.

'Since the start, or had it grown?' Tom continued.

Claire shrugged. The hospital had helped her with legal counsel but when the full extent of her involvement came out, Tom didn't think they'd remain so eager to assist. The man beside her already looked distinctly uncomfortable with whatever his client had entrusted him with.

'I guess he had a crush on me from the beginning,' she said. 'But I didn't breach any ethics. I was always very good to Ethan. I knew he had . . . feelings. It's not unusual. They even tell you about it when you're doing your training. But I didn't have any inappropriate feelings for Ethan and that's all that mattered. He was my patient, nothing more.'

'You had no romantic feelings for Ethan,' Tom clarified. 'But you surely had more feelings for him than for your average patient? You were, after all, having sex with his brother.'

Claire stopped drumming the table. She looked up at Tom, shocked, then her mouth set in a thin line of defiance.

'That's a lie,' she said.

Tom picked up the see-through plastic evidence bag in front of him. He felt no pleasure doing it, but she was leaving him very little choice. Inside was a pair of lacy black knickers.

'We found these in Luke Connolly's room. When we test them for your DNA, do you think we'll find any?'

'I don't know, and even if you do, I can't help it if somebody stole a pair of my pants,' Claire snapped. She was trying to act angry, but really, she was panicking.

Tom looked down at his notes.

'So, you were never in Luke's room?'

She shook her head.

'For the tape, please.'

'No. I was never in Luke's room.'

'You're just an aftershave connoisseur, then?'

Claire looked to her solicitor and back at Tom.

'What?'

'You knew what brand of aftershave Luke wore. Creed Aventus. It's unusual. I've never worn it. Nor heard of it. €250 a bottle is a bit steep for me. I doubt anybody I know is familiar with it either. And yet, you were able to tell me what brand Luke wore. Was that because you'd seen him put it on?'

'No. He must have told me.'

'Okay,' Tom said. 'Let's go with that.'

He paused. She was in denial but her nerves were making her uncomfortable with silence. It was obvious. She could have chosen to not answer his questions. Instead, she'd an answer for everything.

'So you say, on the night in question, Ethan asked you to

drive him out to Little Leaf because he wanted to talk to his brother.'

'Yes.'

'And you did that, unquestioningly.'

'Yes.'

'Did you go into the house with him or wait in the car?'

'I . . . I waited in the car.'

Tom paused and looked up from his notes. Luke and Ethan were dead. She was in self-preservation mode. That was understandable.

'Hmm. Okay. How long did you wait in the car?'

Claire shrugged.

'I don't know.'

'Going by the timeline we've established, it was quite a while. And you didn't go inside, even once? You weren't worried that something had happened?'

'Look, he had no life,' Claire said, a faux dismissive tone in her voice, like none of this mattered. 'Ethan, I mean. He'd been sick on and off for years. He wanted a night out with his brother and his friends. I said I'd help. I'm young, too. I felt sorry for him. I'm guilty of poor judgement, but nothing more. Ethan wasn't a prisoner in the hospital. He was allowed to leave if he wanted. I was just helping him to be a kid. Granting him a dying wish. You see it all the time. Doctors wheeling patients down to the garden to smoke. Bringing heart disease sufferers a pizza. It's . . . normal.'

She laughed, lightly.

Tom took a deep breath.

'Did you think he'd killed his brother when you heard what happened? Did he tell you?'

'No. God, no. He didn't kill him. I'm sure of it. You have it all wrong. You must have.'

'Do I?'

'Yes!'

'Well, if Ethan didn't kill him, did you?'

Claire's mouth fell open, her face clouding with dismay.

'No,' she whispered, her eyes flicking sideways.

Tom sighed.

'You see, I think you're lying, Claire. And I really need to hear the truth from you if you're going to come out of this okay. We're going through the DNA samples in that room right now. I think we'll find yours. You killed Luke Connolly. And I know why.'

Claire shook her head again, adamantly.

'Luke charmed you into bed,' Tom continued. 'And, while he wasn't your patient, he was sixteen when you met him, and you were twenty-two. That looks bad for a professional. But not catastrophic. You might have come through unscathed, even if it all came out. But that didn't happen. What happened is, you fell for Luke. Maybe it was love? Obsession? I don't know what depth of emotion would be required to make you that angry when you found out he was using you. That you were just a body to him. He needed a girl and you were it. A girl he could shag and go back and tell his mates everything was okay with him. He wasn't gay. His *real* girlfriend wouldn't give it up but that was okay, because he'd found somebody who would. And he probably figured, with you being older and in a position of care for his brother, that you wouldn't be clingy, like the girls he went to school with. That he could walk away from you.'

'This is ludicrous,' Claire protested. 'I . . . You've no way of proving any of this.'

Tom held up his hand.

'Let me finish. I don't know how you found out you'd been

used. I strongly suspect Ethan told you. Perhaps he figured it out. He was really good at reading people. And I guess he felt the way to worm his way into your heart was by telling you what a shit his brother was. Not very clever, but maybe he thought he'd be your shoulder to cry on. Teenage boys can be so stupid. But instead of endearing you to Ethan, the truth made you angry.'

Claire turned to her solicitor, helplessly.

He sat up straighter, tried to look officious.

'Do you have an actual question for my client, Inspector?' he said.

'Sure I do,' Tom said. 'I'm getting there. I figure that Ethan, seeing your reaction to the news, decided to tell you more things. To really try to tighten your bond, to make you confidantes. God loves a trier. So, Ethan told you what Luke and his friends had done to that homeless man, setting fire to his tent, nearly burning him alive in the process. I can't imagine what that did to your head. You're caring for a dying boy and there's Luke, waltzing around, hurting people, devastating lives, doing whatever the hell he wants. Jesus, that makes me angry just thinking about it.'

There was a flash of something on Claire's face. A tiny inkling that not everything was buried as deep as she'd like it to be. Tom could feel it all bubbling to the surface.

'So, Ethan tells you he's had a go at his brother for messing you around. We have his texts. "Are you still messing C around?" I thought it was Charlotte, but it could just as easily have been you. You weren't the only girl Luke hurt. And Ethan wants his brother to come clean about what happened to the homeless man. He wants his brother to sober up and stop ruining his life and everybody else's. But he has a problem. Luke is sick of listening to Ethan. So he's stopped visiting. He'd already cut down. We're compiling CCTV but it looks to me like Luke was last in the hospital two weeks before he died, whatever he was telling his parents. And Ethan knew he was deteriorating. He had to speak to Luke.'

'How are any of us supposed to know what was going on in Ethan's head?' Claire said. 'He's dead. I've told you what I did, there's no more to my story. I'm sorry. This is all terrible but . . . it has nothing to do with me. If Ethan hurt his brother, and I'm sure he didn't, we'll never know now. It's done. It's over.'

'I watched him at Luke's funeral,' Tom said. 'Ethan couldn't get up the two steps to the altar. Luke was pushed from the third floor of that house. How do you suggest Ethan got up all those stairs on his own?'

'I don't know,' Claire whispered. 'Ethan had good days. You saw that yourself.'

'If he did get up the stairs,' Tom continued, unperturbed, 'I'm just wondering how he managed to push Luke so hard. You're right; I saw Ethan at his best. He still didn't look like he had the strength to push a healthy seventeen-year-old out a window, drunk or not.'

'Maybe Luke tripped,' Claire said, throwing her hands out, desperation written on her face.

'No,' Tom answered. 'Luke had bruise marks on his chest. Finger marks.' Tom stared down at her hands and back up at Claire. She balled them into fists and took them from the table. 'I think – I can't remember for sure – but didn't Ethan have large hands? He shook my hand before he died. Yeah, they seemed big. Yours look big enough, but smaller than Ethan's. I mean, you being a medical professional, you know how valuable that sort of evidence is. And are you absolutely sure we won't find

DNA? You're positive you didn't touch anything in that room? Really positive?'

Claire paled. Tom was getting close, but he'd yet to deliver his fatal blow.

'I think the worst thing that's happened to you in all of this, though, is Ethan dying,' he said. 'That's where your story comes unstuck.'

'This is ridiculous,' she said, gathering herself. 'Are you going to claim I did something to Ethan now? He died in the care of his doctors, I wasn't even in the room.'

'I don't think you killed Ethan, Claire,' Tom said. 'But Ethan told me you killed his brother.'

Claire's eyes opened wide.

'He didn't.'

'He did.'

'I was there, when you last spoke to him.'

'I know,' Tom said. 'He told me after. He left a message.'

'I don't understand,' Claire exclaimed, distressed. 'He's dead. I don't understand.'

'You see, Ethan was in love with you, Claire,' Tom said. 'So he didn't want you to suffer for what you did to Luke. But Ethan was also a good lad. And he didn't want Daniel Konaté to suffer for it, either. He kept asking me to look at Luke's friends. He wanted them punished. I reassured him I was close and I thought he was right, but facing death can do funny things to the brain. Ethan wanted justice for his brother. I think he wanted to tell me the truth, but, in the end, he couldn't say it. Not when he was still alive.'

Claire looked confused.

'And maybe he felt a little angry with you, after all,' Tom said. 'Because you chose his brother and not him. Maybe at the funeral he remembered that he loved his brother even more than he loved you. So, he left Luke a voicemail. He deleted the call record from his phone so you wouldn't see it, because, obviously, you had access to his phone. But he couldn't delete it from Luke's because that was out of battery and . . . he wanted somebody to hear it. He knew his belongings would go back to his parents.'

Tom picked up the other evidence bag on the table. They'd listened to the voicemails in the hospital after watching the CCTV. It had given them the final piece of evidence needed to arrest Claire.

Tom took out Luke's phone with gloved hands and scrolled through. Then he placed it on the table and pressed the playback icon.

Ethan's voice filled the room.

*'I'm sorry. Claire wanted to hurt you, but not kill you. I wanted to hurt you. But neither of us wanted you dead. I hated you sometimes. I hated you for being with her. For using her. You fucked up. But it didn't matter. Not really. What they're saying about Daniel, though; I've tried to fix it. I don't know if I can. He loved you and you should have treated him better. We all deserved more. But you didn't deserve what happened. I love you. See you soon.'*

Tom took the phone back.

'So,' he said.

Claire's face crumpled. She placed her hands over her eyes.

'I'm only twenty-three,' she said weakly.

'Luke and Ethan are dead,' Tom said. 'Claire, I'll find your DNA. You know I will. Somewhere in that house. I'll put you there, and then all this lying, you know where it will get you. It's better you talk to me. Cooperate. You must know this.'

Claire stared down at the table. The solicitor leaned over and whispered something in her ear. She looked up, met Tom's eye. She was ready to speak now. He could see it.

'I only went up to see what was taking Ethan so long. They were arguing. Ethan was trying to reason with Luke. He was telling him how much of an arsehole he'd been. He actually said to him, "I'm dying. Why won't you live your life properly?" And Luke just told him to fuck off. I mean it. He said, "Fuck off, Ethan." And Ethan swore at him. Then Luke, he . . . he pushed him. He pushed his dying brother onto the ground.'

Tom held his breath.

'Ethan was shocked,' she said. 'He looked at me and it was in his eyes: *Look at what my brother, the one you chose, is capable of.* I felt so ashamed. And Ethan was on the floor . . .'

'You wanted to protect him?' Tom said.

'No.' Claire stopped, wrung her hands. 'Yes. I mean, I wanted to hurt Luke. I wanted to hit him and slap him and make him feel the pain that he was causing. But I didn't see the window. I didn't mean to push him out a fucking window. And when I had my hands on his chest, I could see him looking over at Ethan and he looked so sad, so sorry for what he'd done. He hadn't meant to push his brother. But I meant to push Luke. Just not to his death.'

Claire lowered her head into her hands and groaned – a painful, raw sound, full of regret and grief.

Tom felt like he'd been punched in the gut.

She hadn't meant Luke to die. Neither had Ethan.

There'd been no intent. It was just a stupid tragedy.

Yet another, in Glenmore House.

# CHAPTER 54

The official handing over of the chief superintendent title to Tom was far less officious than the formal goodbye dinner at the police Ball for Sean McGuinness a month earlier.

They popped open the bubbles in Tom's new office, Sean's old one. The team had squeezed in, along with AC Bronwyn Maher, Emmet, Linda and Natasha, who'd brought several bottles of champagne. Tom had been asking her to stop thanking him for over a week now but he suspected it would go on a while. This time, she'd also brought him a card from Daniel. It was typical of a teenager. Two lines. *Thanks, mate. I owe you one.*

Still, it gladdened Tom's heart.

'Well, I'll miss the place,' Sean said. 'No doubt about it. Not so much the place, but the people.'

'Are you planning on dying, or just not seeing us again?' Tom said. 'Because you're due in ours for Sunday lunch.'

'Ah, you know what I mean,' Sean said gruffly. He was emotional, bound to be. It was a big day.

The door opened and Willie Callaghan popped his head in.

'Feels like the smallest party in the world,' he said. 'Room for three more?'

'Three?' Sean asked. 'Are you expecting twins?'

Willie came in. He was followed by Ian Kelly and Jackie McCallion.

'I was just calling over to let you know the DPP has submitted an application for a new trial date,' she said, blushing furiously. 'For Claire Doyle this time, obviously.'

'No, no work,' Sean said. 'I'm finished with all that.'

'I think she meant that for me,' Tom said. 'Come in, Jackie. Take your coat off and have a drink. That's an order.'

'I told you all,' Linda said. 'A reign of anarchy. Just the sort I like.' She looked ten years younger, Tom thought. He made a note to ask her how things were progressing on the Paul front. Something told him they'd turned a corner.

'The Connollys, Jackie?' Tom asked. 'How are they?'

'As expected,' Jackie said. 'Devastated.'

Tom cocked his head, but said nothing. And then everybody was drinking and talking again.

Tom wasn't sure how Rose and Chris would cope with the truth. They would be asking themselves if they should have seen it coming. And when Tom replayed all the conversations he'd had with Ethan, he realised that, yes, Ethan had been unhealthily fixated on his brother's life. Perhaps understandably, to a point. It was, after all, the life Ethan should have been sharing. But it hadn't gone both ways. Luke hadn't had one single photograph of Ethan in his room. It probably hadn't always been that way, but it was as Coach Walsh had said – teenagers were selfish. It was too much to expect Luke to remain the considerate sort for all those years, especially when he'd so many of his own problems, albeit mostly of his own making. His dalliance with Claire had probably been, if even unintentionally, designed to hurt his brother, the recipient of so much attention for so much of Luke's life. Claire had found herself caught in the middle of something that was beyond her and now she'd paid a terrible price for it.

The rest of the Little Leaf teenagers were facing charges for the attack on the homeless man, varying in degrees of gravity. Tom had gone to visit the man. He'd never recover fully and still had months of surgery and skin grafts ahead. A donation towards the man's care had been made from the police fund. The inspector also knew Jacob would face charges for buying drugs. All those young lives, so horribly tainted by sheer stupidity.

'Nervous?' Sean asked, sidling up to him.

'Why would I be nervous?' Tom said. 'Isn't it all about kicking back now and yelling orders at people? Isn't that what you did?'

Sean smiled. Across the room, Louise met Tom's eye. She raised her glass and Tom nodded back.

'I'm kind of looking forward to it in a masochistic way,' Tom said.

'That's good,' Sean agreed. 'Because it is a painful job. We did good, didn't we?'

'On the case? I have to admit, you made a better partner than I imagined you would.'

'I'll ignore that. No, I mean with the department. We've run a tight ship.'

Tom looked around the room at friends and colleagues and loved ones.

'We have,' he said, and he felt quite emotional. 'I'm going to miss you.'

Sean took a sip from his glass before he could speak.

'Ah, stop. You're going to bring a tear to my eye. Right. I need to head. I've got a dance class.'

'Jesus.' Tom laughed. 'Fair enough. We'll take this to the pub.'

'No, you won't,' Sean said, and clapped his hand on Tom's shoulder. 'They can. You have paperwork.'

He pointed over to Tom's new desk and the large pile sitting on top of it.

Tom looked at it and groaned. There it was. His new reality.

From DCI to pen-pusher.

'Give me strength,' Tom said, shaking his head.

He'd have to find a way to work around this nonsense.

# ACKNOWLEDGEMENTS

Nicola, Stef and Rachel. Team Spain. Nobody is as lucky as me.

The whole amazing bunch at Quercus. Bethan, Hannah, David, Milly, Jon, Cassie. My seventh book with you and I hope there are many, many more.

Hachette Ireland, Breda, Jim, Ruth, Joanna, Elaine, the whole gang. You do a phenomenal job.

All my pals, family, friends and neighbours; love the lot of you.

Fern, Mark, Mick, Meg, Frances, Stellan and Gretta, for always believing.

The reviewers, booksellers and bloggers who have helped to share these books with the world, thank you so much.

All my author friends – we get it (you're probably the only ones reading this, right?).

And last but most importantly.

Isobel, Liam, Sophia and Dominic.

Everything is for you.

Read on for an exclusive extract from Jo Spain's new standalone thriller, *Six Wicked Reasons*.

# JUNE 4TH, 2018

You didn't swim in the bay.

The locals knew that.

The sailors who had lost their lives in the South County Wexford inlet over the years had all been from other parts of the world. They hadn't known about the treacherous rocks and tricky rip currents of Spanish Cove, so named for its first recorded casualties – members of an Armada vessel that had blown off course and found itself dashed on the jagged ridge.

Within sight of shore, the sailors, to a man, had drowned.

The tide lifted and pummelled their bodies against the very rocks that had caused their demise, painting the stone crimson.

Some claimed they'd been lured to their deaths by otherworldly creatures.

Other cultures called them mermaids. Sirens. In Gaelic, *moruadh*. Dangerously beautiful beings with icy skeletal fingers and a grip like tangled seaweed.

Superstition. Folklore. The stories that endure in places like these, away from the bright lights and modern cynicism of the city.

The family who'd hired the yacht for the party on the night it happened were all locals.

It would *never* have occurred to them to strip off and go swimming.

Now that family was gathered in the harbour master's office, blankets and crinkled silver foil wrapped around their shoulders. Bedraggled, cold and in shock.

Nine had boarded, only eight returned alive.

There'd been fireworks, earlier in the evening. The strains of music could be heard from shore. Crates of champagne had gone on board, delicious canapés, everything to make it the perfect luxury night at sea.

It was a much-anticipated reunion.

A brother, who had vanished from their lives ten years ago, leaving untold grief in his wake, had come home.

The party to mark his return ended when a body was pulled from the water, already deceased.

The victim's head bore the marks of a heavy blow. The water had washed away most of the blood, revealing an ugly gash, so deep the white bone of the skull was visible.

It was entirely plausible that a boom or some other piece of sailing equipment had swung at the victim, making him lose his balance – except the deck from which he'd fallen seemed free of any such dangers.

He'd been drinking; he could have slipped and banged his head, then somehow managed to topple over the side rail – although it was quite high and designed for safety.

The detective sergeant in charge wanted to know if the victim had displayed any symptoms of ill health, dizziness or confusion? Had he been depressed?

What, exactly, had happened prior to the alarm being raised?

There was a lot of broken glass on deck. Two of the brothers had fought, if their bruises and bloodied noses were anything to go by.

The detective, now living in Wexford town, had once been a local himself. He knew the family, way back. He could have asked to have been excluded from the investigation. But in a small, remote village like this, where everybody ate and drank each other's business, being seen as one of their own was often to the advantage of the police.

Anyhow, this was a busy night for the county police force, with two serious incidents elsewhere in their jurisdiction. There *was* nobody else, his boss cheerfully informed him.

But it would be resolved quickly. An accident, wasn't it?

Wasn't it?

The family comforted each other, as they waited to give their statements.

The unity, however, was forced.

Their brother had returned and now their father was gone.

Frazer Lattimer, sixty-one years of age, native of Scotland, resident in Ireland most of his adult life, was dead.

His children looked at one another, and wondered.

Which of them had murdered him?

# Part One

## ONE WEEK EARLIER

# CLIO

*Adam's home.*

The words still rang in her ears.

Said so casually. Like he'd just popped down to Four Star Pizza and returned with a sixteen-inch deep pan, extra pepperoni.

Or had just arrived back after a long day at work, the headlights of his car illuminating the driveway.

Adam's home.

The sentence hadn't been uttered with the weight it deserved, the gravity that captured the fact their brother had been missing for ten years – at worst, presumed dead, at best, presumed dead.

Clio was still reeling from Ellen's phone call, the imparting of the news.

Adam's home.

*Does he know about Mam?* Clio had asked. *Does he know what he did?*

Once upon a time there was a family.

A father, a mother and six children. They lived in the most scenic part of Ireland, in a beautiful house on a hill, and were wealthier than everybody they knew. Rich in every sense, but mostly in the way that mattered. They had class. They had status. They had each other.

And then it all went to hell in a handbasket.

Clio picked up the photograph that had captured the Lattimers at a happier time – her whole family at the beach.

Her parents sat on scratchy, striped towels. Kathleen's smile came easily; Frazer's was less enthusiastic but even he looked to be enjoying the day out. Clio's sisters, Kate and Ellen, shielded their eyes from the sun as they looked up from placing pretty shells on a giant sand monument that Adam had built. Adam grinned happily, his uncomplicated nature apparent in his features. James was self-absorbed as usual, licking an ice cream he'd made last far longer than any of his siblings'. Ryan had pulled a last-minute cheeky face, tongue out, eyes crossed, fingers in his ears.

And there was Clio herself, a chubby little thing sitting at the front, the baby of the family, adored by one and all.

Who'd taken that photo? She was too young to remember. Probably Uncle Danny.

She placed the framed picture in her holdall.

Then she started to move around the room.

It was years since Clio had done this. Said goodbye to inanimate objects.

Goodbye, bed. Goodbye, alcove. Bye, wardrobe. Bye, stairs.

A little OCD in an otherwise chaotic life.

Her eyes scanned the small apartment for the last time. The tiny, functional kitchenette with the pan on the two-ring hob, still burnt on the base from the time she'd got drunk and decided to make popcorn with barely a dribble of oil. The single bed, half the slats broken. She'd propped it up with boxes but it still creaked like hell whenever she had somebody in it with her. The cracked window, through which the sounds of Bleecker Street seeped night and day, reminding her that, no matter how lonely she felt, she was always surrounded by other people.

This was her world. These days, you couldn't get next nor near Greenwich Village for the rent she was paying for this place. But when Clio had arrived, four years ago, at the tender age of twenty-one, her then-boyfriend had already secured the rent-controlled studio from a departing expat and Clio had clung onto it ever since.

At the time, the boyfriend had told her she'd never grow accustomed to New York. Clio was used to sleeping in the blackest of nights, a blanket of stars overhead, to a soundtrack of lapping waves and gulls.

Bleecker Street was sirens and pneumatic drills and nightclub revellers and car horns.

In the end, it was the boyfriend who ran home. Clio stayed, working in various bars or restaurants, taking cleaning work and other jobs – any position that would pay her cash in hand.

She'd told herself she didn't need much money once the essentials were covered.

Walking along the Hudson was free. The city's art galleries and libraries regularly ran open-house nights. Shows could be seen for half-price if you were happy to queue or knew somebody on the concession stand. Drinks flowed liberally if you found the right barman to screw.

It said a lot about her personality that she could see the positives. Most people who'd been done out of fifty-plus grand on their twenty-first birthday and endured what she had would have been bitter about their circumstances.

Clio zipped up her holdall and looked around the room one last time.

There was a definite nostalgic lump in her throat.

Here, in a small apartment in a big city, she'd found independence. She'd found peace. The space to be just Clio, and not *Clíodhna Lattimer, youngest of the brood, daughter of Frazer and Kathleen, sister to . . . you know the ones.*

But it hadn't all been easy.

In fact, at a certain point, it had been spectacularly shit.

But even prisoners find it hard to leave their cells and face the outside world.

People ran out of empathy, somebody had once told her. They could listen to your pain for a while, but then their worlds moved on. Nobody stayed long in the company of a victim.

So, she would never let anybody know the full truth of what she'd endured.

Clio picked up the white rectangular envelope she'd left on the bed.

She'd taken the letter out of its original envelope. This one was plain, no name or address inscribed on its front.

The letter had started it all. It explained everything.

She'd promised herself she'd get rid of it. If anybody knew she had it, if they read it, they'd learn what she'd learned. But she couldn't destroy it. She needed to keep reading the words, to remind herself why she was returning to Spanish Cove.

She tucked it into her handbag and grabbed her holdall and wheelie suitcase containing the sum of her worldly possessions.

'Goodbye, home,' she said, her voice caught on a sob, and left.

★

The screech of airplanes braking on the runway at JFK airport.

A long line of yellow cabs; a wide expanse of stone-grey buildings; glass-fronted terminals; a mass of travellers, the experienced and the wide-eyed.

Inside, in a tiny office, a twenty-five-year-old woman pretending not to give a damn but, truthfully, trembling like a little child.

'It's Clio. Clio, like the car, you know? Renault Clio? Not Cleo like the queen. But you pronounce it like that.'

'It says here on your passport Cleed-na . . . Clee-odd-ha-na, ma'am.'

'It's Clíodhna. Clee-oh-na. This is exactly why I use Clio. For the love of Christ, is this going to take much longer? Can't you hear the announcements? That's my fucking plane they're talking about.'

'Ma'am, please refrain from using expletives.'

The large black security official's eyes bored into Clio's. She felt the heat burning red hot in her cheeks. She blinked first, lowered her gaze. This small interrogation office she'd been brought to, after being plucked out of the passport control line post-security, already felt like a prison cell. She wanted out.

'You will be accompanied through the terminal to your flight. You will stay in the boarding lounge. You will be . . .'

Clio switched off at that point. She had no rights, no argument to make.

She'd overstayed her welcome in the greatest country in the world and now she was being chaperoned out of it. Make America great again. Deport Clio Lattimer.

It wasn't her fault the plane was running late. Some minor technical fault Aer Lingus was dealing with last minute. Clio tried to tell that to

Betty, the female security official she'd been assigned, hoping it would put an end to the dirty looks Betty kept flashing her. Built like a brick shithouse and humanity-weary, Betty's whole demeanour further diluted the *'You have a nice day, ma'am'* the previous security official had sarcastically bid as Clio was carted off to the boarding gate.

Now, sitting at the sushi bar in terminal two – because Betty recognised Clio was entitled to eat as long as she didn't plan to eat anywhere off airport property – Clio relayed the whole sorry experience to a County Galway man perched on the next stool.

'And their drugs dog ripped a ladder in my tights going past with that stupid thing on his back,' she said. She turned to her guard. 'Didn't he, Betty? Does he need to walk that close? I mean, if he has to get that close to smell the drugs, is he any fucking use, Betty?'

The Galway man, whose name Clio couldn't be arsed to remember, blushed at the security official's obvious irritation. He ordered another two vodka tonics from their server. They arrived in seconds, served up on square napkins. Clio knocked hers back, shot-style. Betty pursed her lips. Betty probably had three kids at home and no doubt just wanted to get through her shift so she could fuck off to Stop and Shop and pick up some groceries. Clio almost felt sorry for Betty.

'So, why are you going back?' Galwegian asked. 'If you knew you'd get stung going through JFK? Did somebody die or something?'

'Why don't you get another round in while I pee?' Clio said. She swivelled on her stool. 'Betty, how about we gals go powder our noses?'

The security official's features were so scrunched they were starting to disappear into themselves. Clio reckoned if the Aer

Lingus flight took much longer, Betty might consider sticking Clio on any plane, going anywhere, just to get rid.

And maybe that wouldn't be a bad thing.

'More vodka for the lady on a mysterious trip home.' Galwegian smiled.

'Oh,' Clio said. 'There's no mystery, really. The prodigal son has returned. My brother. Disappeared ten years ago and now he's back.'

She hopped off her stool.

'Jesus,' her companion said, taken aback at the turn in the conversation. 'He vanished, like? Where was he?'

'God knows.'

'And he just came back? That's incredible. So that's why you're going back. Makes sense. I'd say you're dying to see him.'

Clio felt her breath shorten, her chest constrict.

'Actually,' she said, 'it would have been better if he was fucking dead.'